AX   EE 9/25

by *Shirley Ann Grau*

THE HARD BLUE SKY   *1958*

THE BLACK PRINCE   *1955*

These are *Borzoi Books*,
published in New York
by *Alfred A. Knopf*

T H E
HARD BLUE SKY

The Hard Blue Sky

BY Shirley Ann Grau

Alfred A. Knopf

New York

1958

L. C. Catalog card number: 58–7562

© Shirley Ann Grau, 1955, 1956, 1957, 1958

THIS IS *A Borzoi Book,*
PUBLISHED BY *Alfred A. Knopf,* INC.

FIRST EDITION

A portion of the material in Part VII appeared originally in The New Yorker *in somewhat different form, and portions of Part II and Part IV in* New World Writing *and* Mademoiselle *respectively in somewhat different form.*

THE HARD BLUE SKY

THE

HARD BLUE SKY

PRINCIPAL CHARACTERS

Gus Claverie
Didi LeBlanc
Mercy Schesnaydre } *island kids*
Joey Billion
Burt Richaud

Inky D'Alfonso: *crew of the* PIXIE

Hector and Cecile Boudreau: *a young couple*

Julius Arcenaux, *the grocer* } *Cecile's parents*
Philomene, *his wife*

Perique: *a young man*

Ferdinand and Carrie Lombas: *Perique's parents*

Annie Landry: *a sixteen-year-old girl*

Al Landry: *Annie Landry's father, recently widowed*

Adele: *the new wife Al Landry brings from Port Ronquille*

Claudie: *Adele's son by a previous marriage*

Therese Landry: *Annie's cousin*

Beatriz Valdares: *a South American girl; Annie's roommate at the convent in New Orleans*

Eddie and Belle Livaudais: *parents of*

Henry, *who is 18*

Pete, *who is 16*

Robby: *Eddie Livaudais's six-year-old bastard*

Chep Songy } *Belle Livaudais's brothers*
Ray Songy

Jerry: *Chep's son*

Mike Livaudais } *Eddie's brothers*
Phil Livaudais

Marie Livaudais: *Mike's wife*

Lacy and Andrée Livaudais: *cousins of Eddie Livaudais*

Mamere Terrebonne: *the oldest person on the island*

Anthony Tortorich: *from the other island*

*

BACK in the wide deep curve of the coast to the west of the three mouths of the Mississippi, the Gulf is brown and muddy. Always. Only, when the sun is very bright and the sky a hard blue, the water can look clear. And the fishermen, at least the ones who take people from New Orleans out on charter, pick up a couple of dollars now and then betting on just that.

All along this northern edge of the Gulf there is almost no solid land, just the marsh grasses that dapple in the wind like the Gulf itself—prairie tremblant, they call it—its tracks only an occasional trainasse, a trail cut for a pirogue, and the twisting network of bayous that run sluggishly to the four points of the compass and drain finally into the Gulf. For three or four hundred miles the coast is like that. With one exception: a chain of three islands.

They are right on the edge of the marsh, about a mile apart.

They are a kind of bridge across the mouth of a wide deep bay that extends four or five miles north into the marsh. The islands are all the same shape—a long narrow strip. They are all different sizes.

The smallest of these, hardly a half-mile long, is to the east. It is the lowest too and seems to be sinking. During any storm now the water sweeps right over it.

But there were trees once. If you look around you can see the old roots, bleached white as driftwood. And there is a single stump left, a hollow trunk maybe five feet tall, and splotched by mold. At its bottom there is a pool of water—of rain water. It varies some summer and winter, but there is always a little. Mosquitoes breed there—in spring it swarms with wigglers. And dozens of little lizards, their bodies turned brown against the bark, come and feed on them. Birds come too, mockingbirds and ricebirds and sparrows, and blackbirds, and they hop around in the tough brown-yellow runner grass and pick at the lizards. Sometimes they yank

3

them right off the sides of the stump. And sometimes too a wood-pecker works for the maggots in the bark. Under his steady hammering the old tree shakes. And the lizards all stay out of sight in the roots and the ground. And the other birds have to search through the grass and out along the driftwood and logs that have piled up at the east tip. Out there—in the logs and the twisted driftwood—on sunny days, the gators lie. And sometimes their tails move faster than the birds.

In almost the very center of the island there are two posts, crooked now but still standing. They were put in deep and steady and the storm water has only tilted them a little. The posts are all that is left of a pigpen. Thirty years or so ago, when the island was higher, Ray Hébert brought his pigs across to leave them there during the summer. (His wife couldn't stand the smell of the sty in her back yard. It wasn't any worse than anybody else's, but under the hot July sun they all smelled, people said, like death itself.)

But his pigs were always slipping through the fence rails and heading down to the east end because it seemed marshy there and cool. And the alligators got them, one after the other.

They call it Isle Cochon now, and they leave it to the birds and the alligators and the fiddler crabs and the lizards.

The next-sized island is the one off to the west, called Terre Haute. It is a couple of miles long and fairly high: only during very severe storms and hurricanes does the water wash over it. (During one hurricane the water was several feet deep over the whole island—but that didn't happen often.) And it has trees and grass, even if the grass is mostly brown and the oaks are burned off at an angle by the spray. Oyster fishermen and trappers live there—fifteen houses or so (built high on stilts out of reach of flood water) and enough kids to make them noisy. And on the north side, the bay side, the slips for the four or five oyster-luggers.

The third island, the one in the middle, is the highest and the best. It is only about a half-mile wide, like the others, but it's nearly four miles long, a slow gentle sweep up to a curve at the east end. The land itself rises slowly from the brown sand beach on the south to the little shell ridge overlooking the back bay. There is a heavy bank of oak trees that begin just beyond the sand and an irregular line of very tall palms. (One comes down almost every September in the storms but there always seem to be plenty left.) Under these trees there are houses, better houses than on Terre Haute, good tight houses, built at least five feet off the ground—hurricane water sweeps right over this island too. There are about twenty-five of these houses, tin-roofed and painted, some of them, in bright pastels. And to the back of the island, in the little curve like a toe on the east end, are the wharves for the boats, Biloxi-luggers, they call them, and a small icehouse. Sometimes the shrimp, or the fish, are cleaned and packed on the island.

The houses are all down at the east end, all in maybe a mile-long strip. The rest of the island has nothing but oaks, their trunks and branches twisted by the wind and the spray; oleanders with branches thick as a man's arm, and covered with pink and white and red flowers in the spring and summer—only, their smooth, dark pointed leaves are poison. Hibiscus and its midsummer flowers. Wisteria and bougainvillea so thick you have to cut your way through. Chinaberry trees with their tiny whitish purple flowers in March—and the stifling rotting smell of the yellow berries on the ground in December. And in the marshy spots, reeds that rustle and crackle their hollow stems together in the slightest wind, canes six feet high or more in patches where stories say there were painters once.

The painters were killed off, a long time ago. There is nothing on the island, except rabbits and maybe an occasional muskrat that floats over from the mainland on a tangle of grass.

And the dogs. Whole packs of them. Some nights you can see lines of them sitting out on the sand bars at the western end of the island, howling out across the Gulf at the moon. Trappers a couple of miles back in the marsh beyond the bay swear they can hear the dogs there, if the wind is right. There isn't much to eat, and the animals are always bony: they live on rabbits and birds and whatever they can steal.

When the bitches go in heat, packs roam up and down the whole length of the island, snorting and yipping, rooting under houses, tearing down clothes that are spread to dry across bushes, splashing about in the swampland beyond the back ridge.

They've given the island its name. People call it Isle aux Chiens.

*

THE PEOPLE who live on the island now are a mixture of French and Spanish mostly, though an occasional very dark child shows Indian or Negro blood. They are nearly all related, one way or the other. They are all fishermen, too, and they have the fisherman's dislike of the land: there is not a single large garden on the island, though things grow well. In most of the yards there is only a pepper bush by the door—there'd be no cooking without its small glossy red and green peppers. And on the porches there are ferns in old lube cans. Only one or two of the women have little patches (carefully fenced from the rabbits) of parsley and green onions and chive. And a mirleton vine growing on the fence, some okra and a few tomato plants. There are no flowers except wild ones— with a single exception: Easter lilies. Every house has at least a few bulbs, and the women take great care of them, better care, in a way, than of their children, who have the run of the island, unwatched.

It is an island of fishermen, and when times are bad they turn to trapping. Some of the kids grow up and go into the towns or on to New Orleans, but enough of them stay on the island where their fathers lived and their grandfathers, and back two hundred years. There is not much going on there now, but Isle aux Chiens has had its good times, times when money was easy to get. And all a man had to be was willing and strong and not afraid. Prohibition was one of them.

A man who knew his way through the maze of the bayous could almost name his own price then, as boat after boat of liquor came up from Cuba, unloaded, and slipped in small boats through the bayous to New Orleans.

A young man could make real money. The old men, too crippled with rheumatism to move, sat on porches and watched, enviously, and lied to treasury agents, and lied to the courts and ali-

6

bied their sons and nephews and cousins free—and made a little money for themselves. Some of these old men, sighing at their own helplessness and their creaking joints, began to remember the stories they'd heard, stories of another time when money was easy to come by—stories of Jean Lafitte and Louis Chighizola and Dominique You. Of pirates and smuggling when the island was first settled. When the deep little harbor inside the curve of the island was crowded with sailing-ships.

But that was back before anyone's memory. Even prohibition was a long time past. And the money from it was gone years ago.

THE WHITE AFTERNOON

"GUESS what I seen from the top of that old tree there," Robby Livaudais said, "guess what?"

He was just another island kid, small for his age and thin, with black eyes set too close together over the high bridge of his nose. Like the other boys', his head had been shaved in June; now, in early August, the stiff black bristles stood straight up, unevenly. He was wearing a pair of striped overalls fastened on just one shoulder; the other strap had been torn off. The legs had been cut off, too, when the knees were worn through, and never hemmed. There was a fringe of thread on them now. Whenever Robby had nothing else to do, he would set himself to unraveling a bit.

"I seen a sailboat heading right this way."

"Go way, and quit bothering us," Gus Claverie said.

"I seen a boat and I bet it Jean Lafitte coming."

The other kids did not look around. They were pushing the old tire that Menton Schesnaydre had hung by a rope from the strongest limb of the chinaberry tree.

Didi LeBlanc said: "It my turn."

"Leggo," Mercy Schesnaydre said.

They all yanked at the tire. Joey Billion, who was sitting in it, kicked at them.

"Jeez. . . ." Gus Claverie gave the tire a spin, a hard spin, mak-

8

ing it whirl on its heavy rope. Joey Billion fell out on his back.

"Look at him," Didi giggled, "making a big old puff of smoke."

Joey sat up and, twisting around, began to examine the back of his thighs. He picked out a couple of cinders and flicked them away.

"You know what I seen?" Robby repeated.

Gus put his leg through the tire and pushed himself off. Joey had to fall flat again as the swing whizzed over his head. Gus kicked at him, but missed. Joey laughed and rolled out of the way.

"I get me a knife and cut that there rope."

"Yaaa, toe cheese!" Gus went swinging back and forth, hanging by one arm and one leg.

"What you see?" Didi asked. Her hair was slightly longer and she was slightly taller—except for that, she looked like a boy. She was scratching her head with both hands as she asked Robby: "What you see?"

"A sailing-boat."

"A what?" Gus put down one leg and with a puff of dry dirt stopped the swing.

"Way, way out."

"It ain't there."

"They ain't no sailing-boats," Joey said.

"The *Mickey Mouse* now, that ain't got no sails."

"Not the *Mickey Mouse* nor the *Saint Christopher*, nor the *Hula Girl* nor the *Captain Z*."

Gus pushed the swing back and forth slowly. "There ain't nothing you see I want to look at."

"Bet it's somebody out shrimping and waving a handkerchief."

"Bet it's somebody been blowing his nose and drying the handkerchief," Didi said.

"I seen Lafitte coming," Robby said.

The afternoon got too hot for swinging. Joey went home. The others lay face down in the shade for a while and sweated.

"My Aunt Marie, she been by Arcenaux's this morning," Robby said and stared straight up into the sky. "She got a box sweet crackers. A big box."

They turned and were looking at him. Robby sat up and squared his shoulders. "She give me one to feed the fish this morning."

"What fish?" Mercy asked.

"The ones I'm growing under the house."

Didi giggled. "Got a mess of old half-dead fish."

"They growing all right."

"They stink."

"You got to show us," Mercy said.

Marie Livaudais was lying across the bed, in her slip, dozing on the heat of the white afternoon, and listening to the sounds all around her. The buzzing drone of wasps building a nest under the eaves outside the window. The sleepy squak of the chickens. The muffled talking of kids outside. Then the squeaking board in the kitchen. She did not bother to get up or open her eyes. She yelled: "Get out and stay out! Or I come fix you!"

There was a pause, a little pause and some soft brushing sounds.

"I hear you climbing out that window," she yelled.

Outside a kid giggled softly, behind his hand.

She listened again: nothing. She let herself slide back into her doze, wondering idly what they had taken.

They finished the box of graham crackers and stuffed it in the cracked trunk of the old chinaberry tree. Burt Richaud came, jangling a small net bag of marbles.

"I ain't gonna play," Robby said. Burt Richaud did not pay any attention. With the tip of his bare toe he drew a large circle in the soft dirt. Then he squatted down and stared at it.

The kids came up and stood around, waiting, carefully outside the circle line.

Burt put a single bright blue marble in the center of the circle. Then he stepped back and took out a cat's-eye. He held it up, between two fingers.

"That's a pretty one, for sure," Didi said.

"Never seen one so pretty," Mercy said.

"My papa brought it from Petit Prairie."

"Just a old marble," Robby said, and kicked with his heels in the dust, like a rooster.

"Bastard," Burt said. "Get out of here."

"He ain't got a mother," Didi said, "and he ain't got more than half a papa."

"Ain't so," Robby whispered. But he let Didi push him away.

The kids began their game. Robby watched them from a distance, quietly. Then he walked over to the tall thin palm tree. He squinted up along the trunk which curved very slightly away from the beach. And he began to climb.

Marie Livaudais scratched at her head. The sounds of the kids—the giggling and the laughing—irritated her. And the window shade kept blowing up in the light breeze and the sun flashed in her eyes. She recognized one of the voices: Robby's.

She wondered sometimes why she had offered to take him. As if she didn't have enough kids of her own. . . .

He was a Livaudais all right. Looked like them. She saw that the very first time she ever laid eyes on him, that day the priest from Petit Prairie brought him over to his father.

He was three then, and had been staying with his mother. But she had found a husband. A man from Biloxi, a foreman in a lumberyard and a good steady man. She had told him Robby was her nephew, and just stopping with her for company.

When the time came for her to go to Biloxi, she took Robby down to the priest and told the name of his father, and left the boy there.

So Eddie Livaudais got his illegitimate son to raise. And because his wife, Belle, wasn't one to be kind to her husband's bastards, Marie Livaudais had taken him in.

And me, Marie thought, I got to go opening my big mouth, and go saying I put him with my kids. All together. . . .

It was too hot for the pillow. She pushed it to the floor and bent her arm. The window shade flapped closed again. She sighed and stretched.

Robby was at the top of the tree. He yanked off a couple of the small hard yellow dates and, leaning out away from the trunk, he squinted carefully and dropped them. Didi LeBlanc jumped straight up in the air. The other kids looked at her without moving. She stood with her hands down stiff at her sides, her mouth wide open, her eyes shut, screaming. From the tree Robby dropped another date, but missed: it plopped into the dirt. Didi kept on screaming.

A little gust of wind released the spring and sent the shade flying up. Marie Livaudais heaved herself out of bed, mumbling softly under her breath. The damp slip stuck to her legs and she yanked it free as she went out on the porch.

She yelled at the kids, waving her arms. One of her big breasts popped over the top of her slip, but she did not seem to notice.

Marie looked up the palm tree, squinted, and then stomped down into the yard, hands on her hips.

"Come on down out of that tree there, that's been leaning and shaking in every little wind, before you break you fool neck!"

The boy in the tree did not move. He wrapped his legs tighter around the trunk and yelled: "Yaaaaaa, toe cheese."

She gave one more quick look up the tree and then began to scan the ground. She crossed the yard, pushing aside the kids and stepping through the middle of the circle of marbles.

She found what she was looking for: a piece of brick. She weighed it in her hand, decided it was too heavy and smashed it on an oyster shell. She picked up the two largest pieces and looked up the tree again. Then she closed one eye and very carefully and deliberately threw the first piece. It hit Robby's hip. He yelped but did not move. She walked around the tree and threw the other; it clipped him in the center of the back.

He slid down the trunk quickly. The bark burned the inside of his legs, and he was rubbing them when she caught up with him.

"Sal au pri!" She grabbed him by one arm and almost lifted him up. He began to cry.

She yelled back at him: "I got a mind to shake you till you brains fall out or you get some sense. And there ain't no telling which come first."

His eyes shut tight, he screamed. The other kids came up in a circle, their heads sticking forward on their necks, watching.

"Hey," Burt said. "He's popping blood all around, him."

"Where you bleeding?" Marie said. "Where?"

Robby stopped yelling and opened his eyes. He pointed to his legs. There were long red brushburns down the inner sides, still with pieces of the heavy rough bark sticking to them.

Marie half carried, half dragged the boy up the steps and into the house. "All I got to do is take a rest, me, and you go find a way to mess yourself up good, and come screaming to me."

"You hit me," Robby wailed.

"And you got to say a prayer to the Blessed Mother that you didn't come falling down with that tree that's been shaking at its roots for I don't know how many years, and you jumping around up at its top, like you was a monkey, and nothing come falling down."

She sat him on a kitchen chair. The other kids crowded up to the screen door. She got a bottle of iodine from the corner of the cupboard and smeared it across the brushburns. He yelled. She reached up and got a piece of sugar. "Open up you mouth."

She dropped a lump in and yanked her finger away fast. "Ha! . . . I ain't so stupid I don't know what you thinking." She went back to work with the iodine. "Ain't gonna bite me."

Burt said: "He going to be decorated up like a Christmas tree, him."

"You pay no mind to them," Marie said and glared at them over her shoulder. "They ain't got nothing but dirty feet and dirty noses and not one handkerchief."

He bent over studying the stained skin on his legs, pulling the broken skin apart with his fingertips.

"Quit that!" She moved over to the sink, took down a cup, shook a little bit of Octagon soap powder in it, filled it up with water so that the suds spilled over the rim. "I almost forgot me what you call me, still up in that tree that ain't no more than just brushing in the ground and shaking all over while you was up there."

He began to whimper again. Over at the door, the kids shuffled and pressed their noses on the screen.

She dragged a wood kitchen chair in front of the sink. With her still holding his arm, he scrambled up.

She swished the suds around in the cup. "You remember what you was calling me."

He nodded, his eyes on the yellowish soapsuds.

"You just keep thinking on that, and you start saying the Hail Mary and praying to God you tongue don't drop out with cancer for saying things like that."

He didn't move. He only rubbed one bare foot against the other ankle.

"You started, huh?"

He nodded again.

She released his shoulder and put that hand on the back of his head. She brought the cup of soapsuds up to his lips. He squirmed and kicked. The cup made a little clinking sound against his teeth.

"Quit, you," she said, "before I bust you teeth like they was acorns falling down."

She tilted the cup, and pressed his head back. "Open you teeth or I going to pry them up like a hound dog."

The water was running down his chin and splashing off the chair. His mouth filled. He blew the liquid out, opening his clenched teeth. She poured the rest of the soapsuds down and clamped her hand around his mouth. She shook his head then, just the way she would shake a jar she was washing out. "Jesus, Mary," she said, "you got to get you mouth clean out of words like that, talking like a trapper out in the marsh."

She held his head over the sink and took away her hand. He sputtered so that his whole body shook.

"Now wrench out."

He grabbed for the pitcher of water and took a mouthful from it.

She yanked it away from him. "Ain't you never learned to use a glass?"

She tasted the water and made a face. "Just wasting, and with the water so low that the wigglers is coming out the pipes." She sighed and went out on the porch. The kids scattered back to the edges, but she didn't notice them. She poured the pitcher of water on the four scraggly wax plants growing in the rusty coffee cans by the steps. She picked up the mop from where it hung handle down over the railing, shook the small bright red roaches out of the head and went inside to mop up the soapy puddle on the kitchen floor. Then she hung the mop out of the window.

Finally she turned on Robby. "You ain't moved?"

He shook his head.

"Get out of here," she said. "Go play around a million miles from here. Go feed the gars in the middle of the bay."

He scrambled away. The kids, who were still standing just the other side of the screen, pulled back to make room for him.

Once the door had slammed behind him, he stopped and looked at them. He let his lids fall until his eyes were half closed and he had to lift his chin to see.

"Jeez," Burt said.

Robby blew a little saliva bubble, slowly.

"Look at him," Didi said.

"He still bubbling," Mercy said.

"Jeez," Burt said.

Robby blew another bubble and, crossing his eyes, tried to look down at it. Then, because she was the closest, he grabbed hold of Didi's shirt front and pushed her off the porch. She didn't make a sound, just plopped down into the dirt. He made a wide left-handed swing at Burt, who ducked. He climbed to the top of the porch railing and jumped down from there, rolling over and over. Then he tried standing on his head.

Finally he stood up, blew a couple of bubbles very carefully, and started down the road. The other kids followed, first Didi, then Mercy and then Burt. Robby pretended not to notice them but every once in a while he turned and threw a handful of dust. And he swaggered so hard he wasn't even walking a straight line.

Half an hour later he was perched up on the highest limb of the camphor tree behind the Arcenaux grocery, while the other kids climbed restlessly around in the lower branches. When they tried to come up with him, he kicked them away. Finally they all settled down and watched the white-hulled sloop that was beating toward the island.

*

TEN minutes after he had cast off from the sloop *Pixie* Inky D'Alfonso was approaching Isle aux Chiens. He throttled down the outboard and came in slowly.

Ahead of him was the island, a long low strip, perfectly straight on this side. He didn't remember ever seeing such a straight line before. There was a sand-colored line and then a curving line of green, lifting up to a kind of point three quarters of the way to the east end. The trees looked glossy and heavy there.

He glanced over his shoulder. The sloop was moving east, on a reach now. And the main was luffing. A little. . . . Damn fool had no tiller hand. . . .

The dinghy swayed and quivered. All he'd need, he told himself, was a spill overboard. He was a fool to get himself in a crazy trip like this. Nothing about it was right.

And then he grinned. . . . Nothing was right, except that he couldn't keep away from a sailboat.

He'd quit high school to crew on a West Indies job. And that was only the beginning. . . .

He got a splash of murky sour water in his mouth. He spat and wiped his lips and got back to business.

He came in around the eastern end of the island, through the narrow pass between it and Isle Cochon, where the charts said there should have been a line of reflectors. The sand fringe went around this side of the island too. It looked white and soft to lie on.

But there was nobody on it, not even kids. Maybe the afternoon sun was too much for them. He circled the end of the island and saw that it was a kind of point, jutting northward. Farther down in the circle, he could see the rigging of a lugger. And even at this distance he could smell the tar of the nets.

He swung the dinghy down into the circle. The edges of this side

16

of the island were marshy: he could see the alligator grass and the cattails and the saw grass. A yellow and black ricebird whizzed over his head.

He saw a kind of rickety fishing-pier, and behind it a little path that ran straight into the trees. He eased the dinghy over and made it fast to the last pole. The pier was chest high and only two boards wide. He had to hoist and swing himself carefully sideways. The ragged edge of the board scraped his stomach. He sat for a minute, catching his breath, and staring into the heavy green shadows of the trees.

Somebody was watching him. He could feel it as plain as a hand on his shoulder. It was the sort of thing that made his spine prickle. He could feel himself begin to get angry, could feel it in a certain restless movement of his hands.

There wasn't a thing he could see beyond the oaks and the oleanders and the vines and the low flat leaves of the palmettoes. The ricebird was sitting on the post nearest shore.

Almost as soon as he stepped ashore, he saw the houses, four of them, not a hundred yards from the water. In the fenced yard of the first was a dog, a fair-sized black and white animal who crouched quivering behind the gate, his teeth showing just slightly in a silent snarl.

Inky stopped and talked to him. "Hi, boy." The dog hugged the ground tighter.

"Okay," Inky said, "okay." He looked at the house. Like the other four it was lifted off the ground on high foundations. The front porch was empty. "Hey," he yelled, "anybody home?"

It was absolutely still. Inky waited a minute, scratching his ear. Then he walked to the second house. There was no dog this time and he went up to the front door. He pounded on the door frame. "Nobody here either?" He stuck his nose against the torn screen. He could see a center hall, with a dresser and some chairs in it— but nothing else.

"Nobody here?" He waited perched on the railing, picking the shells from the soles of his topsiders.

There was only the very faintest creak of a board inside. He got up and peered down the hall again. It was empty.

"Hell," he said softly and went down the steps again. He lit a cigarette very slowly and flicked the match away in a high arc.

The other houses looked just as deserted, thin spidery houses with little threads of footpaths between them.

Take the one that goes west, Inky thought. There's got to be somebody sooner or later.

"Somebody who won't hide," he said aloud. He felt better—let them hear him. And if he couldn't get anybody to show them the channel—What did he care? Let Arthur keep sailing the god-damn boat up and down along the coast. God-damn fool who had to stop and wet his finger before he was sure where the wind was.

"You looking for somebody?"

He spun around. For a minute he did not see the woman. And when he did, he blinked and shook his head and looked again. Back under a tangle of bougainvillea and slung from the thick branches of a tough oak was a faded gray-black hammock. She was sitting on the edge, her bare feet dangling.

"It was you yelling down at the houses, no?"

"You heard me?"

She grinned. "You was making enough racket to wake the whole island."

She slipped off the hammock. She was quite short, a stocky figure, wide shoulders and wide hips. But she had a very small waist—the sort you could put your two hands around, Inky thought.

"I'm Cecile Boudreau."

"Ignatius D'Alfonso—call me Inky."

"You come off the boat that's running up and down along the coast?"

"We been trying to find the channel."

"It ain't marked," she said.

"You're telling me," Inky said. "What'd they do? Use it for a shotgun target?"

She was a good-looking woman, he thought. Not more than twenty-five or so. She looked fine in the shorts—good legs and big breasts.

"The charts say it's marked."

She shrugged. "It wasn't nothing but a reflector at night."

She had brown skin—sunburned or not, he couldn't tell—and black hair cut short, very short; and greenish eyes.

"Any sort a mark and we could come in."

She grinned. Some of the teeth on the right side of her mouth

—far back—were missing. "It ain't hurt you being out there."

"Depends how long we got to stay."

"What you coming here for?"

"Look, honey," he said, "I don't know anything. It's not my boat."

She was staring at him directly. He'd never had a woman look at him quite that way.

This one now, she just stood staring right straight at him. Those light eyes began right at his shoes and went all the way up him. That should have meant just one thing. But this time he wasn't sure. The way she was staring—appraisingly, interestedly but sexless too.

And then he knew where he'd seen that sort of look before. Back in the athletic club in New Orleans. (He'd worked there a couple of years, the time when he was crazy to be a fighter.) He'd seen wrestlers look at each other that way just before starting a match.

That was the way she was looking at him. . . .

"Do you know the channel?" he asked.

"Sort of."

"Could you get us in?"

She shook her head. "I wouldn't take a chance with such a pretty boat, me."

"Hell," he said, "you want us to spend the rest of the year cruising up and down out there, waiting for the government to come put up new markers?"

She slapped at a mosquito on her arm. "You find somebody."

"Where?"

"You tried the Rendezvous?"

"You been watching me ever since I set foot on the ground."

"Not watching."

"Okay . . . listening."

"You was making so much noise, I couldn't help it."

A black and yellow ricebird came and sat on the tip of a swaying branch. "He's following me too," Inky said—and found that funny. "Don't people ever come out when you knock on their front door?"

"They wasn't home."

"Hell, no," he said, "I could hear somebody inside."

She slapped the mosquitoes on her bare thighs. "That's the Caillets."

"They don't answer?"

Her light eyes crinkled with laughter.

A door slammed, the sound muffled by the trees.

"That's the Caillets' now, for sure," Cecile said.

"Look," Inky said, "all I want to do is get in that channel."

She clucked her tongue. "I keep telling you go try the Rendez-vous."

"Okay," he said. "Where's that?"

She was staring at him, as if she wanted to remember just ex-actly what he looked like. "I show you."

"Which way?"

There was a rosebush growing at the side of the path, an old climber gone wild, with thorns like a rooster's spur.

"Move," she said, "or I get scratched up."

He hesitated for a moment, not seeing what she meant. She put a hand in the center of his chest and pushed him back, hard.

He started to grab her hand and then stopped. She went on ahead.

"Back this way here."

He found himself staring at the heavy back lines of her thighs. And he found himself thinking: That's not fat, not one bit. That's muscle. If you touched it, it would be hard.

"You find somebody at the Rendezvous, for sure."

"Won't they be out working, this time of day?"

She glanced over her shoulder. "Not all."

They passed between the houses; their porches were still empty.

"You know," he said, watching the way her shoulder blades moved through the thin shirt, "I thought the place'd be full of dogs."

"There plenty of dogs all right," Cecile said.

They crossed the little clearing where the houses were and took another path. There were hackberry bushes taller than a man's head and clumps of thick heavy blueberries.

"They just ain't around now," Cecile said.

"What?"

"The dogs." She turned around and stared at him. "You was the one was asking."

"Oh," he said, "sure."

They came out of the bushes and the trees and were on the beach.

"This here is easy walking," she said.

"The sand is yellow. It hadn't looked that way."

She looked up and down the beach, still not stopping her walk, and pursed her mouth. "Guess so."

He kicked at a big piece of driftwood. "That looks like a telephone pole for sure."

"All sorts of things come up."

"I bet."

"My old man found a rocking-chair, upholstered and all."

"Dry it out?"

"He's been sitting on it ever since I can remember." She grinned, sharp, eager, boylike. (It was funny, Inky thought, with a shape like hers, how she could remind you of a boy.)

They passed a mass of seaweed drying and smelling in the sun. And a small dead starfish.

"Man," she said, and stopped and stared out at the little surf. "I'm seeing things, maybe."

Inky sat down on a half-buried piece of driftwood and rested his head on his hand.

Cecile watched for a few more seconds, then walked out into the surf. She bent forward, peering, and walked a few more feet down the beach. Then she reached forward and picked up something and dragged it back to shore.

Maybe it's the short hair, Inky thought, or the way she moves, but how the hell can she look so much like a boy.

She had the object out on the dry sand now and was standing over it. "Sal au pri!"

Inky looked away. Bending over like that she didn't look like a boy, for sure.

They'd been on the boat for a week now the three of them. And all that time there'd been Helen, in shorts and a halter, or sunning herself on the forward deck with nothing but a towel. Arthur hardly able to keep his hands off her.

It bothered a man after a while.

"Look here."

He got up and walked over. "Looks like a hunk of wood."

She clucked her tongue. "Talking about chairs, I come to seeing them. . . . This piece now, looked like a chair."

"Yea," Inky said.

"The kind with no back."

"I saw it," Inky said. "It looked just that way."

She kicked at it. "Maybe it dry out and be good for firewood." She curled her toes over the smooth round edges. "Ain't good for nothing else."

She grinned again, her bright hard animal grin. Her eyes crinkled up so that she looked more fierce than amused. Inky wondered what it would be like to have her in bed.

"Oh hell," he said aloud. She probably wouldn't be any good, just put her hands behind her head and let him. "Hell," he said again, aloud.

She reached out and patted his shoulder. He almost jumped. "You find somebody to take your boat in, for sure."

"I'm not so sure," he said.

"I can get my husband do it."

"You promising for him?"

"Pay him?"

"Sure," Inky said, "it's not my money."

"He do it, if nobody else will."

Inky stared off at the gray-blue Gulf. The *Pixie* was far down to the east now. You couldn't make out the figures any more, just a hull and sails.

"The charts say there's plenty water down there," he said. "That right?"

"I guess so."

"Jesus," he said, "all we got to do is go aground."

"Somebody would pull you out."

"And pull the keel out too, I bet."

She looked up, squinting her light eyes in the glare. Crinkling up her face made her look old, very old.

He thought: She going to make one of those round-faced old women, with round cheeks and a little round mouth all run together with wrinkles and folds, like a kewpie doll that's been left too close to the fire.

A couple of kids passed them, walking down the beach, feet in the last edge of the surf. They were carrying crab nets, and they looked so much alike they might have twins.

"What you say?" Cecile said to them. A mosquito lit on her knee and she smashed it. "Look at that there," she said, "he's full of blood—been chewing on somebody else real hard."

"He bite you?"

She shook her head hard, so that the short black hair fell in her eyes. She didn't bother pushing it away.

Just back in the trees some kids were screaming, and a dog began to howl.

Inky squinted one eye in that direction.

"It's the Roualt kids," she said, "they pestering the dog again. In a minute or so you'll hear them yeowl too, when they mama comes out and belts them one."

"There's another piece of driftwood," Inky said.

"Nothing but an old plank." She sniffed. "Where do you reckon all this stuff comes from?"

"The driftwood?"

"What do you reckon it comes off?"

"I don't know," he said. He glanced up at the small white spot of sail and wondered if Arthur and Helen were getting impatient.

"And I heard you can tell what the weather is, miles off, from the way the waves come in. From the way they move."

"You can?"

"I was asking you."

"I heard something like that," Inky said, "but I don't remember."

She clucked her tongue. The dog stopped yelping and a kid began to scream, and then another one.

"See," she said, "I told you—their mama got around to giving them a belt."

"You were right on the nose that time." Inky said.

Cecile dusted the sand off her legs, then she began walking slowly down the beach. He got to his feet, brushed off his pants and followed. When he had caught up she said: "That building down there, the one that's kind of sticking out on the beach, kind of half in and half out the trees."

"Yea."

"That's where we going."

"You sure there going to be somebody there?"

"If there ain't," she said, "Hector do it."

"I'll remember that," he said.

They walked rapidly toward the building. Inky began to feel the suspicious ache in the back of his calves. Damn the sand, he thought.

"How do you do it?" he asked.

"Do what?"

"Nothing," he said.

Her heels did not sink deeply in the sand: he turned and looked back at the tracks. She walked markedly slue-footed, but she scarcely seemed to brush over the sand.

He was getting winded when they came to the Rendezvous. It was a narrow long wooden building and not more than twenty feet wide. From the arrangement of the windows he could tell that there was a large front room and then two smaller back ones. In front was a porch.

"This didn't used to be on the beach," Cecile said.

"Where was it?"

"It hasn't moved. . . ." For the first time she sounded annoyed. "But the beach come in to it."

"You're not old enough to see things like that."

"But my old man, he say that when he was a boy, there was a little clump of oaks right out in front of this porch. He used to have a swing on them, that's how big they was."

"They're sure not here now." Inky scuffed his toe in the sand.

"There been two or three hurricanes since then, and no mistake about it." She laughed, softly and differently. Inky looked at her curiously. It wasn't a laugh of amusement at all.

"Pieces of the beach goes all the time," she said, "with the water sucking away at it. And when it comes to a hurricane, big chunks of it goes. All the trees that used to be out here went with one of them, my papa says. And then it wasn't no time till the sand moved up, right up to the porch."

She reached out and patted the bleached, sun-split boards, patted them the way you would a dog or a horse.

Inky said: "I sure wouldn't want to be in this place when a hurricane's around."

"I don't know, me," she said. "I seen old things not lose a shingle and new things get smashed into pieces and sunk in the bay."

"I still wouldn't want to be here."

Cecile shrugged. "I don't reckon it matters much what place you in."

"Hell," Inky said, "I sure think it does."

"Well," she said, "you go see who you can find inside. Just wait around and you find something."

"It's sort of funny to think of Arthur sailing up and down out there."

"You work for him?"

"In a way?"

"You crewing for him?"

"Yea."

"You never did say where you was going."

"Just over to Galveston, that's all."

"Why'd you come to stopping here?"

Inky squinched his eyes tight shut. "Her god-damn teeth."

"His wife?"

"You shoulda heard her moaning and yelling every wave hit the bow," Inky said, "and wanting us to call the Coast Guard or the Navy or somebody to fly out and get her." He scratched his chin and propped up one foot on the lowest step. "And then it comes out that she was having trouble with her wisdom tooth back in New Orleans a month or so ago, but she couldn't stop to do anything about it. Hell, no."

Cecile said: "So you want somebody to take her over to Petit Prairie too, no?"

"You're right, honey. You're absolutely right."

"You better call the dentist there, account of he goes fishing for days on end."

"Now, honey," Inky said, "she wouldn't go to him. They going over to find somebody there to drive them all the way into New Orleans." He watched the sharp bright white points of light on the waves. "The god-damn tooth," he said very softly.

"You stay here with the boat, no?"

"Smart like a schoolteacher. Sure I do. Until they make up their god-damn mind to come back, or send me somebody to sail it out with."

"You give us the most excitement we got in months."

"Hell," Inky said.

She pointed to the front door. "I see Dan Rivé in there. By the back of his head and the way his ears wiggle while he listening to us." She picked up a bit of shell and threw it with all her strength against the wall. "People can be real nice," she said. "For sure." She began to walk away.

"Hey," Inky said, "aren't you coming in?"

"What for? I showed you where it was."

"Thanks," he said. "Thanks a lot."

"You going to be around," she said without turning. "I'll be seeing you, one place or the other."

He watched her for a minute, watched the steady wide roll of her hips. Damn, he said to himself, god damn.

He wondered if he'd been propositioned. For the first time in his life he wasn't sure.

PERIQUE LOMBAS cut across the island, walking fast in spite of the heat, heading for the wharf on the north side. Only one of the little fleet there was in, on its high white bow the red-lettered name, *Hula Girl,* the Boudreau boat. Hector Boudreau and his father, Archange, got it cheap ten years before over at Mobile. And when an accident crippled the old man's hip, Hector bought him out too. That made the *Hula Girl* the biggest boat on the island to belong to a single man. So Hector was proud of her, kept her cleaner than most of the other boats, even scrubbed out the wheelhouse every month or so.

When they worked, the Old Boudreau still went out with them. For a cripple he could move fast—and there were those who hadn't given him much of a chance to walk again. It was two years ago now that he'd got caught between hull and dock. They hadn't thought he'd live when they took him over to the hospital at Petit Prairie, him conscious all the way, but not making a sound, not answering anybody, not seeming to hear, but all wrapped up in a tight little cocoon, just him and the pain.

He was tough and he could still work, but only the light stuff. Perique was the regular crew. He was just twenty, taller already than any man on the island, and very thin, with a long thin face, close-set brown eyes, and a heavy black beard that showed through shaving.

The engine hatch was open now. Hector was squatting in the little patch of shade from the wheelhouse, splashing his face and neck with water from the bucket he had set there.

"Where the hell you been at?"

Perique shrugged. "You shoulda wait for me."

"I can't wait around all day."

"Lets us see what you got."

"Man," Hector said, "not me."

27

"You don't want to do nothing more this evening?"

Hector's face was streaked with oil and his eyes were bloodshot. "I been at it an hour, and I'm ready to quit."

They put the cover back on the engine hatch. Hector emptied the bucket of water over the side. "Here it come—look out, you fish!"

"Bet the heat don't bother them," Perique said.

"How Annie doing?" Hector winked.

"I don't know, me."

"Hell, man," Hector said, "don't let it get you down none."

"It ain't bothering me."

"They get like that sometime."

"Yea," Perique said.

"Only thing you can be sure of, it ain't going to stay that way. They never stay one way."

"You don't see me crying none."

Two small brown pelicans were swimming in a wide circle around the boat. Perique whistled at them.

Hector said: "I seen you over there one day, day before yesterday maybe."

"Lay off," Perique said flatly. And after a pause: "You sure you want to leave them nets like that?"

"Yea," Hector said, and rubbed the back of his neck. "You see the kids down by the cleaning-shed?"

The shed was right on the end of the wharf—just some two-by-fours and a low roof built onto the side of the icehouse. Fish were gutted there, at a big long wood table. And there was a hand pump and a hose that went into the bay about fifty feet away—so the place could be washed clean in a minute, even if it only was with salt water.

There was a bunch down there, in their mid-teens, most of them. Some were cleaning fish, the rest were watching and giggling and slapping each other on the back or trying to get a hand on a girl's breast or thigh.

"Look at the bucket there," Hector said. "They got some croakers they don't want. And they been putting lye in 'em and throwing it to the pelicans."

"Fi d'poutain," Perique said softly.

"I ain't right fond of it neither."

"That plain make me sick," Perique said, "when he swallows it and goes flopping around in those big old circles."

"You did it when you was a kid."

"Don't make me like it more now."

The giggling got louder and the group crowded around the table.

"Fi d'poutain," Perique said again.

"Sound like Charlie Alain," Hector said, "and I bet he stuffing that fish right now.

They saw the group step back. They saw the fish's silvery underside glint for a second as it went sailing out into the waiting beak of a pelican.

Perique turned away and began to pull at the heap of nets. "You want to do something about these, no?"

"In a while, man." Hector kept rubbing at the back of his neck: that was where the sun got you first, sometimes so hard it felt like a rabbit punch.

"I come down here to work," Perique said, "And I ain't gonna sit on my ass all day long."

Hector shifted and stretched and scratched through the buttons of his shirt in the thick hair of his chest. "Go on ahead."

"Why don't I run 'em up, so we can see how bad they torn."

"I know how bad," Hector said.

Perique dragged at the heap of nets. His sweat-soaked shirt stuck to his back and shoulders. He straightened up. "Enfant garce!" He unbuttoned the shirt and threw it to the deck. His body was brown and very thin; the edges of the spine stuck up like knuckles, and the muscles were like cords. There was a tattoo high up on his left arm, almost to the shoulder: an eagle with a flag in its mouth.

"You fixing to get sun stroke for sure?" Hector asked.

Perique did not answer. By the time he'd fastened the net and cranked it up, man-high, by the little hand winch, he was covered with sweat.

All of a sudden Hector looked over the rail and grinned. "Hi, what you say?" He got up and sat astride the rail. "Perique man, look who we got here."

Annie Landry took her pirogue within ten feet of the lugger, and then with a single quick stroke, turned it sideways and stopped it dead on the water.

"See that?" she grinned up.

"Always did say you could handle a pirogue like a man." Hector took a cigarette from his pocket.

"Me, too," Annie said.

Hector tossed one. She caught it with a quick downward motion of her hand. The pirogue bobbed lightly but steadily.

Perique came and stood just behind Hector. "Where you going?" he asked her.

She ignored him and was looking at Hector from under her lowered lids. "No light?"

"Come get it." He pulled a box of matches from his pocket and held them out.

She was looking at Perique now, fluttering her lids. "You want me to fall in the bay, huh?"

"I don't want you to do nothing, me," Perique said. "You was yelling for matches and he's giving it to you."

"How I'm going reach it?"

"That your problem," Perique said.

"Think I can't get it?"

She shifted her paddle and dipped with it. The pirogue jumped almost sideways. The water swirled to the top, but not a drop splashed in. She flicked the paddle dry and laid it across the narrow boat. She waited until the water was quiet and the hull had stopped vibrating. Then she put out her hands, one on each gunwale and lifted herself to a crouching position.

"Sure glad you know how to swim," Hector said.

She shifted her feet slightly; the pirogue swayed.

"If anybody come along now," Perique said, "you go over for sure."

"Bet I can do it." She stood up finally, one foot on each side of the sloping shell. Her head was just above the deck of the lugger.

"Look at that," Hector said, "no hands, even."

She stuck up the cigarette between her lips. Perique struck a match. "Not you," she said. "I wouldn't trust you." The cigarette dropped down again. "You likely to burn my nose off just to get me to fall in the water."

"Me?" Hector asked.

She stuck the cigarette straight out again.

"Okay," Hector said. He snapped a match against his fingernail and, leaning down, lighted the cigarette.

She puffed at it, hard, the way a beginner always does, her eyes squinted against the smoke.

"If you old man knew you smoked," Perique said, "he'd take a couple pieces of skin off you."

She stuck out her tongue, around the corner of the cigarette. "Il vient d'poulailler," she said to nobody in particular.

Perique blushed. The sunburned back of his neck got red. "No more than you."

"Man, man," Hector said, "ain't love something."

"Shut up," Annie said.

She bent her knees and slowly lowered herself back to a sitting position in the pirogue. Then she picked up the paddle and moved off a bit. "So I don't got to look straight up when I talk to you," she explained.

The two men sat astride the rail, looking down at her. It was funny, Hector thought, how quick she'd come to growing up. Last year, or a little before, she'd been a kid.

He remembered her, when her mother died, and that wasn't a year and a half past—a kid with a round fat face and pimples.

Well, Hector told himself, she wasn't a kid anymore.

In the bright white sun, her hair was even whiter than usual. She was the only person on the island with blond hair: her mother (Mary, Rest her soul, Hector thought) had been a big blond German woman from up Bayou Lafourche. Alastair Landry had gone far off to get himself a wife.

It was a pretty girl, for sure, Hector thought. In all the sun her skin just got darker and with a deeper pink glow so that her eyes looked brittle-blue.

"I got business," Annie said, "soon's I finish this here cigarette."

Perique was silent staring over the back bay.

Hector looked at Perique's thin sulking profile and said: "Where you going?"

"Fetch some soft shells, if they biting."

"Where, huh?"

"Over across there."

A few days ago she had stuck some branches, leafy ends down, into the shallow water. And today when she went back and pulled them up, there'd be crabs hanging to them, like fruit.

"I ain't seen your old man today," Hector said, "where he at?"

"Over by Port Ronquille."

"Again, huh?" Hector grinned. "He been there a lot."

"I don't mind," Annie said. She reached up one hand and pushed back her short blond hair. "Me, I got work to do."

She paddled off, with long easy strokes.

Hector shook his head, "I can't ever figure, me, how that kid grow up."

Perique said, "What about that place on the bow—don't that got to be sanded off?"

"Man," Hector said, "that Annie sure is something to bother a guy."

"Reckon I could work on that."

"I ain't ready to paint yet."

Perique got the sandpaper and wrapped it around a block of wood. "If you had a power-sander, man, this would be just fun."

"Going get one." Hector sat down in the shade of the wheel-house.

Perique went up in the bow and knelt down, curving his body over the low wood rail, stretching one leg out behind him for balance, and began to work on the spot.

"Man," Hector said, "it do make me feel good to watch you work."

Perique straightened up, stretched and bent down again.

"It ain't going to be near that hard if you go get my old man's skiff and work up from it."

"I reach it."

"You getting split wide open."

Perique's face was flushed red with large white splotches when he finally finished and came over to the patch of shade. He stretched out full length, face down, on the boards. "Jesus," he said softly.

Hector tipped back his head and stared up into the sky that

was still bright and hot but was getting the darker tone of the evening coming. A small fat sparrow flew down and perched on the swinging nets.

After a while Perique rolled over and grinned. "That is hard work for sure."

"You could have got the chabec, easy as nothing."

"Didn't feel like it." Perique shrugged one shoulder.

"You know," Hector asked, "what I'm thinking about?"

"Nuh uh."

"How I don't feel like drinking beer tonight, me . . . feel like this is a night for whisky."

Perique sat up and rubbed his stomach. "I'm gonna be black and blue."

"Yessir, when we come to get through with supper, I'm gonna get out that bottle of whisky."

"What kind you got?"

"Four Roses."

"Ain't bad," Perique said.

"Hell it ain't!" Hector bent his knee and began to scratch it hard. "Mosquito bites near three day old and driving me crazy."

"Put some Campho-Phenique on 'em."

"You come over tonight and I'll give you a drink too, man. That'll help out you stomach."

Perique straightened up and took a deep breath slowly. "You reckon Annie got the crabs?"

"She ain't come back this way."

"She could gone round and tied up at Arcenaux wharf and we wouldn't seen her."

Hector said: "All I can think of, me, is that bottle sitting home waiting."

"I ain't been drunk in a long time."

"Why you don't come get drunk and go over by Annie's."

"What for?"

"Maybe work better that way than sober."

"I ain't up to bothering," Perique said.

"Hell you ain't."

Perique put his hands behind his head and kicked off his shoes. "Don't know why you making a fuss."

"Cause you ain't moving."

"I got hot pants for her. But there ain't nothing so important in that."

"Okay, man," Hector said.

He got to his feet very slowly and went to the wheelhouse, took the ignition key out and dropped it in his pocket. "You remember the time LaHarpe left his key and the Perrin kids took the boat clean up to Port Ronquille?"

Perique did not answer. He was lying perfectly still looking up at the sky. It was very quiet.

Hector came back on deck, and stood scratching his chin. "Seems like all I can think about is that whisky."

"Leastways, all you can talk about."

Hector nudged him gently with his toe. "Come on, man, and I match you drink for drink."

"Not me."

"Ain't that much work to do tomorrow."

"And I wanted to," Perique said, "ain't no amount of work tomorrow gonna stop me."

"Half a bottle of good whisky."

"Quit kicking me," Perique said.

Hector pulled back his toe. "Man, I hate to see you moping around like that for her."

Perique kept opening and closing his eyes, very slowly. "She going to do something one of these days, and I ain't gonna want nothing to do with her."

"Me, I'm going home." Hector stepped over the gunwale. The pier creaked and shifted under his weight. "Jesus . . ." he said, "I gotta fix this." He tiptoed across the boards.

Perique stared straight up. It was going to be a hot night, and still. The mosquitoes were beginning to come in already.

A seagull squaaked. He turned his head in time to see the white shape spin down and splash into the water. And a second gull follow it.

He sat up. "Jesus, Mary!"

The two white shapes flew up from the water, got only a couple of feet above the surface and splashed back in. This time Perique could see the length of string between them. The kids were fastening two fish together by a couple of feet of string and tossing them into the air where two gulls swallowed them.

"Can you make seagulls drown, mister?" one of the girls mocked in a high, shrill baby voice, "show us how you make seagulls drown."

The other girl whooped and buried her head in her lap.

Charlie Alain was untangling a piece of twine. "I'm working on it, honey." He stopped and picked up one of the fish and waved it around his head. "Look!" he yelled at the gulls, "see!"

Perique stepped to the wharf, looking after them. The mosquitoes were biting, and he stood on one leg, scratching the other with his foot.

"Hi," Annie said.

She was almost beneath him. She had slipped the pirogue almost under the pier.

Perique squatted down. "You get any crabs?"

She pointed to the bow, to a basket covered with wide mulberry leaves. "What you think that is?"

"It didn't take you long."

"You sorry or glad for that?"

"I ain't neither," Perique said. "I was just saying what you was."

The pirogue rubbed against the piling and she shoved it off gently with her paddle.

He shook his head and fished out a cigarette.

"You ain't going to offer me one?"

"Your old man don't want you having one."

"Since when you take sides with my papa?"

He stood up, stretched. "You see all the excitement on the other side?"

"Like what?"

"Sailboat," he said, "hunting for the pass, I guess."

"Here?"

"Go have a look."

"What they come here for?"

"Don't ask me."

"How long?"

"I don't know," Perique said. "About noon, maybe."

"Nobody told me." With a jab of her oar, she moved the pirogue clear of the barnacle-crusted pilings.

"I got to be going," Perique said.

"Where to?"

"I'm getting drunk tonight, me, and I got to go get supper first."

The pirogue had swung back near the pilings.

"With who?

"Huh?"

"With who you going get drunk?"

He winked: "See you."

He went off down the pier, whistling soundlessly into the hot afternoon. He'd have to find Hector and tell him that he'd just given away half a bottle of his whiskey.

Perique looked down at his feet, the way they went flicking back and forth under him. Man, he told himself, man, you are flying for sure.

*

BY six o'clock that day the *Pixie* was in harbor.

Inky and Dan Rivé had made an agreement, sitting there in
the Rendezvous with a bottle of beer. They'd shook hands on it,
drained their bottles, and went off to get Rivé's boat.

It was a twenty-foot hull with a half-cabin, and it stank of
dead fish. And Inky wondered what Helen was going to think of
it—maybe with her tooth she wasn't going to notice.

And in less than half an hour, Inky and Arthur had dropped
the *Pixie*'s sails (lashed the jib to the lifelines, hurriedly, and
left the main uncovered) and were following Rivé back through
the channel under power.

Except for one lugger the wharf was empty. "Where do we
tie up?" Inky yelled.

Rivé waved his hand. "No matter where."

Even before the lines were fast, Rivé had his boat alongside,
and Arthur was loading a couple of suitcases in it. Then Helen
got in, a scarf tied around her head and holding one cheek, complaining: "Don't push me."

The noisy old motor gunned, and the hull swung away showing
the name on her stern: *Dorothy R.* After a couple of minutes it
got quiet, and then quieter, until there was only a faint sound
left and a faint shape that was heading straight across the bay.

Inky was alone with a boat that wasn't his and a fat roll of bills
that were. (Just before leaving Arthur had called him below and
given them to him—"Ought to be enough," he said. And Inky
had put them in the locker in the head, in the center of a roll of
toilet paper.)

Behind him the island was very quiet, with just the faint smell
of cooking. Inky redid the lines; they had been done so fast they

37

were sloppy. A lugger was coming in. He watched her dock. Then got out his own canvas fenders and began to string them from the stanchions on his outer side.

He was so busy and they came so quietly—he jumped when he saw the line of kids standing on the pier watching him. But he just stared back at them, and said nothing, and went forward to take in the jib.

It seemed to him that all the kids of the island were lined up there, giggling and pointing to the fenders he had just put out. Occasionally one of them would put out his foot and pretend to step down to the deck—and the others would roar with laughter.

It struck Inky suddenly that, in a group like that, they had a funny smell, like peanuts. . . .

Finally, one of them—it was Didi LeBlanc—actually jumped down to the deck. Inky heard her land—the kids got very quiet suddenly—but he kept on working steadily. Didi scuttled over to the forward porthole and peeped in. Inky finished unsnapping the jib from the forestay, turned suddenly and with one quick step was across the deck. Didi did not even have a chance to turn around. Inky caught her around the waist and tossed her up on the wharf, the way you'd toss a bag.

She landed on all fours with her back arched, like a cat.

Inky went back to his work. Now that he had started, he found so many things to do. So he did them, one after the other.

One or two of the kids stayed for nearly an hour, watching him. By that time he was groggy with the stifling, late-day heat. It was getting toward sunset and even the light afternoon breeze had dropped. The water had a faint sweet-sour smell, and when you looked at it, it was dark with an almost oily surface, in spite of the Gulf so close.

"Jesus," he said softly and straightening up, rubbed his hands slowly down his back. The dryness was still in the back of his throat and his mouth. The way it felt just before you were beginning to be seasick, before your mouth turned salty and wet.

Harbor sick, he thought, damned if I knew there was such a thing.

What would the kids do, he thought suddenly, if he hung his head over the side and vomited into the water. Which was what he felt like doing. He kept imagining them: they'd all come running back down to the wharf, from wherever they were hiding now and they'd stand there pointing and laughing and slapping their knees.

He shook his head. He could see it so clear: their open mouths —most of them were at that age where they had no front teeth, just red spaces.

Jesus, Inky told himself, I'm getting sunstroke, and I got to get something to eat.

He went below.

The cabin was hot and close. Just the smell of varnished wood baking in the sun. Inky stretched out on one of the bunks. It was Helen's bunk, his own was up forward. There was still the faint smell of perfume on the covers. He'd never seen a woman use perfume on a boat, but she did, lots of it, because, she said, the winds blew the scent off. Over there, in the locker there'd be two or three bottles still—she hadn't taken them with her.

That was one of the first things he'd done—checked all the after lockers, to see what she'd left.

It was a god-damn stupid business, he told himself.

Behind his closed eyes bright little patterns of color floated; little trickles of sweat ran down his cheeks. And just that little odor of perfume. Did she put drops of it on the covers, he wondered. It wasn't a heavy scent, nor musky. He sniffed. It was more spicy. And, he thought, it didn't smell bad on a boat, small and fresh under the smell of paint and tar.

God, he thought, I've got a bad case.

He rolled over.

He'd have to get the topside covers up by tomorrow for sure, before the sun got to the brightwork.

And for a few days or a week he could play at being on his own boat. Until Arthur gave him his orders. . . . He opened one eye and stared at the white-painted wood. It was a pity he didn't have a girl on the island to give the perfume to.

He'd have to spread out the sails tomorrow, the ones stowed up forward—the storm jib and the spinnaker—the ones they hadn't used at all this trip. No use letting mildew get in them. He'd have to get the mattresses up in the sun too. And dry out the cockpit cushions.

I'll have to do that before the sun is too high, he thought.
There's an alarm clock around here somewhere.

He'd have to find it and set it.

He closed his eyes again and listened. There was just the little
sucking sound of water against the hull (and he thought about
the girl—Cecile, she said her name was—who said the Gulf had
sucked away the beach: it was just exactly that sort of sound)
and the little creaks of the mooring-lines. He wiped the sweat
off his face with the back of his arm. Now that he was alone on
the boat, he realized what a large shape it was.

All those planks, he thought sleepily, pointing up to a bow.
And there's a keel right under me and a couple of tons of lead.

Lying there, he imagined he was in the stomach of some big
animal.

He heard the feet jump lightly down to the deck. The boat
rocked a little with their weight. He swung his legs out of the
bunk. He lay for a minute without opening his eyes, trying to
wake up.

It would be the kids, he thought. They never got tired and
they never went away.

He scrambled up the ladder, fast as he could.

Halfway up, his head and shoulders above the hatch cover, he
stopped. There, sitting on the aft seat in the cockpit, grinning
her bright hard smile, was Cecile Boudreau.

"You surprise to see me?"

"Yea," he said, "sort of."

"We just come calling."

"Matter of fact," he said, "I was thinking about you."

"Man, man," she said over Inky's shoulder to the man who
stood on the deck, leaning against one of the pilings. "Ain't you
getting jealous?"

"Ain't nobody else want you, che'," he said.

She threw back her head and laughed. Those missing side
teeth, Inky thought, made her face look more like a child's.

"This is my husband, Hector."

Inky came one more step up the ladder and held out his hand.
Hector's palm was hard, very hard, and very warm.

"Pleased to meet you."

Hector was fairly tall, tall as most on the island, and very broad with a back so heavily muscled it seemed stooped. He was sunburned too, burned until the undercolor was no longer red but gray. He had black hair, perfectly straight, cut short in front and long in back so that it fell over the collar of his paint-spattered shirt.

His face was broad, with black eyes set very far apart. He wasn't good-looking and he certainly wasn't ugly.

Women might find him attractive, Inky thought. And men wouldn't trust him.

Maybe, Inky told himself, that wasn't such a bad way to be.

"And over there on the dock," Cecile said, "that's Annie Landry."

Inky saw a small thin face under blond hair. Just a kid he thought. She had something of the funny pinched look around the nose that kids often have.

"Hi," Inky said, "I didn't see you back there."

Annie grinned and didn't say anything.

"She shy," Cecile said, "don't pay any attention."

"You sure cause a mix-up," Hector said.

Inky scratched the side of his head. "None of it was my idea."

"The damn tooth," Cecile said, "that what you told me yesterday."

"Rivé, now, he going to be right glad to pick up that extra money running them over there." Hector said.

"He ought to be." Inky climbed out the ladder and sat down on the hot bare boards of the cockpit. "He charged them enough to live a year on."

Hector shrugged.

"Look," Inky said, "don't get me wrong. I don't give a damn how Arthur spends his money. Right now, he's spending some of it on me."

"Dan can use some of that, for sure."

"Me, too."

Hector came aboard and walked slowly forward. He was wearing heavy work shoes. They scratched over the boards.

Inky thought: He's walking harder than he needs to.

But he did not turn or look or give any sign that he noticed. To hell with the decks, Inky thought: If that's deliberate it won't bother me.

Hector walked the full length of the boat and turning settled himself on the pulpit rail. "This is a fancy one, for sure," he said.

Inky looked over his shoulder. "Sure it is."

"Teak decks."

"Yea," Inky said, "I noticed."

"Sure looked pretty sailing out there yesterday."

"We had a fair breeze."

"All that white canvas . . . prettiest thing."

"Yea," Inky said, "I like it all right.

Hector didn't answer, so Inky turned back to Cecile who was still stretched out in the cockpit.

"What do you think about it?"

"Me?" She lifted her heavy eyebrows. "I don't know nothing about boats.

"You think it looks pretty?"

"I do," Annie said from her perch on the wharf.

Inky turned around—he'd forgot she was there. "So pretty you don't want to come aboard?"

She lifted up her chin. He wondered if she was nervous or if she only needed glasses.

"It won't sink if you get on," Cecile laughed.

"I got hard shoes on," Annie said, "and I don't want to cut up the decks like Hector's doing."

The kid surprised them, Inky thought. And he rubbed his nose to cover a smile.

"You want me to jump overboard," Hector said, "place of walking back?"

"No," Annie said. There were nervous red splotches across her chin now. "You just got no right to stomp along."

Hector left his seat on the pulpit rail and tiptoed back across the deck, arms stretched out at his sides in an exaggerated balance.

Annie looked off across the bay. Her lip was trembling, but her eyes were dry and staring.

Inky took a quick look at Cecile. She was still sitting draped out across the back seat; she did not even seem interested.

Hector climbed back on the dock and squatted down alongside Annie. "Now you satisfied, no?"

"I didn't say come off."

"Like hell you didn't."

"I just said take off your shoes." She was following the clumsy heavy flight of a brown pelican.

Hector looked over at Inky. "Something, ain't she?"

"I don't know," Inky said cautiously, "you tell me."

"I got a mind to push her in the bay," Hector said.

Annie swung herself out of reach.

"Quit," Cecile said, "she got on a new clean dress."

"That a fact?" Hector tilted his head looking at Annie, "you got all dressed up."

"It's stuffy down there, huh?" Annie said to Inky, pointing below.

"Hot as hell."

"You're going to sleep there?"

"It'll be better when I get the air scoop up."

"What's that?" Cecile said.

"Goes up by the forward hatch—you'll see."

"Where you going to sleep tonight?"

He pointed to the side seats.

"We got mosquitoes," Hector said.

"I got mosquito-netting."

Cecile said: "You could find a place to stay on the island."

"I don't know," Inky said, "I don't think so."

"We got an extra room at my house," Annie said. "You could have that for free."

"Thanks," Inky said. "I don't want to put you out."

"It's no trouble," Cecile said. "They got this empty room."

"Thanks," Inky said. "I just think I'd rather stay on the boat."

Annie was buffing her fingernails against her skirt. "You got the best part of that deal," she said.

"If I had a boat like this," Cecile said, "I'd want to stay on it."

Annie said: "It's just a little old back room that my cousin used to sleep in when he lived with us before he went away. And you can still smell the turtles and the rabbits he used to keep back there."

"Now that just ain't true," Cecile said.

"I live there," Annie said. "I can smell it."

"Hush up, now." Cecile said.

"You wouldn't like this room," Annie said, "I don't know why I ask you."

Two more boats were coming in, heading for the stretch of dock just to the *Pixie*'s stern.

"The whole house got to be scrubbed out," Annie said, still holding her hands in front of her, "only I don't want to ruin my hands doing it."

"Lord, how you talk," Cecile said and stared straight up at the bright blue sky.

"The dirt is just that thick," Annie said, "and I never did look to see what's under the beds."

Cecile began to whistle softly.

"If you don't believe it," Annie said, "just you come see."

"Look," Inky said, "I like living on the boat. I know where everything is and I can put my hand on it. And I can do whatever I want and there's nobody around to get bothered."

"I don't know why I ask you," Annie said, "now that I come to thinking about it."

"There's all sorts of gear on board," Inky said, "that needs looking after. And if anything went wrong, I want to be right here."

Cecile said suddenly: "You tied where the *Bozo* always comes, you know that?"

"Rivé said they're so low they could tie up right here."

"Alongside?"

"I got the fenders out there, if they want to."

"I see, for sure." And Hector rubbed his upper lip hard.

Cecile started to say something, then changed her mind.

"Hector, man!" a voice called.

Hector walked over to that boat. When he had gone, Inky said: "That's a good-looking man you're married to."

"Me, I think so," Cecile said.

Inky looked around. "Where'd she go?"

Cecile grinned. "Annie? She just up and disappeared."

Hector called over: "*Bozo*'s coming back."

Cecile said: "You can hear them engines a mile off."

"I got the fenders out," Inky said.

Cecile grabbed a circling mosquito out of the air and peeped cautiously in her clenched fist. "Sure you got fenders," she said.

"Now what's so funny about that?" Inky said.

Hector wandered back, stopping finally with one foot on the stern mooring-line.

Inky looked up at him.

"You got a fixed keel and no centerboard?" Hector asked.

"Yea," Inky said. "You can come see if you're interested."

"How much?"

"Huh?"

Hector scratched his eyebrow. "How much lead you got?"

"Two tons."

Hector stared at the stern of the boat. "Looks pretty from back here."

"You like it, huh?"

"What you draw?"

"Near five."

Hector shook his head.

"Four eleven."

"There ain't much water that deep around here."

"If you stay offshore."

"Sure," Hector said, "I wasn't thinking about that."

"That's why we had to be so careful with the channel."

The sound of engines was very loud now. The *Bozo* must be nearing the dock. Inky turned around. For a minute he stared at the rough paint-blistered hull of the fishing-boat.

"Jesus Christ," he yelled, "stay off!"

Cecile rolled over slowly and looked at him. She was grinning.

Along the side of the *Bozo,* acting as fenders, was a row of old rubber tires.

"Don't come in here," Inky yelled. "Keep the god-damn tires away."

Hector laughed. "Going to be a big smear for sure."

Inky was jumping up and down, waving them off. The men on the *Bozo* did not seem to notice. One of them waved calmly to Hector. "Hi, Hector man," he called, "what you say?"

Hector waved back.

"Keep the fucking god-damn tires out of here," Inky yelled. He was standing on the cockpit seats now, stuttering with rage.

"All that pretty white hull," Hector said softly, "just all going to be smeared up."

The *Bozo's* bow came around and her engine reversed and she swung gently in. The two hulls touched very gently, the smaller canvas fenders useless against the thick tires. At that precise minute the *Bozo's* engine went into forward and the line of black tires dragged and scraped along the sailboat's freeboard. Then the engine was idling and two men were calmly fastening the lines.

Inky was very quiet now; he stood watching them, his mouth pursed. Then he leaned over and looked at the side of his hull. The white freeboard was a smear of black rubber.

Inky straightened up. "That was real funny," he said, "and now who's gonna help me clean off the freeboard?"

There were three men on the boat. They looked so much alike they might all have been brothers. Inky looked from one to the other.

"Son of a bitch," he said, "who's gonna help me clean that off?"

They went on with their jobs, appearing not to hear.

"There's a whole day's work cleaning there."

One of the men, the shortest one, with light brown hair cut so short it looked almost shaved, said: "You yelling at us?"

"You god-damn right I am."

"You got you fenders out," another man said. He was older, fifty-five or so, and his hair had balded away to a bristly fringe around the edges. "It wasn't none of our fault they wasn't enough."

"Son of a bitch!" Inky said softly.

The third man, who was tying his shoe on the caprail looked up. "What was you calling us?" He was just a kid, Inky noticed; and he had a kid's pimply face, big red splotches across his cheeks and down his neck. He had long thin arms with streaks of muscle and criss-crossing veins.

"What was that now?" the brown haired man said.

The three were looking at him—two were hostile, a clear fighting look; and the older man was looking at him appraisingly, not hostile, but not exactly friendly either.

In its hook by the side of main hatch was the long bronze winch handle. Inky's fingers closed on it softly. He grinned to himself: that would make the fight more even.

He could feel the muscles in his stomach tighten and he hunched his shoulders slightly. He had the silly desire to giggle. He could feel his mouth move around, trying to stop it. The three were staring at him, and he realized he must be making faces.

He forced himself to take deep slow breaths. Inside his shoes his toes curled downward—to get a better hold on the deck.

Slowly the indecision in the older man's face faded. When he makes up his mind, Inky thought, they'll come.

He waited.

Then it changed. All of a sudden. He saw it change.

It was the pimply-faced boy who did it. Inky was watching him. The face that was angry one minute turned confused and then, all of a sudden, guarded.

With that same careful strange expression on his face, the boy straightened up and laughed, a sharp little laugh that made the others turn to look at him.

Inky saw it and wondered. He's remembering something, he thought, you can see him remembering. And it's changing everything. And he doesn't want anyone else to know.

Inky told himself: He's not going to fight. He's not afraid, but he just made up his mind.

"Jesus," the boy said, "it got to be the heat." He gave a shrug with one shoulder. Cut across the *Pixie* and climbed on the dock.

For a minute the others just stared after him. Then the older man said quietly: "Nothing here that won't wait for tomorrow, Chep boy. . . . Lets us go."

"I got to get the cigarettes." Chep got them from the wheel-house and, with the other, crossed over the *Pixie* to the dock. As he went, he lit a cigarette, dropping the match, which flickered for a second on the deck and then went out.

The two of them headed down the dock. Inky picked up the match and tossed it to the water. "Jesus," he said, "everybody takes it out on the decks."

The pimply-faced boy had not gone. He was standing a couple of feet back on the dock, talking to Hector.

Inky picked up the chamois and rubbed the spot: there was a small burned mark. He threw the cloth through the open hatch, angrily.

"It wasn't that bad," Cecile said. She was still stretched out on the cockpit seat, looking as if nothing had happened.

"Everything's swell," Inky said. "Now who were they?"

"Livaudais," Cecile said. "Eddie Livaudais, the old man, and his boy Henry there," she pointed over her shoulder, "and his brother-in-law."

The boy finished talking to Hector and started off. After a few steps he turned and asked: "You know the date?"

"Who?" Cecile said. "Me?"

"It's the ninth," Hector said.

"You sure?"

Cecile said, "I wrote a letter yesterday and I looked at the calendar—that's what it is, for sure."

The boy lifted one hand to rub his cheek, remembered the pimples and dropped the hand again. "Just what I wanted to find out," he said with a little grin. "The date was bothering me."

"How come?"

"I been working enough these days here," Henry said. "And I'm figuring to take it easy for a while."

"Hell," Hector said, "wish I was doing it."

"Can't go getting in a fight," the boy said with that same nervous laugh. And he deliberately didn't look over toward Inky. "Can't go getting bashed up when I'm taking a couple of days off."

"Wish I was doing that," Hector said.

"Going hunting, maybe." And the boy left.

"What I don't get," Cecile said quietly, "is why they changed their minds."

"You got me," Inky said.

"Ain't like a Livaudais."

"You saw it," Inky said.

Cecile shook her head. "And they fighters, them. Tough as nobody's business."

"They could toss you in the bay," Hector said. "Any size pieces they want to."

"Something stopped Henry, for sure."

Hector chuckled and began to move away. "Crazy Livaudais," he said, "that what we always say around here. Whole bunch always been crazy."

"See you," Cecile said.

"I'll be here," Inky said.

Hector was halfway down the wharf. Cecile ran to catch up with him, turning once to wave.

Inky sat down on the sun-warmed cockpit seat and stared at the winch handle. And he felt just a little twinge of regret for not using it.

All the rest of the evening young Livaudais's face bothered him.

*

AS they had planned, Perique and Hector began drinking after supper. They worked on the whisky, sitting in the little screened-in part of the Boudreau porch. Cecile put the kids to bed and went over to the Monjures, next door, visiting. Every now and then they could hear her laughing. Finally she came back, passed by with only a look for them, and went to bed.

They found another bottle and kept drinking, steadily. Shortly after ten they finished all they had. And Perique left, walking slowly along the gravel paths, until he saw the light in the Landry house. He went over and let himself in the gate. The dogs knew him, and whined around his legs. He walked up to the window which was just slightly over his head, and called: "Hey!"

He heard the rustle of the paper as Annie put down the magazine. "Hey!" he called again. She did not answer. But the whisky was singing behind his ears, so he said: "You got company in the parlor."

And went around the front and let himself in.

Annie had been curled up on her bed, her clothes off in the stuffy night, reading magazines: a copy of *House and Garden* that was four months old, and five or six back issues of the *Ladies' Home Journal*.

When she heard Perique she pulled up a couple of copies to cover herself, in case he could climb up on something and look in the window.

She was surprised. She really was. And her skin prickled with a shiver even in the heat. It was a pleasant feeling. She was glad he had come, gladder to see him than she had been in a long while. She slipped a dress on, hurrying, not bothering with panties or a bra. It was a heavy chintz cotton, and there wasn't really any need for it, she told herself. She stopped to put on some lipstick,

49

and brush her hair, and smear a little perfume down the sides of her neck.

He had put on only a single light in the living-room, and for a minute she didn't see him. "Goodness," she said, "it's dark."

"It's your eyes," he said thickly.

He was drunk, she thought. And there was another lovely little goosepimply shiver.

"Papa hasn't come back," she said, "he must be staying the night."

"I figured that," he said.

"I was in bed."

"That's a nice place to be."

"I meant I had to get dressed again, in skirts and all."

"Okay," he said, "let's us talk about your skirts."

"You been drinking?"

"Honey," he said, "I am drunk. You got any beer?"

"You don't need any more."

He got up and walked quietly past her and out to the kitchen. "Know your house well as mine."

She went around, turning on the lights. He came back, three beer cans balanced on one hand, and squinted into the light. "God damn," he tumbled the cans into her lap. "Hold on to these." And he turned them all back out. "Open me a beer," he said.

"I don't know," she said, "you had enough."

"Not going to do it, huh?"

She caught the warning in his voice and shivered again.

"Okay," he said. "Do it myself, me. And that there is one against you."

"One what?"

"Tell you when the time come."

"What?"

He drank the beer in long gulps. "I'm real thirsty," he said. "Whisky give you a thirst."

"Don't I get one?" she said.

"More out there. Go get you' own."

She got up, angry now, went out to the kitchen, and brought a couple of cans for herself.

He was in the big chair. She sat on the sofa, realized that was a mistake, and was a little shy about changing her seat abruptly.

He gathered up his beer cans and came over to sit beside her. She started to move. He dumped the cans quick to the cushion, and grabbed her.

"Don't spill it," she said. "I got a clean dress." She was excited now, she could feel her ears get hot—it was almost like anger, only it wasn't.

"It's a clean dress," she repeated.

"Take it off if you worrying about it."

"No. . . ." She pulled back, but he had her by one wrist and yanked her back down. "Ouch," she said, "you hurt. . . ."

"Don't go whining like a puppy dog." He finished the can. "Hector, he was right."

"About what?" she asked.

"None of your damn business," he said.

He held her on the sofa with one hand, while he finished the three cans. "You didn't drink yours," he said.

"I did."

"I been around here," he said, "I been around here, me, and around here and around here some more. . . . And no this and no something else. And a man get enough somewhere."

He put the empty cans down carefully on the floor. "Don't want to go ruining you papa's rug none." He paused, thinking. Then he stood up. "Come on."

In the hall he staggered, and she pulled free and was almost out the front door when he caught her. They knocked the little tabouret over.

"Jesus," he said.

The only light in the hall was a small bare bulb without a shade. He left that on, and he left the door to her room open. That made a dim yellowish light inside as he pushed her down on the bed and carefully, with drunken precision undid the back buttons.

"Go head and yell," he was saying, "go ahead."

She was more afraid now than anything else. And she held herself perfectly stiff.

He dragged the dress off. "Being careful," he said. "Me, I'm being real careful."

"Not bad," he said in a minute, "I seen better, but not bad."

. . .

And he said: "It's the god-damn likker."

She laughed a little uncertainly.

"Bitch," he said, "nobody's through with you."

She pulled away, but not very hard. Her nipples were burning and her belly quivered.

"Take care of you . . ."

"Your teeth," she said, "they hurt."

"Nothing to what they going to do . . . nothing."

The night was very still and there were mosquitoes singing away in the corners of the room. "God-damn fucking likker," he said, "but it don't matter."

"Jesus," Perique said, "better go pass out home."

He stumbled out through the hall. She heard him cursing the front gate, heard it spring shut behind him, and then heard the irregular rhythm of his steps on the gravel.

Annie wondered what time it was. The Baby Ben clock which always stood on the bureau had got knocked over; she couldn't find it. A round white spot of mosquito bite began to rise on her stomach, and she scratched at it fitfully.

Finally she pushed herself up, and sat on the edge of the bed. She looked back, around her shoulder, at the sheet. She was surprised that there was no blood.

Annie did not see Perique for two days. Then she met him on the path between the grocery and the Livaudais house. She wasn't sure what to say. So she said nothing. She started to look down at the ground and pass by him. But he took her arm and stopped her.

"Look," he said, "don't worry."

Still looking at the ground, she shook her head, agreeing, and wondering what he was talking about.

"I had a load on, me," he said, "but I can tell you just exactly what happened. Like I been cold sober."

She nodded, afraid to say anything. She didn't understand, and she knew she should have.

"Didn't want you worrying about nothing."

"I wasn't," she said.

"Wasn't even near you."

She nodded and tried to think of something to say. "It was the likker," she said finally, echoing him.

He blushed. She stared as the tips of his ears got red. "I had some too much," he said.

"Didn't matter."

His ears were bright red now. "You didn't have a hard time of it," he said defiantly. "You got some fun out of it."

"Sure," she said, "sure."

But he was walking rapidly off.

She stared after him, wondering what they had been talking about.

ISLE AUX CHIENS

* *

~~~~~~~~~~~~~~~~

JULIUS ARCENAUX rubbed his eyes. It was so quiet even the flies weren't stirring; they were just still black spots on the dark ceiling. Way off some dogs were yipping, their cries sounding strangled in the heat. From their tone, they'd be after a bitch.

On hot days, with nobody to talk to in the store all the long afternoon, he had a hard time keeping awake. Sometimes he'd just give up and go to the back of the grocery where he lived and take a nap. If any customers came, they would yell for him.

His wife was always furious when she found him sleeping in the middle of the bed. "Comme cochon," she would tell him, "rolling in his sweat on the bed all day long."

They had been married a little over thirty years, and it had been a long time since he minded what she said.

He wouldn't even open his eyes; he'd just turn over and go back to sleep. He slept better in the bed alone.

Sometimes when he woke up at night he could feel the form alongside him, feel her without touching her. And it would seem to him then that her body filled the whole small room. He could feel her expanding, expanding, blowing up like a balloon. And he would lie with the side of his face pressed hard into the pillow and look up at her silhouetted against the open window, the

54

mounds of her thighs and her breasts. And he'd feel so crowded that he would roll out of bed and finish off the night on the linoleum of the floor.

Julius Arcenaux loosened the handkerchief around his neck. He'd tied it there in the early afternoon to catch the sweat that poured down the wrinkles of his thick neck.

"Ain't doing no good," he told himself aloud. All over, the shirt was sticking to his body. He could hear it squish when he moved his shoulders against the chair back. There were only two dry spots: the upper crease of each short sleeve. Otherwise the yellow cotton was soaked through: he could see the black hairs that covered his chest and stomach.

He changed his shirt three or four times a day in summer. Philomene, his wife, didn't bother washing them anymore. She just hung them over the back of the rocking-chairs on the back porch. It didn't matter to him that the shirts weren't fresh as long as they were dry.

Slowly and tiredly he walked back to the bedroom and got another shirt, dropping the wet one in a small ball on the floor. Philomene was not around. She'd be visiting next door or at their daughter Cecile's, a couple of hundred yards away. One thing was sure: she'd be somewhere close. In the last ten years she hadn't left the island except for her daughter's wedding.

Julius changed his shoes too, because he could feel how wet the canvas tops had got. And went back to the store.

This time he moved his chair over by the Coca-Cola icechest. He tilted back against it, his arms stretched out along the top. There was just a little cool coming through to the porcelain surface. He stared straight up, sighing gently. Right in the path of his eyes was a cluster of shoes, half-a-dozen pairs, their laces knotted together at different lengths, all hanging from a single big hook, the way you'd hang garlic or gourds.

He cocked his head for a minute listening. Then he shouted: "Get off my porch there. And quit doing that." And then the scamper of bare feet.

The kids were just about the only people moving around during the afternoon, and lately they had all wanted to carve their initials on the posts of his front porch. He'd chased them off three or four times a day for the last week. He wondered what was so special about his front porch; but there was no telling with kids.

He listened. Then he called again: "I done told you to get off that porch." There was a pause. "Get the hell off there, you!" And then clearly, the sound of a single pair of feet running.

Julius Arcenaux sat grinning in his chair. The kids never did understand how he knew they were there.

Back when he was a boy he had trained himself to catch the little sounds people make—even the tiny sound of breath. If it was perfectly still, as it was now, he could hear the lightest breathing.

His brothers had teased him about that when he was a kid. "Hey, boy," they'd say, "you in training for a dog, no? You going to go jumping in the water to fetch us duck?"

Sometimes he'd swing at them, but he was too little to win any fight. So most time he'd just walk away, his ears burning and a dry twitching feeling behind his eyes. Once he'd gone straight to one of the largest of the cane brakes. He'd walked in as far as he could, sliding his thin body between the reeds; then he crawled in the rest of the way, his elbows digging into the soft earth.

He lay flat on his stomach in the deepest part of the brake, squinting into the dusty sifted twilight—the bright noon sun never penetrated the thick growth—and listening: the rustle of the wind passing over the top of the reeds far above his head, the squawk of birds, the bumble of insects as they flew between the canes, and the slither of snakes—little grass snakes and the larger blue runners.

He held his breath so he could hear the other sounds: the busy movement of ants on the earth as little grains of mud rolled away under their feet. If he put his ear to the ground, he could hear a murmuring, deep inside. He sat up suddenly, rattling the cane around. He stared down at the ground, at the crumbling mossy worm-scarred surface. Then he put out one hand, almost afraid and touched a stalk. He let his fingers run up and down it, far as he could reach. He bent his head again and listened.

"I can hear the roots growing," he told himself. "Me, I can hear them pushing and growing through the ground."

All of a sudden he was afraid—as if he had come on something he shouldn't have. The same way he felt when he saw Augustin Billion and the girl lying out one night, close behind the big oak tree back of the Landry house.

He went crashing out of the cane brake, his arms beating a path before his face, but the sharp dry edges cut his skin and left him bleeding.

When his mother saw the cuts, she shrugged and put a pot of salt water on the stove to warm. "Boys always fighting somehow, and you ain't no different."

She'd wanted girls; and she'd had boys, six of them. Julius was the youngest and the smallest. "I was getting tired out when I come to bear you," she told him.

The others were the roughnecks of the island. She'd get sick to her stomach sometimes, seeing them come home after a fight, bruised and cut by knives or socks filled with lead weights from the nets. Sometimes they would fight with lengths of chain, swinging them from their hands like whips.

When they came home, Julius was there, watching. The mottled blue skin, the sight and smell of blood—they excited him so that he could not sleep afterward.

"What?" he would ask his brothers. "What happened?" And they would only grunt and curse under their breath.

Once his father was hurt—Julius remembered that so clear, as if it were a couple of months ago and not near forty years. An accident on the boat left a long gash down his father's arm. His mother had taken the finest needle and white silk thread and sewed the edges together. Then she went outside and got the newest strongest spider web she could find and brought it in carefully so that it would not break and laid it back and forth across the wound, to make it hold together.

And then she'd put both hands to her mouth and run out of the room. Julius took over, without anybody having to ask him; he knew exactly what to do. He wrapped the rags around and around the arm, perspiring with the effort, so careful to make them even and comfortable.

His father looked at him with a kind of a grin that was just a little lift of the mouth. "Takes after his mother, him. He is going to be a fine nurse."

His father fell asleep then, right in his chair, even before the bandaging was finished. It was the whisky—his mother gave them all the whisky they could drink before she started work, so that there would not be so much pain.

That day when Julius came out of the cane brake, cut and scratched, his mother asked: "You been fighting, no?"

He pulled up his shoulders and lied: "Oui."

A couple of days later, his brother Raoul was talking about cane-cutting over in Napoleonville. Then spotting Julius, he grinned. "For what do you listen, dogaree?"

"Nothing."

"You don't know what it is about."

"But I do." Julius said something he knew he should not have said: "I know about the cane."

"How do you know?"

"I heard it growing."

"Holy mother!" his brother said. "You never even seen sugar cane."

Julius did not answer.

His father asked: "Where you heard the cane?"

Julius dropped his head and tried to move away.

His father caught him by the shoulder. "Where you heard the cane?"

"Down beyond the Robichaux grocery, I heard it."

Raoul pounded both hands on his knees as he laughed. "We have an idiot who hears things but does not know the difference between sugar cane and all the others. He would try to eat a fishing-pole."

"Let him alone," his mother said.

He followed her outside. "I did hear the cane."

"I got to go get the clothes in. Come along. What else you heard?"

He took a quick look into her face, but there wasn't any laughter there, just a serious question. "What else you heard?"

"I hear the sun come up in the morning; and I hear the leaves come out the stalk; and I hear the worms crawling in the ground. And when I sit and watch a moonflower open, I can hear that, me."

"And what does it sound like, that?"

"It creaks, like."

"Next time," his mother said, "I will listen."

Julius Arcenaux stretched and shifted in his chair. That had been such a long time ago.

He cocked his head and listened to the hum of the mud daubers building their nests on the underside of the drainpipe just above the window.

The dogs were still yelping—they were closer. A man's voice shouted at them.

Julius Arcenaux got to his feet and stood for a minute, hands scratching his thighs. He kept his nails short, very short, or he bit them, and the soft skin made no impression on the khaki pants. "God damn." He rolled up one leg at a time, and methodically scratched. The heat made the skin prickle like a nest of ants.

Outside the man's voice yelled again: "Hi, hi, hi!"

Julius grinned. That would be the dogs, all right. Packs of them roamed all over the island.

When he was a boy a whole pack had gone running over him. He'd lain on the ground, screaming, until one of his brothers jerked him up to his feet and felt him all over, carefully, looking for broken bones, and laughed at him for being afraid.

To this very day, Julius thought, his brothers thought he was a coward because he had never liked to fight and because he hadn't taken his place on the boat with them.

Maybe, Julius thought, or maybe not. "I can't help what I am, me," he said aloud.

And he hadn't been scared that day when the painter had almost jumped him. That had been ten or fifteen years back, when his daughter was still little. He'd taken her into the swamp. They weren't going anywhere in particular, just fooling around because he hadn't wanted to stay home. It was early spring, he remembered, because the girl had reached over the pirogue and pulled a handful of crawfish from under a big fallen branch. He'd taken one look at the grayish things and motioned her to throw them overboard, they were that small.

He'd gone on, paddling the pirogue slowly, until there were too many vines to see the bright sun overhead and the water was still and gleaming with slime and the cypress knees were covered with green mold. He felt a prickling down his back, and out along his fingers, right to their tips. He'd always felt that way about the swamp.

The narrow strip of water passed between mounds covered with thick green bushes and splotches of colored flowers.

He saw the small low hibiscus bush with a single flower, big and yellow as the sun through a Gulf mist. And he wanted it, though he knew it was a silly thing for a grown man to be picking flowers. With one quick flick of his paddle he drove the sharp bow of the pirogue up on the land—it was a shell mound: he could tell by the sound—and started for the flower. The growth was denser than he'd thought. He put his arms up to shield his face and let the weight of his body push through. He took two steps and was considering giving up the whole idea, when something made him shift his arms slightly and look through them.

The painter was right there, not ten yards away, on a low branch about level with his head.

He'd never been so close to a live one before, so close he could see the flecks of color in the eyes and the fringe of tiny burrs on the left ear. And the muscles along the flanks rippling.

The shotgun was back at the pirogue. And the girl was too small to use it.

Because of the god-damn flower, he thought. And because he was so stupid as to leave the gun in the boat.

It hadn't been more than three seconds, all of it. Then Julius found himself staring at an empty branch. He squinched his eyes and looked harder, not quite believing. The painter had disappeared, so quietly that not a single leaf shook.

His eyes still fastened on the place where the animal had been, Julius began backing to the pirogue. Slowly, carefully, his body stiff and erect, he moved back, his eyes jumping around in the leaves and the branches and the vines, looking.

And when he dropped his arm, the girl had the gun ready for his hand.

He let her paddle the pirogue back, while he sat with the shotgun ready and watched.

.   .   .

He hadn't been scared then, though he had been close to getting killed and the girl with him. He didn't even bother telling about it when he got home. It would just scare his wife and make her argue every time he wanted to go out. And as for his brothers, he didn't care what they thought, not any more.

He had once. When he was still a kid. He'd tried his hand at fishing with them. Only, with the slightest bit of weather, with just a little wind, and just the smallest roll to the boat, he couldn't work anymore. The smell of the nets and the fish and the water and the taste of the brackish spray—these made him sick. So sick that there was nothing to do but sit on the deck, hold to the wood rail with both hands and hang his head over the side, while his father and his brothers stood around laughing.

After a couple of trips he gave up fishing and took a job in the grocery.

His brothers thought he was a coward. When he was young, he was almost afraid to go home when they were there. He was that afraid of their joking. Until he thought of a way to stop them.

"You got nothing to laugh at," he told them. "All those days you looking at fish and shrimp, me, I'm looking at all the girls what come down to the store."

That hushed them for a minute. Then Pierre, his second oldest brother, said: "Nobody but a dogaree like you be satisfied with just looking at the girls."

"Me, I ain't said nothing like that." Julius lit a cigarette and slanted his eyes down. "While you all gone they don't just come down to the store to talk, certainement."

"That ain't so," Pierre said.

"You ain't there to see."

In the quiet he walked across the room, clacking his heels on the bare boards, loud as he could, and into the kitchen. He kissed his mother lightly on the top of the head. "What we got for supper, che'?"

She looked at him, her head tilted sideways a little. And the small amused look in her eyes made him swallow hard. He was lying, and she knew it.

A couple of days later, when he was getting his own breakfast in the kitchen, she stood in the doorway. She was a tall thin woman, no hips and no breasts—more like the outline of a woman's figure than the woman herself. It was hard to imagine a man wanting her (though Julius's father did and made no secret about it), hard to imagine a kid growing in the narrow cavity between those thin bones.

"You are late this morning, no?"

"Maybe." He was and did not care. There was a dull ache at the base of his skull.

She walked across the room to the mirror and began combing her hair. She kept it short and clipped—she did it herself with a scissors every Sunday afternoon—while all the other island women wore theirs long and in a knot at the back.

"You don't care if you never see the grocery again?"

"Maybe."

"Poor bébé," she jerked the comb through the thick hair, "you have a harder time growing up than the others."

He stood up. "I got to go."

"Stay . . . when you have put some meat on those bones, the girls will look at you twice or maybe three times. . . . I will fix you some fresh coffee."

Looking back he could think about that time calmly, even be amused by it. Time when every girl that came in the grocery looked beautiful to him, and he kept staring at the bodies under the dresses. Once somebody had said—he'd forgot just who— "Stop undressing me with your eyes, p'tit." And everybody around laughed. And he'd tried to think of something to say and hadn't even found a single word.

"Just like a muskrat," the girls would say, and that was the nickname they gave him. "He got ideas just like a muskrat."

And then he decided to get married.

He met the girl in a strange way. It was winter. The balls of the chinaberry trees were yellow and falling; there was already the faint rotting odor of them on the ground. He was fishing from the end of the pier when he heard the kids come up, heard them laughing and talking and throwing rocks into the water. He glanced over his shoulder: they were from Petit Prairie; they'd come on the boat that brought the priest over for the yearly christening.

Julius went back to staring at his line where it entered the water that was faintly green tinged with floating grass. He closed his eyes and when he opened them a couple of minutes later, there was a girl climbing out of the water, right alongside his pole. And behind him were the other kids shrieking and slapping their knees with laughter.

Climbing out, the girl was shouting back at them, breathless and not so very loud. She didn't seem to notice that he was there, though she grabbed hold of his leg to lift herself over the edge.

He did not move to help her. He was still not sure that he was seeing anything more than the dazzle of the sun in his eyes. He kept staring at her through half-closed lids. She was wearing a pink dress, with little prints in it, little flowers and little diamonds of black. The cotton stuck to her body—she wasn't wearing any underclothes because of the heat. He didn't see her face once. He didn't think to look. There was just the cloth stuck to the skin with little green wrinkles and beads of water and bits of green marsh grass, and under it, the clear outline of her body. As she scrambled to her feet, the oval line of her thigh was right on a level with his eyes.

She'd been swearing like a man when she came climbing out of the water. The words kept coming back to him, each with a tingle of pleasure. Two weeks later when he went over to Petit Prairie himself, to see if she was married, he still didn't know her name.

Every Saturday morning, the bachelors of the island—and occasionally the married men, if their wives couldn't stop them —would head for a week-end at Petit Prairie, a two-hour trip by boat, if the weather was good. Sometimes, if it was during trapping season, they brought along the pelts to sell, but there wasn't much of that. Mostly it was a pleasure trip.

They would take one of the boats and a couple of cases of beer and a bottle of wine apiece.

When they tied up at the dock, the deputies of Petit Prairie sighed and shrugged and went home. They couldn't be expected to object to things they didn't see. So they didn't leave home at all. They worked the gardens that their wives tended all week and did whatever carpentry had to be done, or sat on their own porches, all alone with their wives and maybe one or two of their kids. Nothing lonesomer than a deputy on week-ends, people said.

Julius had gone to Petit Prairie with the other men a few times, not very often, because he couldn't drink that much. Once they had to carry him on the boat for the trip home: he had quietly passed out.

Then he decided to go to Petit Prairie to see about getting married. So one Saturday morning he collected his pay from the grocery and walked down to the boat. He was early; they were not yet ready to go. He sat down on the engine-hatch cover and waited until they lugged the last case of beer aboard, stowed it on the shady side and covered it with a tarpaulin to keep it cool.

It was Saturday, and he was sure that the girl would be at the market or along the single street sometime during the afternoon. Most people would come that way, he knew. So all he had to do was wait.

First he walked up and down the line of stores: grocery, meat market, café, bar, dry goods, dance hall. There were nothing but horses in those days—roads were too bad for cars—and the saddle horses and the carts were tied two deep to the hitching-stands along the banquettes.

One of the island men passed him, and pounded him on the back. "There what you looking for, dogaree." He pointed unsteadily to a house a couple of hundred yards down the street: a house like all the others—small and wood frame, with a paling-fence in front, and a screen porch and shutters to cut out the glare of midday. The girls were sitting in the front yard, in rattan chairs, and wearing bright-colored dresses: red, blue and yellow. And on the steps was the landlady, in black silk, wiping her second chin with a white handkerchief, and fanning herself with a wide palmetto fan.

Julius pulled away. He stopped in the bar and had a glass of beer. He drank it slowly—because it was a hot sticky day—and looked around the room. There were women with their husbands, and some single girls giggling together at a table over in the corner, baskets of groceries on the floor. He finished and went outside, the beer still bubbling in the back of his throat. He spent the rest of the afternoon walking up and down the small stretch of street, not more than three blocks all told, looking. When he got tired of walking, he perched on the hitching-racks and looked. And when he got thirsty, he went back to the bar for another beer.

Finally he saw her, turning into the dry-goods store. First thing he recognized was her stiff-legged determined walk. She was wearing a pink dress again—that must be her favorite color, he thought —and a man's hat stuck on the back of her head. And a necklace of flowers made from the pink tails of shrimp.

He followed her inside and stood behind a table piled with overalls and watched her. She bought a child's shirt. His stomach knotted up as he thought she must be married.

As she left he noticed that the hat sat so far back on her head because it perched on a heavy roll of plaited hair.

He asked the man behind the counter, an old man with a big beer belly and a bald sun-blistered head: "Who's that there?"

The old man just looked at him, squinting because he was nearsighted.

"What she called?"

The eyes narrowed even more. The pointed chin stuck straight out. "For what you want to know?"

Julius hesitated for a minute, then walked out. He spotted the girl down the street, half a block ahead. He followed, casually as he could, hands in pockets, his lips pursed as if he were whistling.

Julius noticed a child playing out on the banquette with a rubber ball, bouncing it and counting. Just as he was passing, she missed. The ball rolled right to his feet. He bent and picked it up. Then he squatted, holding the ball tight in his outstretched fist. The little girl reached out one hand and tapped his knuckles. He kept his hand closed. She pulled at his fingers. With his other hand, he pointed. "What's her name?"

The little girl blinked.

"You tell me her name."

The child turned around and looked.

"Tell me." The hand holding the ball nudged hers.

"Philomene Labiche."

"You sure?"

The child nodded and reached for the ball again.

He held it. "Where she live?"

"Down there."

"Far?"

"Là-bas." The little girl sniffled. Two big tears began rolling down her cheeks.

He gave her the ball and walked quickly away and, following Philomene, found the house where she lived.

He went back to the boat to think out what he should do. He stretched out on the deck, his head propped on the wood rail and stared straight up at the sky while it turned from blue to powdery yellow to gray to black with freckles of stars.

Then, because he had gotten very hungry, he went over to the café for dinner. He still did not know how he should meet her. He had no close relatives in town who could go speak to her father. He had some distant cousins, but a man didn't send a distant cousin on anything like that. Then, while he was eating his jambalaya, he had the idea. He almost choked on a piece of shrimp he was so surprised: it was that simple.

The church was a wood building behind a dried brown square of grass and weeds, criss-crossed by wagon tracks and beaten down by feet. Back of the church was the cemetery, row on row of whitewashed brick vaults. And next to the church was the rectory, a small shingled house.

There was no doorbell. He knocked on the wood frame of the screen door. There were four large holes at the bottom of the screen. On the edge of one a large fly was sitting sleepily. He heard the shuffling steps of the old housekeeper. The face appeared, wrinkled like a raisin, with tiny eyes and hair pulled up into a tight knot directly on top of the head.

"I want to see the priest," he said.

She peered at him, her nose pressed up against the screen of the door, the red tip criss-crossed by the black wires.

"I want to see the priest . . . about my wife."

She pursed her wrinkled blue lips together. "Euuuuuuu." She was enjoying what she was imagining.

"I will talk to the priest."

She shrugged and opened the screen.

He sat down in the parlor, in the middle of the large sofa, upholstered with cracked leather and spotted with mold. There were two other chairs and a rocker to match, all of heavy square oak. Over against the wall, between the two windows, was a square china cabinet, with glass doors. On the top shelf were half a dozen or so books in brown bindings. Julius squinted at them. The titles were almost worn off the backs. He spelled out the letters carefully: St. Augustine. The last two books had fallen down and the others leaned against them. They had been that way so long their covers had warped into that arc. On the shelf below was a cross-shaped reliquary; the glass was wavy and Julius couldn't see much of it. On the last shelf there were two little vases and a sea shell.

The old woman came back. "He be here soon," the dry rattling voice said. "It is almost to the time he go to bed. So he be here."

"I wait," Julius said.

He sat very still and waited, breathing as shallow as he could. Odors of town houses always upset him: a mixture of kerosene from the lamp burning on the table, of greens cooked a long time ago, of faint fish and the sweet-like odor of mice in the walls. For a minute he thought of asking the old woman if he could not sit with her in the kitchen. But he only got to his feet and looked out the window. The church was right there: he looked out at the planking of the walls.

He heard a mumble of voices in the kitchen and then the priest came into the room. The door stuck when he tried to open it: it had warped and he had to put his shoulder to it, so that he came crashing into the parlor, panting a little and tugging at his collar.

He shook hands quickly; his palms were wet and his face smeared with perspiration. "Now . . ."

Julius moved his tongue in his mouth before he tried speaking. "I want to marry Philomene Labiche."

"So?" the priest said. "Does she?"

"No."

The priest shrugged his heavy shoulders. "I can do nothing about that."

"I never met her."

The priest blinked his brown eyes rapidly. "Eh? Eh?"

Julius explained patiently: "I never met her, me. So I don't know whether she would like me or not."

"Go meet her, my friend. Go talk to her."

"I can't do that," Julius said. He took a deep breath. "I want you to go tell her."

The priest was looking at him. One large puffy lid slid down and covered its eye.

"I got no family here. The way some people do. Or they could do it."

"You just seen her?"

Julius nodded.

The eye opened. "Who are you, my friend?"

"Julius Arcenaux from Isle aux Chiens."

"And you can support a wife?"

"You ask people. You ask people what sort of a place I got."

The priest nodded and sucked his tongue through his teeth with a little plopping sound.

"Tell her I want to marry her, me," Julius said, "in church, proper. And tell her papa I will come talk to him."

The priest said, yawning: "They will come to Mass tomorrow. You stay for both Masses. They will come to one or the other. And I will talk to Gus Labiche."

Julius sat staring at the rusty green-black cassock. Of the line of buttons down the front, most were missing. He found himself counting them.

"They will let her marry me?"

The priest scratched his stomach. Another of the buttons popped off and rolled along the floor.

Julius looked, but the floor was so dark he saw nothing. He felt around with the palms of his hands until he found it. The priest nodded.

"It may be they will be glad to see her in a house of her own, and out of theirs."

"And her, do you think she will marry me?"

The priest yawned again. "You look like a man. You find a wife, certainement."

"I want her, Philomene Labiche."

"But he is wood-headed! Mo 'tit, we try. In the morning we try. Now go away."

Julius went back to the boat to sleep. Since he was the first back, he got the single bunk. He lay there, wide-awake most of the night, listening each time one of the other men stumbled from the dock to the deck and peered in the cabin and saw him in the bunk and cursed him and turned around to find a place on the deck.

He lay there with the blanket pulled up to his chin, though it was a warm night. And each time he closed his eyes, they popped back open.

Julius Arcenaux rearranged one can of tomatoes in the display pyramided in the middle of the floor. He stared at the can. Although the shipment wasn't more than four months old, there was already a small thread of rust around the top.

He'd have to tell his wife to get that off with steel wool, or nobody would buy the can. He'd learned that trick from old Jaubert: "Eat their meat faisandé, right when it's full of worms, but they got to have shiny tin cans."

Once, years ago, not long after he'd taken over the store, hurricane waters had swept right through the building. There'd been mud a foot deep on the floor: he'd cleaned it up with a shovel. And there wasn't a label left on any of his stock. But he'd washed the cans off in a big tub of water and went over them with cleanser to make them even brighter and lined them up on the new shelves he'd built and had himself a sale. Mixed-up sale, he called it. And for every three cans he gave one for lagniappe.

He hadn't lost money that time, he thought.

The dogs were closer now, over to the north. They were running in a circle. He walked over to the door and looked out. You still couldn't see anything, just the stretch of grass ending at the oak trees; and the dirt road lined with oleanders; and the paling-fence at the back of the Boudreau house.

By the sound of them, there'd be a whole pack. A sudden metallic clanking: they'd upset a washtub or a bucket. A woman shouted.

He chuckled, staring out at the hot dust-fringed afternoon: all that fuss, some dogs after a bitch.

The pan clattered again. That would be over at the Speyrer house. Efetha would be scurrying around the yard, trying to scatter the dogs that were dirtying the wash. She was a short girl with wide-set legs that gave her a rolling walk and put her tight little rear waggling back and forth softly.

One for each hand—Julius closed his eyes, grinning.

He'd been lying that day, a long time ago, when he told his brothers that the girls came down to the grocery to see him. But it had got to be true. His mother had been right, when he'd put some meat on his bones. . . .

His wife found out about the first girl—he never quite knew how, except that you couldn't ever keep anything quiet on the island very long.

And that first time he'd been afraid. Philomene had gone out on the porch, though it was a blustery November day and there was a cold wind from the north swamps, and sat there, in the single chair, rocking slowly back and forth. He got a little nervous watching her through the front window and went out for a walk himself—around the beaches, kicking at the pieces of gray driftwood and throwing little pieces of shell at the gulls and wishing to hell he'd never got in the whole business.

But when he came back, there was supper on the table waiting. And though Philomene did not look at him as they sat eating, she did not say anything either.

He'd wanted to tell her: "I ain't going to do it again." But he couldn't somehow. She would just go on looking down and answer: "What?"

So he sat and ate his supper, though the food made him a little sick.

And he wanted to ask: "Who told you? Rosalie herself? Or who?" But he didn't do that either. Didn't say one word.

She fed the kids and put them to bed (the oldest must have been nine or ten then) and went to bed herself. He stayed up, smoking one cigarette after the other, huddling next to the kerosene stove for warmth.

He'd been afraid that time and ashamed. After a while he lost his feeling about it. And didn't care what she knew or didn't know.

But she always knew. She found out about the other girls too. He could tell when she did; she didn't have to say. She always sat rocking on the porch a little while, each time. But there was always supper on the table. And they never talked about it.

Sometimes he'd look at his sons and wonder if they had ever had trouble with women, now that they were all married with families of their own. He hadn't heard any talk about them. And he couldn't imagine; he'd never even felt related to his three boys. It was only the youngest, the girl Cecile, he was fond of.

A good kid, her, he thought, with more life in her than any of the rest. A good kid.

When she got married—to Hector Boudreau Julius'd gotten drunk, drunker than he'd been since he was a kid. He'd never been much of a man for likker.

They had gone over to have the wedding at the big church at Petit Prairie. They'd had the celebration at his wife's cousin's house—their girl, in a pink organdy dress and a wide-brimmed hat, had stood up with his own daughter.

After the ceremony he'd got drunk, on a mixture of beer and whisky and orange wine, so drunk that once he almost passed out. He was dancing. It was fairly late then, and he'd been drinking steadily ever since the ceremony. He didn't remember who he was dancing with, did not think he ever looked at her face, but from the feel he knew it was a young body he had hold of. The band—a violin, two guitars, a drum and an accordion—began a fast bayou French waltz. He started turning then. And his own grogginess started moving to the beat. He kept going faster and faster, in tight circles. He heard his partner gasp and try to pull away. But he held tight. He felt his head would pop into a dozen pieces and lie spread around on the floor.

The music stopped. And he gave a few more turns, slower and slower, until he stopped too.

People were pounding him on the back and laughing. "Life in this old dog, boy," they were saying. "Yes, man. . . ." They shoved a glass of something in his hand. He took it, held it, and put it down on a table untouched. Thinking about it made him a little sick. He wasn't sober now, but he was clearheaded. He looked around for his daughter. She and her new husband were gone.

Julius did not close his eyes once that night. After the people had gone, he sat out on the porch. And sat until it was morning and time to leave.

From out one window Julius saw a stray dog run across the road: he'd been forgotten or left behind and he was racing to catch up with the pack. A brown long-haired mutt, with a long loping gait.

Julius grinned and fished another piece of ice out of the cooler and tucked it in the exact middle of his tongue. Then he went back to his chair, closed his eyes and began to doze.

He forgot the dogs, forgot them until the bitch dashed in the open door with ten or fifteen males at her heels.

He woke to see the carefully stacked pile of tomato cans crash to the floor and run off to the corners of the room, like water drops hitting the wood. The bitch—for a single second—stared straight at him, her brown eyes wide and a little puzzled. (He thought she was smiling, but it was only a dog.) With a leap she was over the counter, crouching there, hidden. Little bits of splintered china rolled out after her.

Julius rushed at the dogs, swinging his chair in front of him and shouting: "Hi, hi, hi, hi!"

They scattered to the corners of the room but would not get out. They leaped straight up against the walls, dodging the chair, and knocked down the shelves. Already there was a pile of rice like large sand in one corner. The flour bin rolled out of sight; there were tracks in the white dust where the container had been.

He saw a few more come rushing in the door. The whole pack was there now.

He was cursing, using all the words he could remember. He stepped on one of the rolling cans and lost his balance. He fell on a dog. The animal jumped away, yipping and snapping at his shoulder. From his lying position he kicked at it, and missed. He felt something jab the palm of his hand: the keg of tacks was spilled. The animals did not seem to notice, except for one short-haired white dog, who sat in the middle of the floor, chewing furiously at the pads of his feet. Over all the noise Julius could hear his snorting.

The animals ran in circles, looking. Behind the counter the bitch watched. Julius could almost feel her eyes, eager and moist. He got to his feet and, swinging his arms and kicking at the swirling dogs, he made his way over to the counter; his shotgun was hung against the flat inner side.

Teeth tore through one pants leg but he did not stop or even care. He stumbled again and almost fell. From far away, he heard the sound of his own shouting.

He lifted the gun off the hooks—he kept it loaded—swung it around and fired, not aiming, not looking, but firing both barrels from the hip.

He knew better. The instant he pulled the second trigger he knew better. Too late he ducked his head in his arms and hoped the ricocheting pellets would miss. He heard the dogs yipping in high-pitched screaming tones. And he became aware of sharp flashing pain in his arms and the right side of his neck.

And he remembered with relief that he had loaded the gun with birdshot.

One hand holding the side of his neck, he backed up, until he felt the wall. Then he stood leaning on it, kicking at the dogs. A few had scattered; he heard them running off yelping. But most of them were still milling around the store, as if nothing had happened. Only their movements were a little more excited than before. Saliva was dripping off their jaws and their tongues were a little farther out. The bitch had moved down along the counter and up on a little shelf. She had wedged herself on top of the cartons of cigarettes. Her flanks were quivering.

A half-dozen crab nets, stood up on their long poles like brooms in the corner, smashed down. One of them covered a light yellow dog's head. He did not shake it off; he did not seem to notice: the handle trailed around after him.

Julius was panting now, almost sobbing. Outside, he could hear people come running up and then stop, laughing. He glanced out the window—a little crowd, a dozen or so people, and right in front his wife, crouched down, holding her knees with laughter. If he had not emptied his gun at the dogs, he would have fired at them.

He could feel a trickle on the side of his neck. He looked down at his shoulder and saw blood splatters on the blue shirt. With a fingernail he gouged out one of the pellets and looked at it: a little black bit of lead smeared with red. He dropped it and wiped his fingers on his shirt.

He held to the wall with one hand and kicked at the dogs. They just moved out of reach. He was shouting at them: "There. Behind the counter." He was even pointing. "There. There she is."

The bitch stared at him. Her tongue licked the tip of her nose.

He grabbed one of the dogs and tried to carry it behind the counter, but the animal squirmed free. "There she is. She can hardly wait for you. Behind the counter." He grabbed for another dog and missed.

Two of the dogs were snapping at each other on top of the ice-chest over by the window. They lunged, lost balance, and crashed through the glass to the ground outside.

Now through the broken window, he could hear even more clearly: the talk and the chorus of laughing outside. And his wife calling to him: "Julius, hey!" And her laughing, louder than the rest.

It would take him twenty years to get over this story; they would be reminding him of it whenever there was a chance.

The bitch came creeping out from behind the counter, her eyes bright as oil. Silently she jumped through the broken window. The nearest dogs followed, smashing the remaining panes.

The pack swirled for a minute and then flowed away, some through the window, more through the door. A single can rolled across the floor and came to rest against the wall. He saw the bright red label and the word PEAS. He walked over and picked it up, looking for rust stains without thinking what he was doing. There was a terrible pounding ache in his head, so bad that he could hardly see. From the drawer under the cash register, he took a bottle of whisky and swallowed as much as he could stand.

That helped a little. He looked around. There wasn't a thing left of the floor displays. Even the magazine racks had been turned over. And on the wall shelves, only the contents of the very highest ones were left.

Still holding the bottle in his hand, he walked out of the wrecked littered grocery to the back where he lived. The door had been closed tightly so that the dogs had not come in there.

It was time somebody did something about the dogs, he thought. He would take his gun and go after them.

He took another swallow of whisky and set the bottle down on the dresser. His neck did not hurt anymore, just a kind of stinging. With the proper kind of mirror he could even fix it himself.

But, no, his daughter would be the one for that. He would walk over to her place. She would be there.

He unbuttoned his shirt and dropped it on the floor. He opened the dresser drawer that held his handkerchiefs, jerked it open so hard that it fell to the floor. He did not bother picking it up. He took a single clean handkerchief and knotted it around his neck. He touched the wounds lightly. They would have to be cleaned out at once. He'd seen kids ignore birdshot wounds and come down with blood-poisoning.

He could hear his wife laughing and shouting to him: "Julius, hey, Julius, what happen? What happen to you?"

"Moment," he called. "Moment."

He would have to put on a clean shirt before he went outside.

*

BY the time he had walked out of his bedroom, Julius Arcenaux had a fresh shirt and freshly combed hair. He had even poured some tonic on it: his hand hadn't been too steady so some of the liquid had run down his neck. The whisky was getting to him now, and he felt better.

He jerked open the door and went out into the grocery. And in the middle of the floor, turning around and around on her heel to survey the damage was Mamere Terrebonne. He was startled. He didn't know what exactly he had expected, but it wasn't the old lady. She was so old she was a little queer: she would see things and talk to people who weren't there. Kids swore that when the moon was dark they'd seen her out on the long south sand bar waiting for the loup-garous to come and talk to her. Maybe so, maybe not. Nobody was afraid of her, not even her great-grandchildren, who took turns sleeping in the house with her so that she would not be alone.

Even so, Julius was startled when he saw the thin bent figure and the brown wrinkled face, thin and hawked as a gull's.

"They have made you a mess, yes?" Her voice wasn't like an old woman's voice. It was low and soft and a little husky. You could almost hear the young woman she'd been once.

"Um," he agreed and shook his head slightly. He looked around. There was really no one else inside. He glanced out a window. Sitting in a chair in the shade of a sweet olive bush was Philomene, her hands folded across her big stomach. She was talking to someone, a man, but Julius did not recognize the back. He could see though, how brightly she was smiling. And how, now and then, she would look over at the grocery and laugh out loud.

He would have to fix her, he thought, and answering himself he demanded: How? And he realized suddenly that there was nothing he could do. He could not hit her, his own sons wouldn't

76

stand for that. If he found a new girl and told her about that, she would just shrug—she'd found out about others. He could put her out, but she would just move in with one of the kids.

"Nothing you can do, p'tit." He jumped. Mamere Terrebonne was grinning at him. There wasn't a tooth in her mouth, just the bare and bright pink gums.

Julius walked quickly out the door. On the porch he felt glass crunch under his shoes—the front window *was* out. He'd been crazy to use a shotgun inside. With glass costing the way it did. . . . Maybe he'd just put a regular window back in—be safer in hurricane season too.

But there were things he had to do first.

He went down the steps, not looking at the people gathered in the yard, not paying them the slightest mind. His throat was tight and burning, but he kept his head up. And he was very careful of his feet. He had to be steady, he thought; one foot after the other, one almost in a line with the other, but not quite.

And behind him, he heard his wife say: "He must be drunk, him. He don't walk that good sober."

He kept walking on, not looking down, letting his vision be a kind of triangle, from the sides of the path to a little way ahead. He watched the bushes and the trees pass him; he saw each leaf terribly clear, and each flower. As he walked he counted the petals on a red oleander. And saw the designs in the bark. In the top leaves of a little scrub oak a hummingbird was sitting, his wings closed, resting.

"I will kill the dogs," he said.

And he went on.

The gate to his daughter's house was closed.

He kicked it in with his bent knee. He walked up the path that was carefully swept with sand and lined with big shells: his daughter was a fine housekeeper, he thought; a fine girl.

He wondered if she had heard about the store. A thing like that went around the island fast as a brush fire—with kids running in all directions, carrying it.

The way rabbits spread a brush fire, he thought, on their own coats.

He reached the porch and, crooking one finger to his daughter to follow, opened the screen door and went inside. In the sudden duskiness he could see nothing. And he knew exactly what chair he wanted. He would have to ask.

"Where is the big red chair?" The words were an effort that left him breathless. A hand on his arm led him and another on his shoulder pushed him down. He felt the chair, sat bolt up right for a minute studying it to be sure it was the right one, and then passed out.

*

THE NEWS moved fast with kids to carry it from door to door.

It wasn't half an hour before everybody on the island knew what had happened down at the grocery. Most of them went down to see for themselves so that all afternoon there were plenty of people around. It was almost like a picnic or the pirogue races over at Lafitte. Philomene sat in her chair, nodded and smiled.

The three Livaudais men—Eddie, Henry and Pete—went down together. Henry was in his pajama pants (he had been napping when Pete yelled the news up to him), and he hadn't bothered changing. He didn't even bother pulling the cord tighter, until the girls began to whistle.

Eddie said to his son Henry: "You got a girl, no? That why you don't want to get cut up?"

"I ain't turn chicken," Henry said, "don't you sweat about that."

But just then Robby came running up and Eddie turned away to shadowbox with him. When his wife wasn't around, he was always happy to see his bastard.

All that afternoon, until long past suppertime, Mamere Terrebonne hung around the grocery. It was hard to tell exactly what she was doing, but whenever anybody saw her she was busily walking around the building, or digging in the heap of glass on the front porch. She circled the building at least three times, moving slowly and carefully, looking at almost every board in the walls. Then she poked around with her cane in the heap of glass on the front porch, until she had sorted it all out into four piles, according to size.

During the afternoon there were plenty of people there, but around suppertime they left. And only the kids came back later.

79

But it wasn't until about eight o'clock, just when it was getting good and dark, that Mamere Terrebonne pulled her hat down, low so that it almost covered her eyes, and started home.

Maybe it was all the excitement. Or maybe it was just the way things fall out. But that night Mamere Terrebonne had another one of her attacks. And the worst one yet.

She lived alone, in the same house she had lived in ever since she was married, in the cluster of houses that belonged to her relatives, her children's children. (Her children had grown up and died, some of them, and her husband too, and even some of her grandchildren.) She cooked for herself—she ate very little now, and that mostly fish, like a seagull. And she cleaned house for herself, and she padded around in the little front-yard garden, not growing much, hardly doing more than stirring up the soil with a stick.

At night she would light the lamp (she had never had the house wired for electricity), and she would sit under it, making flowers of the fins of shrimptails, twisting the flowers into wreaths and bunches.

She was never alone at night. Her family saw to that. After all, who would know if the old woman died during the night, or needed help? Every night one of her great-grandchildren slept there.

There were plenty of them, half grown, from six to twelve. And they took turns. All day long they played and ate at their own houses. But at bedtime they headed for the little canvas cot in the corner of Mamere's bedroom, next to the big old feather double bed that she slept in, the one that had belonged to her mother. And they would go home for breakfast.

They were company for her too, those nights when she'd napped so much during the day that she wasn't at all sleepy. Then she would put away her flower-making and take the lamp and go into the bedroom, where the kid was already asleep. She would wake him up, prop him up in bed, and talk at him. If he fell asleep in the middle she didn't particularly seem to care.

It made her family feel better to know that the old woman had somebody with her. And she got on a lot better with kids than with adults. They had more patience with each other.

. . .

Mamere had had her first attack two winters back, when she fell out of bed and lay on the floor stiff as a board and not able to say a word. Steve St. Martin was sleeping there that night and he sat up, holding the cover around him, because it was a cold night in February and there was a little skim of ice on the fresh-water pans left on the back porch. He stuck out one toe and gave the figure on the floor a little prod. Then he hesitated for a minute, chewing on one corner of the quilt, not quite sure what to do. And anyhow he was so sleepy, his eyes kept closing. He lay down again but didn't sleep. He kept seeing the figure half wrapped in the covers lying on the bare floor boards. He reached over and touched one hand. It felt cold.

He got up, dragging his quilt with him, and lit a fire in the round barrel-shaped kerosene stove. The wick smoked; it was too high. And the crank stuck. He had to use both hands to turn it down. The quilt fell off his shoulders. Though he slept in a pair of cotton overalls and a sweater, he began to shiver. He pressed his hands to the outside of the stove. The tin was still cold; there was only a faint beginning tinge of warmth. He looked again at the blanketed figure alongside the bed. And backed out of the bedroom. The front door was closed and latched against the cold. He couldn't manage it alone. So he climbed on a chair and opened a window and pushed back the shutter. He clambered through it and dropped down on the porch.

It was so different at night. He stopped for a minute and looked around, trying to be sure of his directions. There wasn't a thing stirring; it was only cold and dark. A single bright star was caught in the top of the oak tree.

He ran all the way home. And inside of ten minutes there were flashlights and lanterns coming from all sides and somebody had started out to get the priest from Petit Prairie. By mid-morning, by the time the priest had come, Mamere was sleeping quietly with a little smile on her face. She had won. Only sometimes she muttered something about M'sieu Mort.

That was the way it happened the first time. And the second time was just like it. Except that it was late summer. And the kid was Addie Monjure.

He woke up when he saw that the lamp was still burning. And he took a good look at Mamere and went racing out of there.

He'd always been a kind of nervous boy, and this upset him so that he began to scream. He had the whole end of the island up in no time at all. Some of the men came out with their shotguns; they hadn't been exactly sure what was happening.

Perique Lombas took his little launch, the *Tangerine,* and went off to fetch the priest, while the women did what they could for Mamere.

And Addie Monjure, he ran right straight home, and got under his own bed, though it was so low you wouldn't have thought that there was room for a single living thing underneath. He stayed there, scared and sniffling a little. And nobody could get him to come out. And his mother finally couldn't take the sounds any longer. So she got his father and his biggest brother to lift the bed right off from on top of him. And a tough time they had of it too, for Addie got hold of the slats, and held on with all his strength. And when they finally got the bed up, he came with it, hanging like a crawfish under a log.

And his mother had to sit and hold him in her arms all the rest of the night and promise him that he wasn't ever going to die. She didn't have a minute to get over to Mamere's until the morning came.

By that time Perique had come back with the priest. And it was just the way it had been before. Mamere was alive and asleep. So the priest gave a long look at Perique, and thought of his lost sleep, stifling a yawn.

And Perique shrugged, for he knew what the priest was thinking, and he said: "If you had seen her when I leave here—you think she would be dead by morning too."

So the priest opened the door of the bedroom and peeped in. Rita Monjure, who was watching alongside the bed just then, stood up and bowed politely to him. He said a quick prayer and made a quick sign of the cross and closed the door.

The priest was a young man, named Ryan, from New Orleans. He had a square head on a thick neck, and legs that were so far apart that he rolled when he walked. He had been to the island before, many times. He was the youngest and the huskiest of the priests over at Petit Prairie, and he always got the distant night calls.

But he was a good-natured man, and he didn't mind. And anyway he was young and very strong and sleep didn't mean too much to him. So he came out on the porch and took off his coat, because already the day was getting hot, and took out his handkerchief and wiped the dust and the sand off his black bag which contained the holy oils and the holy wafers. Then he ran the handkerchief over his own face which was turning sweaty-red in the heat. And went across the way to Ferdinand Lombas's house, and had a few whiskies with the men there.

THE LIVAUDAIS weren't related to Mamere Terrebonne—
not directly anyhow—so that when she had her attack, their living
wasn't changed much. The whole family went to the house the
following morning and asked after her, but that was all.

When they passed by Marie Livaudais's yard and saw Robby
playing there, the four pretended not to see him. The kid ducked
around under the porch: he would always disappear when his father's wife came by.

Eddie was going straight from Mamere's down to the boat. Pete
was going with him, and Chep Songy was all ready and waiting at
the dock.

"You change you mind, huh?" he asked Henry.

Henry shook his head. "Going home with Ma."

His father took off his cap and scratched his bald top. "You got
so much money you don't have to work anymore?"

Henry grinned. His teeth were narrow and pointed and slightly
irregular. "Maybe," he said.

"It going to be a good day."

"I'm tired working," Henry said.

Belle Livaudais chuckled. "Livaudais men," she said, "stubborn
like crabs."

Eddie looked annoyed. "When he running lucky . . ."

"Me, I was born lucky," Henry said and put one arm around his
mother's shoulders. "And I'm going home with my girl here."

Belle smiled more gently and her thin, almost Indian face
cracked into wrinkles. "Crazy," she said, "all the Livaudais. . . ."

Eddie shifted from one foot to the other. He wanted Henry with
him. Needed him on the boat. But he was a man now, for all that
he still lived at home. . . . Eddie was hesitating on the edge of
ordering him to come. . . .

"Oh hell," Pete said, "we get along without him." For all that

he was sixteen—two years younger than Henry—Pete was broader
in the shoulders and weighed a good twenty pounds more.

"Sure you do," Henry said, "You get along fine without me."

"Oh hell," Pete said and scratched his underarm, "you come
along." His thin pimply face sulked.

"Not this time, man."

His father shook his head and didn't argue. The boy was a
strange one, for sure. Always was. Wanting to go off and be by
himself. A kind of wild one.

"Jesus," Eddie said, "leave the son of a bitch here. And let's us
go make the money."

Grumbling, Pete followed his father down the path. He stopped
once and looked back at his brother, hopefully.

Henry and his mother went home. They did not talk much on
the way. They didn't have to.

On the porch, with the screen open in her hand, Belle said:
"That Pete now, he going to miss you being with them."

"Maybe," Henry said.

"You feel all right, no?"

"Sure."

"I hear about the way you don't want to fight down at the dock."

"Jesus," Henry said.

"So," his mother said.

"I ain't been scared," he said.

"So."

"Look, I been telling you. I ain't scared."

"I been hearing you."

With the Arcenaux the Livaudais had always been the roughnecks of the island. All those who had the name, right down to
second cousins, were always the first men in a fight, always
loving it.

"Hell," Henry said, "I'm plain tired being tough. I'm gonna rest
up and then I'm going out hunting."

His mother shrugged. "All stubborn too. They got to do what
they got to do."

"Yea," Henry said. "That's me, for sure."

He spent most of that morning right in the side yard, under the
mulberry tree, cleaning and fixing his two shotguns. And he spent

most of the afternoon sleeping stretched out full length in the front-porch shade. He ate supper early—his mother fixed it specially for him—and he went upstairs straight after, pulled off his pants and his shirt and went to bed. He didn't even stir when his father and his brother came in around eight o'clock, yelling at each other and furious after a bad day.

Pete finally climbed up to the attic where they both slept and stuck his head inside the little partitioned cubbyhole where Henry was. (Henry had built that himself not two years ago. He had wanted a room for himself. So he had divided the attic exactly in half. He had even painted the wall—one coat of pale yellow.)

"Hey," Pete said, "listen at me."

Henry, who was sleeping face down, turned over. "Jesus . . ."

"You shoulda come with us."

Henry grunted.

"You give us bad luck."

"Jesus."

Pete sat down on the edge of the bed. "Ma said you been fixing the guns. . . . You going out?"

"Yea," Henry said with his eyes still closed.

"I'm coming too, me."

Henry shook his head.

"Old man ain't going out tomorrow," Pete said. "I got nothing to do."

"Not with me you ain't."

"Aw," Pete said, "sure I can."

Henry didn't answer.

"You think I can't take it?" Pete asked.

"Sure, kid," Henry muttered finally.

"Be more fun with two, huh?"

"No," Henry said.

He had always gone alone, ever since he was twelve and big enough to have a shotgun and handle a pirogue.

"Ah, hell," Pete said.

"No," Henry said.

He had never worked on the boats more than he had to. He didn't like fishing. He was a hunter. Because of him the Livaudais had meat when nobody else did.

He always came home with duck and sometimes with deer, all

neatly cleaned and stowed up in the bow of the pirogue and wrapped up against the flies. When he brought back deer it meant only one thing—that he had gone beyond the salt marsh and into the swamp that lay to the north of it. Very few people ever went in there, and almost none went beyond the edges.

There was some talk when he first brought back a deer. But people got used to it.

After all, they thought, it was the kind of thing you expected of a Livaudais. They were real tough. All of them.

"You said you was going to take me." Pete sat down on the foot of the bed.

"Get off," Henry said, "I got a clean sheet."

Pete hopped up. Henry rolled over on his side and closed his eyes again.

The following morning Henry went down to the grocery to get supplies for his hunting trip. His mother saw him leave with the empty oyster sack slung over his shoulder.

"You don't got to buy stuff," she said, "when we got it here."

Henry put one hand on the door frame and stretched himself carefully. His thin pimpled face looked younger this morning with its high cheekbones and the deep hollows under them in which a definite beard line was beginning to show. "I got money," he said. "I'm gonna eat it, and I'm gonna buy it."

The grocery had been cleaned up. It was even hard to tell that anything had been wrong, if you didn't look too close. Cecile had picked up the glass and buried it. And two of her brothers had come and boarded up the smashed windows. Julius himself had straightened up the inside. He'd spent the whole preceding day in there, clucking and muttering to himself.

"Looks all right, no?" Julius asked.

Henry took the cans he had bought from the counter and dropped them in the oyster sack.

"Man," he said, "you still hold on tight to them paper bags."

Julius stopped on his way to the cash register and squinted over his shoulder. "They didn't send me bags with the last order —I only just barely got enough."

"Yes," Henry said, "ever since I remember, you didn't have enough bags, except when people come in and yell for them."

Julius rang up the sale and did not answer.

Henry put the last of the cans in the sack and swung it up on the counter. Then he propped his elbows on it and, bending down, put his chin in his hands.

Julius came back with the change.

"I wonder," Henry said, "how much you make on them bags."

"I been telling you," Julius said, "they ain't sent. . . ."

"Jesus," Henry said, "I can go right now and put my hand on a big pile of bags."

"I got to have some," Julius said, "for big orders."

"Gimme my change." He held it in his hand for a minute, rattling the coins, staring straight ahead at the tarnished silver buckle on Julius's belt.

"I reckon I need some sunburn cream too," Henry said.

"Huh?" Julius fingers tapped the buckle.

"Tube of sunburn cream."

"Who for?"

"Who you think?"

"I don't think nothing."

"I'm going out for a while."

"You don't want it, sure."

Henry straightened up slowly and went around the counter and took down the lotion. He stood looking at it, turning the box in his hands. "Hey," he said, "this is fancy for sure."

Lengthwise across the box was a sticker that said: "Arcenaux Grocery. Always the Best."

"Bought 'em," Julius said. "Got to use 'em up."

"Right glad to see somebody could sell you something."

"Waste," Julius said, "sinful waste."

"How much this?"

"Forty-nine."

"Vieux couillon . . . that a dime more than over in Petit Prairie."

"I got to pay freight." Julius rubbed his belt buckle. "Couté les yeux d' tête."

"Okay," Henry said and held out a half-dollar. "Quit crying. And gimme the penny back."

Julius walked heavily across the creaking floor to the cash register.

"I wonder where you got it hid," Henry said to the thick sweat-streaked back.

"Huh?"

"All the money you got."

"You talking like a crazy kid."

Henry sat on the edge of the counter. "Lemme figure now. You don't go to the bank at Petit Prairie more than once a month, most times. And you must have a heap of money around."

Julius waved his arms. "Like all the people—telling me, Julius, you got so much money, Julius, what you going to do with it? And me just barely making a living out this place."

"Yea?"

"And the whole building near to going down with the next strong wind."

"Tough titty, man."

Julius sighed and handed him back the penny.

Henry added it to the change he held and rattled the coins in his closed fist.

"You know," Henry said.

"What?"

"I'm going to get me one of them cigars there."

"First you buying sunburn lotion and now you buying cigars."

Henry opened his fist and picked out a nickel and a dime. He put them down on the counter. "You going to sell me one?"

Julius opened the back of the case and picked out a cigar. When he held it out, Henry shook his head.

"Gimme the box and let me pick."

Julius got the box out.

Henry picked carefully, turning the cigars over and over. "Looks like the mice been at some of these."

"Ain't no mice in that there case," Julius said shortly.

"This one'll do for me." Henry put it in his shirt pocket.

Julius put the box back in the case. "I seen Pete around here just before you come in."

Henry swung his legs back and forth, kicking the counter with his heels. "Maybe he can figure it."

"What?"

"Where you keep all you money."

Julius hissed.

"Maybe we ought to go hunting for it."

"Maybe," Julius said.

"And you be the son of a bitch to take a shot at us."

"I wouldn't be surprise, me," Julius said.

Henry tilted back his head and stared at the ceiling. "Maybe you got it buried in you back yard."

"Maybe," Julius said, and went over to his rocking-chair by the window and sat down.

"You could be keeping it most anywhere on this island, no?"

"Maybe," Julius said.

Pete came in the store. "I been looking for you."

Henry scratched his close clipped head. "What you want me to do?"

"I got this motor, and I can't get it right."

"I said you was crazy to buy that."

"Come look at it and see."

"Ain't got time now."

"Say . . ." Pete stared. "How come you buying cigars?"

He reached out to touch the cellophane wrapping and his brother's fingers grabbed his wrist.

"Leave it alone," Henry said.

"Since when you buying fifteen-cent cigars?"

"He did today," Julius said.

Henry said: "I been trying to get him to tell me where he keep all his money."

Julius lit a cigarette and settled back in his rocker.

"Let the old bastard alone," Pete said, "and come fix that outboard."

"I been telling you no." Henry swung the sack of groceries to his shoulder.

"Jesus," Pete said. "All *that*."

"I'm taking my time," Henry said.

Julius chuckled. "You got enough for two week."

Henry held the bag on his shoulder. "I'm tired eating the stuff Ma buys."

"She going to like that like a hole in the head."

"Ask him what he going to use the sunburn cream for?"

"Huh?"

"Squibb sunburn cream," Julius said. "You ask him."

"What you buying that crap for?"

Henry started for the door. "Jesus," he said, "can't I do anything?"

The two boys walked home.

"When you going to smoke that cigar?" Pete asked.

"Don't know."

"Sure you do, or you wouldn't bought it."

"I tell you," Henry said, "when I get all through shooting and I got a pirogue full of duck, then I'm gonna sit back and have that cigar."

"Man," Pete said, "for two cents I'd come with you, me."

Henry shrugged and did not answer.

"I get the screen, man." Pete held open the door.

Still carrying the sack over his shoulder, Henry crossed the hall and began to climb the steep ladder-stair that led to the attic.

"You ain't going to put the stuff in the kitchen?"

Henry shook his head. He disappeared through the small square hole in the ceiling.

Pete went over and yelled up the steps: "Just out in the back yard if you want take a look."

A thump on the floor and Henry answered: "What the hell you talking about?"

"The outboard, man."

"Screw you."

"Come take a look, huh?"

"I'm trying to get going." The bedspring creaked.

Pete laughed. "Man, I hear everything you doing—you flat out on you back."

"Look," Henry said, "I'm gonna be up all night and working. I got to get some sleep."

"Just take one look."

Henry said: "When I get back."

"You fix it?"

"Yea," Henry said. "When I get back." He lay still and breathed the heat and the quiet. Finally he began to count his own breaths.

. . .

It was near five when Henry left the house. He had slung his two shotguns in their leather-and-canvas cases over his left shoulder and he carried the sack in his right hand. Pete was just coming in. His shirt was streaked with grease.

"Be a son of a bitch if I can do anything with it," he said.

"You quitting?"

"I got a date, man. I got to change my shirt."

Henry started down the steps. "You going to get any?"

"How'd I know?" Pete shrugged.

"Who you going out with?"

"None of your business."

"Efetha?"

"Maybe."

"You ain't going to get none, man."

"Quit," Pete said.

Henry walked along the docks, the planks shaking under his steps. One of these days, he thought, somebody would fix the boards, but that would be a long time coming.

He passed the sloop, where they had nearly had the fight a few days earlier. It was a pretty hull, he thought, and somebody sure spent a lot of time painting at it. Those would be teak decks too, he thought. It was something to see with the *Hula Girl* tied up alongside: the big high bow that was kept painted all right, but looked like somebody had whittled it out of a big block of wood, and hadn't done a very smooth job at that.

The man sitting in the cockpit of the sloop nodded to him. Henry nodded back, wondering idly what kind of a fight he would have made that day.

He was kind of sorry now that he hadn't. Kind of sorry . . .

He could feel his shoulder tighten, and he hitched the shotguns higher. "Jesus," he told himself silently. And for just a minute his steps slowed down.

Then he remembered and began to walk even faster than before.

It would be stupid, he told himself, when he wanted to get going. . . .

At the end of the dock, Henry picked up a coil of rope, dropped it into the sack, then headed along the island. He kept his pirogue over by the little rickety landing his father had helped Al Landry build.

He walked along the top of the shell mound that ran the length of the north side, a kind of levee for the island against the back bay. The sun was beginning to go down and it would be an almost cool night, with maybe a little breeze. That was good, he thought, it would help with the mosquitoes.

Fifty feet or so in front of him a long dark shape slipped over the shells and into the marsh of the bay side. He wondered if it were a cottonmouth.

He put the sack carefully in the bow of the pirogue. A couple of bronze-colored mosquito hawks that had been perched on the pier flew up around his head with a tiny, dry crackling of wings and bodies. He watched them: they had found a pillar of gnats, almost stationary in the air, and they shot back and forth through the pillar, dipping, weaving, eating. Higher up in the sky a couple of pelicans pumped slowly along.

He put the shotguns in, and got in himself. Then slowly he paddled through the marshy grass into the open water of the bay. The hollow shell of the pirogue danced on the tops of the sharp little waves. He shipped his paddle and let the boat swing around until it was broadside to the island. And he listened. There was a cow complaining; and some kids were screaming. Funny, he thought, no matter when you listened around the island—day or night—there'd be a kid yelling.

He looked down at the water: there were pieces of seaweed with orange berries. He fished one out, looked at it and smashed one of the berries between his fingers.

He wondered how it would taste to the fishes. He sniffed, but the berries had only the faint smell of decay.

He threw the tuft straight up and watched the sea gull dive after it. And miss.

He laughed. "Ain't so fast as all that," he said aloud to the small white body and the widespread fanning wings.

He looked back at the island, let his quick black eyes run back along the arc to the far end where the riggings of the boats stuck up into the small piled heaps of the evening clouds. There were little faint flickers of heat lightning up there.

He wiped the sweat off his lip with the back of his hand. He lifted his paddle and squinted out along its surface. Then he dipped it in the water, turned the pirogue and headed across the bay, with long slow strokes, not hurrying but moving just the same, and not looking back.

Inky shifted uncomfortably in his seat, and scratched at his ear irritably. He had got out the paper to refinish the little rough spot on the cowling that had been bothering him. But he didn't feel like doing it anymore.

The afternoon sun was slanting down low now so that the rigging of the fishing-boats made criss-cross shadows on his own deck.

He stood up stretching and looking across the bay. Halfway down the curve of the island he saw Henry's pirogue. He shielded his eyes and looked again. Then because he had nothing else to do, he went below and got the field glasses.

Inky recognized him. Damn, he thought, I'm seeing him everywhere. Coming or going. Solemn like a pelican.

After a few minutes Inky got tired of watching and put the glasses away.

*

AROUND six o'clock, when the yard was mostly in shade and it had got a little cooler, Belle Livaudais dragged the charcoal pot from under the back-porch foundation. She tipped it over, sending sprawling out into the light the beetles and spiders and fat black roaches that had lived inside. Then she took a broom and swept clean a spot in the yard, about twenty feet from the house.

"Henry," she called. "Henry, hey!"

She put the charcoal pot in the center of the swept circle. "Henry, hey, Henry, hey, c'here."

Inside the small white-painted house with a steep tin roof, a voice yelled: "He been gone this last hour."

She straightened up, put her hands on her narrow hips and sighed. "You got to come then," she said, "I ain't got the back for hauling water today."

"Okay," the voice said, "okay, lemme get my pants on."

She stood alongside the charcoal pot and rubbed her hands up and down her back.

Funny, she thought, how it had never been right since after the last baby. Not a hurt, no, but a little ache . . .

"You coming right down out here, no?"

"Lemme get my pants on."

She stretched herself now. She was a tall woman, with narrow shoulders and narrow hips. All in one line, like a pencil.

She sighed again. That had worried her once, when she was a girl, a long time ago. A very long time ago; she could hardly remember being young.

She looked at the kids sometimes, never walking when they could run, never sitting if they could stand; and then tumbling down asleep when they got tired. She had trouble sleeping; it had started after the last baby died—nights when she'd lie in bed, eyes

95

wide open, not tired, not even restless, just content to stare up at
the black ceiling. And she could dream, even awake, even with her
eyes wide open. All the things she'd wanted to do. All the things
that she'd wanted to happen to her. And hadn't.

She got the bag of charcoal from the porch and shook some into
the pot.

She almost laughed now, remembering. She'd been so worried
about her figure when she was a girl. There was just a cracked
piece of mirror in her bedroom. (It had got smashed when she and
her sister had one of their fights; and they each took half.) Some
days she would slip off her dress and her shift and stand looking
at her hard bony chest with the strips of muscles running up cross-
wise under the arms. And she'd be almost ready to cry. Somebody
told her rice was the thing to eat. And she'd made herself almost
sick, eating it.

She'd got herself a husband though. Best-looking man on the
island in his day, and a Livaudais too, tough as they come. He
wanted her spare hard body. She was lithe and muscular as a boy.
She did a boy's work too, every day of her girlhood.

She went to bed with him, demanding no promises, asking for
nothing, not even love.

Then she stopped seeing him. All of a sudden. Not another man
—she knew as well as anyone Eddie might have killed him. She
just stayed home, and every evening he could see her sitting on the
porch with her parents. If he came near, she went inside.

So he married her.

Belle Livaudais squatted down and started the fire in the little
pot. A mosquito settled on her thigh. She slapped and then
scratched away the black speck with her fingernail.

The old women had been so upset when she'd come to get preg-
nant. They'd gone to her husband Eddie and told him to move out
of the house quick or the mother and baby would die, for sure.

She could remember that, so clear, though it was near twenty
years ago. . . .

She'd been over at her mother's. There was a hammock in the
yard there, hanging between two mulberry trees. A regular ship's
hammock. Her father had got it somewhere. (Nobody ever asked
where he got things: he just picked them up when he was away

from the island.) And she'd been lying there swinging gently, and staring up at the little green nubs of the berries (it was early spring). She'd been laying with one hand on her belly, trying to feel the life in there. And when she'd come to going home, Eddie wasn't there, just two old women, her own grandmother and another one whose face she'd even forgotten. They both lived there with her until the child came. And Eddie, he had moved down to the other end of the island, to stay with his brother's family. He wasn't allowed to come back to the house at all.

The old women had worried about her narrow hips . . . but she hadn't. They rubbed her belly with lard every morning while she dozed. She was very calm. Nothing came near to her. Not even the gossip that Eddie and the Hébert girl were sneaking something at night. Nothing.

And the baby was delivered so easy. She smiled to remember.

It was true, she thought, that she hadn't had many. Only three, and two had lived. But they had all been boys, fine healthy children. Even the one that had died. . . . He'd been the prettiest of all, she thought sometimes. Though she couldn't close her eyes anymore and bring up his face, smooth and round and white. Yes, she nodded to herself, time was playing tricks on her again.

She blew on the charcoal.

Time worked that way. Like the sand and grass over in the marsh. Whatever stood on it slipped down into it and disappeared. Not so fast you could see it going. But still after a while, it was gone.

She hated time, she thought. Forever cutting off things behind you, and then in a while cutting off what you remembered of those things. And leaving you just a little narrow spot of present and near past to stand on.

She stared down at the smoking coal. She felt herself balancing on a narrow point. With time behind her, gobbling up her connections with the past. Time pushing her ahead.

"Nothing left to see behind," she said aloud, "and nobody could never see forward."

She stirred the coals with a thin twig. "Except they was a saint," she added.

"Jesus, Ma," her son said, "you ain't so old you got to be talking to yourself."

She looked around at him, not really seeing him, but still balancing on that point time had left her.

"Jesus," he said again, "what the matter?"

She shook her head, very slightly. "Ain't nothing."

"You looked at me so funny."

"Nothing," she said. The dizzy balancing feeling was gone now. And she was back squatting on the ground alongside the charcoal pot, her eyes smarting from the smoke. And a job of work to do.

"You can get the big washtub for me, no?" she asked.

"Okay," he said, "want me to fill it?"

She sat down on the ground. "And what I going to do with an empty washtub?"

"Okay," he said.

"Fill up the tub at the pump," she said.

"Jesus," he said, "why can't I use the bucket?"

"It ain't clean." She stirred the coals again. "It had oysters in it."

"I wash it out," he said.

She shook her head. "Ain't going to be clean enough. And I want clean water, me."

He shrugged. "I give up."

He got the tub off the back porch, filled it almost full, and then grabbing both handles, staggered across the yard with it. The water sloshed and splashed on his stomach. He lowered the tub down on the charcoal pot and more water splashed to the ground and made little round balls in the heavy dust.

He said: "What you doing that got to be done just so fine?"

He noticed the small pile of white cloth under the chinaberry tree and went over to look. His mother was still blowing gently on the coals.

"First Sunday coming," she said, "and they get used for Mass."

He lifted up first a long narrow white strip of cloth embroidered along one edge. Then the other, a long white lacy gown—a priest's surplice. He dropped them back in a pile again.

"So they get used," he said. "But why you washing them?"

"They got dirt in them."

"They got mildew on them. I can smell it."

"More reason."

"Jesus," he said, "and that what I near to broke my back lugging the water for."

She didn't answer. While she waited for the water to boil, she went and found the one spot of soft grass under the mulberry tree, smoothed it with her hand as if it were a bed or a sofa, and sat down.

Pete went over and patted her shoulder, letting his hand rest there for just a minute. "Don't knock youself out."

"The pants is torn."

He glanced down at his knee. "They been torn."

"Why you ain't said something to me?"

"They all right."

"Ain't no son of mine going to walk around with his skin showing."

"Make it cooler," he said.

She glanced up at his face, saw that he was teasing. "Go on," she said, "go back to what you was doing."

"Your water ain't boiling."

"Ain't no water boil in a minute."

He squinted up into the sky. "Jesus," he said, "look at that hawk there."

"Where Henry go to?"

"How'd I know." The hawk had disappeared, but he kept squinting, trying to see it.

"He didn't say?"

Pete laughed. "He don't ever."

"Why he ain't told me he was going?"

Pete grinned. "You was down at the church."

"He like to be alone sometime, him."

"He want to be alone a long time, this time," Pete said. "I seen the load of stuff he took."

"Maybe he get us some deer."

"Yea," Pete said.

"Be nice to have some deer, no?"

"Yea," Pete said.

"Shake up the fire some, che'."

He did, and then headed back into the house.

She called after him: "Maybe this time I cook it with wine, no?"

THAT was the night it rained—a short, hard storm, with little square stabs of lightning and a stiff, chill wind.

Old Boudreau shook his head and said that it felt like a little hurricane and that meant a bad September for sure.

Eddie Livaudais, when the thunder woke him up, thought of his son (safe up in the marsh he would be, sheltered from the waves, but wet anyhow). And he chuckled to himself—teach the kid to stay home, maybe.

Down in the brakes and the hackberry thickets around the houses, the dogs began to howl. And Rita Monjure who was staying with Mamere lit all the lamps in the house, and looked at the clock every ten minutes to see how much longer it was to daylight.

When morning did come, the wind was still blowing hard, but it was bright and clear—just some little straggly bits of cloud that disappeared in an hour. And the wet ground and the leaves steamed under the sun.

Around noon, in the hottest part of the day, Mamere began to stir around, and to mumble. And Rita Monjure, who was going home just then, dead tired from no sleep, walked the extra distance over to the grocery to tell the people there that the old woman was pulling through. Then she plodded on home, chased the kids off her front porch with a mop and a series of yells that scared even them, drank four cups of cold coffee and went to bed herself.

Mamere Terrebonne opened her little eyes that were tucked way back in her wrinkled brown face (for all the world like the face on a gingerbread doll), and she called for some anisette. When the women who were watching up with her—Cecile Boudreau and Justine Landry—said no because the doctor had told them so the last time, the old woman fell to swearing softly.

Cecile clapped her hand over her mouth and went over to look

100

out the window. She found it funny—this old woman who had been almost dead, and who was lying in the middle of her bed now, covered with quilts in August, and cursing in the old fashioned roundabout way.

Justine Landry was shocked. "You been so close to God," she told her grandmother, and went to get some of the medicine the doctor said to give if she got excited.

The hands were curled on the edge of the bedsheet. One on each side, Justine thought, like the claws of a bird that was lying on its back, dead.

"God, He is close to me," Mamere said, though she was panting just a little. "He never leave me, Him."

Justine got one hand behind the old head. "Take this, Mamere."

The old woman made a face and then drank. "Tastes of the henhouse. . . ."

"And only day before yesterday," Justine said angrily, "the priest was here for you."

Over at the window, Cecile turned around sharply. They had agreed not to tell the old woman that.

"Ha!" Mamere said explosively.

Justine looked over at Cecile and shrugged. "I forgot. . . ."

"Ha!" Mamere said, "if he had wait, just a little, I could have a drink with him."

Cecile grinned. "You don't get none now."

"You been sick," Justine said, "you got to keep still."

"Which one it was?"

"The one named Ryan."

"Sal au pri . . . and he come to bury me."

"No," Justine said.

"And him he come to put me in the ground."

"You got to keep still."

"Sal au pri . . . he come all that way. Maybe got wet too. And he got all that trip for nothing.

"Mamere," Cecile said, "how you know it was raining?"

"I got ears. I can hear. . . . Son of a bitch . . ."

"She couldn't hear nothing," Justine whispered. "She was like to dead."

"How'd she tell?"

Justine shrugged.

"I bet she smelled it," Cecile said, "smelled it in the air this morning."

"Son of a bitch. . . ." Mamere said. "But somebody gave him a drink, no?"

"I wouldn't be surprised, me," Cecile grinned. "Over by the Lombas place."

"You didn't go with him?"

"We was busy with you," Justine said.

Mamere clucked her tongue. "I need none of you . . . when you could have been having a drink with that handsome priest. . . ."

"You were sick, old lady," Cecile said. "No matter what you tell us."

Mamere stared at her and grinned, suddenly, a toothless happy grin.

"You sneaked by," Cecile said, "now don't go making so much noise or maybe he come back for you."

"Raide comme une babiche," Mamere muttered.

"Maybe so. Maybe not. You got to stay where you're at."

"And that Ryan, he could not even stay to pass the time of day with me."

"Maybe," Cecile said.

"Comme une babiche."

"Ain't no whisky or nothing in the house," Justine said.

And the old woman fell back to cursing under her breath, softly, until her eyes closed and she was asleep.

Cecile said: "Henry went hunting." It was late afternoon and on the porch rail the moonflowers were beginning to open.

"Henry who?"

"Ain't but one Henry around here."

"I forgot that," Justine said.

They had moved away from the old woman out to the next room, which was the parlor.

"Something smells funny in here."

Justine pointed to the picture of St. Joseph. The candle burning under it had fallen over into a little bunch of shrimp-tail flowers.

"Shrimp shells burning," Justine said.

"Anyhow," Cecile said, "ain't no son of mine ever going to do that. And leave me wondering where he's at."

"How you going to stop them?"

"I'm going find a way."

"That what my mama say when my little brother he starts coming up," Justine laughed. "She didn't have no chance."

"I'm going find a way."

"First it was like: Mama, can I have a BB gun? Mama, all the other kids, they got BB guns. . . . And from the minute they get that, there ain't no keeping them in the house. They got to be out getting something."

"If you ain't careful you going to be waking the old lady."

When Mamere woke up her mood had changed. She was not cursing nor grinning anymore. When Justine and Cecile peeped in, she was staring at them with solemn eyes. "I want the priest," she said.

"You feeling worse?"

"I want the priest."

She closed her eyes and would not say a word more. Justine raced out of the house to the Lombas place.

The house was empty except for Perique on the back porch. "Go get you papa," she said breathlessly.

In half an hour or so, the porch of Mamere's house was crowded with people, while their kids played in the yard.

Nobody went in until Ferdinand Lombas arrived. And he was slow coming. Perique had hunted for almost an hour before he located him, clearing the eels out of his traps on the north shore. He came just as he was, sweaty and smelly, and with the white slime from the eels on his pants and shirt. He only stopped in the front yard long enough to take a drink of water and wipe the sweat off his face. Then he went inside to talk to his grandmother.

"Mamere," he said softly, and her little brown eyes popped open.

They were bright little eyes staring at him, bright as a crab's eye is. And mentally he crossed himself—some people said she could do gris gris.

I never believe that, he told himself. But he crossed himself again, to be sure.

"Mamere," he said, "you want something?"

"I want the priest, me."

Ferdinand stopped and scratched his head. "You feel weaker?"

"I want the priest."

Ferdinand rubbed his hands together. The smell of the eels began to fill the room. "But the priest has just been here."

"He did not come in the room."

"He look in the door," Ferdinand said, "and you was sleeping and better, so we took him home."

"Go get him."

"We should get the doctor too, no?"

She clucked her tongue and it rattled like the shell of a crab. He had heard of crabs sometimes that lived to be nearly a hundred. Like her.

"The doctor, no?"

"I have no need for the doctor."

"But why the priest?"

The eyes blinked. "You go get him."

Ferdinand rubbed his hands together harder. The water he had gulped down in the front yard was beginning to pour out of his body. "But we just took him home not hardly more than a day ago."

There was a crowd of faces in the doorway now, reaching almost from the top to the floor. Those who had got there first squatted down to make room for others behind them. "What she saying?" somebody whispered.

Ferdinand thought for a minute.

"For what do you need a priest," he asked finally.

The little black eyes moved on him. "He leave without a blessing."

"But you are better?"

"Enfant garce," she said. "How can I get better without a blessing from a priest. How can I never leave my bed without I have it?"

It was very quiet, except for the hoarse breathings over in the door and the muffled giggles of the kids outside.

"You don't feel yourself sinking?"

Mamere lifted her head on its skinny neck. "Everybody pushing me," she said, picking her words carefully and slowly. "Pushing me, pushing me down in the ground, down-down, until I got nothing to do but make grass."

Ferdinand waved his hands again.

Mamere's head stuck up even more sharply on her neck and her voice got stronger. "I ain't going down there."

"Nobody say . . ."

"Now you ain't getting me a priest."

"Nobody . . ."

But Mamere had put her head back and closed her eyes.

Ferdinand backed away until he got to the door, then he turned and pushed through the people.

Ferdinand went over to the Arcenaux grocery and had two beers.

"They on the house, man," Julius Arcenaux told him. "You got enough to worry about."

"I got troubles all right," Ferdinand said and belched because he had gulped down the beers so fast.

"And what you going to do about them?"

Ferdinand shook his head. "I got to think about it." He reached in the cooler and got a third beer.

"Now that ain't on the house," Julius said. "I roll you for it."

They were making a couple of tosses, lazily, just warming up their arms, when Ferdinand's wife, Carrie, found them.

"You old Mamere dying and you playing . . . son of a bitch!"

Ferdinand held the dice behind his back. "We was thinking. She say we got to get her a priest."

"So you are getting her a priest, sitting here?"

"Look," Julius said, "your cousin, he's the pastor."

She frowned at him.

"You got to ask him."

She scowled.

"Now that is a first-class idea," Ferdinand said and rubbed his hands on his stomach. "A first-class idea."

"Mother Mary," Carrie said. "I got to go all the way over to Petit Prairie?"

"No," Julius waved his hands around his head. "You forget."

"What?" Carrie asked suspiciously.

"The telephone," Julius said.

There was one phone on the island, and that was hardly used. Nobody quite knew why the telephone company bothered to run a line out to the island, except maybe to say that they had. Julius Arcenaux had built a little lean-to at the back of his grocer and had a pay phone put there. People used it occasionally. Julius would telephone his orders to Port Ronquille because he hated writing letters. When Hector Boudreau's sister over at Biloxi had twins she called her mother. And when Stanley Waguespack was in the army and away at Fort Dix, he'd call his mother the first Sunday in every month, and talk for a little while, though he hadn't much to say ever, because he hadn't got on with his parents, and it was strange that he called at all. And from New Orleans the afternoon of every Christmas Day, Sister Mary Margaret called her family. Since she was related to so many people, and didn't particularly care which one of her family she talked to, nearly anybody could answer that call.

Most of the year people forgot that the telephone was there.

"I don't know, me," Carrie said. She was thinking of the quarters slipping down into the little black box.

"Call you cousin and tell him to send that young Ryan out here. How we going to work," Ferdinand said, "if I got to spend all my days here, watching to see if she going to die, or if she ain't. How we going to eat?"

"Okay. Okay," Carrie said. "Gimme the money."

"Me?"

"Gimme."

Ferdinand emptied the pockets of the pants. "Two bits."

Carrie said: "That all you got?"

"You got eyes, you can see. . . ."

It was a good ten minutes before Carrie came back into the grocery.

Ferdinand said: "You ain't been talking all this time?"

She wiped her nose on the back of her hand and then scratched the top of her head. "You god-damn fool telephoning!"

"What's the matter, huh?" Julius asked.

"Don't you go soft talking at me!" She slammed the screen door

behind her—so hard that the handle which said Bond Bread in big
blue letters shook loose and fell to the floor.

And Ferdinand had to follow her all the way back to the house
before she would talk to him. Right at the front gate she turned
and said to him: "God-damn telephoning."

And Ferdinand looked around quickly at the other people who
were listening, and said: "Huh?"

"He asks, is she getting well? And I say yes, Father. What in
god's name I'm gonna say. . . . And he say he is pleased to hear
that . . . and all the while I can hear the operator listening. I can
hear her breathing, me. . . . And he say again how glad he is
and she is a fine old lady. And I say can he get the young man to
come out again. And he say for what I need a priest when she is
getting better."

Ferdinand leaned on the gate post with a sigh. The circle of
listeners was drawing up closer.

"So I say, Father she say she need a priest . . . and he say
why . . . and what I'm going say then? Am I gonna tell him
how the man goes running off without a blessing so he can drink
whisky with you?"

"We ain't had more than a drink or so," Ferdinand said.

"So I tell him. There wasn't nothing I could do but tell him.
And then he says that he can't send Father Ryan back on account
of he's got to coach the basketball team at the school that's got a
special game coming up and how he got to do the Forty Hours' De-
votion too. And how there's just old Father Manent who's up in
the years and he gets seasick anyhow. And there's himself, and he's
got the rheumatism. . . . And he says there ain't nobody he can
send. And we say good-by. And it cost eighty cents."

"Jesus," Ferdinand said.

"Go talk to her," Carrie said. "Maybe she feel different now."

So Ferdinand hitched up his pants and slapped a stray mosquito
on his ankle and went inside.

When he opened the bedroom door the old woman did not
move or open her eyes. For just a minute he was scared. So he
tiptoed closer, the boards sighing and creaking under his weight.
And then he saw that while her eyes didn't move they were only
partly closed. From the crack the brown irises watched him.

"Cecile, she say you been wanting me."

"I been wanting you for a long time."

He sat down on a little cane-backed chair. "Mamere . . ." he said.

"I been waiting."

"We call up the priest."

She did not answer. The lids did not lift. He wasn't sure she hadn't fallen asleep on him.

"On the telephone, we call him up."

One finger moved very slowly, beckoning.

He leaned over, both hands on his knees."

"Fi d' poutain."

He sat back and rubbed his hands up and down his thighs. "I been trying to tell you."

Outside a mockingbird was singing at the top of his voice. God-damn bird, he thought, he can strangle and choke on his own tongue.

"We talk to him on the telephone."

Outside a kid yelled and somebody hushed him.

"What they think I'm doing," Mamere said, "that a kid, he can't yell and empty his lungs. What they think I'm doing, dying?"

"We talk to him on the telephone."

"So?" Mamere opened her eyes just a little bit more. "And for what I got to care how you talk to him."

Ferdinand sat back in his chair. "He say you going to get all right without no priest."

Mamere stared at the ceiling where a couple of fat black flies buzzed.

"Ain't no priest you can trust," Mamere said and then spat in a little arc down to the foot of the bed."

"Now," Ferdinand said, "well . . ."

"Sal au pri . . ."

Mamere began to moan very softly. "Son of a bitch of a priest . . . how I'm ever going to get out of this bed."

Cecile came to the door. "What's the matter with her?"

Mamere stopped moaning. Cecile and Ferdinand scurried over to the bed to see. The sharp black eyes were peering up at them.

Cecile whistled. "You give us a fright."

The lids that were like rice paper blinked. "You got to go get him."

"Huh?"

"Go get him."

"Who?"

"The priest."

"Look," Ferdinand said, "he say he ain't coming and he ain't."

"Go get him."

"You mean go make him come?" Cecile said.

Mamere's little eyes closed again.

"We can't do nothing like that," Ferdinand said. When Estelle Abadie's baby was born and the women took one look at it and saw it couldn't live more than a day or so, the men went for the priest, even though it was the middle of the night. They got him out of his bed and into his cassock, him fussing and arguing all the time. Paul Travigno, who had been an altar boy once and knew what was needed, packed up the little black bag.

They'd have done the same with a doctor, if they needed him.

"You ain't that sick," Cecile said.

"Ain't never going to get from this bed again," Mamere's eyes didn't open.

"Sure you are," Ferdinand said.

"Got no time. . . ." And she stopped speaking and would not give any other sign, no matter what they said to her.

It was Julius had the idea finally. Though he didn't say anything about it until the following day. His wife heard him chuckling in bed that night. But she didn't bother asking him. She didn't really care.

The next day he found Ferdinand chopping away the grass around his front door with a sickle. They talked for a minute there, with Ferdinand on his haunches and Julius bent over, but with his head lifted. And in a few minutes Ferdinand stuck the sickle point down in the ground and headed out the little gate. Julius watched him go, and then looked down at the sickle. Finally he picked it up and went to work. In ten minutes or so he had finished the grass. It was one of the few things he liked to do.

Mamere was lying with her eyes open all the way, staring at the ceiling when Ferdinand came in the room. She looked just a little sad.

"With who you tripoté last night, while I am lie here?"

Ferdinand paid no attention. "I have everything fixed."

She sighed. "There is nothing fix."

But she was not yelling at him, he noticed, so maybe . . .

"You want a blessing from the priest. . . ."

"If I have told you," she said, "I have told you a million time."

"Alors . . ." he interrupted. "I know how you can have the blessing."

She turned away and stared at the wall.

"A blessing from the priest himself."

"It is nothing to make joke about," she muttered.

"Now listen . . . we take you over to the store. Four, five, six of us men, many as it needs to carry you. On the bed."

Mamere turned to him, frowning uncertainly.

"Now listen," he said. "You don't got to get out the bed, nor move. And we take you down to the store. And by that time, Carrie she got the priest on the telephone and he is all ready. And you pick up the phone and say it's you. And he give you any kind of blessing you ask for."

"Enfant . . ." Mamere began.

And before she could finish he ducked out the door.

Ferdinand ran all the way. He sent his wife scurrying over to start the call, and he found four men to help him with the bed. It wasn't five minutes before they were carrying Mamere out the door. And it wasn't ten minutes before they were carrying her back, and her with a big smile on her wrinkled raisin face.

* * *

SEA CHANGE

~~~~~~~~~~~~~~

THE NEXT few days were like all the days of all the Augusts, white-hot and dusty. Way out, on the rim of the Gulf, was a chain of thunderheads, shining in the sun, their black underbellies flickering with heat lightning now and then. They seemed to stay there, all day and all night, unmoving. The island was dry and brown-looking. The dust from the white shell paths rose up in clouds from under each foot, even the lightest of the children's, and coated the trees and bushes and got into all the houses. After a bit the women stopped dusting their furniture; it wasn't much use: in an hour the same gray film would return. On the *Pixie* Inky had put canvas covers over all the brightwork and washed down the decks carefully, every day. At night it was too hot for mosquito-netting. He smeared himself with repellent and lay down on the bare decks, without mattress or pillow, with only the slope of the bow lifting his head a little.

Yvonne Songy, who had always had asthma, came down with a bad case, so bad that her older brother Jerry took her in specially to Petit Prairie. She would live with her aunt there until the rains came in September and settled the dust.

Henry Livaudais had not come back yet. But no one worried or thought any about it. He had been out as long as five days before. That was just his way. The boy was a born trapper, he liked the feel and the smell of the marsh and the swamps. And he knew

111

how to handle himself too: when he'd come back, his face and hands would be just as clear, not so much as a single scratch from the sawgrass on them.

And people went on pretty much the way they had before, only they went about it more slowly, and they got tired a little quicker.

Annie Landry let herself into the Boudreau living-room, and finding no one there, went to the bedroom. Cecile was changing the baby.

"Hi," Cecile said. "Where you been keeping yourself?"

"I been around."

"I was talking to you papa, just last night he come by."

"I could gone crabbing with Perique and made some money, only I didn't want to."

"They buying crabs again, huh?" Cecile finished the diaper and flipped the baby over on his stomach. "Try that way for a while, macac. . . . I'd gone," she said.

Annie just shook her head.

"And I didn't have these two," Cecile said, "you see how fast I go to pick up money that easy, me."

"Perique's been talking about getting a job in Petit Prairie."

"I been hearing him talk like that for years."

"Maybe he's going to."

"Maybe. And maybe not."

Annie squinted one eye at the baby. "Man, has he got heat."

"Don't tell me," Cecile said. "I been knowing about it."

Annie had pulled her white-blond hair back into a ponytail, held by a thick red rubber band. "You like it this way?"

Cecile looked. "Makes you ears stand out."

"No."

"You need it hanging soft and loose."

"No," Annie said.

"You ask me."

"Course I only got a rubber now . . . when I put a ribbon and some flowers on, it'll be better."

Cecile shook her head. "Won't change your ears."

Annie rubbed both ears, hard. "They're like my papa's."

"Wouldn't be surprised."

"Kind of long and thin."

"All you got to do is let the hair fall over them."

Annie made a face.

"You got nice hair—nobody got blond hair like yours around here—and you don't want to go slicking it back."

"I could be making a lot of money today."

"Shoulda gone."

"No," Annie said. "What do I need money for?"

"Don't be plain ga-ga," Cecile said. "Everybody always need money."

"I don't."

"Come get some coffee," Cecile said, giving the baby a final pat.

"Rather have a beer."

"Got that too."

"I can't," Annie said, "I get too fat."

"Then stop bothering," Cecile said.

"Can't do that either."

"Okay," Cecile said, and went into the kitchen.

"I don't know why people got to rush and drink something all the time."

"Me, I sort of like it," Cecile said. She touched the big enamel coffee pot with one finger to be sure it was warm, then poured herself a cup. She carried cup and pot both into the living-room, and seated herself carefully with the pot on the floor beside her.

Annie followed her.

"Gives me time to get my breath before I start to think about supper."

Annie made a face. "Always eating."

"Huh?"

"Didn't you ever think about it. . . . Spend all you time cooking and feeding people and more people."

Cecile hesitated just a minute with the cup at her lips. "I think of that," she said quietly.

"Just putting food in mouths," Annie said. "That all."

"That has come to me, sometimes," Cecile said very quietly, "and I have wondered about it."

"So what?"

"Nothing," Cecile shrugged softly. "And you, do you have the answer?"

Annie was a little upset by her tone, but she went ahead. "It's dull," she said, "just plain dull."

The clipped black head nodded gently.

"Me," Annie said, "I left the dishes from breakfast. And they still there, cause I couldn't wash, I was so tired of them."

"They be full of ants," Cecile said.

Annie stamped her foot and the coffee pot rattled on the floor. "You know what I'm talking about."

Cecile nodded again.

"Always feeding something. . . . Plain stupid."

"Maybe."

"So what do you do?"

"Nothing," Cecile said. "And what you do?"

Annie let her breath go out in a sigh of annoyance that ruffled her lips together. "I'm going back to New Orleans." And she was a little surprised, because until she said it, she had not thought of it at all.

"Maybe."

Annie was quiet for a bit as she walked slowly around the small room, staring curiously as if she had never seen a single object before. She walked from wall to wall looking at the pictures: one on each wall. On the south wall, there was a picture of the Crucifixion, a lithograph in red and black. (All over the island, religious pictures were always hung on the south wall, no one could say why, and no one changed.) On the east wall was a brown-wood-framed print with a tiny brass nameplate: *Firelights* —a beautifully dressed woman, with high-piled hair, gazes dreamily into the fire from which a vision of her lover-to-be smiles at her. The picture was water-stained; they'd found it on the beach four or five years ago, when they were first married. On the other walls were pictures Cecile had done herself with colored pencils: a head of her son when he was about two; a sketch of the wharves when the boats were gone: empty planks and hanging lines and the empty waters of the bay.

Cecile had always been quick with her pencil. She still sketched sometimes, when there was time. She had a way of hitting off likenesses.

Annie said: "Do me sometime."

"Sure, just as soon as I get a minute or so."

"And I can put it with the one you did of me, before I went off to school."

Cecile blew on the top of her coffee and sipped it. "Okay."

Annie went over to the window that was set so low in the wall that she had to bend a little to see out. All the windows were built that way—built for sitting people. From a chair in any room, you could see out comfortably.

"I wonder," Annie said, "I wonder why they go and build windows like this."

"They build like that even in the old, old houses."

"There got to be a reason."

"I sure don't know, me." Cecile said.

"We always go and do things different on the island."

"Maybe living out here make it different."

"They don't build windows like that, even in Petit Prairie, not even in New Orleans."

Cecile drank her coffee and did not bother answering. The baby cried in his sleep.

"Does it hurt as much as they say?" Annie stared at the picture of the empty wharves.

"As what say?"

"Having a baby."

"No," Cecile said. "It ain't bad at all."

"It seems like it would be terrible."

"No," said Cecile, "why you want to know?"

"No reason."

"What you do?" Cecile's light green eyes peered intently over the coffee cup. "You get yourself a baby?"

"No."

"You worried about it."

"No," Annie said, "I ain't worried."

Cecile went on staring at her stomach. "Nothing showing."

"I ain't," Annie lifted her voice with annoyance. "I told you I ain't. I'm just asking."

Cecile picked up her cup and walked out to the kitchen. She was staring into the icebox, when Annie came and stood behind her.

"I didn't mean to yell," Annie said.

"Just studying dinner."

Annie said: "I was just trying to figure out something. I got to have babies, I guess." She hesitated. "You listening to me?"

"I'm listening to you with both my ears."

"Only it seems like your body would come bursting apart with a thing as big as a baby trying to get out."

"It ain't so bad," Cecile said.

"It seems like it would hurt."

"Sure it does." Cecile measured out a cup of rice and began to wash it at the sink. The hard white grains slipped back and forth between her brown fingers. "Hurts and hurts til you think you go flying right out you mind each time the pain come back. And then it's all done and finished."

Annie pulled a chair from beneath the board counter and sat down on it. "Cecil'. . ."

"Huh?"

"Don't you ever get afraid that this whole island is going to slip right under the water?"

"Nuh-uh."

"Just sand and trees, no rocks to hold it."

"It's been here a long time, sure."

"But if there ever was a real big storm, with waves big enough . . ."

"Then I reckon maybe we drown."

"You're making fun of me."

"I'm not, che'."

Annie stared out the window at the sand walks, the sand-dusted oleander bushes. "I been thinking," she said, "I been thinking a lot."

"Like what?"

"All sorts things. Like the way things are here and the way they must be somewhere else." She tilted back on one leg of the wood chair. "Like what it's like in California, and what it's like just over on the ocean side of Florida."

Cecile was leaning against the sink, listening. Her green eyes under the fringe of uneven dark hair were very serious.

"And if you went straight out from here, if maybe you took the sailboat that tied up here and went straight south, where would you go? And not just where neither. What it'd be like."

Annie poured herself some coffee in Cecile's cup and drank it

quickly. Cecile strained the cloudy water off the rice and poked at
the shiny white grains with the tip of one finger.

"So many things I been wondering about," Annie said. "Funny
things. And I never saw them before I come back this summer.
. . . When I come back it was all different. And I wasn't gone a
whole year even."

"Like what?" Cecile said and rolled a single grain between her
fingers. "Like what?"

Annie put the cup down very carefully. "You ever notice," she
said, "how they don't ever talk about the fishing? How you never
know what they were doing all day?"

Cecile nodded.

"And it's kind of like they got on the boats and went out and
disappeared in the morning. Disappeared and then come back.
And they weren't anywhere real at all."

"I notice."

"And the beach out there—and nobody swims. Not even the
kids."

Cecile was silent for a minute, remembering. "And when the
moon's out," she said, "you got to put your head under the pillow,
even with all the heat, cause the light's so bright."

Annie said: "And the water all around you, so you can't go
anywhere. And it such a little island."

After a long pause, Cecile said slowly: "You need something
to do."

"I got plenty to do."

"You aunt, now, she could find you something in New Orleans,
for a while."

"No," Annie said.

"And you find a man. No girl pretty as you going to stay alone
for long."

"I don't want to get married," Annie said. "I just don't want to."

"Nobody says you got to."

"I want to stay here. And everything to stay just like it is right
now.

"Bébé, what a thought you got."

"The way things keep changing . . . I hate that most of all."

"Sometimes they get better."

"No, they don't," Annie swung around, her hands jammed in

the pocket of her jeans and her dark face flushed with anger. "They get worse and worse. Just when you get to like people one way, they turn around and go another."

"You don't got to yell at me," Cecile said. "I hear you."

Without a word Annie turned and left. Cecile glanced out the window and watched her. She swung over the porch railing and dropped to the ground without using the steps. She hesitated in the yard for a minute, then began to walk away, faster and faster. By the time she reached the road, she was running.

"Jesus," Cecile said softly to herself. The baby was crying in earnest now. So she went into the bedroom and picked up the sugar tit and tucked it into his mouth. "Feels kind of like a hurricane been through here."

She stood looking down at her own hands for a while, her square strong hands, the only ring a thin band of gold that was already a depression in the hard brown flesh.

"I used to worry with things like that," she told the baby. "Then I got married, me, and there wasn't time anymore."

Annie had made her vaguely sad. So she tickled the baby's foot and grinned back down at him. "Seems like there's just time for all the business of living and nothing else."

She's not doing anything right now, Cecile thought, not even living. When she starts that business, there won't be any time.

She went back to fix supper, Hector would be coming home. Even as she worked, the little feeling of irritation and unhappiness moved along with her.

She stopped and shook her head. Maybe I'm getting ready to menstruate, she thought, feeling this bad. Or maybe the sun.

She put the rice on to boil and had another cup of coffee. If it was the sun, she hadn't noticed it before.

*

ANNIE was sixteen that summer and her figure had just begun to fill out: she was slow for the island.

She wasn't the prettiest girl on the island that summer, by far, but there were men who wanted her, who looked at her out of the corner of their eyes when she went past. There were two or three she could have had that summer, if she had known how to go about it. But they were waiting for her to give some signal, and she did not understand. As for Perique, she had hardly seen him since the night he had come drunk to her house.

She was alone most of the time—her father was hardly ever home—and she did not seem to mind. She took to sewing: to making great full gathers of skirts in brilliant cotton . . . and to letting out her other clothes, for she was putting on a little weight that summer. You could see her angular body begin to soften and take on curves.

When her Aunt Justine (who had taken care of Annie since her mother's death over a year before) noticed the change, she was relieved. "She begins to look like a woman, no?" she asked her husband one day when Annie had just left their front porch.

He cocked an eye. "Not to my taste—non."

His wife sniffed. "And there was times when I thought, me, that she wasn't going to make it."

"Girls is hard to kill."

"Last year, when I think she is going crazy, I wouldn't give a picayune for her chance."

"With the other girls her age she is still a runt."

"All the same," his wife said, "Annie, she is growing up. And only last year I have wondered about her."

For the two months after her mother died—from taking castor oil with a stomach-ache—Annie Landry wandered around, aimless, with a lost and frightened look. There were times when she did not even seem to see where she was going.

Her father said: "She will die if she keep up this way."

"No," her Aunt Justine said. She was a calm practical woman, with close-set blue eyes and a big well-shaped head on top of a long rangy body. Since his wife's death, she did the housework for her husband's brother, along with her own. She was a strapping fine woman with muscles that never got tired. "I will see what I can do."

So she scolded the girl, as much as she dared. "Look at you . . . look how you droop around the house like a sick gull. Doing nothing all the day long, and your poor papa working and worrying too. He must do the cooking too, without me. You, you do not lift a finger nor stir."

Annie did not say anything.

"Look at me!"

She lifted her eyes. There was no expression in them at all.

"Mother of Mary," her aunt said and waved her hands. "You do not even have the pride to get angry, you."

Annie's pale blue eyes stared at her, without blinking, their lids just a little puffy.

Her aunt left, upset in spite of herself. "She don't feel nothing, her. She don't feel nothing."

When she'd gone, Annie walked down to the beach, found a large piece of driftwood, kicked most of the sand off it, sat down, and stared out at the empty Gulf.

During those weeks, her face broke out in pimples. Her aunt treated them with oil of camphor. And scolded. At first Annie said: "Let me alone"—but finally she did not even bother. She spent most of her days lying on the grass in the sun, even the white hot noon sun, where she could feel the warmth go through her body and reach the hard cold center of her stomach and melt that too. When she was soft and warm all through, when the sun was so hot that little white spreckles would dance in front of her closed eyes and she could feel the day all around her like a sea— then she would fall asleep.

If her aunt or her father called her, she would put both fingers in her ears and go back to sleep. If they found her and shook her, she would only get up, moving slowly to keep the wonderful world intact around her, and walk away, unanswering, to find another spot.

"She is losing her mind," her aunt said and threw up her hands. "And so young a one to do that."

During the short hard early-summer rains, Annie went out just the same, so that the rain would make a mat of her short blond hair and run down over her ears and into her eyes. She would cock her head and squint her eyes and stare straight up into the falling points of light. When she came back finally, her jeans and shirt would be soaked through, and covered with mud. Her aunt tried to make her wear a bra.

"It ain't decent, her showing through the cloth that way," she said. Annie only shook her head.

"Let me alone," she said, tiredly. "Just let me alone."

The nights were worse. She would toss and whimper until she fought her way back into consciousness. There was one dream, recurring and recurring: three balls, yellow, bright yellow each one; she could see them rolling across the ground. And she could see the ground clearly too, she could see the little round nasturtium leaves and the full pink clovers.

Even when she was sitting bolt upright in bed, her eyes wide open, she gasped and shivered: the shapes followed her right into the room.

Sometimes, when it was bright moonlight, she would wake up and find herself staring at the knob on the door. Her eyes were stuck so she couldn't seem to move them. And she could feel a knob growing inside her, growing and growing, deep in her stomach, growing and pressing on her insides and pressing on her lungs until she couldn't breathe. And she would have to stagger up and pull open the door and send it slamming back into the wall, before she could catch her breath again.

Once there was an oblong piece of light on the ceiling over her bed—coffin-shaped. And there was a shadowy face at one end. She held her breath, and stared at it, afraid to blink, afraid that if she did, the tiny hold she had on the world would break and she'd go tumbling into the place where the dead were, without light and without feeling.

She did not call, though she could hear the steady hard breathing of her father in the next room. She waited until the shadow was gone and the fluttering in her stomach had stopped. Then she got up and, holding her eyes wide open with the fingers of one hand, she went outside.

There was the small damp smell of the one rose bush, a yellow climber, and the winey odor of the sweet olive. There, the tall dark green bush by the edge of the porch. She squeezed the tight waxy flowers between her fingers and sniffed. The sharp odor went through her head and she felt better.

Two cats were hunting, she saw their flattened shapes slip across the shell path. Something scratched across the tin roof of the house: a bird or a rat. And beyond everything was the sleepy sound of the Gulf. She stretched and rubbed her hands down along the sides of her body. She pulled up the top of her pajamas and scratched her stomach, slowly and hard, so that her nails left long red marks.

There was a handline out on the porch, curled in a circle on the flat top of the railing. Her father had forgotten it. He'd been checking his lines the evening before, talking about going up to Lake Catherine, where the croakers were running.

She picked up the line and left, her bare feet making a brushing sound over the dewed grass. The cats leaped away, yeowling.

She looked after their sound, not seeing anything in the dark, smelling only their heavy musk. "You just look at me and yell," she told them in a whisper. The cats made no sound or move. She went on talking to them, enjoying the sound of her own voice in the empty night. "You go ahead and yell. You can't do anything to me. Not a thing, not a single thing, you."

She stooped and rolled up the legs of her pajamas to keep them dry and went on. She heard the cats rustling in the leaves behind her.

It was getting toward morning—there was the clear feel of day in the air—but the stars were still as bright as midnight. In an opening between the high oleander bushes she stopped and stared up at them, the millions of worlds spinning in big circles: it made her dizzy.

The night was very quiet, just the rustling of the hot night breeze that smelled of salt and swamp—the sweet thick odor of swamp. Mosquitoes sang around her ears and a big night beetle got tangled in her hair. Her fingers found his round hard body with the frantically clawing legs and threw him down on the ground. Then she left the path and cut through the fields, little meadows of creeping tiny yellow flowers with round leaves, to one side the line of oak trees, to the other the slight rise of shell mound that marked the north end of the island. Beyond that was a few feet of salt grasses and then the bay and then more salt marshes on the mainland.

A lean brown rabbit jumped from almost under her feet. She stopped and tried to follow his path, but the stars were not bright enough. She bent down and pulled a leaf and licked the dew from it. The trees on the edge of the field all slanted back away from the sea spray, flat and angled like the roof of a house. And right over them, just barely touching them, was the thin sliver of a new moon. Annie turned her back, closed her eyes, and made a wish.

She walked until she came to a rickety landing, just a couple of boards to make a narrow fishing-catwalk. She had been there so many times and she did not need to hesitate or feel her way. Balancing easily, she walked out to the end, squatted down, and dropped her line.

Just the smell of dust and sand moving on the night wind. And the flat stretch of island with its little oaks and its tall skinny palm trees, more like skeletons than real trees.

With her free left hand, she began snapping splinters off the boards and crumbling them between her fingers.

The little piece of moon was reflected in the quiet water under the landing. Squinting through the boards she could see it. There were little flecks of stars reflected too. She stared at the water until she wasn't sure any more which was up and which was down; and she was afraid to let go of one moon for fear the other would be gone too.

Across the reflection of the moon, her mother's face floated, sharp and dead, a funny smile stitched into the lips.

Annie whimpered, deep in her throat, the way a dog would.

The line jerked, cutting into her palm. She forgot the moon and the face. She'd hooked an eel, a big one. She slipped off the top of her pajamas, wrapped it around her left hand, and shifted the line there. She sucked at the gashes on her right hand and spat the salt taste of blood down into the water.

She didn't kill it. She carried it back to the house. It squirmed the whole way, splattering her body with slime. She put it on the kitchen table and went back to bed.

The eel was refusing to die; she heard it fall from the table and beat against the floor. She heard the muffled cursing of her father, and, as the thrashing in the kitchen continued, his slow stumbling steps. She peeped out the window: the earth was still black, but the sky over to the east was turning gray with morning. She rubbed her cheek and the tip of her nose against the pillow and went to sleep.

A couple of days later her father decided to send her to the Ursuline convent in New Orleans where her great aunt was Mother Superior. He was afraid to tell her, himself, so he sent his sister-in-law.

Annie listened and then said, dry-eyed: "Sure."

"Now you are being sensible." That was her aunt's favorite word. There was even a little bit of praise in it. "Too much grief for you here."

"I don't care," Annie said.

(That evening her aunt said to her uncle at supper: "You think she been fond of her mama, her, with all the taking on she is doing. After her pestering the life out of that poor woman, rest her soul, never giving her a minute's peace. They spoiled the girl, sure, spoiled her rotten.")

"You feel better when you get away. It be good for you che'."

"Yea," Annie said.

"I call your papa."

He came so quickly, they both knew he must have been standing out in the front yard waiting. He came hurrying into the room, stumbling a little over the high door sill, his eyes squinched almost tight closed, one hand rubbing his gray mustache.

"I'm going," Annie told him.

He tugged at the ends of his mustache, trying to curl them up. "That's good. That's good."

He couldn't think of anything else to say. His sister opened her mouth, then closed it, and finally said: "That's sensible, che'."

Annie walked away, very slowly. They didn't look out the windows, but for a long time they could hear her crying outside.

. . .

So she went in to New Orleans with her aunt. Her father did take them up to Petit Prairie in his boat: they could catch a bus there for the five-hour drive to the city.

There were heavy rain clouds in the east and it was beginning to drizzle the way it did every afternoon in July. Flickers of lightning jumped from cloud to cloud.

"Lot of heat lightning there," her father said as he carried the bag over to the bus—a blue-and-yellow-painted job: one of the old public-service buses from Baton Rouge.

"It is just like always," his sister-in-law said.

The first heavy drops fell and smattered in the dust as he put the bags inside the bus.

"What you say?" He nodded to Gil Carnot, the driver, who was leaning against the front bumper, smoking a long thin cigar.

Gil nodded back.

"Well," her father said, and rubbed his hands on the sleeves of his shirt, "now we fixed."

Her aunt said: "You will come get me tomorrow some time."

Her father nodded.

Annie looked from one to the other, her eyes suddenly focusing. "I won't be back tomorrow."

They looked at her, startled by the tone.

Then her father said: "I got to get going. I got things to do."

"I take care of her," his sister-in-law said.

"And you have a comfortable ride, Justine."

She tapped him on the chest with her palmetto fan. "We will be all right." He kissed her good-by.

He hesitated in front of Annie. "Be good," he said. She did not answer.

"I will take care of her," Justine said. He nodded and left.

Annie turned and watched him walk away—a short, almost bowlegged man—toward the dock where his boat was. "Bye!" she shouted. He looked over his shoulder and waved. His mustache was smiling.

Justine settled herself carefully, arranging the back of her skirt so that the light silk cloth would hold its sharp-pressed pleat. "A lady should know how to sit. . . ."

Annie did not answer, so she nudged her. "Your skirt is right?"

"Oh sure," Annie said.

"It does not look right," her aunt said, "you have a big bunch there in your lap."

"It's just like that."

"Stand up and I see."

"No," Annie said.

Her aunt shrugged, and began to use her palmetto fan hard, the muscles of her forearm rising. The little beads of perspiration on her upper lip, among the short black hairs, disappeared. Then, when the driver climbed slowly into his seat, and the whole floor of the bus began to vibrate with the engine, she closed her eyes, turned on her side, and fell asleep, snoring gently.

Annie shifted in her seat. The skirt felt strange—she hadn't had one on since her mother's funeral—and the stockings were burning hot on her thighs. There was a funny little ache behind her eyes and a kind of bubbling feeling in the middle of her head.

She had been to New Orleans once before, for Holy Week. That same great-aunt had got them tickets for the Holy Thursday and Good Friday services at the Cathedral. She and her parents went in especially for that—for the long services full of chanting and organ music and incense in thick white trails like ribbons. She hadn't been more than ten then, so small that she got stepped on in the crush to get in the church, so small that she had to stand on the pew to get one glimpse of the altar: three gold domes sparkling under dozens of candles. The rest of the time she'd sat very quietly and listened and smelled and stared up at the ceiling with its pink and blue and gold angels. And when the procession passed down the aisle right by her, one of the altar boys, the one carrying the incense bowl, began to sneeze.

She did not remember the trip in. So all the way, she sat almost without moving, her elbow bent on the window sill, her head leaning out the window.

When, after the long stretch of swamp, she saw the city, gray and smeary with rain, straggling out along the east bank of the river, she shook her aunt. The woman woke with a gulp and a little cough.

"Look."

Her aunt rubbed her eyes. "We are there." She combed out her hair with her fingers and settled her hat straight. "Fix your stockings, che'."

Annie straightened the seams without taking her eyes from the window.

"And comb your hair: You have been holding your head out the window, no? I can tell."

"No," Annie said.

Her aunt sat, staring straight ahead, her lips pursed as if she were whistling, her fingers tapping the slightly worn edges of her purse. Her gold-rimmed glasses had slipped far down, almost to the end of her nose.

The bus passed the edge of the convent's grounds. They got off.

"Now," her aunt said, "there. That is some place. no?"

There was a wire fence and line upon line of pecan trees, that had been planted in precise straight rows years ago and had grown very tall and dense. The ground under them was dark and mossy and without a speck of grass.

"The gate is this way here," her aunt said. "You take the big bag."

It was drizzling very lightly. Annie could hear its soft whispering sound in her hair. They walked around the corner following the fence, and passing a church with a high pyramid of steps and a brass rail running down the middle.

"There," her aunt said. "Over there we are."

She had to lift her head to see: the heavy carved-wood doors set in a gray cement arch. There were two narrow iron stairways curving up to it, one on each side.

"You go that way," her aunt said pointing to the left, while she herself started up the right.

Annie climbed slowly. Halfway up, she had to put the suitcase down, and rest, the stairs were that steep.

She stayed at the convent for ten months—until one day, almost without thinking about it, she wrote a letter to her father, saying she was very homesick—but looking back, she couldn't believe it had been that long. Probably because she didn't remember it as a whole. She remembered just little bits and pieces. Her great-aunt's face, brown and wrinkled with a crinkled quivering little chin and a sharp beaked nose, with a white circle of starched linen for a cap and a wider circle of shiny smooth linen for a collar. The long dark halls, with black linoleum in a narrow strip down the center. The dark formal parlors, wood-paneled and smelling of furniture polish, with straight high-back chairs of heavy oak, claw-footed. And the windowless vestibule before the leather-padded chapel doors: dark pillars and black-red carpet and a single red vigil light burning. And Mass on winter mornings, before the heat had come on, when her knuckles turned red with little white criss-crossings, when even the candle flames looked cold and unsteady.

She was tired all the time. Mornings when the bell rang to wake up the convent, she could hardly open her eyes. Her body seemed so long and heavy on the bed she did not think she could raise it up ever again. She fell asleep during Mass, even in the cold; once she slipped out of her pew and clipped the side of her head against the floor. All that winter she felt that her body was not part of her at all. She felt stiff and strange, her legs and arms hurt. And when she looked in the mirror she saw under her eyes heavy black circles with little cobweb lines of veins in them.

Evenings she learned to crochet because there was nothing else to do. She finished a pale green stole, folded it in a drawer and did not wear it. Then she began a bedspread, the same color, because it was the only yarn the convent had.

She shared a room with a South American girl whose name was Beatriz Valdares. She was short and very dark, with the figure of a nursing mother. Her family had sent her out of the country when the rifle bullets of revolutionaries crashed into their living-room. So Beatriz waited impatiently, writing long letters home, four and five pages at a time, in violet ink. Though she had been at the convent three months, she had learned hardly any English.

She and Annie disliked each other immediately. They divided the room by a chalk mark down the rug. And when Beatriz left for the week-end—she was always gone visiting friends—she would point to her side of the room, double up her fist, and shake it.

The very first week Beatriz went to her cousin who was a nun and complained that Annie talked in her sleep all night long. But there were no empty rooms in the convent and so she came back in worse humor than before. That night she shook Annie so hard that her fingernails dug into her arm, and left little blood marks.

Annie lay quietly, and tried to remember what she'd been dreaming. Finally she pulled the covers over her head and tried to go to sleep.

Lying there, without moving, she heard Beatriz get up. There was the faint rustle of a taffeta robe and then the very faint creak of a door. Annie sat up and switched on the lamp to be sure: the other bed was empty. She looked at the clock: it was five minutes to twelve.

Annie turned off the light. Her head was hurting, and she felt too tired and sick to be curious.

Occasionally during the months that followed, she would wake up and find that Beatriz was gone. She noticed that it was always the same time—a few minutes to twelve—and that Beatriz would be gone a little less than an hour. Annie did not care. It was a long time before she was well enough to be curious.

Then, one night, in the very early spring, when she heard the door close softly, she got up and followed. She did not stop for a robe or for slippers, though the floors were icy cold and she shivered inside her flannelette pajamas. She caught only the tiniest flash of the robe down at the far end of the dim hall, so she followed, walking on her heels to keep the boards from squeaking. She did not realize where she was going until she got there: down the narrow side steps to the door that led to the back garden, the dark grove of pecan trees she had seen on her first day. The door was open about an inch. She tried peeping through, then put her shoulder to it and pushed. It grated softly—she turned and raced up the stairs to bed. She was asleep before Beatriz returned.

It was not until the next day she figured out what had happened. It was so simple, she should have thought of it sooner. Beatriz had a man waiting for her. It couldn't be anything else.

When Annie saw her next, she couldn't help staring at her.

The girl frowned. "Que rayos te pasa?"

Annie looked at her, imagining what it must be like those cold nights down in the dark of the pecan trees. And she started giggling. Only it wasn't so much a giggle as a laugh that caught somewhere back in her throat. Finally she had to turn over and pull the pillow over her face to stop.

The next time Beatriz slipped away, Annie got up too. She stopped to pull a sweater on over her pajamas. She peered down the hall, but remembered the outside door and the sounds it made when opened. She went back into her room and leaned out the window, leaned far out, trying to see. No use: they would be around the corner of the building.

It was a bright night, with an almost full moon. There was just a sliver gone. The trees, which came up to the level of the second story, were still and silver-colored. The peaked bell tower of the church was spotted and moldy in the light.

And she saw something else: the broad ledge of the window sill continued like a belt around the building, trimmed here and there by grinning gargoyles and curly-maned lions.

She swung herself out on the ledge, and stood up, slowly. She balanced herself carefully, swinging her weight from one leg to the other, back and forward, getting the feel. The ledge was too narrow for balance with both feet together, but with one hand holding to the brick wall, she could walk easily, her feet crossing one over the other.

She stopped to rest at the first of the gargoyles. She hooked her arm around his cement neck and looked about. Straight down, through a break in the trees, she could see the clipped grass. The moon was so bright she could almost pick out each single blade. Above—she craned her neck back—the brilliant misted sky with only faint touches of stars. And quite suddenly she wondered what it was like on the island—it was a clear night; the bay would be flat and gleaming, with just little wrinkles like an old mirror. And on the boats the rough decks would look soft and smooth as teak; their stiff tarry nets would be soft delicate folds.

She sniffed. But there was no smell of salt or marsh. Only the clean odor of cut grass and the faintly murky odor of the old building.

She inched on until she had reached the corner of the building. She peeped around, down into the pecan grove. She still could not see anything. A lion's head ornamented the corner. She stopped for a minute, thinking. She would have to step around that projection; she would have to make the right angle turn without losing balance. For a minute or so she stared at the lion that blocked her path. In the moonlight she could see every grain of cement that made up his face.

Then she turned, facing the building, put the fingers of her left hand in his eyes, hooking them for a little balance. Her right arm reached around his head. And hugging the concrete, she stepped.

For a second her foot touched nothing, and she felt a little flutter of panic in her stomach. She was reaching too high. She brought her foot down along the edge of the building until it found the ledge. Then very carefully, spread-eagled on the corner of the building, she shifted the weight to her right foot, then brought the left leg over. She felt the cloth of her pajama knee scrape and tear, but she did not even bother looking. Her fingers were tingling with excitement, as she straightened up on the other side and let her breath go out in a hissing sigh.

She forgot why she had come. She forgot to look down into the rows of pecan trees for the couple. She forgot everything except the feel of the concrete under her bare feet, the wind, and the bright hard moonlight. She could feel how sharp and cold the wind was but she did not care. She was as warm as if she had a heavy coat.

The tops of the trees were on a level with her feet, soft trees, still as a painting. A car went by on the street; the headlights flicked along the trunks and broke into little snatches of light in the leaves.

She was moving with more assurance now. Her feet seemed to have learned to find the way. She spread her toes flat and broad and clutching as she moved. Her body felt so light, so very light. The air up here was different from the air down on the ground. It held her up.

She stopped for a minute and closed her eyes, the better to feel the air all around her. "If I let go," she said aloud, "if I let go . . ." The air would take her and lift her, even higher. She could hold her arms stretched out, and the air would lift her, the way a bird is lifted, though he doesn't move his wings, floating in great swooping upward circles, right in the path of the light that was funneling down from the moon.

There was a faint smell of jasmine vine. Her mother had always used that. She'd put whole flowering strands in the armoire with her clothes, so that she always smelled of summer. Her mother who was dead. Her mother who was gone for good, who would never come back.

She began to cry with her eyes still closed.

Her fingers were loosening under the soft pressing of the wind. Her left hand patted the bricks of the wall, gently. And she took a few more steps forward, waiting for the wind to pick her up, for the wind to lift her up, for the wind to carry her away. She was holding her right arm straight out and a little back, in the arc of a bird's wing. And her left hand was brushing the wall lightly. She was moving back and forth to the touch of the wind. And the faint sound of the trees beneath her.

There was a loose piece of brick on the ledge: it had fallen out of the crumbling old wall. She stubbed her bare toe against it, knocking it from the ledge. It snapped through the little branches and thudded dully into the ground. There was a strangled sound over to the right, and then everything was very quiet again.

Annie clung to the wall with two hands, laughing softly to herself, feeling the two pair of eyes that were fastened on her from below. She forgot about the wind and the way she had wanted to lean on it and be lifted away. She made her way across the side of the building until she came to the flat ladder workmen used when they were repairing the roof: three rungs up to the slant of the roof and then a single long piece of board flat on the slates, with short cross-ties for steps. She climbed quickly, sitting at last on the peak of the roof. Her toe was hurting. She twisted up her foot, trying to see in the bright moonlight. There was a little blot of black blood on the big toe. She squeezed; the little spot grew.

A car engine started. She looked up and around. Over at the edge of the grounds, over on the dark back street, she saw a car drive off. A dark car, without headlights.

So that was how he came, she thought. She'd frightened them off. She giggled softly. "Nearly dropped it right on their heads," she said aloud.

She sat up on top the roof, pressing her sore toe and looking out over the trees and the little peaked roofs of houses and the straight lines of streets and the little spots of electric lights—frilled, most of them, by the trees; and down a little way, the green and red glow of neon signs; and still farther, the tall buildings of the city itself. She stared for a long time at one with a peaked tower, a point sharp as a needle.

She turned her head slowly, keeping her shoulders straight, and she swung around the horizon: more trees and little irregular heaps of houses, and here and there a taller apartment building. And over, way over to the right, the moon picked out the arches and the criss-cross bracing of the river bridge, thin little spiderweb lines.

She sniffed the air. Just the musty night smell of an old building. The smell of jasmine was gone. And then she remembered that the vine did not bloom this early, there would be no flowers in March. . . . She looked over her shoulder and up in the sky; and was surprised to find it empty.

She got to her feet, unsteadily, and swaying just a bit. She backed down the ladder, one foot after the other. Halfway she stopped and looked up, up the steep black angle. She saw how the slates were cracked and chipped and how some of them were blown up by the wind. And she looked behind her: the same slates slanting down at a sharp angle and where they ended, little puffs of trees.

She got to the ledge and stood holding to the ladder. The wind blew in little gusts; she shivered and held tighter to the wood. She stood without moving until her legs began to cramp.

"Hey," she called. "Hey, hey, hey, hey." She waited. Nothing. "Up here, up here."

Then she remembered: no one slept on this side of the building. Just the library and the reception parlors and the little private visiting-rooms. There was no one to hear her. The back of her throat began to ache. She started to cough and almost lost her balance. She began to inch her way back, slower this time and uncertainly, her left hand waving straight out for balance. By the time she got to the cement lion at the corner she was covered with sweat; it was running in long trickles down her back; it covered all her face in little round blobs that turned icy cold in the wind.

She stood hugging the lion with both arms, whimpering softly, shivering each time a gust of wind hit her body. It did not occur to her to call again.

The moon had gone down a bit. She stared directly at it, then closed her eyes, seeing the green moldy reflection.

Hugging the lion as tight as she could, she stepped out and

around the corner. Her foot missed: too low. But before she
realized it, she was down on one knee, almost. She had to drag
herself upright again. Her leg muscles burned and one of her fingernails snapped back and off. She took a few short breaths. She
was beginning to panic: she could feel the fingers run across her
scalp. She was almost crying as she tried to swing around the corner again. Her foot reached the other ledge. She tested it: solid
and balanced. Her stomach was quivering, fluttering as she swung
her weight around and over. Her hands were so wet they slipped
a little and she dragged the right leg too closely over the concrete:
she could feel the flesh all along her shin tear. But she was on
the other side. Right down the way, not too far now, was her
window. She could see it even, the white curtains blowing out like
the skirts of a dress.

She began to move quickly now, too quickly. Her fingers caught
at the window frame, and she bent down. One foot slipped. Her
toes made a final grab: there was only air.

She pitched herself forward, hard as she could, arms out straight,
reaching. She fell across the sill, her elbows hooked inside. The sudden pain made her eyes reel. She shifted her balance, wearily, until
she tumbled headfirst into the room.

The floor was cold under her cheek, and her body ached in puls-
ing waves. Her closed eyes were dazzled by light, little crumbly
points of light like grains of sand.

She could only think of one thing, and her body quivered with
disappointment as much as pain: I didn't get to see them, I didn't
get to see them at all.

*

ANNIE came back to the island in early summer—in May. She had learned three things at the convent: to chant the responses and the hymns at Benediction, to do some very fine embroidery, to crochet in wool. She came with her suitcases full of stoles done in green wool and tablecloths of unbleached linen covered with leaves and birds until there was hardly a piece of cloth showing.

She had learned to sit very straight at table. "Now," her Aunt Justine said when she saw her, "that is the way a young lady sits, for sure." And she brought her own daughter to see. "Sit at the table, che'," she told Annie, "so Therese can see how you do."

So Annie pulled the straight chair up to the table.

"See," her aunt said, "you should do like that. Sit like the nuns."

Annie had been home a little over a week when her spine relaxed.

"But you forget all you have learned!" her aunt said.

"But she look better this way," her father said. And he put one arm around her shoulder.

Annie slipped away, pleasure burning in her stomach, but her face frowning and her manner brusque.

"What the matter with her?" her father called after her.

She did not look back. She ducked around the corner of the house and around behind the little shed where he kept his skiffs and pirogues out of the weather. Then she sat down on the ground.

From there she could hear her father and her aunt talking—she couldn't make out the words, just the sounds of the voices.

She picked at the ground with her fingers. A blackbird flew down to watch. She put her head on her knees and began to cry.

She could not, for the life of her, have said why. She cried easily that summer, mostly when there was nobody to see her. The tears came spurting out and she felt better for it. Her eyes didn't even seem to get red.

A FOUR-HOUR trip from the island—almost straight east—is Port Ronquille. It is a larger town than Petit Prairie, because of the sulphur mines. One whole tract of land around the plant —a good ten acres square is colored bright yellow. Everything yellow, the ground, the trees, the little scraggly tough chinaberries, the machinery, the wood sides of the buildings, the barges into which the stuff is loaded. They say that for twenty miles around the sun is yellower than anywhere else—but they like to talk.

The town itself is about two miles from the sulphur plant. It is maybe a mile long, strung out along the bayou. And three streets deep: that is all the solid ground there is here. Beyond is the swamp.

The houses are good and tight and painted. The yards are fenced with palings all about the same size so that it looks very neat. There are chickens in the yards, and ducks, and now and again a cow. You can see the kids in the morning, driving the cow out to the open grass on the edge of town, the side away from the plant. All the youngest kids, six or eight maybe, in one hand a switch or a whip, in the other the coil of rope for a tether. On the main street, which is right along the bayou, there is the sea food plant where the luggers bring shrimp and oysters. And right next to it, but across the dirt street, is the ice company. A broad wood chute slung about ten feet above the street, connects them. When the plant is working, the chute shudders and grates as the ice flows down it.

There are four groceries and half-a-dozen bars, one a big barn-like structure where the dances are held on week-ends.

When Al Landry took to going over to Port Ronquille every single week-end, people on Isle aux Chiens began to whisper and shake their heads. Such a thing for a man to do, they said, who'd been grieving for his wife only a while before.

Once or twice, maybe—that they could have understood; that was nature. But every week, nearly. . .

For Port Ronquille is known all along the coast for its fine whorehouse, the fanciest and most expensive south of New Orleans. It is the largest building in town, seven rooms. There are lace curtains on all the windows, full three-yard curtains that reach right down to the floor. And in the front parlor, there is a picture window, new last year, framed by yellow satin curtains and in the exact middle, on a little round brown table is a very large lamp with a yellow shade. The shade still has its cellophane wrapping and the lamp has never been lighted: there are no outlets close enough. The madam is a short Italian woman from New Orleans. Her sister runs the one beauty shop.

It was his cousin, Roy Gaudet, finally asked him.

Al chuckled quietly to himself. "Man, man," he said. "They too expensive for me. I can't have nothing like that for a steady diet."

"So it ain't a whore," Roy said. "But you got a girl, no?"

"Man," Al said, "since when you believe all you hear?"

Her name was Adele, and he had not even held her hand

WHEN he'd gone over to Port Ronquille that first time, he had not been looking for any woman, whore or virgin.

He went because he couldn't stand the island any more. One morning (six months after his wife's death and four months after Annie had gone to the convent), when he had finished fixing his nets, he came back to the house to find a can of paint. He'd put it in the kitchen or under the house. But he never found it; he never got to look. He stood in the middle of the empty quiet house and rubbed his forehead with both hands. He was so tired of working; and he was tired of going to Petit Prairie. He knew every inch of the street, every plank of the lands, every little single piece of dust that blew around in the air.

He would go see what they were doing in Port Ronquille. He had not been there in years. Without telling anyone that he was going, he walked out of the house and down to the landing, cast off his lines and started the engine without even first using the blower, he was in that much a hurry.

It was November, but hot. The people who'd gone up to work in the cane fields would be having a rough time. Sun like that could put a man on his face in no time at all, if he wasn't very careful. He'd seen eggs fried on pieces of slate in the November sun. They'd thought that was a great joke, back when he was a kid, working in those fields: breaking an egg on a flat piece of rock and leaving it there to turn white and milky and cooked. And when they came back and found it, they all stood around laughing and slapped each other on the back, and tried to talk somebody into eating it. But everybody knew that a sun-fried egg wasn't good for the stomach; so much of the sun had made it bad, even while it cooked it. But they stood around and poked their fingers at the egg, and thought it was a fine joke.

Looking back, he could remember that time, but he couldn't believe it. Couldn't believe that he had been like that, been the sort of kid he knew that he was: ready for a fight or a joke, and always laughing. Nothing could have stopped him laughing, no matter how hard the work was.

He sighed and the sigh hurt him—in his chest. That had been a long time past.

People got old, he thought, and their chests got heavy and there was no more fun. Not the sort he used to have when he was young, even when the work was hard in the fields during grinding. He remembered the smell from the mill, the stifling smell of the crushed cane.

They'd be having hot work there today, he thought. Maybe someday he'd go take a trip and have a look at the fields again. Maybe he'd do that.

Thinking like that, he came to Port Ronquille. For a while after he had tied up the boat, he wandered around the streets, not quite knowing what he should do.

He passed the church, a yellow brick building, with a gold-colored cross over the door, and he went inside. It was twice the size of the church at Petit Prairie, he thought with satisfaction. And the pews were painted white and the kneeling benches even had little red pads on them. The stations of the cross were white-framed colored figures. The altar was all white and gold. And hanging behind it was a gold curtain.

Al went to the first pew and knelt there. He said three Hail Marys. He tried to remember some other prayers, like the Creed or the Glory-Be, but he couldn't. So he added the only other one he could remember: "Her soul and the souls of the faithful departed rest in peace, Amen." He made the sign of the cross and left. He walked down the street and looked in the window of a dry-goods store. He kept walking, not thinking about anything much, feeling the ground pass under his feet. He passed the school, a yellow wood building with its screens broken and hanging in long rips. He stopped a minute and listened to the kids: a steady murmur and now and then over it, a single voice, in a call or a wail. He walked until he came to the edge of town, until there were the empty fields stretching off toward the sulphur plant. He looked down at the ground and thought he could see the blackness begin to turn yellow already.

He turned and walked back. A woman, who had finished washing dishes on her tablette, a shelf outside her kitchen window, dumped the water down into the yard. The chickens came squaaking to peck up the little bits of food from the ground. She had been there when he walked out. Now that she saw him coming back she smiled and waved.

He took off his cap and bowed.

He walked back through the main street of the town, past the icehouse (where a single skinny little boy played with a lizard on the steps), past the sea-food packing-plant that was empty now, past a café, and a bar, and the big dance hall, and another café. He stopped, staring in the same dry-goods store window. This time he went inside and bought himself three handkerchiefs with the red initial A on them. When he had the box in his hand, he felt a sudden twinge.

I got no call to go wasting a dollar like that, he thought.

He was standing in the door, wondering if he could ask them to take the stuff back, if he could tell them he had changed his mind, when somebody behind him called: "Al, hey, Al." He did not turn. The voice was familiar. So he stood quite still looking straight ahead, trying to remember.

Then somebody whammed him on the back, and put an arm around his shoulders, and pumped his elbow up and down. "Hey, brother-in-law, what you say?"

He had to look at the man before he remembered the name: Dan Cheramie. Sure. Sure.

Cheramie gave him a slap on the shoulder that sent the parcel flying out of his hand. "Man, I ain't thought to run into you here."

A little boy had scurried from out the back and picked up the package. He stood holding it out, silently, without a word, looking from one man to the other.

"My friend, I ain't seen you in ten year or so."

"That is right," Al said. "Not since the army, no?"

Dan slapped him on the shoulder and shook hands again. He was a tall thin man with the long thin face of a tired old horse. His teeth were long and square and yellow like a horse's too.

His reddish hair had thinned until there was just a curly fringe over his ears and over his collar.

"Man," Al said, "I thought you was working in New Orleans, the last I heard."

"Been back quite a time."

"Ain't been over here in maybe five years," Al said.

The little boy nudged his leg with the package. Al jumped, looked down and grinned. "Okay, bugaree, I take it."

"That's my sister's boy," Dan said, and pulled the tufty hair on top of his head. The boy had had a crew cut some weeks past. It had grown out now, ragged in all directions like a worn-out broom.

Al winked at him. The boy grinned and ducked away.

"Like my place, huh?" Dan said.

"You ain't had a store when we was in the army."

"Man, I ain't had nothing when we was in the army."

Al shook his head. "If this don't beat hell."

"Man," Dan said, "Man. . . ."

"When you get this here store?"

"Two, three years ago. When I come back from New Orleans."

"Don't that beat hell."

They moved out of the way to let a woman in the door. Dan bowed to her politely. A short red-haired girl got up from her seat behind the counter to wait on her.

Dan said with a wave of his hand: "I got four kids, me."

"I only got one girl."

Dan nodded and clicked his tongue lightly.

"She is staying for a while in the convent in New Orleans."

Dan shook his head and rubbed his upperlip with his finger. "You know . . . my mother, she had seven and when one left —my first brother, the priest, I have told you about him, no?— the little ones did not know he was gone. And my mother, she cry for a week or so, but she get over it. There still so many left around in the house. But where there is only one," he sighed hissingly, "God should not be so jealous."

"She is coming back," Al said.

They stood on the top step, just outside the door and watched up and down the street. Nothing was moving, except far down, a brown-and-white-spotted dog. A kitten pattered out from under the steps to chase grasshoppers in the weeds by the foundations. The little boy who was Dan's nephew slipped between their legs to grab the cat and carry him back inside. It was quiet, the way it always was about two o'clock, before the kids came streaming and shouting and giggling along the street out of school. It was the time the old people took their naps and got ready to scold the kids when they should come in the houses.

Dan turned his head suddenly. "But I am stupid me, I forget to ask about your wife. How is she?"

Al stared down at the crinkled green leaves of the little palmetto that was growing right at the edge of the last step. "She been dead."

The other man jumped he was so surprised. "That pretty little blond-haired girl, that come up to New Orleans to see you when we had that leave?"

Al nodded.

"And she been dead."

A man walked by on the street, carrying a crab net over his shoulder and a fish trap by his left hand. He had a straw hat pulled well forward, so that its brim almost touched his hooked nose.

Dan slapped his hand to his head. "But what do you think of me—I am forgetting to ask you to come to my house."

Al shook his head. "I got to be getting back."

"What for?"

"I got work to do."

"There always work to do. . . . This time maybe you have a drink with a friend."

Al nodded and stroked his mustaches. The hot weather made them hard to keep in line.

It was a good house, whitewashed, with green-stained shutters and a paling-fence. Somebody had started to whitewash that too, but decided it was too much trouble. About ten feet of the part fronting on the street was white, the rest gray-brown. The kids were not home from school yet. Dan's wife, Francine, a big tall fat woman with arms thick as a man and as muscled, was taking a nap. She came to the door of the living-room, her dress wet

with perspiration and crinkled up over her knees, smiled sleepily
at Al, and went back to bed.

They sat in the living-room and first had an anisette and
Seven-Up, then a couple of beers. The kids came back from school
and raced through the door. Their father shouted: "Get the hell
out of here!" And they scattered.

Al could see them sometimes peeping around the corners of
the door and giggling outside. Then Dan brought out a bottle of
whisky.

The afternoon was almost over. Francine got herself up, combed
her hair, put an apron over her crinkled dress, and went into the
kitchen to start supper.

"I got to get going," Al said.

"You got to stay for supper now. You can't go back hungry."

Francine looked out the kitchen door. "If he wants you to
stay, you just stay. We going to have a good supper."

Dan slapped him on the back and poured him another drink.
The oldest boy came into the room and had a beer and a cigarette
with them.

When Francine called: "It is ready," Dan shouted back: "We
ain't ready yet."

Al's stomach was shriveled up with hunger so he took another
drink. She fed the kids first. They could hear the sounds from the
kitchen. The clattering of plates and forks and the clink of glasses.
The swinging of feet on chairs and the snorting little breathings.
And the scrapings of chairs being pulled back and forth to the
table.

By this time Al forgot he'd been hungry. When the woman
came back in the room and said: "And you, you not hungry
either?" he answered: "Non, I thank you."

They did not eat supper at all. They both got so drunk that
they sat leaning hard against their chairs, sat sunk way back in
their chairs. And after a while Al cried for his dead wife, and
cried and cried, and felt better for it. Then he fell asleep. He woke
once to hear Francine giving Dan hell, opened one eye, saw that
Dan was peacefully sleeping through it, and took another swallow
of his drink. It was, he noticed, beer. He did not remember having
switched from whisky.

Francine put him in one of the kid's beds. Vaguely, from far-away, he heard the kid fussing as he was moved to the living-room sofa.

Al started to object: "I don't want no kid's bed, me. I sleep on the floor." But somehow, though he said the words, no sound came out. Francine half dragged, half guided him to the bed. He tried again. "I don't want no kid's bed." She pushed him down. He was asleep almost before she'd got his shoes off.

He woke up with the sun falling in his eyes. The room began to spin in slow circles. And there was something inside his head that was pushing against his eyes until they were almost ready to pop right out. And that same something was beating against the inside of his skull. His tongue was twice its size and he was ter-ribly thirsty.

He sat up on the edge of the bed, and his ears ached. He opened his eyes just a slit, shielding them with the lashes, and peered out. It was a small room, with a single window directly across from him. On it was a bright yellow print curtain—he looked away: it hurt his eyes. There were two chests on the wall by the window. And three beds, that was all. Two cot-type ones and the full-size iron bed in which he had slept. He bent carefully, keeping his head up, and felt around for his shoes. His fanned-out fingers reached a little face, touched a sharp nose and a soft mess of hair. He straightened up and put both hands on his knees. "Jesus Christ, what you doing under the bed?"

The kid made no answer.

"Come on out of there. I ain't in no mood to play games."

The kid scrambled out from under the foot, wriggling on his stomach like a snake. He bounced to the nearest bed and sat cross-legged on it, grinning.

Al looked at him through half-shut eyes. "Enfant garce . . ."

The kid grinned even wider.

He looked vaguely familiar. They sat and studied each other while Al rubbed his face with both hands: the skin was tight and sore to the touch.

"I remember me now. I see you at the store."

The kid grinned and bounced a few times on the bed.

"Why ain't you answering me? A gar ate up your tongue?"

The boy giggled and rubbed his nose with the back of his hand. "No."

"Find me my shoes, huh."

The boy dropped almost head first off one bed and stuck his head under the other. He backed out with the shoes. He put them carefully on the bed, one on each side of Al. Then he scooted out the door.

Al put on the shoes very carefully. Then he stood up, testing his weight first on one foot, then the other. His legs were steady: he was surprised.

Dan was in the doorway grinning. "Beer is a mean thing, man."

Out of sight, his wife snickered. "Beer ain't got nothing to do with it. If you going to try to drink the Mississippi dry, you sure going to feel it the next day."

Dan just grinned with the corner of his mouth. A screen door slammed.

"Now," he said, "she went."

"I hope I ain't done nothing."

"Hell, no, man, come get some coffee. Or milk maybe, milk is fine on a hangover."

Al just shivered and swallowed hard.

"It fix me up," Dan said, "but you don't got to have it. My sister she is here. And she fix whatever you want."

That was the way he met Adele.

At first he felt so bad he did not notice her. He just saw her hand, with the plain gold wedding-band, reach him cup after cup of coffee, and finally a plate of grits and hot milk.

He felt better then, and lifted his head out of his hands, and blinked at her, ashamed at being so weak. She wasn't beautiful, not at all; her features were too irregular. But he looked at her again. Her skin was olive, perfectly even without a hint of color. You almost thought she was wearing a very heavy make-up— the skin was so tight and clear and colorless, it was almost like a mask. Her face was a long oval, from a small pointed chin to wide-set brown eyes, heavy-lidded and set at just a little slant under straight brows. She was not wearing lipstick; her lips were very pale and thin.

He looked again and saw that she was not young; there were little crepy patches of skin at the edges of her eyes and on her hands the veins stood out clearly.

"I hope I ain't been trouble to you."

She smiled and her teeth were small and square and even. "No," she said.

"It was your boy wake me up this morning?"

"Yes."

He leaned across the table; his elbow knocked the coffee cup. The blackish liquid slushed into the saucer, but he did not notice. "He ain't never said a mumbling word to me. I wasn't even sure he was big enough to talk, him."

She smiled, a little bit of her tongue showing through her square teeth. "Didn't you never have children?"

"Sure," he said. "Only I never noticed how big she was before she got to talking."

"You want some more coffee?"

He held out the cup. "I be turning green and yellow from it soon, but it's good all the same."

She asked: "Where's your girl now?"

He watched the dark liquid come out of the blue enamel spout. "New Orleans."

"Oh," she said.

"At a convent."

"Oh," she said, "she went to the church."

"Hell, no," he looked up quickly. He put three teaspoons of sugar into the coffee. "She just went there for a while. So she can get over her mother's dying."

He was surprised that it didn't hurt him to talk about it.

"She been dead, but not long."

He drank his coffee slowly. The little boy stuck his tousled head around the corner of the door. He stared at Al for a while, sucking up his mouth. Then his thin body followed his head inside. He was holding a kitten to his stomach. He slipped around Al and went up to his mother.

"Make bo-bo," he said.

She took the arm he held up. There were three long scratches down the forearm.

"The cat do that?"

He shook his head violently.

Al grinned at him. "He ain't going to say nothing, him."

"No," she said. "Nothing against that cat."

The kid giggled and then sobbed when his mother put iodine on the scratches.

"Hi there, boy," Al said. "Look at me. You papa give you that cat, no?"

The boy looked confused. The cat got away and he scurried off after it.

"He got no papa," Adele said.

Al stared at her, not understanding.

"He was killed two years past." There wasn't a flicker in her face. Her eyes didn't even blink: they were brown and dry.

"Oh," Al said and looked down at the floor. "Nobody told me that . . . or I wouldn't have said nothing, me."

"It is all equal," Adele said.

In the quiet, they could hear the cat yeowling outside, and the little boy begin a singsong chant to it.

"It is strange, no, the way things go," Al said and rubbed his finger around the edge of the coffee cup. The coffee had stained the white china.

"It is strange, for sure."

"I have sat and tried to figure it out, sometimes. And it don't come out."

"No," she said.

"I marry twenty-three years—a long time. So I can't hardly remember what it is like before I got married, when I was courting the girls."

"We was married four years," she said.

He took a long guarded look at her. She'd be near forty now, from the shadows around her eyes. And that meant she hadn't got married until she was an old maid.

He stood up. "I got to be getting back. I got work to do."

"I never been out to the island."

"It ain't bad," he said. "I like it better than any place I seen."

He went down the steps, then turned and looked back over his shoulder. "Thanks for the breakfast," he said. "It put me back on my feet all right."

"It wasn't anything," she said. "Just fixing breakfast."

He had turned to walk away when she asked: "Do you ever come back this way again?"

"Maybe," he said. "Maybe I might."

It was a month or so before he did. But he went back. First thing, he looked for Dan at the dry-goods store. He was not there. Only his wife was keeping store.

"I don't know where he is, me," Francine told him, "but it wouldn't surprise me none if he was having him a couple of beers someplace."

Sure enough he found him, in the second bar he looked into, a fair-sized building, neat and painted, and called the Tipsy Kitty. Al had only just peered inside the dusky room, past the red glow of the juke box, when he heard Dan holler: "Hey, brother-in-law, boy, what you say?"

He stood blinking. The large square room had only one small window over the bar cash register. Gradually he began to make out the pool tables on the left side of the room, the worn floor of the empty dancing-space, in its exact center a slot machine, and finally Dan, perched up on a stool and leaning against one of the tin-foil covered posts that supported the roof.

"How you doing, man?"

"I been just looking for you," Al walked over and pulled a stool alongside. "This time I'm wanting to buy you a drink."

"Always welcome, boy." Dan slapped him on the shoulder. "If I heard you was coming, I'd be doing something stronger than beer, me."

Al poured the beer, tipping his glass so that there was just a thin little line of foam. "I been hearing about your sister's husband."

"Which one?"

"One married your sister, what's her name, Adele."

"Jeez," Dan said, "he was a funny one."

"Heard he got killed."

Dan finished his beer and reached for the next one. "All Saints' Day, two years ago—ain't likely to forget that."

"Seems I heard."

"I bet you ain't heard all about it."

"I don't know," Al said, "what's all about it."

"He was driving a truck. His truck. I don't know exactly why he went and bought a dump truck—he was postmaster here. But he got this truck, got it cheap too, had to go all the way over to Lafayette for it. And for two solid days it stood in his back yard in the rain, while everybody sat and tried to figure out what he was going to do with it.

"And Adele she tried to figure it out too. And she asked him but he wouldn't tell her either." He stopped and took a swallow of beer. Hesitated, tasted and took another long drink.

"What'd he have it for?" Al asked.

Dan swallowed. "He wouldn't say. Only on All Saints' Day, it stopped raining. And everybody is fixing to go to the cemeteries and some people is all ready there when they see him—Bob was his name—go driving out the road in his new truck. And nobody could make any sense out of that either. And then Adele and the boy come down to the cemetery, and they didn't know either. Only for a long time we could hear the motor. He must have been gunning it like crazy, we could hear it so long.

"And after a while we sort of forgot him. There was lots of flowers to put up, and lots of people to talk to. And for sure, old lady Billion goes and has the fainting fit she has every year when she looks at the grave of her husband and her boy that died when he was a baby.

"Then we hear this damn truck again, hear it far off, roaring and coming fast. And in a little while we can see it. One of the kids is standing out in the road and he yells: 'Là-bas, she come.' And he goes scurrying out of the road as fast as he can. And this fucking truck comes right down the middle of the road, so fast you can see daylight under the wheels—he's hitting the bumps that hard. He's flying, man."

He finished the rest of the beer out of the bottle, pushing the glass aside. Then he twirled the bottle in small circles by his finger tips.

"We want a couple more," Al said.

"Don't shake them up," Dan said and wiped off the foam from the bottle neck with his finger. He carefully sucked it dry. "That's a plain waste, man."

"Then what happen?"

"Why, man, he come along the road until he get right to the edge of the cemetery lot, and then he blows a tire—ain't never no good tire on a second-hand truck. So he goes off the road and over that little stretch of grass there—you could see the skid marks burned in the ground, until the grass grew up so high last summer—and right into that oak tree there . . . man, this here is real cold beer."

"Me, I want some oysters," Al said.

"Not here, man," Dan waved his hand, "I show you where they got some nice fat cock oysters."

For all that it was the middle of the week, the main street was crowded. Dan knew every person they passed; he nodded or waved or smiled.

They passed the bank with its green-painted door and barred front window. "This is a big town, now," Al said.

"And, man, it sure the place for business," Dan said. "You ought to quit fishing. Ain't no money in that."

Al stopped to tie his shoelace. "No," he said. "There ain't. But I reckon you do what you're used to. And I'm accustomed me to that."

They ate the oysters in silence, opening them themselves, spearing them up with the tips of the knife, and draining the liquor from the shell.

Dan said: "You asking about Adele's husband—he always cut his nose to pieces drinking out of oyster shells. I remember me one night when we musta had six dozen a piece. And our noses was bleeding." Dan rubbed the tip of his nose slowly. "You know," he said, "they didn't get on much."

"She wasn't no girl when she got married."

"Hell, no, man. She was living at home. And they thought they never would get her out the house. She just didn't seem much interested in any boys, nor them in her. Never knew where she met him. But one day she just walks into the parlor with Bob Reynal. And they say they going to get married. . . . Alors, they get married."

They finished the last oysters and tossed the shells into the heap already in the pail.

"He was a hard man, him. Lived around here all his life, but nobody knew much about him. His family been dead, and he was just another kid around here, when I was a kid. Then he worked at the ice plant for a while, and then he got to be postmaster and then he got married."

"Do you reckon," Al asked, "she would mind if I went calling on her?"

"Find out for yourself, man," Dan said. But all of a sudden, the voice had a different ring.

Al left him then, trying not to notice the change.

He saw her then, and he went back every week-end he could manage. When Annie came home in May, he said nothing to her but went as often as ever. But he never had a drink with Dan again, nor went to his house.

He could figure out what the trouble was. Town people—people who had a store and were headed places in the world—wouldn't want their sister going with a fisherman. But he kept coming just the same.

He asked Adele once if they'd said anything about him, and she just shook her head and said: "Nothing. They ain't said nothing much or important."

Her son had fallen asleep underneath a chair in the corner.

"If he ain't just like a kitten," Al said, "curling up under things and going to sleep."

She picked him up and carried him to bed. Al followed.

"He sure is a pretty little boy. And me, I don't even know his name."

"Claudie."

"That is a nice name."

She took off his overalls without his waking. She took off his shoes and socks and put the thin little body in its underpants on the bed.

"I wish he'd put a little flesh on him." She pulled the cotton blanket up. He did not even flicker an eye.

"He will," Al said. "Why, I bet he grows up to be the fattest man you ever did see."

"Maybe," she said.

"Why sure he will," he said. "My wife, she was the skinniest little girl you ever saw." He hesitated and wondered if he should have said that.

They left Claudie's room and closed the door behind them. "Was she pretty, her?"

"Like I was telling you, from being the skinniest kid she turned nice and round when she grew up."

"She was very fine?"

"Yes," he said slowly, because he did not understand. "She was very fine, her."

"And she always had a good time, always laughing?"

"I don't know, me," he said. "Maybe."

"And my husband, he was fine too. Only he did not laugh much. He was a quiet sort."

Al nodded as they sat down again in the living-room. "They do say those people, they are born on a day when the sun don't shine."

"And you believe that, what the old women say?"

"I don't know," he said. "Maybe."

"And maybe not."

The quick hard tone of her voice startled him and he stood up. "But you got other things to do without just talking to me."

Almost before he could blink she was on her feet, and she had one hand on his arm. "Ain't you got time to drink a beer with me?"

While she got the bottles he glanced out the window and saw the lights in her brother's house next door. "They finished supper and gone into the parlor," he said.

She glanced out briefly. "Looks that way."

He smiled slowly. "They don't seem to have no love for me, somehow."

"That ain't so," she said. And he jumped a little, her voice was so flat and stiff you could almost touch it.

The whole island was watching him. They didn't follow him over to Port Ronquille, because that way they would have found out for sure, and they preferred to talk. (Annie just shrugged and forgot about it.) The old women shook their heads; and the young girls giggled and felt a hot touch in their parts. The young men wondered what sort of a girl would have anything to do with Alastair Landry, who was an old man of forty-two or -three and who had heavy, thick, drooping black mustaches that he waxed so carefully.

He had not even so much as held her hand, though he hadn't had a woman in months and it bothered him. He hadn't even kissed her until after they'd decided to get married.

They were sitting in her living-room on a hot August evening. He had had supper there—he had left the island in mid-afternoon to get there in time.

They were just sitting with the radio playing and he wasn't thinking of anything in particular, just fanning himself slowly with a latanier—the towns were always hotter than the island.

He didn't quite remember afterwards how the talk had come around to that. But she'd said flatly and calmly: "What do you think people say, if we was to get married?"

"I don't know, me," he said automatically.

"What was you to say, if we did?"

"I don't know."

"We ain't young kids, can't say we don't know what we doing."

For one second he thought: We ain't doing nothing. But he didn't say it.

The chickens in the yard were flurrying and squaaking. A cat must be after them. He wondered if he should get up and see.

"Do you think we are old enough to know what we are doing?"

"Your family don't like me."

"Let them go cook in hell."

In the pause, it was very quiet. The chickens had settled down now. On the front porch the kid was playing. You could hear his level monotonous singing.

"Look . . ." he said and stopped.

"Maybe," she said slowly, "you don't want to."

"No," he said.

"Maybe you are sorry you asked me."

But I didn't, he started to say and changed it to: "But I ain't."

She sat without answering, staring down at her lap. She had put her hands out flat, one on each knee, palms up, fingers curling a little.

He found himself staring at the thin limp fingers. Then almost without meaning to, he said: "But maybe you ain't wanted to marry me?"

She did not answer nor even move. He looked away. He was just thinking that maybe he ought to get up and leave when she touched him on the shoulder. She had said something.

"I ain't heard what you said."

She sat down on his lap. "I said I would me."

He kissed her, surprised to find how cold his lips were on her dry, hot ones. She reached up one hand and tugged on his left mustache, pulling until it hurt.

*

IT was two weeks later, the twenty-first of August, a Thursday, that they were married. Al came in late Wednesday night, and slept on the boat. Thursday morning, after the seven-o'clock Mass the priest came back to the altar and married them. The rest of the morning they spent putting her things on the boat. He'd hired a couple of boys to help.

They came back, late that afternoon. And that was the first anybody on the island had ever heard of Al Landry's new wife.

Except Annie. And she only found out by accident.

She had come back to the house in the early afternoon on Wednesday to change to her oldest working-clothes, when she heard her father moving around in his bedroom.

"Hey," she called, "you home?"

And after a minute Al answered. "Yea."

Annie scrambled into her torn shirt and a pair of navy pants that had once belonged to her cousin. "The *Popeye* coming in," she said through the walls, "and they got to do the packing here—Petit Prairie all jammed up. . . . You hear me?"

"Yea," Al said, "sounds like you going to make some money."

"For sure I am." She tied the shirt in a knot on her stomach and went around and into his bedroom. "I'm going get me enough money for a radio."

"We got a radio," Al said.

"Little one for me, white, so it goes by my bed . . . Jesus!" She stopped suddenly and looked at him. "You all dressed up."

He was wearing his one dark suit, you could still smell the moth balls on it faintly. He took off the jacket and hung it over the foot of the bed, folded carefully so that it wouldn't muss. He pleated a handkerchief and put that in the pocket.

"What goes on?"

He took off his white shirt, and folded it on top of his jacket.

155

"Go away," he said, "I got to change my pants."

Annie went out in the hall and waited. When he came out again he was wearing his old khaki pants and an undershirt. But he still carried the good suit and shirt over his arm.

"What goes on?"

He walked through the hall toward the front door. "I be back tomorrow evening."

"I'm still asking what happening."

"I'm getting married," he said. "I'm going over to Port Ronquille and get married."

Annie just stood staring after him. And when the screen door slammed shut right in front of her, shaking dust into her eyes, she didn't even blink.

*

IT was the strangest day in Claudie's life. They had been traveling such a long time. And he had been sick twice. Twice his mother had to take him out of the wheelhouse and sit down on the deck with him and put one hand under his forehead and hold his head over the side. Each time, when they finally came back, the man laughed and slapped him on the back.

It was the vibration of the engines and the way the boat slipped and jolted on the surface of each wave. Not that he hadn't been on boats before—he and the other kids of Port Ronquille had gone scurrying over each fishing-boat that came in the bayou and tied up. But those boats had been steady, only bobbing a little with a passing wake. He'd never been on a moving boat.

He was so tired. It had been a funny day. When he woke up first, and went wandering into the kitchen, nobody was there. He looked into the plates stacked on the table and rubbed his fingers over them. Then he hunted through the rest of the house. His mother was always around—only this time she wasn't. She just wasn't. He went out to the back steps and sat down and planted both elbows on his knees and whistled for his cat. The sun was warm and high: he had got up later than usual, he could tell.

When his mother did come, she was all dressed up in a blue hat with yellow flowers on the brim, and a blue dress with a white lacy collar that he hadn't seen before. He hugged her legs and felt that she was wearing stockings, which she almost never did. There was a man with her. His name was Al; Claudie had seen him around the house before. Each time he came he brought a present. The last had been a big red ball—only some dogs had taken it off the front porch and chewed it up.

She gave Claudie his breakfast on the back porch—bread and jelly and a cup of hot milk with a couple spoonfuls of coffee.

157

The minute he had finished eating, she washed his face at the kitchen sink and dressed him in the white cotton suit he wore only to church on Sundays. He started to say something, but she hushed him quickly. When he was dressed, she took his hand and led him outside. And they watched, while some men he didn't know took the furniture out of their house and put it on the deck of this boat—that looked and smelled like all the other fishing-boats. They tied it down and covered it with black tarpaulins.

His Uncle Dan left the store and came down to the dock, standing off a little on one side, watching, not saying anything. His mother hadn't noticed, she was so busy scurrying back and forth, and watching to see how each single piece was put on. But the man Al, who was with his mother, he had noticed, though he didn't give any sign: Claudie could tell from the sidewise flicking of his eyes. He had bright black eyes and sometimes they scurried over to one corner for a quick peep and then jumped back to the middle.

And for some reason—he didn't quite know why—Claudie imitated the man, never looking at his Uncle Dan directly, but only peeping from the tail of his eye.

When everything was ready, his mother took his hand and got on board with him, while the man freed the lines and dropped them on the deck.

His mother looked around for the first time, just as the man went in the cabin and spun the wheel and the bow swung away from the dock. His uncle turned away—twisted around on his heel and walked back to the store, spitting in the bayou as he went.

His mother turned around too, and went into the wheelhouse. And in front of everybody, because they were still so close to shore that everyone could see, she kissed the man.

For a couple of minutes Claudie stood on the deck and watched the way the land pulled back and shrank. All of a sudden his mother came popping out and grabbed him by the hand and took him in the little cabin and hugged him. "Poor bébé, I have almost forgot about you!"

"See," the man said to him, "the house where you use to live."

His mother stood him up on the little bunk and pointed. "Là-bas."

Nothing looked familiar.

The man reached down and pulled his hair. "I can whittle, me. I going to make you all sorts of things. Make you a dog. With a real tail. Hear me?"

Claudie stared at the man. Already the white shirt, and the way the little whiskers sprouted out into a mustache was beginning to look familiar.

"Answer him," his mother said; "he's you papa now."

Claudie looked at the face very carefully—at the way the eyebrows straggled out at the edges to meet the hair.

Claudie hugged his mother. He reached up far as he could. Her thigh and her hip felt warm and hard and familiar, the way they always did. He buried his face in her shirt and pushed his face in hard, until the cloth hurt his nose and mouth. And then he took a deep breath, smelling her, smelling the warm musky mother odor.

He would have liked to stay there, his eyes closed, his hands pulling the cloth around his head, but his mother pushed him away. "Sit up here," she said, "and look out the window."

He could see some houses, like the pictures in the books he had at home. "You used to live there," his mother said.

He shook his head. He did not believe it.

The man laughed. "Don't!" his mother said.

Claudie looked at the houses again. They were pictures. If he could just get closer to the window, he could touch the paper. And rustle it.

"You remember the house?" his mother asked.

He hung his head. There'd been a bed once—he got out of it this morning, a long time ago, that had a cover of red-and-white and blue-and-white squares. And a picture that hung on the wall and a candle under it that his mother lit every night. And there were the doodlebugs that he'd brought in yesterday, all tight in a ball and put under his bed. He'd meant to look for them again this morning, but he hadn't got chance.

"You ain't going to be sorry?" the man said.

His mother didn't answer. She tossed her head and dropped her eyes a little bit and her finger played a steady little tap-tapping on the wood of the door.

Claudie began to cry. The tears spurted out of his eyes and

dropped on his shoes. His mother talked to him, but he was so busy crying he did not hear her. Finally she shook him, hard, so that the tears splashed out of his eyes and he could see again.

"Mickey," he said.

"Oh God," his mother pushed back one strand of hair that had fallen across her forehead.

"What's the matter?" the man said. "He get hurt or something?"

His mother straightened up—she had bent down to talk to him—and kept pushing back the hair with short jerky strokes. "The cat."

The man whistled, long and low.

"But it's his cat. And I meant to bring it."

"Well," the man said, "you want to go back for it?"

His mother was quiet for a minute. "No," she said, "I wouldn't go back in that store and ask Dan where the cat is at. I'd just as soon have the gars chew me to pieces."

Claudie began crying again softly.

His mother picked him up and put him on her lap as she sat on the bunk.

"Listen, 'tit macac, listen at me."

He twisted around and looked up in her face. He reached out one finger and touched the hair over her ears.

"You tell me what color that minou was."

He frowned.

"You tell me now."

He thought for a minute . . . the cistern in the back yard where the shingles were falling off. There been a snake there one day, wriggling across the damp ground.

"What color Mickey was?"

"White."

She laughed. "How you like that now . . . all the fuss and you don't even know what color."

She got up again and went and stood alongside the man as his hands moved the little wheel back and forth. A wheel so little that it looked like his hands could smash it.

Claudie curled himself back in a corner of the bunk, between two packages and right next to the gilt-framed mirror his mother had wrapped in the quilt from her bed.

"Don't you break that mirror," his mother said.

The man glanced over his shoulder and grinned. "Seven years' bad luck, boy."

Claudie pulled away a little. He shook his head—violently, so that his ears began to buzz. And because that amused him he kept it up.

His mother put her hand down on top of his head and stopped him. "Quit that, fou-fou. You shake your brains out."

He giggled and pulled his knees up to his chin and then rested his chin on them. He sat quietly for a while and sang a song to himself: "White cat, white cat, white cat, white."

After a little he yawned and went to sleep.

He woke again when the boat began to pitch. He scrambled out of the bunk and grabbed his mother's leg.

"What's the matter with you? We just come out the bayou. Nothing more."

The boat was moving like a rocking-horse. He climbed up to his mother's waist and clung there, so he could see out of the window. No land on either side. Only water, bright blue under the sun. He squinched his eyes from the glare and twisted his head. A little bit of spray, like rain, spotted the windows.

"What you want to see, dogaree?" the man said.

"The island going to be right over there," his mother pointed. "You watch for it."

He climbed down and started to walk across the deck. But the tossing confused him and he lost his balance. He sat down hard.

The man laughed. "You break it, dogaree?"

He sat on the floor with his hands out one on each side of him, and studied his mother's face carefully, to see if she was afraid. She wasn't. She was excited; he had never seen her so excited; she could hardly sit still; her foot kept tapping the floor or her fingers the glass. When one part of her became quiet, another part began to move.

He sat still, where he had fallen and thought about it. And then he felt his ears get cold and his mouth get salty. His mother heard his little choking and she grabbed him up and got him outside, but not quite far enough that first time. He was sick on the deck.

His mother dragged him back inside, him feeling light and empty. "He ain't going to make a sailor," she said.

"He get used to a boat," the man said. "It just take a little time with some people."

"Poor bébé," his mother said. She pulled out a brown paper bag from among the other bundles. "I got maybe something for you." Her hands rummaged around and paper rattled. "Here. Yes." She held out a handful of the small round oyster crackers. "These make you feel better."

He took them and held them in his own hand. He put a single one on his tongue and let it melt there until there was just a pulpy flour-tasting mess.

He did not move until he was sick again.

This time his stomach kept turning itself over and over and emptying air into his mouth as his mother held him there, over the low wood rail. When his eyes were open he could look directly down at the water. He saw how it came in flat bits, like the kaleidoscope toy he had got at Christmas, that shifted and changed and was never still for one minute. It wasn't blue either, but a kind of gray-blue, streaked with froth, and you couldn't see down through it.

His mother pulled him to his feet and took him back to the cabin. "Mary Mother," she said, "maybe he's going to do that the whole way."

"It ain't far," the man said. "It ain't far at all."

"He ain't got anything left to throw up," his mother said.

Claudie stood, swaying back and forth with the motion of the boat, letting his head hang and swing too, so that the floorboards passed back and forth in front of his eyes.

"Stop him swinging his head like that," the man said. "That just making things worse."

His mother picked him up and sat on the edge of the bunk and held him in her arms, all the rest of the way. He put his head as far under her arm as he could.

The man said: "There it is."

His mother almost dropped him down on the floor, she was in such a hurry to get up.

And he scrambled up her leg and made her hold him too, so that he could see.

There was land on two sides now. On the right, the thin green line of marshes, an edge of grass that reached back, far as you could see from here, without a single tree or a single rise of ground. Just grass, shifting and moving and showing little shadows when the wind blew over it. Ahead was the island, thick clusters of oak trees and a few thin tall palms.

"It look nice," his mother said slowly and in a very quiet voice. Claudie cocked his head and looked at her; he could tell she was uncertain. And he waited to see if they should turn around and go back.

"It's a fine place," the man said. "You'd know if you was ever out before."

"No," his mother said; "I never thought to come here, me."

Claudie kept staring at her. He didn't understand her tone. He had never heard it before.

She turned down to him, giving him a swat on the rear. "Why do you stare at me, macac?"

The man picked him up in one arm. Claudie had not been this close to him before. He could smell the strong sweat odor from the white shirt. He squirmed a little and tried to get down. His mother did not smell like that. She had a soft warm smell, not sharp and metallic. But the man paid no attention to his movements.

Claudie looked over the shoulder to his mother. But she was staring straight ahead and there was just a little bit of a smile curling up the corners of her mouth.

"Which end is your house?" she was saying.

"In the middle," the man said. "But back from the landing. Way back. Where there's a little shade on a hot day."

Claudie squirmed and kicked, and the man let him down. He ran for his mother and tried to pull her skirts around his head, but she only lifted him up too. He hung his head and whimpered.

"What the matter with you, dogaree?" she said. "Don't you want to see where you going to live?"

He thought about that for a while, until finally understanding, he lifted up his eyes and frowned at her.

"Ah . . . that got a rise out of you, no?" she pointed. "There. That where we going to live."

He shook his head.

"Yes we are."

He shook his head again. That wasn't where they lived. The place where they lived had a street of gravel out front and a front porch and four cane rockers on it. And his room had yellow and blue linoleum on the floor.

He shook his head.

"Sure," his mother said. "That other place," she said, "we don't live there. It wasn't no more than a picture."

He whimpered again and put his face down in her shoulder. He wasn't sure any more.

"I'm sure glad we put that tarpaulin on the stuff," the man said. "There's more spray than I figured on."

"I reckon it's dry."

"Sure," he said. "They fixed it so it would stay dry in most any sort of weather."

"Maybe," his mother said slowly and doubtfully.

"Look, che'," he said, "nothing got spoiled coming across."

"I wouldn't know what to do without I got my things."

"Look," he said. "They all there. Nothing gone overboard."

She smiled suddenly and slipped her arm through his. "I ain't nothing but sort of edgy."

He kissed her on the cheek. His breath, heavy with tobacco, reached over to Claudie. The boy sniffed and then sneezed.

They were coming to the dock. The man let the boat in slowly, the engine idling. The hull touched with a soft bump. He opened the door and shouted: "What you say, there, Perique!"

The tall thin boy, who was sitting on a keg on the dock, had not moved until then. But he stood up and got the stern line and dropped the big loop over the post. Then he slowly secured the one at the bow.

"Perique, hey, come here," the man called. "I got somebody for you to meet."

Perique came back, his rubber-soled shoes making soft little padding sounds on the boards.

"I got married. And this is my wife, here."

Perique grinned. "Vieux couillon! If you ain't the one." He bowed very formally to Adele. "God make you happy."

"And now, man, how about us taking some of this stuff off?"

"Sure," Perique said. "Let's us go." He saw Claudie standing in the middle of the wheelhouse, right where his mother had set him down. "And who the hell we got here?"

"That's Claudie," his mother said. "My son."

"How you, dogaree?" Perique said. Claudie slipped behind the door. "He don't want to talk, him."

"He's scared," his mother said.

The two men began pulling back the tarpaulins. His mother came and took Claudie by the arm, and sat down on the deck close to him. "Bébé, listen at me. I got something to tell you."

He looked at her. Now that the boat was steady he was beginning to feel much better. He even grinned a little bit.

"No," his mother said, "listen at me."

So he looked at her, looked at the thin little lines that ran from the edge of her eyes up toward her eyebrows and down toward her cheeks.

"I didn't tell you before, because I never had chance."

"Let's us just take these bags here," the man said, "and we can come back for the other stuff later."

"When we got some extra help," Perique said. "Sure."

"Adele," he called, "come on!"

"Moment," she said over her shoulder. "I am busy."

Claudie was watching a big fat green fly that circled around the door, landed on the deck. He jumped after it, with his foot raised, and missed.

"Listen at me, macac." His mother took his shoulder and turned him around. "That man there, the one who just called. You know which one I mean?" Claudie nodded. "He is your papa."

Claudie shook his head.

His mother sighed. "I got no time to play with you . . . You got to call him Papa."

Claudie scuffed the toe of his shoe along the deck.

"Say it now. Say Papa."

He hesitated, opening his mouth. And he remembered. Gene, the boy who lived next door, and had a big mole on his upper lip, used to point out a field, full of low whitewashed brick vaults and stones with names and dates on them, and say: "There's your papa, boy. Out there he is." And once he'd gone over just inside the gate and squatted down, almost hidden by the long grass. He'd looked all around him carefully, but the grass was just grass and the mud was just mud like it was around his back doorstep. There were a couple of big black crickets but they got away before he could catch them. So he left, without seeing his papa.

"Go ahead," his mother said. "What you going to call him?"

He looked at her.

She stepped back away from him and sighed with annoyance. "Mary Mother, I got no time to be playing games with you. . . . Tell me or we leave you right here on the boat and don't take you with us. We leave you here alone and don't come back for you. . . . Tell me!"

He looked down at the toes of his shoes, white shoes that she had polished just yesterday. There were scuff marks on each toe.

"Tell me what you going to call him!"

"Papa," he said. Hesitated a minute because it was so easy to say, like any other word that came out of his mouth. And then began to cry.

"What the matter with him?" Perique said.

"Completely ga-ga," his mother said.

The two men carried the bags; his mother tucked a brown paper parcel under her left arm and with her right took hold of his hand. For the first few steps she had to drag him, crying. But then he forgot about that, and looked around him, at the strange new place.

They left the dock and walked along a white shell road. Claudie picked up one of the shells and tossed it at a palmetto leaf.

"Come on," his mother said and pulled him to his feet.

Perique glanced over his shoulder. "Come on, boy. Pick up your feet and move. This ain't feathers we're carrying."

They turned off the shell road to a narrow path. There were trees now, short thick trunk oaks and under them scrawny oleander bushes. In the open places the oleanders grew heavy and full, tall almost as the oaks.

Claudie wanted to look around, but his mother kept dragging him so fast that he would stumble sometimes and fall but she had such tight hold that he just swung along in the air until his feet hit ground again.

His mother slowed down, so that he had chance to see. There were houses, a couple of hundred feet apart on each side of the path, houses built high off the ground on brick foundations. And there were people sitting on the front porches, sitting with their chairs tilted back against the wall, or sitting and rocking. His mother was looking at these people. He could see a smile beginning at the corners of her mouth.

The man slowed his pace and dropped into step alongside her. "You getting tired out, honey?"

She looked from him to the people on the porches. "You know them there?"

"Sure," he said without looking. "Ain't so many people on this island you can't know them."

"You don't want to stop?"

"No," he said, "let's us get on home."

"If they friends of yours . . ."

"No," he said, "Perique tell them."

"You didn't tell them we was getting married?"

"It wasn't none of their business. . . . Let's us get on home."

"You ain't even going to wave to them?"

"No," he said. "Let's us get on home."

"What they going to think?"

"Don't tell me how to do things, che'."

Claudie had found a black dog on one of the porches. A small dog with shiny hair—it was lying right on the edge of the porch with its muzzle sticking out. He was just about to whistle to it when he felt his feet fly off the ground and he had to start running to keep up with his mother. He didn't have breath to whistle but he did wave, hard as he could.

The dog did not lift its head.

When his mother let go his hand, they were on the porch of one of the houses. Claudie walked over to the edge and peered down and around the corner. There was a big oak there, growing close to the house. And an old tire on a heavy rope swung from one of the low branches. A big fat green caterpillar walked along the edge of the railing. He flipped it down with his finger and squashed it with his foot. Then he crossed the porch to peer around the other side. There was just a cistern there and a small pile of lumber, neatly stacked up on sawhorses. With his hands behind his back, he walked up and down the porch a couple of times. Inside he could hear the voices—his mother was laughing. He had never heard her laugh quite like that before: high-pitched and giggling. He went to the screen door, but the handle was too high for him to reach. He stepped back and thought for a minute, then began to kick the frame of the door hard as he could with his left foot, yelling all the time.

Perique came to the door. "Quit that, dogaree, before you smash in the screen and fill the house up with mosquitoes."

He opened the door and Claudie ran in, brushing past his legs.

The smells of the strange house confused him. He followed the voices to a room on the right of the hall. His mother was there, all right, sitting on the man's lap. Claudie could see his drooping heavy black mustache over her shoulder. He went up to her and tugged on her dress.

She tickled him under the chin. He jerked his head away. He hated that; she knew it.

"Look him jump," she said. "Fraidy cat."

He stepped back and looked at both of them.

"What you staring at, boy?" the man said.

"Come sit here," his mother said.

She put both arms around him and hugged him. Rubbing softly he tucked his head in the familiar place under her chin and stretched out his legs. Then he looked down. The man's other hand was patting his mother's thigh in a nice steady rhythm. Claudie caught at one of the fingers. The hand turned up and grabbed.

"Want to play catch, no . . . I got you."

He pulled on his hand to free it. The man just laughed. "I got you."

He pulled harder, whimpering a little. "Al, let him go," his mother said.

The hand did not loosen. "I ain't hurting him."

"He want to get loose."

"I ain't stopping him," the man said.

Perique came to the door. He was such a tall thin boy that he

never stood straight if he could lean on anything. Now he braced
his feet on one side of the door and put his shoulder on the
other so that he stood criss-crossed.

"You want to go get the rest of the stuff, man?"

"No," Al said. "Let's us wait until it is cooler, tonight."

"Okay," Perique said. "I got nothing better to do." He pulled
himself to a standing position and disappeared.

"So," the man whistled softly, "we get everything done. He
go to see about the truck and he tells everybody we are married.
It is that simple and easy."

His mother tried to smooth down the hair on top of Claudie's
head. "And will they come back, do you think?"

"By nighttime we going to have a full house here."

Way far off some kids were shouting, and an acorn fell off and
rolled down the tin roof.

"Don't you want to see the rest of the house, che'?"

"Sure," she said. "Most certainly I do." She pushed Claudie off
her lap.

"That's the kitchen, right there," he said, "and the back door.
And the rest is over here."

They crossed the little hall. When Claudie tried to follow them,
they closed the door.

So he went and looked out the back door, then he turned and
walked the length of the house, scuffing his heels as hard as he
could. He stopped at the door, staring out, rubbing the tip of his
nose against the screen, sniffing in the sharp odor of dust. Then
he kicked it wide open, so hard that it banged against the wall
of the house, and went outside.

There was a girl on the porch. She was sitting in one of the
cane rocking-chairs with her bare feet propped up on the railing.
Claudie was so surprised that he just stood and stared at her for a
minute. Then he turned to run inside, but the screen had slammed
shut again. He kicked at it and jumped for the handle, and
though he had it between his fingers once, he could not open the
door. So he turned around and, with his back and both hands
pressed against the screen, watched the girl.

She did not take her feet down, or move her body in the
slightest. She turned her head very slowly. "You want to get
back in, huh?"

He kept staring at her, not moving, just watching her large very pale blue eyes.

"I'll open the door when I come to getting up." She turned her head back and stared straight ahead. Her right hand patted the side of her chair. "Come on over here."

A big mockingbird came down and perched on the porch steps, his long thin tail jabbing the air. She hissed at him and he was gone in a second.

Claudie tiptoed across the porch until he stood by the chair.

"Want some gum?" He nodded. She took a yellow package of Chiclets out of her shirt pocket, shook out one and handed it to him. He popped it in his mouth. "Don't swallow it, idiot. Just chew it, see?"

He noticed that the shell path went by right in front of the house, just outside the little wire fence. And that on the other side of the path was a thick clump of oleanders, their leaves shining and green.

"You're her boy, huh?"

He was so busy watching the grove of oleanders that he hardly listened as she went on talking to him. "They put you out? Are they in bed now? Are they?"

He looked at her quickly and looked away, shaking his head.

"No," she said, "I guess you wouldn't know."

Another girl passed, peddling slowly on a bike, the dust rising in little low white tracks after her. And in the top of the oak tree two mockingbirds began to fight. Claudie bent back his head far as he could and tried to spot them.

She said: "If you keep on looking straight up for birds, like that with your mouth open, they going to drop right square down your throat."

He closed his mouth with a gulp and looked down at his feet.

She laughed. "Frog eyes! . . . What's your name?"

He was still staring at his feet. "Claudie."

"Oh sure," she said, and scratched her knee.

He went back to watching the small things that moved in front of him: a green grasshopper, with legs thin as wire; a couple of big red ants.

A young woman passed, a short stocky woman with black hair

that had blue tints in the sun. Annie called: "Hey, we got a wedding here, come on over."

The woman waved, but kept walking.

Annie ran down the steps calling: "Cecile, come on . . . they're beating those old bedsprings to pieces."

Cecile turned and walked to meet her then, shaking her head. Claudie could hear the angry murmur of the voice, but they were too far off for him to get the words. Then Annie turned and walked back to the porch, swinging her shoulders with her steps. She sat down again and jammed her feet back up on the railing.

Claudie watched her; for a moment he'd thought she was crying, the way she passed the back of her hand across her eyes.

"What are you staring at, idiot?"

He looked away quickly.

Perique came back. He was just opening the front gate when she shouted out to him: "My old man got married again, did you know? Must be some widow from Port Ronquille."

Perique came up the walk and stood with a foot on the first step. "I was down at the dock, me, when they come in."

"That's her boy there."

"Yea," Perique said, "I know."

"Man," Annie said, "you can hear those old bed slats creaking."

Perique did not answer. He looked down at the tips of his shoes.

"What's the matter," Annie said, "you don't think I got any reason to talk like that?"

"Oh hell," Perique said.

Annie hissed under her breath.

"Picking a wife's his own business."

"Okay," she said. "Okay, mister jackass."

Perique sat on the top step, beside Claudie. "I don't know, me," he said. "She look all right to me."

Her bare toes stretched and curled. The mockingbird came back to the far rail.

"Come on," Perique said. "Come on have a beer with me."

Claudie looked up eagerly. He liked the taste of beer. He'd always drunk the warm liquid that was left over in the bottles.

"Go away," Annie said.

"You come with me."

"I want to stay here, right here," Annie said, "until him and that scrawny woman come out."

"The kid's right here," Perique said in a whisper.

"What do I care?"

Perique got up and left without a word. Claudie watched his faded tight jeans walk away. There was a knife hanging from his belt, a thick red knife. Claudie wished he had one.

He looked over at the girl but she was staring straight ahead, her face not moving. He sighed lightly. It was very quiet in the whole afternoon with just the faint burring of crickets and a tiny stirring in the leaves.

He was tired. He stretched out on his side, his back against the railing, his head on his arm, and went to sleep.

He woke up when the glass broke. He heard the crash and then the little ripple of the pieces falling. And people laughing. And one woman screaming almost: "Eh, là-bas!"

He sat up and looked around. He was in a room, a small room, he could see the walls dimly. The door was there, straight ahead, with a little thread of light around it. He was in a bed, a narrow, rather hard bed—he could feel it shake with the stomping. He got up and went to the door. First he tried peeping through the crack, but there was just a blur of light. Standing on his tiptoes, he stretched up to feel for the knob. It was an old-fashioned latch—jumping at it a couple of times, he pushed up the little metal bar. Then he pulled the door toward him and slipped out. He was in the narrow hall that went down the center of the house. The hall was empty: there were only a half-dozen empty beer bottles lined up very neatly on the little half-table under the picture of the Sacred Heart. Down to the right was the door to the living-room: there were people in there. And somebody was playing a piano: he stopped and listened carefully: he had not noticed one in there before. He walked down, very slowly, along the wall, his head twisting to right and left as he went. There were lots more people out on the porch; he could hear them talking. He went first and peeped out the screen, but he couldn't see very much. So he went into the living-room instead.

He stood just inside the door, and a little to one side, and watched. His eyes found the piano, over in the corner with a bunch of straw flowers on top. He couldn't see who was playing it. There was a girl, in a tight-fitting green silk dress, singing. Her hair was very black and short and brushed straight up with a green flower right on top. And in the little clear space in the middle of the floor some people were dancing. He couldn't see them, just their feet moving between the legs of the people standing in front of him. The room was so noisy that his ears hurt a little. But he got as close to the people as he could and then squatted down and peered between their legs.

He stayed that way for quite a while. Then the couple standing directly in front of him, a short stocky man with a short, almost fat girl, turned and stumbled over him. Claudie yelped.

"Jesus," the girl said.

The man picked him up and held him high over his head. "Here one boy who come to a party in his drawers!"

Claudie looked down: there was nothing but nubs of faces. He kicked and screamed.

The man held him tightly. "Anybody want him, before I throw him out the window?"

Everybody laughed. Claudie bent his head trying to bite the hands that held him around the middle, but he couldn't reach.

"He's a painter, him."

He could see the teeth in all the open mouths and the faces tilted up to him.

"He's mine. Give him here."

"You want him, man? You sure you want him?"

"Sure I do. Give him here."

"Okay."

The arm brought him down. Claudie thought that he was going to be put back on the ground, and he stretched out his legs to be ready. But instead, the man shifted his grip to one arm and one leg.

Claudie felt himself swing back and forth a couple of times and then the hands were gone and he was falling backwards through the air. He arched his back and his legs began running, but he couldn't even get himself straight up. He did not even have time to cry.

Somebody caught him, caught him so hard that for one minute

he couldn't breathe. He felt like his stomach had been flattened. Then there were floorboards under his feet, and his papa was shouting in his ear: "Scared you, boy?" And his mother was hugging him. She looked tired; there were dark shadows under her eyes. She'd been drinking too; he could smell that on her breath as she hugged him. Her eyes were very bright and her cheeks had a high red smudge to them.

"What the matter, bébé?" she asked. "Why you pull back from me?"

The piano started again.

"Hey, look," his papa said.

One of the dancers, a short thin man with a tumbled mass of black hair, a little black mustache, and a receding chin had put a drink on his head and was waltzing his partner in tight fast circles. The girl was giggling so that she could hardly keep step with him. "Watch it, che'," he told her, "or you make me waste this here good whisky."

The girl only doubled up more with laughter. But she did not once lose the beat. And the level in the glass hardly moved. They ended with a tight whirl; the music stopped. He carefully finished the glass at a single gulp. The girl sat down right where she was on the floor.

Claudie pulled away from his mother and backed up until he felt the wall behind him. Then he let himself slide along it until he was sitting down on the floor too.

They had forgot about him. So he sat there, his knees drawn up under his chin, and watched.

Once his mother came over and stooped down beside him and said: "You got to go to bed."

He shook his head and flattened himself even more against the wall. "No," he said and pulled away.

"Al," she said, "I can't do nothing with the boy."

"Let him be."

She stood up. "He ought to be in bed."

"Us too," he said. And everybody howled. Even the piano stopped for a minute when the player took time out to laugh.

Claudie pushed himself along the wall until he had wedged himself against a big red plush upholstered chair. There was a man sitting in it with a girl in his lap. Her legs hung over the arm.

She had nearly kicked off her shoes: they dangled from her toes. Claudie stared at the dirt-streaked inside of the shoe.

Somebody put a half-empty beer bottle down right along side him, and patted the top of his head. He did not look up. Carefully, his left hand reached out and got the bottle and put it to his lips. He rolled the warm bitterish liquid around on his tongue before he swallowed it. After that he drained all the bottles he could reach.

When he got so sleepy that he knew he could not hold his head up any longer, he crawled behind the chair, between it and the wall.

The lights were all out. For a minute he couldn't tell whether his eyes were open or shut, so he fluttered them to make sure. He still could not see a thing. He felt the chair on one side and the wall on the other pressing him, catching him. He scrambled out as quick as he could, scuffing his knuckles against the rough plaster of the wall. He saw light then, the soft blue light of a night sky beyond the opened window.

He stopped and stood very still, catching his breath, both hands holding his stomach, to try and stop its twitching.

There was a soft rustle on the floor over in the corner: too light for a rat. A couple of big roaches must be running there.

He stood on a chair and put his head out the window. The porch was black shadow, deep and thick. Only one of the ladder backs of the chairs stuck out against the moonlight. You couldn't see very far, not much beyond the white shell path which was so bright that you could tell when a rabbit flashed across it.

Claudie took a deep breath of the sour-sweet swampy air. The rabbit set his body tingling, even down to his fingers. If he had a gun, he could go get the rabbit or maybe two or three and then he would have them for dinner tomorrow. If he had a gun . . . he would have to get one soon, one of his own. His fingers tingled even more when he thought of touching the barrel, so smooth and cold. This man now, maybe he would let him have one tomorrow.

A mockingbird stirred sleepily in one of the bushes and a sudden light breeze blew the curtains out around his head.

He got down and, walking carefully, made his way to the hall.

Once he tripped over a glass or a bottle: he couldn't tell which, and he didn't stop to see.

The first door he tried was locked. He pushed and jiggled the latch hard as he could. Then he stopped and listened: heavy slow breathing.

The next door was ajar. He went in. The moon was coming in through both windows and he stared around. It was the same room he'd wakened in. There, hanging by its string from the footpost of the bed was his model boat. He turned it carefully over and over, to be sure that it was all right. He ran his fingers along the hull. Somebody had whittled it for him, a long time ago; he'd forgot just who. He unwrapped the string from the post and carried the boat over to the window sill. He put it in the exact center, very carefully, and climbed into bed.

He lay watching the shadow his boat made on the floor. The bright moon through the window only made the far corners of the room darker. He tried to keep watching the boat but his eyes began to swing over to the dark corners, the corners he had never seen by daylight. His stomach started to twitch.

He got up and went back to the window: the moonlight was warm and the night smelled good—there must be a night jasmine somewhere close.

And by the open window he could hear clearly: somebody crying, very softly, as if they had been doing it for a long time and were tired out. He stood on his tiptoes and listened. There was some sort of a box at the corner of the window: he climbed up on it and stuck his head out. The sound came from the window right next to his.

He jumped down and scooted out the room. That next door was closed. He took a deep breath and jumped at the latch. It lifted and the door swung open.

Annie said: "What do you want?"

He did not answer. Her bed was right under the window, right in the light. The moon made a kind of a halo around her hair.

He could see the outline of her head and when she bent forward to whisper to him, he could see the outlines of her face.

"Let me alone."

The room smelled good; she must be using some sort of perfume, spicy and soft and faint.

He climbed into bed alongside her. She rolled away, and then turned, pushing him out, hard, so that he landed with a thud on the floor.

He stayed there for a minute, sniffing: there was the same odor his mother had, but fainter.

He went up to the bed and started to climb back. She kicked at him. He stepped away and waited, rubbing the tip of his nose. When she had stopped sobbing, he tiptoed over, and very carefully, so that he should not shake the springs, he climbed in.

She pulled away, taking the sheet and the pillow with her. He did not mind. He grinned into the dark, put his head on his bent arm, and went to sleep, balancing himself on the very edge.

BY seven o'clock the following morning, Annie was on the back porch, eating a watermelon. She was blowing the seeds out over the railing into the yard—there was a trail of shiny wet seeds to her chair. And there were a couple of big wet stains on the front of her yellow shorts.

She'd found the melon in the kitchen when she'd gone looking for breakfast, and she'd just about finished it in the two hours she'd been alone, sitting in the little spot of sun that came through the thick mulberry trees.

Though she rarely did, this morning she'd put on make-up— she'd spent nearly an hour at it. And it was a good job. Only in the bright hard light, if you looked close, you could see the dark circles and the puffy eyelids.

It was the beginning of another hot summer day, but she stayed in the sun, even moving her chair about as the rays shifted and changed. She'd felt chilly that morning, and she'd been shivering until she'd come outside.

Every once in a while she squinted up at the bright white light streaking between the leaves—and blew a watermelon seed up at it.

By nine o'clock only one person had passed down the path that went by the house: Cecile Boudreau, wearing a big floppy straw hat and carrying a fishing pole. She waved and called softly: "Want to come with me?"

Annie shook her head.

And Cecile had laughed, softly too, so she wouldn't wake any sleepers. "I ain't going to catch nothing, but I got to try."

While Cecile was there, a couple of kids passed. Annie didn't see who they were. She just noticed the shiny black tops of their heads go past the bushes.

There'd been lots more people, Annie thought, if it hadn't

178

been for the party. It had been a good party, she admitted, with everybody drunk, and all the island there.

Annie hadn't been there herself. She'd spent most of the night wandering around—down to the west end of the island, all the way down to the sandbars, where you could see the lights on Terre Haute; over to the wharf, where the *Mickey Mouse* was tied, her decks still piled with tarpaulin-covered boxes and furniture. And around and around all night, until she couldn't stand up anymore. And then she had sneaked into her room, though the party was still going on in the front of the house.

She threw the rind of the melon down into the yard and the chickens came to peck at it.

It was so quiet, nothing moving or stirring, except the birds and a couple of dogs. It'd be a day lost. . . .

Annie cut another slice of the melon. Small black ants were beginning to come. She stepped on them.

The smooth cool stuff slid down her throat. Her eyes burned a little, but she didn't feel bad, she noticed with surprise.

"I don't feel anything, me," she told the morning.

The sun shifted slowly, leaving her in shade again. She heard the scraping of a chair and the splashing of water inside the house.

She lifted one leg straight out and stared at the toenails.

"It is nothing to me," she told herself.

A gull wailed overhead. Annie picked the seeds from the last piece of melon and threw them at the hens.

Adele came out on the porch behind her. "You been up early?" she asked.

"I like to," Annie said. I got to find a place and take a nap, she told herself.

"You can see the paths now," the woman said and pointed. "Last night it look like there was nothing but woods back there."

"Sure there paths," Annie said, "and houses too."

"You can't see them from here."

"They're there all right, whether you see or not."

"Lots?"

"A good many," Annie said.

Al began to whistle inside.

"He's shaving," Annie said.

"While he's whistling?"

"He always does that," Annie said and she could see him, standing in front of the little mirror, his face white with lather, moving the straight razor carefully, trimming his mustache just so.

"You like the mustache?" Annie said.

"Yes."

"It's getting gray."

"Everybody's hair gets gray."

"Not niggers."

"Yes, they do," Adele said.

"You seen them in Port Ronquille, huh?"

Adele nodded, her eyes searching around in the trees and bushes.

"Way back there we got a couple pigs."

"I can smell," Adele said.

"You ought to smell it sometimes," Annie said.

"Ummm," Adele said.

"Hey there," Al called, "there is no breakfast."

"There's coffee dripping on the stove," Adele said. "And I be there in a minute."

"Je peux pu 'ttendre." He was chuckling.

"I be there," Adele said, more softly.

"Everybody got up late today," Annie said, "I been watching and hardly nobody passed."

"Account of the party?"

"They were all here," Annie said.

"Not everybody."

Annie stared across the parched bleached ground of the backyard. "That's all there is on this island."

"Everybody?"

"Except Mamere Terrebonne who don't go out at night. And maybe some more old women."

"Oh," Adele said.

Annie gouged out a few more seeds and tossed them at the hens.

"How many hens you got here?"

"I never counted," Annie said.

"I brought three or four—big reds."

Annie rubbed the tip of her nose.

"They were in a crate on the boat."

"Then I reckon they still there."

"Somebody ought to feed them, or bring the cage up here."

"Ask him," Annie said, jerking her thumb over her shoulder to the house.

"They were talking about a sailboat last night." Adele leaned on the railing and stared into the trees.

"You won't find no sign of it there."

Adele let her eyes run around the fenced in yard, at the chickens pecking away at the shell of the watermelon, at the bicycle wheel that had been leaning so long on the side of the house that the spokes had almost rusted away.

"There is one here?"

"Yea," Annie said, "down at the dock. You didn't notice it, coming in?"

"All the time it stays there?"

"Just came in two weeks ago."

"Oh," Adele said, "I thought somebody here had a sailboat."

"Wouldn't nobody on the island have a thing like that."

"Oh," Adele said.

Inside Al was saying: "Hi, boy, boy, boy."

"I'll fix breakfast," Adele said.

"Not for me."

"You haven't had any."

"Yea."

Adele looked at the last piece of melon. "Just that, no?"

"I don't want anything."

"You got to eat something."

Annie stared at a mamselle that perched on the railing. "If he was just a little lower down the chickens get him for sure."

"I fix you something."

"Look," Annie said. She caught the mosquito hawk and threw it down to the chickens. "Let me alone."

"I find Claudie asleep in your bed this morning."

"Nothing bothers me," Annie said, "because I don't care."

Adele went inside, slowly and without another word.

Annie listened to the clatter of pots and two voices talking, and the high-pitched patter of the boy. Then she got to her feet and stretched herself all over, like a cat. She took a running start and jumped the low yard fence. She followed the path for a little while, but the crushed shells were too hot to her bare feet. So she cut back into the trees, walking slowly, and looking for a cool place to have a nap.

After just a couple of minutes she heard somebody else, heard them whistling away behind her. The man from the sailboat was coming along the path too: she caught a glimpse of him first. So she stopped at a tangle of muscadine vines, waiting for him to catch up.

"Hi," he said.

She turned and grinned.

"I know you," he said.

"I reckon so." She went on searching for the round grapes—the birds and the worms hadn't left many.

"You were down with Cecile—what's her name? The first day."

"It's a mighty fine boat you got."

"Isn't mine," Inky said.

"Same thing."

"Hell, no."

She had a palm full of grapes and she began to eat them slowly.

"What's that?"

"You never saw muscats before?"

"Oh sure," he said, "my sister's got a back yard full of them."

"You never ate them?"

"Never thought about it."

"Taste one."

He reached for her hand. She jerked it away. "Pick your own, mister."

"She called 'em scuppernongs." He reached up, took one and squashed it on his tongue.

"How's it?"

He made a face. "Sour as hell."

She laughed and, cupping her hand, rolled the grapes into her mouth. "No such thing."

"My sister used to cook them up."

"Where she live?"

"New Orleans."

Annie nodded and began picking among the higher clusters. She could feel him looking at her and she wondered if the make-up had smeared in the heat.

"Foucher Street."

"Oh sure. . . ."

"Know where it is?"

"Yes," she said. Pretending to brush away a gnat, she ran her fingers along the side of her face. The make-up felt smooth.

"You used to live there?"

She nodded.

"Where?"

"I was staying in a convent."

"I'll be damned," he said. "You don't look like the type."

"What type?"

"That goes in a convent."

"What *do* I look like?"

"I don't know . . . a good type."

She giggled and popped away some nubby green grapes between her thumb and finger. "I was just staying at the convent. . . . I wasn't studying to be a nun."

"Well," he said, "that makes me feel better."

"It was fun," she said.

He rubbed his chin. "I heard about all the fun that goes on in convents."

She shrugged, not understanding and not wanting to admit it.

"You have a boyfriend used to sneak in at night?"

"My roommate did."

"Tell me."

"Nothing to tell." She tucked her blouse inside her shorts. "I couldn't even get to watch them."

"Bet nothing went on."

"I don't know," she said, "I never did see."

"You didn't have a boyfriend?"

She looked at the ground. "That's nothing to talk about." She hoped her voice sounded right.

"Tell me about that."

There was an old brown leaf on the ground, all shriveled and curled like a cocoon. When I'm old I'm going to look like that, she thought, and she shivered.

"What's the matter?"

"Nothing," she said.

"You shivered like you had malaria."

"I was thinking."

"About the guy?"

"Yes," she lied.

She leaned back against a mulberry tree, not bothering with the big black ants that were crawling up the trunk. "He was nice," she said.

And her mind began to form a picture: he would be only middle-size, he'd have black hair and blue eyes and he'd look sort of Irish, only he'd be German. "His name was Warren," she said. And was a little surprised that lying came so easy.

"That's a fancy name."

"He came from a fancy family," she said. "If I told you his last name, I bet anything you'd open your mouth for surprise."

"Go ahead . . . surprise me."

"I can't do that." The story was coming easier and easier to her. Now when she closed her eyes, she could see Warren, as plain as if she were really remembering him.

"What'd he do?"

"He went to school," she said smoothly. "To Loyola—and that was where I met him. I went over to one of the dances at the school."

Inky said something, but she did not listen. The story was growing, almost in spite of her now, and she was caught up in it. "He was going to be a lawyer like his father—he's a politican, a big one, too."

She let herself slide down the trunk until she was sitting cross-legged on the ground. Inky still stood, looking down at her. "He had black hair," she said, "but he had blue eyes too."

"Now we're getting to the exciting part," Inky said, "how'd you get him in the convent?"

She lifted her head, staring at him, but not seeing him. And remembering Beatriz . . .

"We had lights out around ten-thirty. And I'd take a flashlight and go down the corridor and down the stairs. And there was a side door."

And as she remembered, she was almost sure it had happened to her.

"There were lots and lots of trees out back there . . . a pecan orchard somebody planted a long time ago. And there was a little street that went across the back, a mud street and not very good, so not many people used it, just the ones who had houses there."

"Be damned," Inky said, "that's beginning to sound all right."

"You could park a car there—and he'd always come in with his lights switched off, just to be extra sure. And there was a piece of the wire fence that just lifted up—it was old wire and rusted through. It was so dark with the trees. And the streetlight way down at the corner."

She was crying now, she felt the tears on her cheeks. She stopped, wiped them away. The feeling of elation was gone, and she was back staring at the short slim dark man who had come in to the island on the sailboat. He was wearing a white sweat shirt with a big rip on the shoulder and his pants had grease stains.

And she wondered if the tears had smeared the make-up. . . .

"You had a rough time, huh?" Inky said.

She noticed with surprise that he was looking at her legs and without thinking she drew them closer under her.

He noticed and grinned. "You got nice legs."

"Warren used to say that. . . ." but the fun was gone from the story. And there was only a dry taste at the back of her mouth.

He was carrying a long switch of willow in his hand. He flicked it back and forth like a whip.

"Look at me," he said, "I'm working to get in the circus."

"You got nothing else to do?"

"This is the life," he said, "man, this sure is."

"Nothing to do."

"That's what I like, honey." He squinted at her. "I never had very much of that in my life . . . and I like it now."

She pulled a long blade of grass and began to suck it.

"I heard the racket from your party last night clear down to the boat."

She had almost forgot—the party, the wedding-party.

"You didn't come?"

"Nobody ask me."

"It was sort of a family thing, I guess."

"I figured that."

"You coulda come."

"I guess."

"People are all right, when they get used to you."

"That girl now, Cecile something or other, she seemed like a nice sort."

Annie nodded, threw away the blade of grass and reached for another.

"She was the first person I ran into on the island."

"She's all right," Annie said.

She was beginning to feel the lack of sleep. There was a little headache starting and her shoulders felt heavy.

"What sort of a guy is he?"

"Who?"

"Her husband."

"He's nice too." The few tears made her eyes burn. She blinked rapidly.

"She's good-looking."

"Don't you let Hector hear that."

"Why not?"

"Just don't."

"Don't he know what she look like?"

"Sure he does," Annie said, "only he's not going to like anybody else looking."

"Okay," Inky laughed, "I got it."

Annie yawned and shook her head.

"Party got you too?"

"Guess so."

"Say . . ." Inky said, "it was your old man? The guy who got married?"

"Sure."

"How'd you like that?"

"I liked it fine."

"Two women in the house."

"I'm not likely to be in the house long." No one had used the word woman to her before—she felt a little jump of pride.

"How come?"

Annie shrugged and yawned again.

"You getting married or something?"

"Could be."

"I was crazy not to see it," Inky said and scratched his curly short-cut hair. "A good-looking gal is bound to get married."

It's me he's talking to, Annie told herself.

And she lifted her head and, very carefully, smiled just a little to herself.

The way Beatriz must have done. . . . And for a minute she could feel the long black hair waving down to her shoulders, hanging down her back.

She lifted one hand, and touched her own short blond hair.

And she wasn't Beatriz anymore. She was back on the island. And Inky was in front of her, grinning.

"You sure do go off in a trance."

"Oh," she said, vaguely.

"Was he that good?"

"Huh?"

"You get that look in your eyes when you think about him."

"I don't."

Inky got a new pack of cigarettes out of his shirt pocket.

"How long you going to be here?"

"Until somebody tells me to get going."

"He pay you?"

"Maybe," Inky said.

Annie put both hands behind her head and laughed. "I'm not trying to find out how much money you carrying around."

"He didn't pay me, but he will all right."

"I don't believe that," Annie said.

"I can't make you."

"You got sense not to go flashing a roll."

"If I had it, I wouldn't do that."

Annie got up. "I got to see about getting me a nap."

"Can I come?" Inky grinned and lit a cigarette. "Want one?"

She took it. "Just one match." She put both in her blouse pocket.

"What's that for?"

"My papa'll hit the roof if he sees me smoking."

"You going to sneak it?"

"Sure."

"Where you going to take your nap?"

She shrugged.

"I'll come keep you company."

"What for?"

"Watch you." Inky blew smoke in a small ring that the wind broke. "Maybe take a nap myself."

There was a tingle in Annie's stomach and for a minute she wondered if she was going to be sick. "No thanks."

"Okay," Inky said, "I was just asking."

Annie yawned again.

"I was taking a short cut," Inky said, "and sort of got mixed up—which way's the grocery?"

"Right down there . . . and you turn when you see a red-painted cistern, and keep on going."

"Thanks," Inky said.

Annie ducked back through the blackberry thicket. She could move through the tangle almost as quick as a deer could, and just as silent. That was why she always found more berries—she could go farther in than anyone else.

She came out of the thicket and cut across the little swampy spot. She pulled a leaf from the jonc plat and chewed on it, wondering why the muskrats liked it. She stopped to spit out the reed, and wiped her mouth with the back of her hand. A whole cloud of grasshoppers flew up from her feet. She climbed the slight rise of the shell mound and was in the shade of the chinaberry trees. It was a kind of island here, with swampy stretches on all sides. Under the trees the black ground was covered with the crinkled gray seeds, a few heaps of white shell, and a clump or two of nicomus daisies.

She stretched out flat, the seeds crunching and shifting under her weight. And she stared straight up at the blue white sky through the umbrella-shaped clumps of leaves.

Did Beatriz do this, she wondered, Beatriz who had sheer flowing nightdresses. Annie closed her eyes and could see her. The lovely gown, and the heavy beautiful figure. Annie craned up her head and squinted at her own body: she would never look like that.

There was a dry taste in her mouth. From the jonc plat, she thought.

"I shoulda brought some water," she said aloud.

And she was terribly sleepy. . . . She thought about her father, who was married now. He had done it, she thought, and that was all.

There was the warmth of the ground under her, and the heat of the day all around her. She closed her eyes but didn't sleep. There were just pictures floating across her lids. Beatriz with her hair in curlers. . . . Inky's brown eyes, that were too large for his face . . . the way the flat mulberry leaves looked against the sun. . . . The chipped front tooth Inky had . . . her father's mustache, and his teeth that were white and perfect . . . the breeze that went past her, flowing like water, and the heavy jasmine odor. And the feel of the stone on the convent's roof. . . . The blue shirt that had faded almost white except at the seams. . . . An ortolan skimming right over the green pebble-like buds of a crepe myrtle. . . . The shirt bright blue at the seams, and a pack of cigarettes in the pocket. Inky's shirt . . . A bayou whose name she'd forgot, thick heavy water, like oil almost, breaking in slow waves from the boat's bow, water that was black and heavy from all the dead things in it. . . . The brown-haired woman with her hair drawn back so smooth it looked like it was painted there over her ears. . . . The dogs, one black, two brown-and-black-and-tan, loping down the beach, just inside the little surf line. . . . Beatriz, peering out of the window, while the wind swirled her robe and her heavy perfume.

Annie rolled over, rubbing at her eyes.

How did it start, she wondered, this man that Beatriz met? And what had happened? What were they doing now?

"I'll write her," Annie said, and even she did not believe that.

Where did she meet him? Or did it just happen?

Like Inky, maybe?

"He needs a woman," she said aloud and her eyes popped open in surprise. She had not thought of it before she said it. She would not have believed it. But now, being said, it seemed true.

So, she thought, so . . . that was how it started.

Still, maybe. And how did you find out. How did Beatriz find out? It wasn't something you could ask. And it wasn't something you could push. How did you know? And what did you do?

Without opening her eyes she picked up a handful of the little chinaberry seeds and began tossing them in the air one by one. The steady cricket calls stopped abruptly.

Maybe you just waited and waited and nothing happened. And maybe if you tried to hurry it it would go all wrong and he'd go running away a thousand miles.

She should have asked Beatriz.

But that wouldn't have worked either. That wouldn't have worked.

Maybe there was something she was supposed to do and she wasn't. Maybe it was something right in front of her, lying right in front of her eyes. And maybe he was cursing her for a fool.

She wanted to cry but her eyes hurt too much from last night. So she kept very still and listened to the crickets come back one by one, until the whole hot afternoon was filled with their dry rustling.

She was a cute kid, Inky thought. And she needed a man worst way. They all did at that age. It was kind of funny the way they couldn't quite figure out what was eating on them. The story about Warren now . . . it just didn't make sense. She was probably just sleeping with some island guy. And that was her way of dressing it up. Or, maybe, he paused, rubbing his chin and smearing grape juice on his jaw . . . maybe it was true. Hell, no, he thought.

She was almost grown up. Figure was pretty good: he had noticed. And she did have one thing—a gal he'd once dated had named it for him—a blouse full of goodies. She had quite a face too, with those big light blue eyes.

But she just wasn't the type he went for. Not his type at all.

That same afternoon he got to feeling restless. The island was so small. And the mosquitoes. And just now a cloud of biting gnats. When a lizard ran out on the deck, he smashed it savagely —and then had to clean off the smear.

Finally he marched over to Arcenaux's to use the telephone. The grocery was crowded, and he knew that all the people would

be listening, but he didn't care. He got three dollars in change
from Julius and then went into the little phone room.

He called Arthur first at his office. A voice said that he had
gone home, a soft gentle voice with a touch of Alabama drawl—
Inky recognized it. He had seen the secretary once, when he'd
had to go to the office; a good-looking redhead. He'd wondered
then about Arthur. What man wouldn't give that a try. . . .

Inky called the house. He got Helen, then Arthur. By this
time the irritation that had prompted him to call had worn away.
And he listened to Arthur patiently.

"Okay," he said finally. "One more week."

He hung up the receiver and went back into the grocery. No
one was standing anywhere near the wall—no one was listening
—but Inky could have sworn that he had heard the rush of feet
just a second before. It didn't really bother him.

*

HENRY had been gone for six days before the Livaudais started to worry.

In the morning Pete was very nervous. He had got up five or six times during the night to check his brother's bed. When during the afternoon he finally got into a fight with George Manint, he felt much better for it.

And when Eddie came home that night, Belle was waiting, standing just inside the front screen door. "He ain't back yet," she said.

Eddie stopped just where he was, halfway up the steps, for a couple of minutes. Then he nodded. And walked away.

He was back again in maybe ten minutes. They did not have to say any more. Before light in the morning, he and his brother Mike went out.

And within a couple of hours the whole island knew that Henry was lost in the marsh and that the Livaudais had started to look for him.

That was on Friday.

*

WEEK-ENDS there were dances at the Rendezvous. On Friday night there was a piano and an accordion and on Saturday there was a five-piece band—they came down from Petit Prairie every week. And on Sunday night there was nothing but the juke box.

Late on that Friday afternoon, Inky finished scrubbing the jenny. It had gotten mildewed, stowed away. So he had put it out on the wharf, and gone over it foot by foot, with a bucket of Clorox and soapy water and the garden hose he'd found down by the sea-food packing-plant. (It was the only place on the island had a well and a pump.)

Even the well water was almost warm, Inky thought, and he had an idea. But first he lugged the heavy wet sail on board and ran it up, leaving it to hang almost limp under the bright sun. He stretched and rubbed his back. Scrubbing like that, on hands and knees. . . . God damn.

For a while he watched the streams of water drip down into puddles on the deck and then the puddles themselves turn into streams down the slant of the bow.

Then he rubbed his back again, went below, got a towel and a bar of soap. He took the hose and pulled it as far back into the shelter of the trees as it would go—it wasn't very long, just three twenty-five foot sections put together—and fastened it to the limb of a locust tree. He had a shower.

He scrubbed himself—even his hair. And when he remembered it had been days since he'd had a bath, he rubbed even harder. He got soap in his eye and by the time he'd got it out and opened his eyes again, there was a circle of kids watching. Not giggling, not moving, only staring, solemnly.

For a minute they startled him, but he kept perfectly still. Then he went on with his shower. The damn kids, he thought, they were everywhere on the island, all at once.

193

He finished and, reaching up, turned off the nozzle. When he looked again, the kids were gone. They could come and go without making a sound. Sometimes at night he'd take a look out the forward porthole and he'd be sure he saw a little form up there in the bow. But by the time he'd got up, there wouldn't be a thing. And there wouldn't have been a sound.

"Talk about ghosts," he muttered to himself.

"You are beautiful now, no?"

Inky spun around. Julius Arcenaux was sitting on one of the old sawhorses that had been left behind the sea-food plant.

Son of a bitching fairy, Inky thought . . . and then stopped. He had seen Julius pinching the girls when they passed behind the counter in his grocery. That wasn't any fairy—but he had been sitting, watching.

Inky said: "I was beginning to smell like a goat."

"All dress up for dancing, huh?"

Inky wrapped the towel around his waist and knotted it. "No?"

"No," Inky said, "I'm not much for dancing."

"You should go," Julius said, "maybe you find a girl could teach you, huh?"

"What I want a girl for?"

Julius shrugged. "You are grown big enough to know that."

"Thanks," Inky said.

Julius stretched his great fat body until the buttons on his shirt gaped open. "Never can tell."

"Where's the dancing?"

"Only one place."

"Where's that?"

"The Rendezvous."

Inky ran his fingers through his wet hair, combing it. "I go down there for a drink, sometimes."

Julius pursed his lips. "Go do some dancing, man."

"Maybe," Inky said.

"Here come a couple of nice little girls, man." Julius pointed over Inky's shoulder.

There were two girls coming along the wharf—and a kid with them. Inky recognized Annie.

"They must be coming for the late show," he said.

"Huh?"

"I got to go get some clothes on."

"Wait a minute, man, and meet them. . . . I introduce you."

"No, thanks," Inky said, and headed to the boat.

"What the matter with you? Ain't you a man?"

Inky swung over the lifelines. "I'm just shy," he said.

About eight o'clock he decided to go over to the Rendezvous. He'd been thinking about it for an hour or so. And the more he thought the better a glass of cold beer got to taste. He had whisky on the boat. He even went and got the bottle and poured a couple of jiggers over the cubes of ice he got from the refrigerator in the little galley. And he sat out on the deck under the little tent of mosquito-netting that hung from the boom, and drank.

And with each swallow he thought about the beer.

"When I finish . . ." he said aloud. Only I won't hurry.

So he drank the whisky slowly and looked around, though you couldn't see very much through the netting. And it was a good hour before he left the boat.

The beer was cold. He drank three bottles before he caught his breath. Then he put both elbows on the bar and stretched and took a deep breath.

The Rendezvous was crowding up. There were three or four men, like him, standing at the bar. He had seen them before, and he nodded to them. They made a little lifting motion with their glasses and looked away.

The tables that were usually pushed back against the wall were set out now, in a kind of big circle around an open dance floor. The band wasn't playing—they had gone out somewhere. To have a drink: they always carried their own liquor—orange wine in gallon jugs. Heavy sweet wine that could make a man drunk and sick both, if he wasn't used to it.

Most of the island would be here, Inky thought, at least all of them young enough and strong enough to dance.

Somebody was waving; he stared harder. It was Cecile. Sure it was. Only she was wearing an off-the-shoulder white blouse and a full red skirt, and she had a sprig of some pink flowers in her hair. If she hadn't waved, he wouldn't have recognized her. And the man with her, the heavy-set man with the long black hair glistening with hair oil and water, that was Hector. Inky nodded. Hector bowed politely.

His eyes were getting used to the dark. There was no light in the room at all. Only the red reflections from the four Jax beer signs hung in the front windows. The end of the long room was almost completely black. There weren't even shapes back there, only giggles now and then.

"You come, huh?" Julius was at Inky's elbow.

"You can see."

"Tonight a big deal night, big week-end, for sure."

"How come?"

"They started drinking last night at the wedding," Julius grinned. "Don't look like they going stop."

"Everybody?"

"Except maybe the Livaudais."

"What's wrong with them?"

"Don't feel like it," Julius said. "They got a boy been gone too long out hunting."

"The beer's cold," Inky said after a pause.

"My daughter looks nice and fine, no?"

"Sure," Inky said. "And she's got a good-looking husband, too."

Julius snorted. "You see back there." He pointed to the far end of the room.

"Who can see back there?"

Julius laughed and poured the last of his bottle into his glass. "You not supposed to see."

"I figured that," Inky said.

"Back there, it is like being all alone. Only you got music."

"Yea."

"Things that go on . . ." Julius clucked his tongue. "Rosalie Conte, she say she got a baby planted in her. And right back there."

"She didn't yell for help," Inky said and dipped the tip of his nose in the foam of his glass.

Julius shrugged. "She didn't need help, maybe."

Inky was drinking the bitter beer in little short swallows and counting them.

The accordion-player came back in the room, and wiping his mouth on the back of his hand, took his seat. He sat rocking back and forth on the unsteady legs of the cane chair and frowning down at the floor.

"Looks like he's about to cry."

"Always look like that," Julius said.

"Where's the other guy? The piano-player?"

"He be around before too long."

"Hot in here."

"Summer, man."

"Jesus!"

"You got a right to ask any girl to dance and nobody get offended."

"I keep telling you over and over again," Inky said, "I'm not going crazy to dance."

"Okay," Julius said.

"I just want to get drunk, not much, just a little."

"No more?" Julius leaned forward so that his little close-set brown eyes were only a foot from Inky's.

Inky turned his back. "I still don't want to get laid."

Julius clucked lightly way down in his throat and walked off.

Inky bought another bottle of beer. The piano-player came ambling back in the room. And began to play something using only his left hand. His right arm held up his head.

For an hour or so Inky stood at the bar, his back to the dancing. He heard the shuffling feet and the laughing and the light panting breaths. He did not look. He drank his beer steadily and slowly. When the man next to him yelled across the room: "Hey, brother-in-law! What you say?" and stumbled away, Inky hitched himself up on that empty stool.

"You feet bearing a heavy load, no?" Lacy Livaudais, the bartender, said. He was a short dark man with a wide round face (like most of the people on the island). A curly shock of hair stood straight up in front of the little cap made from a woman's stocking that covered the hairless back part of his head. Below the cap and down his neck you could see a slick whitish scar.

"You nearly got killed once," Inky said.

"Me?"

"You in the war?"

Lacy laughed. "And if I was, I'd have me a nice fine wig."

"I guess you would," Inky said.

"Gas fumes in the bilge."

Inky nodded. "I sort of figured that."

"Blew the face clean off the other guy."

"I seen what they can do."

"We was just kids."

"Yea," Inky said. "Kids get careless."

He turned around on his stool and watched the room. It must be getting late, he thought, most of the old people had gone. There were two girls dancing together. He blinked and looked again. Two dark girls. And terrific dancers, he thought, watching their high-heeled shoes. He'd seen Lesbians dancing together before, but that was down in the special places in the French Quarter in New Orleans. . . . He watched the girls again.

"You think that funny, huh?" And Hector was standing right alongside him.

"Jesus," Inky said, "nobody ever makes a sound or walks straight up to you."

"You think that funny?"

"I never saw anything like it before, if that's what you mean."

Hector grinned. His long carefully combed hair was tousled and hanging in greasy pieces over his forehead. He brushed it back and tried to pat it in place.

"They say there ain't any man on the island a good-enough dancer to keep up with them."

Inky scratched his ear. The beer had cut down his vision so he had to peer hard to make out the figures of the girls in the half-light.

"Maybe that's so," Inky said, "they're doing some mighty fancy steps."

A girl came up to Hector. (Through the beer mist Inky struggled for her name: it was Annie. Sure, he told himself, sure.)

"Cecile and me," she said, "we going on home."

"Wait for this and I go on with you."

"Hi," Inky said.

"Hi." You couldn't tell from her face whether she remembered seeing him before.

"You get the grapes?"

"The what?" Hector asked.

"She was off hunting grapes at her special spot."

Hector looked at her grinning. "Nobody eats muscats much, cost too much to fix 'em."

"I wanted some, me," Annie said.

Hector went on grinning. "It wasn't grapes you was after."

Annie spun around on her heel and ducking between people and dancers, disappeared. Hector kept on chuckling.

The accordion and the piano were playing faster and faster.

"Watch 'em now," Hector said.

The other dancing couples had stopped trying to keep up. They stood around at the edges of the floor and watched. The two girls were still following. Inky squinted to watch their feet, but all he saw was a blur.

"Jesus," he said softly.

"That something, no?"

"Sure is," Inky said.

Over on the little bandstand, the man with the accordion was grinning widely, his two gold teeth flashing.

One of the girls was calling, or grunting. "Hu, hu!"

"Keep you breath," a man called, "you going to need it, for sure." And somebody laughed.

Inky gave up trying to follow the dancers. He stared up at the rafters and reached behind him for the beer. He was drunk enough now to be able to float off, away from his body. And he was out, somewhere, up with the dark beams by the roof tree, when he heard a couple of rapid heel taps, a soft thud and a swishing. And then the whole room cracked up with laughter.

He came back within himself and looked out of his eyes. Some of the watchers had rushed to the center of the floor. One of the girls was still standing, shrieking with laughter. The other was out of sight.

"She fall?"

"Didn't you see, man?" Hector said. "Always happens, but I seen her do better than tonight."

They had her on her feet now, and her doing up the bun at the back of her neck and calling for everybody to look on the floor for her hairpins. Some guys got down on their hands and knees and began to crawl around.

And a couple of the boys got a hand under each of her elbows and pushed her over to the bar. She was limping. . . . Inky looked down: one foot was bare.

He got off his stool and stepped back. The boys lifted her up on it, still by the elbows.

She was a good-looking girl, Inky thought. A little too short, but a good figure. And the highest heaviest breasts he had ever seen.

"I lost my shoe," she was saying, still panting, "I lost my goddamn shoe."

"Give the lady a beer," somebody said.

"Pour it so there's foam," she said, "I like the foam."

When it came she put her nose in the froth and then lifted her face, grinning. "Real cold!" And she began to drink, so quickly that some spilled on her breasts.

Inky found himself staring at them, wondering what sort of a bra she wore, and whether her skin would have little red crisscross marks from the stitching.

Then he remembered what he was thinking, and turned away, tossed off the last swallow in his glass, and left. He noticed Julius sitting at a table just inside the door and grinning at him, as he left.

He felt a little brittle the next morning. He did not work all day. He sent a kid over to the grocery for a sandwich at noon. He took a pillow up under the trees and one of the paper-back books he'd bought nearly two months ago and hadn't looked into. And in the heat of the day he'd dozed off.

He came flying out of his sleep, sitting straight up, and feeling that there was somebody staring at him. But there was nobody there and not a sound—not even a cricket or a locust.

So there had been somebody there, he knew. He got to his feet and looked around, but in the tangle of bushes and vines and wide palmetto leaves, he could see nothing. And after a minute or so the crickets began again.

He looked around for the hose—some men were scrubbing out the wheelhouse on one of the luggers tied down the wharf a way. And they had just started dragging the hose there.

So he put on his trunks and walked across the island to the open surf side. The sand was a muddy color, but it was smooth as he waded out and there were no rocks. A hundred yards farther out two porpoises were playing, their shiny black backs rising, arching and disappearing. A game of tag, Inky thought.

The sand dropped away. It seemed he had stepped over a ledge. And for a minute he went under the water, then he was treading, shaking his head to clear his nose and eyes. Then he started in a slow crawl down the beach, trying to mimic the slow rolling motion of the porpoises.

The water was very warm, he noticed. If you swam too hard, you could feel yourself begin to perspire. So he turned on his back and floated, trying to see if he could lift both his feet clear out at the same time.

In a few minutes he was winded. Jesus, he thought, the damn cigarettes. So he headed in. This time for fun he swam as high up the beach as he could. His ankle hit something, and he turned to see. The little surf was too muddy. But he felt by the way the water moved that there was something beneath him. A porpoise, maybe, playing games with him—a few strong strokes sent him up on the sand. He was walking out hitching up his pants, when he noticed the tall thin man standing and watching him.

"Water's on the warm side," Inky said.

"Bet it is for sure."

He wasn't a man, Inky thought, just a boy. Very tall, very thin, with a long thin face and a heavy black beard that showed through shaving.

"Why don't you go try it?"

The boy shook his head. "Go swimming a couple times a year."

"Yea?"

"When I fall over." The small pointed white teeth laughed.

"I been seeing you down at the dock," Inky said.

"Name's Inky," the boy said. "I know. Mine's Perique."

"I left my cigarettes back on the boat," Inky said. "You got one?"

"Don't smoke," Perique said. Though there was the shape of a half-full pack in his shirt pocket.

Inky didn't look. "Won't kill me to wait."

"Not many people around here go swimming."

"Wonder why?" Inky said. "Water's good."

"Work on it all week," Perique said, "and you don't want to go floating around in it on your day off."

They stood and watched the empty expanse of Gulf, bright blue. The porpoises were back; there were three this time.

"What's that?" Inky pointed to the flurry of white caps off the west end of the island.

"Shallows."

"No pass there?"

Perique shook his head.

"It makes it look pretty, all right," Inky said. "All that white water off to one side."

High overhead, a hawk and a catbird were fighting and screaming. A couple of feathers floated down and settled in the surf.

"Funny thing," Inky said, "coming in just now, thought I kicked up against a rock."

"Didn't know there was a rock anywhere along this coast."

"Okay," Inky said. On his wet body the sun was burning hot, and in the glare he could hardly open his eyes. "So what's out there?"

"Timbers, I reckon."

"There?"

Perique nodded and scratched his upper lip.

"Ship went ashore?"

"*Charlotte L.*"

"Musta been a long time," Inky said, "Sand's most covered it."

"When it blows the right way sometime," Perique said, "you can see the hull stick up."

"Took a blow to put her up there."

"Did, for sure."

"Kind I don't mind missing," Inky said. "Be seeing you."

He went back to the boat and began to fix supper. And he cut himself three extra slices of bread; he was planning to do some drinking that night.

. . .

He had switched to whisky. Lacy Livaudais just grinned. He had on a different cap, Inky noticed, a school beanie this time in dark green with the initials TU on the front.

"You doing serious drinking tonight, beau," he said.

"It's been coming for some time," Inky said.

"Get a bottle," he jerked his thumb over his shoulder at the rows of pints and fifths. "I'm thinking it going to be cheaper for you."

"Okay," Inky said, "and no charging for the water."

"What label you want?"

Inky squinted at the names. "No Scotches?"

"Sure." The head turned so that Inky was staring at the thick white-scarred back of the neck. "There."

"Just one bottle?"

"Who going to drink Scotch?"

"Not me," Inky said. "Gimme the P.M."

The room was noisier than the night before. It was the band: the piano and the accordion from yesterday, and a guitar, and a set of drums, and a violin.

Inky found himself listening to the violin. "Jesus," he muttered under his breath. There wasn't a string that was tuned right. Sounds like that were enough to twist your ears off. . . . But nobody seemed to mind or even notice.

He was sipping away at the whisky, drinking it neat. He'd always liked the blends better than the straights. It was a matter of what you got used to first. . . .

Even now when he was spending Arthur's money. He slipped one finger over his wallet in his shirt pocket, a good fat wallet, fatter than he'd ever had in his life; all of it to take care of a boat, a narrow mean hull and some canvas overhead. Boat that had more care than most people, he thought.

And he thought of Helen and the bottles of perfume that were still on the boat. She'd left a heavy musky woman smell around the cabin for days.

He closed his eyes and sniffed the whisky and tried to imagine her. Maybe it was the sharp smell of the whisky or maybe it was the noise in the room behind him, but he couldn't seem to manage.

I came real close to getting stuck on her, he told himself. And he answered himself: What else was going to happen, shut up in a boat with her like that.

"God-damn bitch," he said aloud.

The bartender heard him and leaned over in his direction. "Who that?"

"Girl I used to know."

"Good looker?"

"Man," Inky said, "you'd dream about this one for a piece of strange."

The bartender chipped a sliver of ice and dropped it into Inky's water.

"Only she was fooling," Inky said.

"Huh?"

"She wasn't all that fond of her husband."

"Never are," the bartender said.

"Hey, Petie, hey!" somebody shouted in the room.

"She wasn't having anything to do," Inky said, "not with any-body." Man, she lay herself out on the deck, smearing oil all over herself. And you'd see her put it on and rub it all over and turn around and take off her bra. And you could tell by the way her back moved that she was rubbing it in her breasts—she'd rub herself all over and squirm because it was so good. She didn't need a man nor anybody else.

And Inky turned around and leaning back on the bar, began to watch the room.

Julius was waving at him. Inky nodded back.

Julius came up to him. "I been calling you. You gone deaf?"

"I didn't hear nothing."

"Sure I call you. I say: 'Petie, hey.'" Julius stopped and began to grin. A little grin that began at the corner of his mouth and kept spreading until it turned into a laugh and he had to bend over and slap his knees. "That ain't your name!"

"What?"

"Petie."

"No," Inky said.

A girl passed within arm reach. Julius patted her behind. She spun around. And glared at Inky for a minute.

"Look, lady," he said, "it wasn't me."

Julius chuckled. Her eyes swung over to him and hung still

for a minute. Then she began to giggle as she backed safely away.

"How'd you keep from getting your ears flattened?"

Julius waved his fat pink hands. "Me? Nobody going to take old Julius serious. Not no young man, he ain't going to get mad."

"I take you serious," Inky said. "I wouldn't let you get in ten feet of any woman of mine."

The little hands folded together solemnly. And Julius pursed his lips.

Inky worked away at his bottle steadily, not slugging himself all at once so that he would turn groggy. He was working himself into a beautiful glow. He hadn't had a good drunk like this in months.

"You getting a load there, man," Hector said.

"Don't you worry about me," Inky said.

"Long as you ain't a mean drunk."

"Me?" Inky said. "Who's drunk?"

"Okay," Hector said.

Cecile came up and rubbed her chin on his shoulder. "How's he making out?" she asked Hector as if Inky weren't there.

Inky said: "Ask me."

Those light-colored eyes of hers crinkled up in a grin. "How you doing?"

"Just great," he said. "Just plain great."

"Yea, I can see . . . you sure you don't want to dance?"

"How many times I got to tell everybody . . ."

"Okay," Hector said.

"If you do," Cecile said, "there's them around wouldn't find it any great trouble."

"Yea," Inky said. "I noticed one eying me for size."

Cecile laughed, out loud. "He don't need us," she said. "And I got to dance, me," Cecile pulled at Hector's arm. "Can't keep still."

They sidled away through the crowd. Inky went on drinking, carefully, building his glow.

That one girl, the one he had noticed, kept finding excuses to walk back and forth in front of him, never looking at him, but always looking him over. Inky tried to catch her eye, but she was far too quick.

She was good-looking: dark hair, dark eyes, and dark olive skin. There'd be Negro blood in her somewhere, Inky thought. She was wearing an orange dress—bright orange, the color of life-jackets—cut very full, so that it was always moving around her, always swirling, as if she were just stepping out of it.

One of the neon signs began flickering. Lacy Livaudais shook it, hard as he could. Steve, the other bartender, went over too, and tapped it with his fingernail. Nothing happened. So they both shrugged and forgot it.

The uncertain light made Inky's eyes twitch and burn. A tear went dripping down his left cheek. "Jesus," he said softly. He started outside, remembered and reached back for his bottle and took it along.

It was a hot night, moonless, with stars so bright and low that you'd think they were caught in the trees. It was still too, all you could hear was the high singing of mosquitoes and the little sucking sound of the surf, not fifteen feet away. The steps of the porch went down into the sand.

It'll go in a hurricane, Inky thought.

But what about the whole island, he wondered. There wasn't any height or real-looking substance to it. The wind and the Gulf together could lift it right off and scatter it all up and down the coast in a million billion pieces. But it hadn't gone—and nobody remembered to count the hurricanes that had passed while people were living here.

It made you dizzy, Inky thought, all the generations that had lived here and all the wind that had blown over them. . . . It was thoughts you never had unless you had a few drinks too.

Inky scratched his head and half sat on the railing. Over in the far corner of the porch on a little wicker settee a couple was necking. They did not seem to notice him.

The Gulf had turned black. Where'd the porpoises go, the ones that he had seen playing in the afternoon. Maybe some bigger fish was chasing them. He tried to remember. Maybe a barracuda.

The screen door opened behind him, but he did not bother.

"Man, you are a foxy one," a woman's voice said, "don't even leave his bottle out on the bar while he's gone."

The words and the voice registered slowly. When he looked there was only the back of the bright orange dress.

Son of a bitch, he told himself. And went back inside to the bar.

His glass was still there. And standing next to it was the tall thin boy he had met on the beach. Inky said: "You know anything that eats a porpoise?"

"Huh?" Perique just stared.

"Nothing," Inky said and felt his ears go hot, "I was just talking."

"What eats what?"

The ice was melted. Inky leaned across the bar. "I need some of this, might need a chaser." And to Perique he said: "I was just talking crazy. Forget it."

"Sure," Perique said.

There was a girl with him too, Inky had noticed her trim form. And now he noticed her face, and shook his head and looked again. "I sure do keep running into you."

Annie said: "You look like you having a good time."

"Come on," Perique said, "have a dance with me."

"Quit ordering me around," Annie snapped. "I didn't come with you."

"Who'd you come with?" Inky asked.

"Nobody," she said, "I'm big enough to find my way home."

Inky took another sip out of his bottle. "I guess you can if you want to."

She turned away from him, abruptly. "Let's try one," she said to Perique.

The girl in orange kept crossing back and forth.

She was alone too. Or at least, she was never alone. But she was never long with any one man.

The dress was cut low in back. You could see the two little points of her shoulder blades.

Inky finished his bottle. Lacy asked: "You want another?"

"Hell," Inky said, "I don't want to pass out."

"You got work to do yet tonight?" He scratched his bald skull through the felt cap.

"Maybe," Inky said.

A big brown hard-shelled beetle bumbled into his shirt and hung there. Inky flicked it down to the floor.

"Hey," Lacy said, "don't step on that. It's a stink bug."

"Get me a drink," Inky said.

"A bottle?"

He shook his head.

"Man, you losing ground," Lacy said.

The girl passed back again. Her legs were a little too thin. She was getting rid of her dancing partner.

"I got to get home," she was telling him. "I got to sleep sometime."

He was tugging at her arm, a thin wiry fellow. "C'mon, no? Best dancer in the place."

She pulled away. "Where I leave my purse?"

It was down at the far end of the bar. As she headed to it, Inky tossed off his drink and ducked out the door. He moved into the dark clump of little trees to the left of the building. Then he squatted down on the ground to rest. His head was singing, just a little.

She came out, finally, brushing back her hair with one hand. She came down the steps, and then stopped and took off her shoes. She giggled softly to herself as she walked along, holding them one in each hand.

Inky got to his feet very slowly.

"I'm coming," she said, "don't hurry me!"

How can she see me, Inky thought, unless she's got eyes like a cat. But he stepped out and touched her arm. She jumped back, gasping.

Inky stood looking after her, trying to understand, shaking his head slowly. "Wha's the matter," he asked her. "Wha's the matter?"

She took a couple more steps back until she brushed against a hackberry. The swirling skirts caught up on the heavy thorns.

Inky still hadn't moved. Something was wrong. And he was trying to understand, drunkenly. And then he noticed the other shadow, just down the path a little. Or maybe he heard the very faint click of the switch-blade knife.

He was too drunk. And fighting with a knife wasn't one of the things he wanted to do sober. So he didn't move.

The girl in the orange dress was keeping very still. You could hear her heavy breathing. You could tell she loved a fight.

Inky tried to stop his head swinging, tried to hold it still so he could see better. He used both hands finally, propped them one on each side of his chin.

The man had taken a step out into the white crushed-shell path. You couldn't see the knife, but he'd be holding it low.

The woman began carefully pulling her dress off the thorns. "Jesus," Inky said softly.

"Who you looking for?" the shadow said.

Inky rubbed at his eyes, and shuffled his feet on the ground, trying to be sure of his balance. For a second the red neon of the beer signs caught and reflected something. Button, Inky told himself. Or the blade.

He rubbed furiously at his eyes, trying to clear his head. He moved his shoulders: they felt stiff.

The woman still hadn't got her dress free. She was half bent over, twisted to one side, and she was working gently at each one. Calmly, as if she'd been out for a walk on a Saturday noonday.

"Son of a bitch," Inky whispered.

The man came out into the center of the path. A step or two closer. He wasn't hurrying, but he was coming.

And then there was somebody calling him. "Inky . . . Inky . . ." A soft little call. "Inky . . ." For a second he was not sure. He cocked his head, listening.

When the girl turned up at his side, he did not recognize her in the dark. "I been looking for you," she said.

He opened his mouth to answer and then closed it again.

She glanced up the path, as if seeing for the first time. "George?"

"What you come busting in for?"

"Whose busting?" She giggled. "I got as much right here as you," she said. "I got a right to meet my date, no?"

"What you coming here for?"

She just giggled. Inky went back to rubbing his eyes.

"Everybody real loaded," she said. And she slipped her arm into Inky's. "So dark you can't see much. . . ."

She turned him around, and they crossed in front of the Rendezvous and began to walk up the beach. "Let's go over to my porch," she said loudly.

They felt the other eyes following them down the beach. Inky stumbled in the sand. The girl laughed. "You real drunk. . . ."

They walked down the beach, almost half a mile. Inky felt the soft sound of the surf in one ear, and in the other the soft murmuring sound of the land life.

They turned inland. "This whole island's full of the god-damn paths."

"Sort of," she said.

They crossed under some twisted oak trees and were starting across a little meadow.

"Wait a minute," Inky said, "now wait a minute."

There was some kind of small flower underfoot. You could see them faintly in the dark.

"Wait a minute," he said. And he squinted at her face. "Be god damned," he said. "Annie."

"Let's go," she said.

"Thanks, kid." He would not move. "That was a real fine job."

"You know the way back to the boat?"

"Which boat?"

"Yours."

"Thought you said we were heading for your house."

She giggled nervously. "I was just talking," she gestured, "for them."

"Why not?"

"Well," she said, and paused for a minute, "my papa wouldn't like that."

"He's got a new wife," Inky said, "he won't notice."

You could feel her stiffen in the dark as the hurt got to her. She began to walk away.

He stumbled after her. "Sorry, honey," he said. "I'm drunk or I wouldn't say that."

She stopped but didn't answer.

"Show me the way back to the boat," he said.

*

HIS arm through hers was heavy and sometimes it seemed she was dragging him along. Now and then she had to stop for breath. He didn't say a word the whole time.

Once she said: "Watch where you step." And he didn't even seem to hear her.

They passed the Arcenaux store where a little light was still burning by the back door. Philomene always left that for Julius so he wouldn't trip when he came in.

Annie looked at the light when they went plodding past, the little glow behind the drawn shade. Philomene, now, Annie thought, she was a patient wife. What did they have to say, she wondered, on the nights when Julius stayed home.

Inky tripped again.

"That was a root," she said. "Pick up your feet."

They came to the wharf and there was the bay black and still with little points of stars reflecting, and the outlines of the luggers. And one tall mast.

"Come on," Annie said, "we're almost there."

Their feet were like hammers on the boards. They must be waking everybody on this side of the island, Annie thought, and she tried to move slower.

A couple of cats, who had been prowling around on a lugger, jumped over the side and scooted away between their legs.

"What the hell was that?" Inky said.

"Nothing. Cats."

If he fell in, Annie thought, what would happen? And she held on to his arm a little tighter.

We'd both drown . . . she thought. He wouldn't let go, and we'd both drown and in the morning, they'd find us, and they wonder what we were doing to fall in. . . .

And because she'd had a couple of drinks too, and the whole

211

world was shimmering and sad, she began to cry. Not sob, but cry. The tears were pouring down her face. Then, quick as they began, they stopped.

"Can you get aboard?"

He stepped slowly and carefully over the lifelines. "Can't go falling in the water."

He'd been thinking that too. Or maybe he could tell what she was thinking. . . . "No," she said.

She followed him on the deck. "Can you manage?"

He sat down for a moment on the carriage roof. "Don't worry, honey, I made it a lot drunker than this."

"I'll go light the lamp." The matches were by the stove, and the lamp right above. The light and the recent tears hurt her eyes and she stepped back. It was just a little pool of light—just a kerosene lamp—and she could stand on the edge of it.

"You can come on now," she said.

He swung himself down the hatch, not bothering with the little ladder.

"You did that the hard way."

"Never bother with ladders, honey," he said; "they really trip you."

He was leaning against the little icebox and fingering it as if he had never seen it before. Suddenly he tapped it sharply. "Let's have a drink."

"I had enough," Annie said.

He didn't seem to hear. He got two paper cups from a holder on the wall, found a bottle in one of the cabinets and poured a couple of drinks. "Even got ice." He got a couple of cubes and dropped them in.

"We so fucking fancy," he said and hesitated, looking around. "How come?" He pointed unsteadily to the lamp. "We got electricity."

"Didn't know where the mainswitch was," she admitted.

"Knew I wouldn't leave it on, huh?" Inky grinned. "Smart girl, smart like a schoolteacher . . ."

"This is lots of light," Annie said.

"Sure . . . but it's there, right there, under the ladder, see?"

"It's a nice boat," Annie said, "but I got to go home."

She wanted to leave, but the passageway was narrow and he

was standing in the middle. She could have pushed by, he didn't seem in any mood to stop her, but all of a sudden she didn't want to touch him.

"Sit down," he said.

There were two bunks, one on each side. She hesitated for just a minute. She felt strange sitting on a bed. . . . There's nowhere else, she told herself.

He handed her the cup, and then sat down on the opposite bunk. She felt relieved, and, way down, a little disappointed.

He did not say anything. There was just the very small sound of the almost still water against the hull. And a couple of night birds.

The lamp smoked for an instant, then cleared. The cubes of ice bumped against the paper cup she held in her hand. And the silence bothered her. She could feel herself breathing it in. Almost like being under water, and drowning.

She said, because she had to find something to say: "You really been drinking."

And then she was sorry, and wondered if he was going to be offended. He was slow in answering and she tried to think of an apology.

"I been drunker," he said.

"Nearly got yourself cut up." She sipped and looked at him over the rim of the cup.

"Son of a bitch," he said softly.

She watched him, sitting under the kerosene lamp, the yellow light making a kind of halo

"Tell me about your boyfriends," he said suddenly.

She frowned. And had a little flutter of panic. "You asked me that before."

"Tell me about the rest of it."

"I can't do that," Annie said.

"Answer my questions?"

"Maybe."

"Start with that tall thin fellow, the one tonight."

"Perique?"

"Yea."

She laughed and her fear relaxed a little. "Oh, him . . ."

"He's your boyfriend?"

"In a way." She felt better now, now that she'd had time to think. She could remember now and tell him, tell him carefully so that there wouldn't be any contradictions. She had thought it all out, long ago, all about the different ones who had been her lovers. She could close her eyes now and see some of them, she had imagined them so clearly. She could remember how they had kissed her even . . . but that was as far as she could feel. Even her daydreams had ended here. Had left her irritated.

"What way?"

"Huh?"

"You heard me," Inky said. "Don't be a sneaky little bitch."

"Well," she said and stared up at the carefully polished beams of the ceiling, "I didn't go to bed with him."

She watched Inky carefully. Her answer had surprised him. His face showed it. She felt better, more confident.

"He's a nice boy," she said, "but I just didn't feel that way about him."

"You got to feel that way?"

She said: "Don't you?"

"Sometimes," he said.

"And sometimes not?"

"Finish your drink," he said. "Don't make me waste it."

She took another small sip.

"Too strong?"

"Hell no," she said.

"Where'd you learn words like that?"

"Nowhere." It was hot in the cabin. She wondered how he could sleep here.

"In a convent?"

"Maybe," she said. He would live in this cabin, not the forward one—she was almost sure of that. But there wasn't a sign of him anywhere—not a jacket nor a cap, not a paper nor a book. The cabin was clear and spotless, like a picture advertisement for a boat.

"Tell me what it was like, in the convent."

"Sort of dull," she said.

"How many of the sisters made passes at you?"

"Well . . ." she did not quite understand. She was afraid to say yes and she did not want to admit a no.

Then she understood. "No," she said quickly. "Course not."

She began to wish she had stayed home, that she'd stayed home and not started the evening at all. Whenever she looked back now, she'd have to remember the unpleasantness. It was this business of remembering that annoyed her.

The evening had changed and there was a bad taste in her mouth.

"Didn't want to hurt your feelings," Inky said, "I was just asking about what I'd heard."

"You know some funny people," she said. She sounded peevish though she hadn't meant to, and she was sorry.

"Forget it," Inky said.

The first thing she knew she was crying was the little splash of a tear on her hand. She looked at it in surprise. "What sort of night is it?" She went and looked out the hatch, and wiped her eyes while her back was turned.

"Come on," he said. "Tell me more about your boyfriends."

"Well," she said. And she turned her memory back on the big gray stone building, with its stained-glass windows in the long halls, and the little red glasses of vigil lights in all the corners, and the smell of furniture polish so strong in closed rooms you could hardly breathe. And Beatriz, lovely and old for her age, moving down the corridors with a slow step and a soft wiggle of her behind that no amount of nuns' scoldings could change. Beatriz, with her heavy-lashed eyes, that she mascaraed secretly every morning.

"No," she said, "it wasn't me."

But the more she thought the more she remembered: the dark wine-red color of Beatriz's robe gliding down the black linoleum-floored hall. And the ring Beatriz had pinned to her bra. And the lights of the car flickering through the leaves and the trunks for just a second before they switched off.

And looking back, she *was* Beatriz. She could feel her lips form the characteristic half-smile, sleepy and alert all at once. And when she turned away from the open hatch, she had the slow walk and the soft little wiggle.

"I don't want to talk about it," Annie said and her voice had taken on a very faint accent.

"Why not?"

She sat down on the bunk and her fingers touched the left bra strap, the way Beatriz did.

"It was sad," she said, "and I don't want to remember it." She felt so confident now.

"What happened?" Inky frowned in the effort to see her more clearly. "He go off with somebody else?"

"Please. . . ." She hissed her s's just slightly and looked away in disgust.

"Why didn't you keep him?"

"There are some things—" she hesitated just a little, "beyond help." That sounded good so she repeated the phrase: "Beyond help."

"Why?" He was pouring himself another drink. "He leave town or something?"

She was fingering the little clasp on the strap; it could have been a ring. "He left—in a way."

"You sound like he died."

She was a little surprised: the idea had not occurred to her. She stood up and peered out the little porthole, and she lifted her chin the way Beatriz would have done.

Of course he had died: he was killed in a car crash.

She was crying now, really meaning it now. But still she held her chin up.

The tears were very warm on her face and she could feel them spreading out, spreading out, until her whole body was warm and tingling.

She was so busy with her make-believe grief that she did not notice Inky until he came and sat beside her. She jumped—just a little. She couldn't help that.

"Have a drink," he said.

She shook her head, but he took her cup and filled it.

"Look," he said, "you got troubles, I got troubles. Nothing so different in that."

She hardly heard him. She was thinking clearly—so clearly that it seemed like she was talking out loud—If I'm going, I have to go now. And if I stay, I can't cry tomorrow. Because I'm sober enough now. And I could go up that ladder and go straight home.

She thought about that: going up the ladder step by step. She could feel that hard surface under the balls of her feet. Then the deck, then the wharf boards.

She stared down at the brownish-yellow mixture in her cup. "That looks strong," she said, and leaned back.

Inky's arm was across the back cushions. And her neck rested on it at an uncomfortable angle, but she did not move. It would look too funny, she thought.

"Want some music?"

"You get anything this late?"

"All-night station in New Orleans."

"Where's the radio?"

"There." He pointed to her left.

"Okay." He reached his right arm across her. "Can't make it," he said. "Got to move."

His arm brushed across her throat. "Lemme get one swallow first," she said, forcing herself to sound calm.

His arm stayed where it was. "Move," she said. She took a couple of swallows and sat up.

He leaned behind her this time and turned on the radio. She could feel the heat of his body and she wondered how anybody could sleep down in the cabin.

She asked him: "How can you sleep down here?"

He straightened himself up. "Sleep on deck," he said.

The radio was on, very softly. Annie cocked her head listening. "I'm real glad to know about that station."

"Nice in a car at night."

She sipped at her cup, not quite sure what to say.

"Drink up."

She hesitated.

"Won't hurt you."

She swallowed quickly, shivering a little as the liquid burned down her throat and chest.

He grinned. "Feel that?"

"Right here." She put a finger to her chest.

He put a hand on top of hers. "There, huh?"

She nodded.

"Rubbing helps." He began to massage her hand around, a small circle in the middle of her chest, rubbing fairly hard so that she squirmed a little as the bra straps cut her shoulders.

"Quit," she said.

He got up and fixed her another drink without a word. She stood up too, shaking out her skirt.

"One thing been bothering me," he said.

"What?" There was a stubborn crease in the skirt; she tried to pull it out between her fingers.

"Story about the guy in New Orleans—that true?"

"Sure it is," she said.

"You been to bed with a man, huh?"

She gave a little snickering laugh, more from embarrassment than anything else. And turned to look at the papers on the little hanging table. There were a couple of pens and a bottle of India ink and some water colors there.

"You been drawing?"

He did not answer. She shuffled the papers. For a minute in the dim light, she did not believe what she saw.

It was an ink sketch, done with great care—a naked woman, lying on her back, her legs open.

"Got a better one," Inky said, and hunted until he found it: a nude sleeping on the sands of some beach, her sun hat over her face.

"Oh," Annie said.

"They bother you?"

"No," Annie said. And that was the truth. She was surprised, and she was startled by the beauty of the women's bodies. Do you suppose, she asked herself, I'll look like that someday?

"I get five bucks or so for these," Inky said, "in New Orleans."

"You do?"

"Sure," he said, "They color 'em up for the tourists."

"Oh." She took the drink from his hand and went back to the couch. The radio was still playing.

"Pick up a lot extra money that way."

She put her nose down in the paper cup, sniffing the bourbon. "Didn't know you could draw."

"Sort of," he said. "Want me to do one of you?"

"Like that?"

"Sure," he said, "I wasn't ever very good with faces, never could get a likeness."

She shook her head.

"Why not?" he said. "I bet you got a cute shape."

She buried herself in the cup, blushing with the compliment. Her ears were singing now, very steadily. "No," she said.

"Okay," he said. "It's a shame."

She was a little groggy and very hot. "I don't see how you can take it down here," she said. "I'm burning up."

"Slip off the dress," he said. "It's too pretty to get it sweaty and wet."

She was thinking that over when his fingers were quickly opening the buttons of the blouse. By the time she'd decided to say no, he had the blouse thrown back and the soft fingers were dragging the bra down.

"No," she said uncertainly.

"Listen to the radio," Inky said, "and finish your drink."

The fingers fastened themselves to her nipple, coaxingly.

"Look," he said, "why didn't you tell me, for Chrissake?"

"What," she said, "what?"

"I ask you."

"What?"

"If you'd been to bed with a man before."

"I was."

"Oh sure," he said, "oh sure. . . . Look at the cushion."

"I'll clean it."

"God damn," Inky said thickly. "I didn't want anything to do with a god-damn virgin."

Even through the whisky she could feel that hurt.

"It gets light early," Inky said.

She was barely listening. The whisky had worn off, leaving her with a sodden heavy feeling. I'll feel god awful tomorrow, she thought.

And then, surprised, she had to add, tomorrow is here now.

"Know what time it is?"

She shook her head.

"Just about four-thirty."

"You don't have a clock."

"There." He turned her head, so that she saw the little green luminous numbers. "See."

She yawned deeply.

"Don't you think you better get home?"

She was so tired she could hardly hold her head up.

"You don't want people to see, do you?"

She kept thinking, tomorrow is here now.

"C'on, honey. I'll walk you home."

The gulls were beginning to scream. It must be near morning. She wanted so badly to go to sleep.

His hand on her arm urged her up the ladder. On the deck she stopped: the little fresh air made her feel better. "Give me the comb," she said.

He handed her the one from his shirt pocket. "It's clean, all right."

She jerked it through her hair quickly. "That'll do."

Did he kiss her good-by, she wondered. And was too unsure to look at his face to see. Or maybe she was supposed to do something. She tried to think but her thoughts kept scattering like water drops. There was something . . . something . . .

"Don't fall," he said when she swung over to the dock.

"Water might feel good," she had a tired little smile. She tried to put the faint little accent back in her words, but somehow she couldn't manage it.

"Can you make it?"

She took a couple of sharp breaths. Her body ached all over. Standing up brought a pain to the pit of her stomach, a pain she hadn't noticed before.

"I'll walk you home."

"No," she said. "You stay here."

"Now look . . .

"You couldn't find you way back in the dark. And maybe George got a real drunk on—wait for him to sober up before you run into him."

There was something that should be done. There was something that needed to be done. And now knowing, she began to feel restless and embarrassed.

"Can't let you do that," Inky said and he scratched his close-cut brown hair.

"Oh hell," Annie said. Her head felt clearer. She wanted to stay and she wanted to leave. "I can take care of myself."

"Don't be mad," Inky said.

"Who's mad?" She wasn't. She swore she wasn't. She tried to remember Beatriz, tried to imagine herself Beatriz again. She closed her eyes to try. She would have the image for a minute, but then it would fall to pieces.

"I just didn't want people seeing you here."

"I can take care of myself." The pain in her stomach was making her sick. She wanted to go home.

"I don't know," Inky said doubtfully and scratched his ear.

"You'll just get lost," she said, and she had already turned away with the nasty taste of confusion in her mouth. "Me, I'm used to it."

She moved off down the pier, stepping carefully on the rickety boards. Inky watched her out of sight, but she did not once turn or wave.

As she got to the end of the wharf and turned off it to the path, she noticed somebody sitting quietly on the big rusty windlass that had been abandoned there years ago. Somebody waiting, out of sight of the *Pixie*. She noticed without any emotion at all that the sitting figure was Perique.

She passed within five feet of him. For a minute or so she wondered whether he was going to take a knife or his fists to her—if he were drunk, he might. He sat with his feet tucked up under him and his arms wrapped around his knees. He was not asleep, she was sure of that, but he didn't move at all when she passed him.

The dogs were barking down at the western end of the island. From the sound they'd have something treed.

The barking always sounded muffled at night, she thought.

Against the uneven shells of the path, her shoes slipped and jogged.

If I take them off, she thought. But her fingers, hanging down from her hands, felt stiff and heavy. So she didn't bother.

I'm moving hard, she thought, but I'm not moving fast.

From a chinaberry tree an owl stared down at her, and then flapped silently away.

Evil eye, she thought, that's what they used to say. Owl looks at you, devil looks at you.

She crossed herself with a small vague movement.

You weren't supposed to kill an owl. They said if you did,

you'd be killing your three-times great-grandmother. Boys did, sometimes, but never on purpose, and though they fell to laughing and joking about it, they had a different and a scared tone.

A cricket now . . . that was the same sort of thing. He was your three-times great-grandfather, they said. If a cricket got in the house you weren't supposed to kill it, the way you did roaches and ants. You chased it out, but not with the broom, with the feather duster.

There were crickets all around now, singing. They'd hush when she passed, and then take up again when she'd gone. It was like she was moving in a well of silence, carrying it with her.

And if a cricket got to singing in the house . . . and if a cricket sang in the house during the night, that was a death.

Before her mother had died, hadn't she woke up one night to find a cricket sitting in the corner of the room, singing. And hadn't her screaming gotten the whole house up. . . .

They were the color of death, black, shiny black, like the limousines at funerals in New Orleans. And when you looked at them close, at their nubby head and their bone-thin bodies, they were the shape of death too.

There'd be a time when one would come and sit in the corner of her bedroom, and wake her at night with his singing, his coming, his singing for her.

Her thighs hurt so, and the bottom of her stomach. She pressed both hands to it as she walked along. Her head was hurting now and her eyes felt dry and burned.

There was a little breeze had come up, a little warm breeze that was off the swamps to the north. You could smell the swamps in it: the heavy sweet-sour rotting. A rooster gave a sharp loud crow.

The breeze would drop soon, and it would be so still that the mosquitoes would come in clouds. And first there'd be a greenish sky and then the sun would come up, white and burning.

Even as she kept moving, she was watching the sky. But it was still all dark, except for the stars and the pale old moon that was just beginning to rise.

She passed her own gate. She had to turn and go back to it. She had trouble with the latch. Her fingers didn't seem to be strong enough to pry it open. The big black dog her father had trained to be a hunter came out from under the house, growling.

"Sh. . . ." she whispered. The dog flattened, his head stretched out, fawning. She patted him. "Sisss. . . ."

I'm sneaking home, she told herself. Like I was still in the convent. . . . "There's nobody here to mind," she told the dog aloud.

At her words all the crickets for a hundred yards around stopped suddenly, and the dark got thick and silent. She could almost feel them—and all the other creatures that lived in the brush—staring at her, watching her, waiting for her to leave.

She patted the dog again. And she began to feel fear tickle up her scalp. She turned and hurried into the house, tripping on the top step and falling full length on the porch. She was in the front hall and hobbling down its length to her room when she remembered that she had lost one shoe. And went back to get it.

The black dog came in with her, squeezed in between her legs. She heard him pad into the living-room and wheeze with contentment as he stretched out on the sofa.

"You'll catch it in the morning," she told him aloud. "He beat the hide off you."

The hall was dark too, and she tripped again on the little piece of rug in front of her door. But she got inside and stretched out on the bed, in her clothes, watching the ceiling go past like a merry-go-round. After a while, when the sky was beginning to lighten and the chickens were stirring around in the yard under the window, she sat up and pulled the dress over her head.

She ached. She ached all over, and she was nauseated. Her stomach hurt, like there was something inside moving, tearing her. She was terribly hot, and she was too tired to take off her slip. She lay very still and felt the sweat run down the curve of her body.

She wanted to cry, but she couldn't. Her eyes were dry and wide. It was broad daylight—and had been light for several hours —before they sagged closed.

* * * *

THE MARSH

~~~~~~~~~~~~

THAT Sunday started the way the fourth Sunday in the month always started. Jack Roualt (it was his turn) got up at six o'clock, shook the hangover out of his head with cold water and a whole pot of coffee, and started out in his little boat—the half-cabin fifteen-footer—to get the priest.

He got there a good two hours before the priest was ready to leave. And he spent the time walking up and down the street, watching the girls as they came out from Mass. There was always a line of men, leaning on the rail outside the church. (It had once been a hitching-rail.)

Around ten o'clock the priest was ready, and they headed off top speed for the island. The priest was going to hear confessions before Mass, say Mass quick as he decently could, and go hurrying back for his late, and warmed-over, dinner at the rectory.

And just about that time too, Eddie and Mike Livaudais dropped into their beds for a couple hours' sleep before they went on with the hunt.

That particular Sunday, no different. Except, maybe, that people got up later than usual, feeling brittle from the alcohol. None of the boats went out working. And the kids played in whispers around the houses or went off to the west end.

. . .

224

It was a little after ten when Al and Adele Landry finished breakfast. One corner of the kitchen was stacked with grocery boxes full of her stuff—she had not had time to unpack that. But there were new curtains at the window—her curtains, from the other house—and her china was on the table. Not bad, she told herself, for two days.

They were quiet, breathing into the hot thick silence of the morning. Adele could almost feel her mind running from one job to the other, deciding what to do and which to do first. And coming always back to the thing that was bothering her.

Finally she said it aloud: "It's not like you knew where she was."

"Who?" Al asked sleepily.

"Annie."

Al stretched and yawned and kicked the table so that the coffee cups rattled and the brown liquid sloshed into the saucer.

"You didn't hear her," Adele said, "this morning?"

"Maybe," Al reached out and patted his wife's hand, "maybe."

Adele looked worried. Her heavy brown eyebrows were crinkled. "And that means she was with some man, for sure."

Al nodded. "My girl, she is not queer, che'."

She clucked her tongue. "She is a nice girl. But she is too pretty for that."

"Never too pretty."

Adele spread her hands out on the oilcloth. "Look now," she said. "Me, I can be a little careless where I go. I am not so young anymore. And I am never pretty."

"You out of you god-damn mind."

"No." She shook her head. "I know this for a long time, and it does not bother me."

Al tilted his chair back and stared at her, at the smooth clean lines of the brown hair pulled back from her face into a roll. "Face like a 'tit ange . . ."

She got up and, taking the frying-pan off the stove, put it in the dishpan. "I am worried about it."

"I can tell, me," he grinned. "You just went and put the pan full of grease in your dishwater."

She yanked it out.

"You are worried, for sure."

She dipped the pan back in so hard that suds sloshed over the edge of the sink. "When her own father does not worry . . ." She stopped and began to scrub out the grease.

Al took a little crayola-shaped cylinder off one of the shelves, went over to the big mirror by the sink, and began to wax the tips of his mustache.

"And we going to fight so soon. . . ." Her voice was a little unsteady.

"Who fighting?" he asked. "I ain't."

She didn't answer. He put the cover on his tube of wax and put it back on the shelf. Then he came over and patted her behind. "Look, che'," he said, "what I can do to stop her?"

She did not answer. She hung up the pan.

"See," he said, "you can't think of nothing. I can't think of nothing. There is nobody nowhere can think of anything to stop the kids from doing what they bound to do."

"Won't do her no good," Adele said.

"Maybe," Al said, "maybe not. Nothing to do about it. Like the hurricane, no? Nothing to do."

Adele went to church. She left the minute the bell began to ring, and that was the minute the priest stepped off the boat.

Al turned on the living-room radio loud and took a rocking-chair out on the porch. There was a baseball game coming from New Orleans and he didn't want to miss it.

Adele did not go to confession. She couldn't think of anything that she had done, anything that might be a mortal sin. And she never went to confession just for venial sins, though a priest had told her once it was a good idea. After all these years she was still afraid of going into that little black box with its musty velvet curtains, and the face behind the little wood lattice.

But she liked going to church. Back home she went to High Mass every Sunday. . . . The priest came only once a month and there was never a High Mass on the island, Al said. The priest didn't bother; there weren't any trained altar boys, and there wasn't a choir. Maybe, she thought, on Christmas Eve or All Saints' Day or Easter, Al will get the boat and take me over to Port Ronquille. . . .

The incense and the singing, and the organ roaring so that her ears tingled—she always sat way back in the church, under the organ loft, so that she could hear the loudest. She would carry the sound in her head for hours after.

The island church was small and white painted. And in black letters over the front door the words *Maris Stella*—there was more to the inscription but it had washed away because nobody bothered repainting more than the two words. The church was set up on the same high foundations as the houses. Under it a couple of chickens and a nanny goat were grazing. The bell was hung from a ten-foot scaffolding built just to the right of the front door.

The steps of the church at Port Ronquille were always crowded just before Mass—people gossiping, people getting a last cigarette before it was time to go inside. Here there was just a stray dog sleeping in the shade of a jasmine bush.

Inside the confessional was empty: she hesitated a moment by the dusty curtain. The church was nearly empty too. Up in the front row, strung out like black beads on a thread, were four black-scarved women. Old women, from their hunched shoulders.

Adele sat down in the second to last pew. A small boy came in the sanctuary, a lighted candle in each hand. He put both on the altar, made a little ducking bow and disappeared.

Up in the front row wood rosaries clattered on the seats. And one of the old women began to whisper to the other, in a high-pitched hissing voice.

And then the priest came out, moving with great long steps that swirled his cassock and shook the whole building. One of the candles went out. He lit it impatiently from the second. Then he sighed and began, pausing only a breath for the responses no one was there to make.

Adele could not follow him in the missal. His words were not clear enough for her to understand. She closed the book and put it on the seat behind her. And watched. He had just whirled to the right side of the altar and began what she knew must be the epistle, when the crowd of people came in. They scurried up the center aisle and stumbled into the pews: women, all women, Adele noticed, and children. Only some half-grown boys. And not a single man.

Adele folded her hands and turned her eyes back to the altar.

The second candle had gone out again. But the priest did not seem to notice or mind anymore.

Why did there have to be candles, she wondered. But there were, whole batteries of them, at big weddings and funerals and big holy days. When she got married the first time, there'd been whole lines of candles on the altar and a priest in white, white satin vestments with little tracings of gold thread. She had been close enough to notice that.

It was hard for her to remember now what Bob Reynal looked like. And it wasn't that long, she reminded herself. She felt a twinge; maybe she should have. She shook her head, very slowly, to herself: she didn't and that was all there was to it. A year after he died, she had slipped the wedding-ring off her finger—because she was afraid of losing it, she told people—and had rarely put it back. She lived very quietly, and she was no more lonesome than she had been before he'd appeared.

The house, the pension, the boy Claudie—she should have remembered him better. But the house looked just like a dozen others in the town of Port Ronquille; and the money came from a government check; and the boy was her image and nobody else's.

He was gone, clean gone, the way chalk is when a blackboard's been wiped with water.

When she thought about it, looked at it that way, she had a funny feeling. She was almost angry with him. He had cheated her. He had not made her miss him. He was just gone. And he had taken his memory with him.

She got to her feet for the Gospel. Some of the people around her stood, leaning against the pew in front of them. Most did not move.

For a minute she was uncertain. But of course not, she told herself. If there was one thing she knew, it was what to do at Mass.

She'd expected a sermon: she rather liked them. But the priest just whirled around and with a *Dominus vobiscum* went on to the Creed.

She sighed very lightly. And went back to her own thoughts.

Al now, if anything happened to him—and she crossed herself quickly—she would miss him.

Nothing will happen to him, she promised herself. He was just one year older. It'll be me die first, she thought.

A couple of pews in front of her there was a boy Claudie's age. She found herself watching him. Looked like a nice boy. Was the water on the island good, she wondered. Back in Port Ronquille people said the water was bad. But most of the kids around looked healthy. . . .

And would they play with Claudie, when they got used to him? They weren't now, for sure. And it almost broke her heart yesterday to see him stand in the front yard or on the porch and watch the kids go past, busy at something, with never so much as a glance at him.

"They get used to him," Al told her when she asked him. "Let 'em alone. Kids like to go slow."

And he said to her: "He don't look the picture of misery."

It was hard to tell about the boy, she thought, but he seemed happy. And he had taken such a great liking to his stepsister.

One evening over in Port Ronquille, when Al was visiting her, she'd asked about his daughter, was she pretty. And Al had looked surprised and said no. But maybe Annie had changed in the year she was away. Or maybe her father just didn't notice.

Adele remembered the stumbling steps she had heard in the hall early this morning. That was natural enough. For a pretty girl. She herself had never done anything like that: she'd never had more than three drinks at any time in her life. And she had never come home just before daylight on a Sunday morning.

But then, Adele thought, you had to be fair. Nobody had ever asked her. She went to the dances at Port Ronquille sometimes when she was a girl. There were always men to dance with her and take her home. But she'd been so quiet and shy and—even in her thought she hesitated at the word—not a bit pretty. There never was anyone hanging around, feeding her drinks, trying to go to bed with her.

"I got to be fair," she whispered to herself. "I can't take it out on her."

And maybe too, as Annie got a little older, she'd get prettier. And there'd be more men.

What was that like, Adele wondered, having all those eyes on you. . . . She ought to have been sorry that she'd missed that.

But she wasn't. She was still shy.

And who was it last night, she thought. Maybe that tall, terribly thin boy—what was his name—Perique.

She blinked and shifted her eyes back to the altar. The last Gospel . . . so soon . . . she stood up. And then the prayers . . . for the Intentions of the Holy Father, for Peace. The beginnings of each prayer cut across the ragged responses to the preceding one. The priest was in a hurry.

Everything will turn out all right, she told herself. Only a crazy fool worries like me.

Just the same maybe a special prayer. . . . And she tried to think of the proper saint . . . St. Ursula maybe, a young girl too. And Annie had stopped with the Ursulines in New Orleans.

But the Mass was over and the people were filing out. And she did not like to stay kneeling while they passed and looked at her.

She knocked over the little prayer bench in her haste. Even at that she was among the last.

Everybody was going home, even hurrying a little in the heat. Everybody except a group standing over by the bell. They had not been in the church, she was sure of that, but now they seemed to be waiting for something. For the instant she stood above them, on the top step, she noticed that they were not wearing hats—though everybody else did in the summer sun—and their hair was combed and shining.

It was a struggle to keep herself from staring at them as she walked slowly past. She was even afraid to look hard enough to see if she knew them . . . nobody else gave any sign of noticing them.

She did see that they were dressed up. In the hot sun she could smell the clean cotton as she passed by. And even with downcast eyes she could see the sharp fresh creases in their pants.

She would have asked . . . but there was no one. People bowed to her and smiled, but not one of them stopped to talk.

Because there was nothing else to do, she walked home.

*

THEY were all Livaudais men—there was Eddie and his son Pete, and his brothers Mike and Phil, and Phil's three sons; and there were relatives by marriage: Chep Songy and his son Jerry, and Ray Songy too, both of them brothers of Belle Livaudais.

There were ten of them that Sunday morning, standing in the church yard after Mass. They waited until the church was empty, then they went around to the sacristy door. The priest was just coming out, in his hand his little black doctor's bag. His face was red with perspiration, and he had taken off his stiff Roman collar.

"A scorcher," he said gaily.

The men did not smile. Eddie Livaudais cleared his throat, "Father," he said, "we got business with you."

"On a day like this," Stanislaus Ryan grinned, "nobody should have any business, except sitting down."

"We got business," Eddie repeated.

"And it is so pressing as all that?"

Eddie nodded.

"Well then, man," Father Ryan said briskly, "we'll talk about it walking down to the boat."

They started off then. Eddie and the priest walking ahead, the others following two by two. Pete came last. He walked slowest, and every now and then he stumbled over his own feet.

They met a group of women on the path, who stepped aside to let them pass. Even the kids stopped playing to stare after them.

"And this must be a very serious matter," Father Ryan said.

Eddie nodded. And from behind Mike said: "Serious for sure."

The priest did not interrupt his brisk pace. "And everyone seems to know about it."

"People come to find out," Phil said.

"And there is something I can help?"

"In a way," Eddie said slowly.

231

"If you don't tell me I'll never find out."

"I'm trying to," Eddie said, "only my mind don't work so fast when I got to walk too."

The priest stopped dead in his tracks. In the close ranks behind, the men scuffed toes, bumped into each other and stopped. "Now tell me."

Eddie took a deep breath. "I got two boys. One of them standing back there, right back there."

The priest turned around. "And where is he?"

The other men stepped aside to the edges of the path, and Pete Livaudais was hustled up through the passage. The boy kept looking at the ground, but he stuck out his hand.

"A fine boy," the priest said, noticing the carefully ironed shirt and the black hair plastered to the skull with water and oil.

The hand he shook so heartily was cold and damp—on a steaming day.

"Another Livaudais," Eddie was saying, "name Henry."

"Sure, sure, sure, sure," the priest said. "Though I haven't caught sight of him in some little time now."

Eddie shook his head, silently.

"He ain't been seen," Mike Livaudais answered for him, "for eight days now."

The priest put his black satchel down on the shell path. "What?"

Mike took a deep breath and let it out in a sigh. "He gone hunting. He take his shotguns and his pirogue."

"So that's it." The priest's voice was hollow, all of a sudden, and flat.

Mike nodded. "And he don't come back."

"God have mercy on him," the priest said automatically. He turned and stared, through the riggings of the luggers, over the expanse of bay, to the saw-grass prairie, greenish yellow under the hot sun. "And does nobody keep the kids at home?"

"A boy sort of got to go out and look around," Eddie said, and the group mumbled agreement.

"He wasn't even a man." The priest got a handkerchief and mopped his face.

"He got lost, him," Phil Livaudais said softly—sadly but without anger.

Damn their resignation, the priest thought.

"A boy got to look around," Chep Songy said.

"And does he have to go killing himself." The priest slapped at the circling flies with his handkerchief.

"We got to die," Mike said, "for sure."

Father Ryan rubbed his face again, even harder.

"Maybe," Eddie said quietly and almost patiently—as if he were explaining something to a very young child. "But we been living like that all our lives, and we ain't like to change now."

"Maybe he ain't dead," Pete said softly.

Nobody answered. And nobody looked at him. It was all very still—just the jays screaming at each other in the mulberry trees. Then the priest picked up his satchel quickly and walked down the path.

They followed him without saying a word—only the far-off crying of kids, and the squaak of a cat—until they had got to the wharf itself.

"Who is it now," the priest said, "to take me back?"

"He wasn't married, for sure," Chep Songy said, "but he got a family."

"And why do they always go?" the priest asked and his voice shook. "Only a month ago, there were three of them in the swamps around Petit Prairie."

"Got to die, one year or the other."

Stanislaus Ryan shook his head. And turned to the line of moored boats. "Not so many of you are working on a Sunday," he said.

"We stay home," Chep Songy said, "to look. . . ."

That was just so much money less, the priest thought with a start, for the living. So much less for the living to eat because of the time it took to find the dead.

And none of this was thoughts he should be having. . . .

"You talking like he's dead," Pete said. His voice, normally high-pitched—the voice of a boy—was squeaky and shrill. "Maybe he ain't."

A little more, the priest thought, and the boy would be hysterical.

Mike reached one hand up, scratching in the hair that grew so low it gave him only an inch of forehead. "We come to ask you something."

"I will say a Mass for him in the morning."

Eddie waved an impatient hand at the interruption. "We got to die," he said, "but we don't got to leave ourselves lay out in the swamps."

The men murmured agreement.

Mike said: "My nephew, he was young and he make a mistake, but he don't have to stay out in the marsh like a muskrat."

"Animals eating his clothes and his skin and his meat."

"My bones," Pete said, and his voice was quavering like a woman's. "I can feel it like it was me."

Somebody mumbled a reply.

"Stop it," the priest said and swung with his satchel at the big green flies. "If he has died, God will take care of him."

"When old Anton, he drowned," Eddie said quietly, as if he had not heard, "they went back into Orange Bay, you remember?"

The priest shook his head.

"Maybe that was before you come . . . and they took candles and a priest with them."

The priest smashed a fly against his trouser leg, leaving a smear of blood.

"And they put the candles on squares of wood and lit 'em and set 'em adrift," Chep Songy said. "And the candles they draw Anton up from the bottom. They draw him right up to them."

"And maybe, they don't do that, they show us which direction we start looking in," Phil Livaudais said.

"Such a big prairie to find a man in," Ray Songy added. And that was the only word he said the whole time.

A gull circled overhead and gave its long trumpeting call.

"The candles showed them where he was." Pete's body was shaking all over, like a malaria chill.

"Ferm' ta babeche!" somebody muttered.

"And you want me to do that?"

They nodded.

"And if there was any use to it," Father Ryan said, "I'd stay and do it. . . . But it can't work. And there's the CYO meeting tonight that can't go on without me. . . . And there's no use in any of this," he added.

Eddie, Phil Livaudais, and his three boys turned and walked away, without a look over their shoulders, without a word.

Their silence bothered Stanislaus Ryan. "I'm not telling you no," the priest said. "The poor boy's got a right to rest in holy ground."

Chep Songy left. One arm over Pete's shoulder, he turned him around gently. The boy was still shivering.

"If God wills," the priest said, "you will find him, right here, without any candles or any hunting."

Jerry and Ray Songy turned off and disappeared around the ice-house. Only Mike was left.

"And you're the one to take me home," the priest said.

Mike nodded. They went to his boat. The priest put his bag in the wheelhouse and looked around expectantly. Mike had gone over and lifted the cover of the engine hatch. His chin on one hand, he was looking inside.

"What's the matter, man?" Father Ryan said.

"Nothing," Mike said, "only I got a bit of trouble here."

The priest went back to the wheelhouse and sat down. Mike studied the engine for a few more minutes, then got to his feet.

"Where are you going?"

"Maybe it the battery," he said. "I got to go see about getting it checked."

He jumped over to the dock and hurried off. It was then about one o'clock.

*

IT was around one o'clock too when Annie finally got out of bed. She picked her good dress off the floor where she had dropped it and she put her shoes under the bed. The slip in which she had slept was wet through with perspiration. She took it off, yanking it roughly when it stuck over her shoulders. She hung the slip and bra by their straps from the loop of the window shade. Maybe they'll dry out fresh enough, she thought. Probably won't, she answered herself.

Annie went and looked out the window. She put both hands on the sill and leaned her weight on them as she stretched out the window. There was nobody in sight. Even the hens had gone into the shade.

If there *was* anybody there, she thought, they could see me. Wouldn't they be shocked to see me, standing in the window naked on a Sunday afternoon.

There was a wide slant of sun just barely touching the sill. Thrusting out her chest she touched her nipples to the white warmth. It tingled, way up under her armpits. She tried to touch her breast with her mouth. She doubled her neck and craned her tongue and pushed up with her hand. If they were just bigger, she thought, if they just were . . .

Nose to shoulder, she sniffed at her skin. A faint odor of sweat, and saliva and a heavy sweet odor, mostly tobacco. She crinkled her nose. That was enough to make you sick. If bodies just didn't smell so. And if you just didn't have to keep taking baths. Back at the convent there had been a long room, white tiled, walls and floor, with a row of white tubs, five of them. Every day she had gone in, carrying her towels and piece of soap. She could tell in a second if the tubs were busy or not; she did not even have to look in them. She was too shy to look directly, but she could tell in a second if there was an empty tub. Her eyes would flick down

236

the wall at the row of black nuns' robes hung on white hooks against the white tile. If there was a vacant space in the row she scurried down and took it. She only felt relaxed when she was stretched out in the tub, staring straight at the ceiling.

Sometimes when the room was empty she'd spent half an hour in the tub, stretching and sloshing the water over her body. . . . But here on the island she didn't like bathing at all; she did no more of it than she had to.

She sniffed again at her skin. And now she would have to.

Her father called at the door: "Game's on."

"No thanks," she said, "I'm busy."

"You used to like it."

That was true. She'd always listened with him on a Sunday afternoon.

"I got plenty to do," she said.

He put his head in the door.

"Hey," she said, and felt her ears go red, "get out of here."

"What eating on you?"

"Get out," she yelled, "I'm dressing."

"Jesus God," he said quietly, "I been seeing you without no clothes ever since you was a baby."

She rushed at the door and slammed it closed. There were no locks in the house, so she leaned against it.

"Jesus God," he said again slowly.

"I ain't a baby," she yelled through the door, "you got to remember I ain't a baby. . . . You got to quit walking in . . . I'm getting a lock."

He went back to the porch: she heard the rocker begin.

She stood leaning with one shoulder against the door—she didn't know how long. She wasn't thinking of anything. She was just listening: to the little house sounds, to the sounds of the still afternoon, to her own heart pounding. Finally she heard the quick light steps of Adele.

If she comes in, Annie thought, I'll throw her out. And she's not so big I can't do it either.

But the steps stopped still out in the hall. "Annie?"

Annie let her call two or three more times before she answered. "What?"

"Are you sick?"

"Jesus!" Annie leaned her head back against the door and shrieked. "Jesus Christ . . . there's nothing wrong with me. Nothing at all."

"You going to eat dinner with us?" Adele's careful speech did not change. She did not seem the slightest annoyed or upset.

"Sure," Annie said. "I got to eat. . . . Don't I live here? . . . Don't I get to eat here?"

"We getting ready to eat dinner."

"You inviting me?"

Adele did not answer. Annie listened while she walked away. "Al, I'm putting dinner out," she heard her say.

Annie turned back in the room. And put on a pair of shorts and a shirt. Without washing her face she dabbed on some powder and lipstick, gave her hair a quick brush. Then she closed the door very carefully behind her and went to the porch.

They were there and seated at the table, the boy Claudie between them. He was the first one to see her; he flashed his wide baby-tooth grin, and they looked around.

"Hey there," her father said, "we didn't think you'd make it until tomorrow."

"I thought she would," Adele said quickly. "I told you she'd make it."

"I owe you a nickel," Al said.

"Don't put any money on me," Annie said and swung her leg over the back of her chair. "Jesus . . . chicken!"

"Thought you liked that," Al said.

"Now I just thought of something," Annie said. "All our names begin with A . . . excepting frog-eyes here."

"That is right, for sure," Al said. "And we all got the same last name."

"Haven't we got any *coffee?*" Annie asked.

"Right in front of you," Adele said.

Her father laughed and bending over whispered loudly in Claudie's ear: "She's got herself a hangover."

"Maybe." Annie sipped the top of the coffee, loudly.

"You have a bit too much?"

"It wasn't too much," Annie said.

He chuckled again. He was in fine humor.

Claudie laughed too, imitating him.

Annie finished the cup and reached across the table for the blue enameled pot. She knocked over the jar of peppers.

"It's all right," Adele said. "The top was on."

"Wouldn't care if it wasn't." Annie poured the coffee in a thick splashing stream.

"Man, man," her father said, "she sure got herself a bad head this morning."

"I can't do anything," Annie asked, "without people talking about it?"

"Bébé, you got to know that much. . . ."

From the radio inside there was a burst of static. Al jumped up and went to fix it. Annie chewed on a piece of chicken. "It's tough."

"You got a bad piece," Adele said, quick and eager, "take another one."

"All tough," Annie said.

"What we had was fine."

"Tough old rooster."

"You talking about me?" Al had come back.

"Annie says the wing is tough." There was just a little edge of nervousness in Adele's voice. Annie felt a funny little quiver of satisfaction, and she almost grinned to herself.

"That right?" her father said. "Wasn't nothing wrong with mine."

"Like leather," Annie said.

"Pelicans leading by four runs in the seventh," he said.

Adele gave him a quick little uncertain smile and glanced back at Annie.

"Two out and two on," he said. "Don't pay any attention to her, che'. She don't feel too good this morning."

"I feel fine," Annie said. "Why do people keep telling me how I feel?"

"You was asking me the other day," Al said. "Thought we'd go take a look at Bayou Cantaque."

"Hell," Annie said, "I been up there a hundred times."

"Wasn't talking to you," Al said. "You want to, che'?"

"I never been up there," Adele said.

Al waved his hands, like a priest. "So we go."

Annie said: "Thought you'd be sick to death of boats, being on 'em all week long."

For a minute Adele looked like Claudie when he was going to cry.

"God damn it," Al said, "Don't nobody ask me? I want to go, me."

Annie drank the spilled coffee from her saucer, feeling again the twinge of satisfaction.

"I don't think I'm coming," she said.

"Okay," Al said.

"You sure you don't want to?" Adele asked.

"Told you I been a hundred times."

"She wants to stay and see her boyfriend," Al said.

"You don't know nothing," Annie said.

"You think so, bébé?" her father pulled the ends of his mustache, curling them carefully.

"Yea," Annie said and licked the last spot of coffee off her saucer.

"You want me to tell you what I know about what you was doing last night."

"Yea," Annie said and curled up her lip.

"Okay, bébé," Al said. "George Manint, he been by this morning, asking if you get home all right."

"Talk," Annie said, "all people do around here—talk, talk, talk and talk. Times I think I'll go to New Orleans to live."

"You was asking me," Al said, "and I'm telling you. . . . George got a real fine hangover, him. Can hardly open his eyes. And he feel sort of bad . . . he took a swing at Marie Louise and she's beginning to get a bruise on her jaw, and she threw a can at him, only it went out the open window instead. Anyhow he's feeling sick and he don't see how he can go home, things being the way they are there."

"I could get me a job in New Orleans," Annie said. "Easy as anything. At the telephone office."

"And there another thing he feeling bad about. . . . Seems he nearly cut up you boyfriend account of he thought he was waiting for Marie Louise."

Annie was staring up into the blue-white sky, her lips curled back and smiling.

"So," Al said. "And when you come home you stumbling around. Nobody got to be smart to put that together. . . ."

Annie continued staring up in the sky. "I don't care," she said. "I don't care the least bit."

Al got to his feet. "If we going, we got to go soon."

Adele said: "I'm all fixed."

When they were gone, Annie sat lazily following the flight of a green mosquito hawk. He perched finally on her knee and softly she got hold of his wings. She held him up then, close to her eyes, watching the waving legs and the straining arc of the tail.

"Sh——oo," she said and blew at him.

Under her fingers the wings were crisp and fluttery and dry as paper. She stared into his goggle eyes. "Sh——oo."

She threw him up into the air. Her aim was bad. He hit one of the porch posts and fell into the yard. A fat jay swooped down and gobbled him in a minute.

"All they do is talk," she told the hot afternoon. "You go to the can and somebody knows it. . . . I don't care, me."

But she did. If everybody knew it, something was spoiled. She shrugged and got up, went inside and turned on the radio.

They had ruined it, she told herself bitterly. They ruin everything. . . .

She stretched out on the sofa. Her head was aching and her eyes felt funny. She began to wish she hadn't taken the chicken.

What was it like up in Bayou Cantaque, she wondered. What it was like in all of them, she answered: grasses that were always moving slightly and rustling slightly even when there was no wind, and water that was thick and black and so still—if you dropped a leaf, it sat motionless on the shiny surface.

The shiny surface that reflected back at you like a mirror. And you could no more see through it than you could through a mirror. But you could guess what was under it. Alligators, for one; they came up sometimes to kill muskrats on the bank with one flick of their tails. And Congos, the long black snake that swam like a fish, people said, and had a bite that would kill the strongest man alive in just three hours. You'd see their heads standing up sometimes out of the water, and looking for all the world like a plain dark stick. And the creatures lines and nets brought up: gars whose scales made belts tough as leather; big catfish with whiskers and twin barbs; and eels, their mouths filled with sharp white teeth.

She shivered and swallowed a couple of times. She was glad she wasn't a man and had to work those waters.

I'd as soon give up and go in to Port Ronquille and get a job at the sulphur plant, she thought. Even if the sulphur got in your lungs and killed you, little by little, it was better.

And then there were people who had never done anything. Not one thing their whole lives long. Like Beatriz, who couldn't even do her hair. Who hardly knew how to brush it. Who had never seen an iron. Who learned to use it with floods of Spanish words. If I had just remembered them, Annie thought.

And what would Beatriz be doing right now? This same minute. She might be still at the convent. Or she might have gone home. Annie had thought about that home sometimes; she could imagine the place (Beatriz never talked about it, but one of the nuns had told Annie the little bit she knew). The shadowy rooms, one stretching after the other in endless procession, tremendous halls lined with mirrors, a court where mimosa was so sweet and heavy you could hardly breathe.

Annie thought over the picture slowly, touching here and there, smiling to herself. There'd be closets so crammed with clothes you couldn't shut the door. And the curtains at the windows would be satin. In her room there'd be blue satin, pale blue, at the sides draped up by big gold hooks, and over the window part there'd be white lace, sheer as organdy, and billowing out in the small steady breeze. And there'd be white bearskin rugs on the floor, changed every day so there was never a speck of dirt on them. And a dressing-table, all mirrors with tall thin bottles of perfume, so many that you'd forget about the ones in the back.

Annie stretched and drifted back to the island. That would be the life, she thought. How did some people get it, she wondered. How were some born lucky. . . .

She liked this house better when it was empty. She walked from

room to room. It wasn't a bad house, the way island houses went.
And it was pretty cool in summer. She'd seen worse places in
New Orleans, and that was for sure.

In the kitchen she found some left-over coffee and poured it
into a dirty cup. She drank it, watching the fat sparrow that
perched on the tablette outside the window.

And all of a sudden she was facing her big problem, and it
was plain as the dumpy form of the bird: did she put on some
lipstick and take a walk down to the wharf or did she wait for
Inky to look for her?

Adele had left a pack of cigarettes on the table. She took one
and lit it. She tried to inhale, choked, and gave up. She held the
cigarette to her knee and watched the white thread of smoke
crawl over her skin.

It wouldn't do to let him think she was too eager. . . . She
half closed her eyes and tried to look bored. . . . She'd just have
to wait until he came. Of course there was nothing that said she
couldn't go down and have a peep, if she stayed behind the
palmettos and was careful that he didn't see her.

And if he forgot, maybe she could think of an excuse to send
somebody down there, her father, maybe, or Cecile. Somebody who
would remind him, without saying, of her. . . . She could work
something out, if she had to. But he wouldn't forget.

The cigarette was out. She must have knocked off the coal.
She got another match from the back of the stove and lit it. . . .
A holder would be nice. She was crazy not to bring one from
New Orleans. . . . Maybe she should wash her hair today; it
was beginning to have a little sweet-sweaty smell. And what sort
of shampoo. . . .

She'd just have to take a walk over to Arcenaux's and have a
look at what he had. She'd try a new one.

She dropped the cigarette into the last little bit of coffee. And
then she remembered something else: Inky did not know where she
lived.

She ran her fingers under her hair, fluffing it up.

She could go then. She could just happen along the dock. That
was better than his coming up to the house anyway. Because of
Adele.

She was an old maid, Annie thought as she started another

cigarette. She should have gone to the convent; they'd have loved her there. She even sat like a lady or a nun—straight up, so straight that her back curved a little. Jesus. . . .

And what was it the nuns had told her: a lady never spills things in her lap. If she spills, she spills on her bosom. . . .

Annie dropped the half-smoked cigarette into the dish water. Let Adele object. . . . If her hair was going to be dry by tonight, she'd have to get going.

She got a chair and climbed up to the top cupboard shelf. There was a coffee can there. She opened it, reached below the dark brown grounds and got a dollar bill.

She started to leave, hesitated a minute, then went back to the coffee pot and shook it thoughtfully. She drank the little that was left through the spout, not bothering with a cup.

*

FOR a while Father Ryan waited patiently on the *Bozo,* sitting in the little shade of the wheelhouse, reading his breviary. But he came to the end of that, and he put the book on top of his coat, which he had taken off and folded carefully on the deck, stood up and looked around.

The wharf was completely deserted—not even a seagull or a pelican moving—with one exception: a young man by the sail-boat a couple of hundred feet away. He wore bathing-trunks and his body was shining with sweat; he was finishing his washing in a big tub set on the dock. Father Ryan walked over. "Hot work," he said.

The young man looked up briefly. "Yea," he said.

There was a line running from forestay to mast, and hung over it were some long pieces of foam rubber, mattress-shaped. Other lines from spreaders to mast held blue-and-white-striped cotton covers.

Inky straightened up. "This is no day for work."

The priest nodded. "Most people wait till early in the morning."

"I spilled some coffee on the covers," Inky said, "and I had to get it out before it stained." He tipped the tub and poured the water through the cracks in the wharf. "Mildew got in some," he said, "so I did the lot."

"A fine-looking boat."

"Yes," Inky said, "I just work on her."

(Annie had come up just then and stopped behind the heavy tangle of bay trees and palmettos. She held the bottle of shampoo in her left hand and with her right she lifted a single palm leaf to see.

She saw the freshly washed covers hanging limp in the still air. And she could feel first her ears, then her whole face go bright red.

245

It was the sunburn, she told herself, she'd have to get some grease on it before she got sick.

She backed out of the thicket and walked home slowly. She did not want to do her hair any more. She stretched out, flat on her back, on her bed, and cried small angry tears.)

"A racing-boat?" the priest asked.

"And cruising."

"I used to go to the races on the lakefront sometimes when I was in New Orleans."

"It's fun," Inky said. He hung the tub upside down over a piling. "I got some ice below," he said, "how about a drink?"

Father Ryan nodded and came on board.

"Up in the shade under the covers," Inky said, "it'll be cool enough."

They were sitting there, cross-legged on the deck, when Mike Livaudais came back. He did not seem to notice them. He walked on to the *Bozo*. Father Ryan got up to follow him.

"Better luck this time," Inky said.

Mike was staring sadly into the engine hatch. He straightened up when the priest came aboard. "I offer you my house," he said, "instead of the hard deck."

He was different, Stanislaus Ryan thought; he was less sad now, and more determined. The priest wondered. He took off his glasses and polished them on his sleeve. "How long will it take you to fix the engine?"

Mike shrugged. "It is old, yes, and, like old people, it get funny things wrong with it."

"Was it the battery?"

Mike threw out his hands. "How can I tell? Can I look in the inside of the case and see what is going on there? Can I see through lead?"

The priest was scratching his chin with his glasses. "You were going to get somebody to test the battery."

Mike waved his hand around again. "And that Story LeBlanc, I have looked for him. I have looked all up and down for him. Everywhere I could think of, I look for him. And he is not there."

He walked twice around the open engine hatch and stood looking down. "I got to do the best I can, myself, me. I got to get to work."

"And how long will that take?"

Mike shrugged.

"And the other boats now . . . do you think they could be taking me back?"

Mike straightened up and stared down the line of moored luggers. "Hector, now, he is working on his hull."

"Where?" Father Ryan asked, "I don't see."

"From inside," Mike said. "And the *Mickey Mouse* got something wrong with her rudder. And the *St. Cristopher*—that the same Story LeBlanc I am looking for and don't find. . . . And for sure we don't want to take you back in a chabec . . . but no! That is just too much a risky business. And what would everybody say if we drown the priest. . . ."

"Yes," said Father Ryan, "for sure."

"And then there is Al Landry's boat, the last one—là-bas," he pointed, "and he is out taking his new wife for a ride somewhere."

The priest nodded.

"And you do not ask me to steal a man's boat while he is gone?"

"No," Father Ryan said. "No."

"And you see the other boats, they gone working."

"I see."

"But you be cheerful," Mike said, "I get this fixed."

Father Ryan stifled a yawn in the heat.

"Why you don't come back to the house with me? My wife she be proud to have a priest in her house."

The priest got to his feet slowly, one knee at a time. This was a different man, he thought, from an hour ago. Altogether different. . . . And he was beginning now to see what was happening. And he wasn't sure he liked that any better.

Mike slapped one hand to his forehead. "But I have forgot . . . you must not have any dinner. . . . How the dogs they must be growling inside you."

Stanislaus Ryan was a young man, but he felt very tired. "I suppose I am hungry."

"I got to have my head examined, letting you starve in front of my very eyes."

Mike got him by one arm and helped him over the rail like a cripple. "Mother Mary," Mike said, "how I going to talk to myself for doing this."

"It's fine," Father Ryan said. "I'm fine."

They walked up the path to the house. They did not meet anyone on the way, Father Ryan noticed, though there must be plenty people around.

And all the time Mike was talking. "I go find that Story LeBlanc . . . sal au pri—excuse," and he crossed himself. "And I make him tell me why he go and hide so nobody can find him on a Sunday. . . . And I take my engine apart, I got to fix it . . . and maybe LeBlanc he take you, if mine don't go."

Soon as they got in the front gate, Marie Livaudais came rushing down the steps and got Father Ryan by the other arm. They led him in the house, both talking now. And he had the feeling that had he stopped, they would have just dragged him along and not even noticed.

There was dinner—ready, and not touched. Father Ryan looked at it, scratched his chin again, and kept on wondering.

They got him to the table, urged him to sit down. They pushed the chair persuasively against the back of his knees.

"Now," Mike shouted, "la neigre, she will feed you good, no?"

Over by the stove his wife said something without turning around.

"And don't you bring none of the children in here." Mike yelled out the window: "When we got a priest for dinner you got to eat later."

There was a murmur and then crying of kids.

"They must be hungry," Father Ryan said.

"Bunch of cannibals," Mike scowled. "Not more than two days ago, when we was having shrimp . . ."

"Boiled shrimp," Marie said, "plain cold boiled shrimp."

"And one of 'em, he can't stand the sight of another one, and he pick up a shrimp and throw it. And before we got chance to grab anybody, that dish—big, big platter, you can put four duck on it and no spilling over—that dish is all gone and the shrimp they is all over the room."

"Got on the wall," Marie said. "Smell."

Father Ryan sniffed. "I can't tell," he said.

Mike patted him gently on the back. "The Father, he is so polite, him!"

"It's the seminary, for sure," Marie said. "They teach to be polite in the seminary."

Stanislaus Ryan opened his mouth, then closed it again.

Mike bent down, staring into his mouth. "You was going to say something, yes? Shut up! the Father, he going to say something."

"I wasn't," Father Ryan said. "Nothing."

Mike looked disappointed and straightened up again.

A couple of black heads appeared at the window. "Filez d'ici!" Mike roared.

"They must be getting hungry," the priest suggested.

"Don't go being sorry for them," Marie said.

"And you shut up too," Mike said, "with us waiting for food and getting fainter and fainter." He waved his hands again.

"Mo' pere, don't go being polite, just to save our feelings. . . ." He opened the armoire that stood in one corner of the kitchen. Down on the bottom, behind the dresses and coats that were hanging there, was a bottle of wine. He took it out, a gallon jug, and held it to the light. "Marie, her cousin's husband, made it."

She had the glasses on the table. Mike poured them. Father Ryan tasted carefully.

"Oh . . ." he said, "orange wine."

"Shu . . ." Marie nodded. "My cousin's husband don't make nothing but the orange wine."

"And the best, che'," Mike said. "Let's us not go forgetting to say that."

"How you like it?" Marie asked.

"Very fine." The wine was strong and very sweet.

"And you have nothing like that back where you come from?" Marie asked.

"In New Orleans?"

"That where you from?"

He nodded.

"You not from Ireland?"

"Marie, you getting mixed up, for sure," Mike said. "That was the priest before, name of Gillespie."

"Oh," Father Ryan said.

"He went and left." They had found him one morning tossing oyster shells at imaginary cats in the church yard.

"Thought it was you," Marie said.

Father Ryan shook his head.

They had dinner while the kids stood outside and watched them, and occasionally squabbled among themselves.

"And do you think you're going to get that engine fixed this afternoon?"

Mike slapped his forehead. "I have forgot. I am having such a fine time eating dinner with you, it had gone out of my mind entirely." He jumped to his feet, knocking the table so that the dishes rattled together.

"I'll come with you," the priest said.

"But no . . ." Mike picked up a rocking-chair and carried it to the front porch. "Down at the boat it is hot and there is no reason you should sweat like me. . . . You sit here, and my wife, she be out to keep you company when she finish cleaning up back there."

"I could help."

Mike smiled, sadly, so that the missing-teeth gaps at the sides of his mouth showed. "And what you know about engines?"

"Well, now . . ."

"You know about God," Mike said; "me, I know about engines. . . . I come get you when I have it fixed."

He bowed Father Ryan into the rocking-chair and left him.

Stanislaus Ryan put his elbows on the arms of the chair and his chin on his hands, as he watched Mike out of sight. You could hear people laughing and yelling far off, but around the house it was very quiet. Even the children, back in the kitchen, were quiet; they must be getting fed.

There was a telephone on the island somewhere, he remembered. Later on, he would have to use it to tell the housekeeper back at the rectory at Petit Prairie that the CYO would have to meet without him—if the engine didn't get fixed in time. And he didn't really think it would.

Marie came out, carrying some sewing in her hands, a bright yellow and red piece of cotton. He looked from her to the spot where the steady, square, plodding back of her husband had disappeared. "Such fine liars," he muttered.

"*Pardon,*" she said and cupped a hand around her ear. "But I did not hear, me."

"It was nothing," he said. "And I wasn't talking to you."

It was nearly six o'clock before the engine was fixed. Mike sent a kid up to tell Father Ryan.

"It sounds right now, no?" Mike asked him.

Father Ryan cocked his head and listened. "You didn't have a hard time with it."

"Mother Mary, but I had a time, for sure!"

"You didn't get dirty," he pointed out.

"Ah, but I am smart and the Marie she get mad if she got to wash too much. . . . I take off my clothes."

"All of them?"

"Down to the underwear . . . right now my underwear, they are filthy."

Father Ryan shook his head and got on board.

"I been thinking," Mike said.

"I know," the priest said.

"You know what I been thinking?"

"Only maybe," the priest said.

"It being so late now," Mike said, "and it ain't far out the way to Catfish Bay . . . it wouldn't take long."

And the technical charge, Father Ryan thought, what would it be: kidnapping? He had heard of this happening—to doctors, to priests; and there'd been the stories back in the seminary. . . . But he'd imagined it somehow as more dramatic.

He almost chuckled. Well anyway, he thought, a sense of humor helps. And he could see that he was going to Catfish Bay, like it or not.

For a second he wondered: What would they do if I said no? Would it ever get violent. . . .

It was a silly idea, he thought, but it wasn't sinful. There was no reason why he shouldn't. It was irregular, and maybe it wasn't done in the best religious spirit, but then what was. . . . And God would be one to understand. . . .

And if he said no, there'd be more engine trouble for sure

again. And just as sure he wouldn't be getting home tonight.

If you started looking into people's motives too closely—well, who would you admit . . . They'd just as soon keep him here all night. And he had the five-o'clock Mass. If he didn't turn up, the old boy would be furious, and so would the other assistant. And they'd be as rude to him as they could without sinning. It wouldn't be very pleasant all together.

"I think we might go by there," he told Mike.

*

MUCH later that night, toward midnight, the *Bozo* came back and docked quietly. There were five or six men on her, and they had the lines in place in a couple of seconds. They left the boat then, walking off their separate ways quickly. The moon had made the white shell paths bright, almost, as daylight.

Mike said: "Quit asking me . . . and get the god-damn kids outa here. Why ain't they in bed? They oughta be in bed."

Marie hissed at the kids, who disappeared. You could hear them scuffling softly in the loft overhead.

"I need a drink, me."

Marie moved to the armoire.

"No, god damn . . . I don't want no wine. . . . Where you hide the bottle whisky?"

She reached under the sink, behind the boxes of soap powder, and got out the bottle.

"Right there?" he said. "Right out in the open where every kid can get at it. . . . You losing you mind?"

"Did they find it now? . . . You tell me did they get any? . . ."

He looked at the bottle and grunted. "Full soap powder."

"Wipe it off," she said. "Ain't nobody making you eat it."

He poured himself a drink. "Quit asking me. . . ."

"I ain't said nothing."

He took a couple of swallows of whisky straight. "There a way for doing things," he said, "and a way not. We did it wrong. . . . The priest now, he didn't want to go. And when we got there, he was in a hurry to get off again. And the candles, they kept going out. And there wasn't nobody could tell which way they was pointing."

He put his feet up on the kitchen table. Little bits and pieces of mud crumbled off the soles and scattered on the oilcloth.

253

"Tell me I'm messing you kitchen," he said and squinted at her with one eye tight shut, "go on and tell me."

"You hear me saying anything?"

"Good thing," he muttered into the glass. "I push you head around back."

"I ain't said nothing. . . . You hear me saying nothing?"

"Jesus God," he said. "And then the priest, he says, 'I told you it wouldn't do no good.' . . . If he wasn't no priest, ordained and in church, I push him over right there and let the gars have a work at him."

He crossed his feet and a little more dirt fell on the table. "We tried," he said, "no son of a bitch going to call us not men for trying."

Overhead the kids giggled softly.

"Ain't they asleep yet?" he said.

"They all excited for sure," she told him. She was standing over by the stove, hands on her hips, her bare feet planted far apart. That was the way she did when she expected to stand a long time. "And I expect they are listening."

"Good!" He banged down his glass on the floor by his chair. "Pour me another drink. . . . And maybe it learns them to stay out the swamp. And maybe it don't. . . . You pour the whisky like an old aunt." He yanked the bottle away.

She did not answer. She went back to her position in front of the stove. He drank the whisky in short nibbling gulps. The kids were very still, and there wasn't a thing moving outside.

"And that Eddie . . ." he shook his head.

He was silent so long that she finally asked: "What about Eddie?"

"I come back, the pit of my belly froze up. Only just now the likker is warming me."

"What about Eddie?"

"I wouldn't want to be him," he said. "Looking at his face from the outside, I wouldn't be inside him for nothing." He stared up at the dark uncovered beams of the ceiling, stained almost black by years of cooking under them. "Not for nothing."

"You go back tomorrow?"

He nodded, very slightly.

"And the shrimp, they are running too. I hear that from Gary Alonzo."

"Maybe," Mike said, "I hear the same thing. The other men, let them go out. The Livaudais, they got something got to be done."

"You want another drink?"

He shook his head. "Can't have no hangover on me in the morning."

"Listen," Marie took a couple of steps toward him, "you going to talk to the kids, no? You going to talk to them?"

"What for?"

"While this is all in their minds, you going to talk to them about not going too far back in there. Like . . ." she hesitated for a moment, "Henry done."

"Yea," he said, "only not now."

She clucked her tongue. "I wasn't asking you to do it now. Only sometime."

"Yes," he said. "For sure."

She picked up a rag out of the sink and went over to wipe the fingerprints off the door of the icebox. They were greasy. She sprinkled a little soap powder on the rag and worked at them.

"We go again."

"You think," she said still scrubbing away, "he might be living yet?"

"He shoulda know better. He know enough not to go so far he can't get out. Whyn't he stay where he knew his way?"

"He wasn't a stupid kid," she said.

"He knew better, for sure. . . . If he stay where he knew."

"You think . . . maybe?"

He just shook his head to answer.

"Quit looking like that," Eddie said to Belle. "I'm going back, me. First thing in the morning."

BEFORE light the following morning, Hector Boudreau and Al Landry were down at the dock. And a few minutes later Eddie Livaudais came, a gunny sack of food over his shoulder, a shotgun in his hand. He was dressed for a long day's sun too: a long-sleeved heavy white cotton shirt, a pair of white cotton pants and a wide-brimmed straw hat.

And not three steps behind him came his brother Mike, his wife's brother Chep and Chep's son, Jerry.

Al and Hector moved over to meet them. Eddie was walking along with short jerky steps, his eyes on the ground right in front of him; so he didn't see them until he almost walked into them. Then he looked up sharply and waved his hand. "No," he said, "we don't need no help."

Al Landry pushed back his own cap. "Me and Hector was just wondering."

Eddie shook his head sharply. "Four do much as six or eight."

"No offense," Hector said.

"Hell, man, no," Mike said, and glanced at his brother. Eddie was terribly nervous; he could hardly stand still at all. "If we need any, we call for you sure."

"Look," Hector said, "lemme run you over to Catfish Bay. . . . I been wanting to try out that engine."

"That's an idea, for sure," Al said. "And it save you that much paddling."

"Maybe . . ." Mike turned to Eddie, "you the boss."

"You going to paddle far enough," Hector said, "once you get there."

"That's the idea," Al said.

"You got enough paddling," Hector said, "without making more."

Eddie's eyes were bothering him. He kept blinking very fast. "Okay," he said.

256

Hector got the blowers going. Chep and Jerry put their shotguns and their gear on board and then went to get lines to the
two pirogues.

Eddie did not offer to help. He just stood and watched, blinking.

"You don't want to put the sack on board?" Al asked. And
Eddie was surprised to find he still had it slung over his shoulder.

"Hot as hell," Jerry said.

Mike chuckled. "You ain't seen nothing, kid," he said. "That
bothers you, you might just go home straight off."

Jerry tested the muscles in his right shoulder. "Don't reckon I
will."

"You ain't seen nothing," Mike said. "Vieux couillon! But this
ain't nothing at all."

Annie Landry sat in front of the mirror and undid her curlers.
She brushed out her hair carefully—the shampoo gave it red tints,
all right, she thought, but that wasn't bad either. Then she made
up, very carefully, even to the mascara.

Earlier that morning, she had climbed up to the top of the
largest oak tree, the one that grew way in the back, by the pigpen. And from its top she could see the wharf—the boats were all
out working, except for the Livaudais's two, and the *Pixie*.

She finished her make-up and stuffed the shirt down into her
pants. She ran one finger testingly up and down her legs: she
had shaved this morning and her skin still prickled a little.

Then she walked slowly across the island.

Inky was in the little clump of trees that reached right down
to the wharf. He had got a canvas chair from somewhere, and he
was sitting and reading.

"Well, hi!" he said. "I was beginning to think you'd disappeared
for good."

"I've been around."

"Not down here, you haven't."

"I was down yesterday," she said, "but you were busy washing . . ." she stopped, remembering she shouldn't have mentioned
that.

"You damn right I was." He began laughing, slapping his
knees. "That was one on me," he said. "Spent all yesterday morning
washing."

Already she was wishing she had not come. But there was no way back, so she went on recklessly. "I'm real sorry," she said, "but it never happened before."

He laughed harder. "You damn right it didn't." The book fell off his lap and he stopped to pick it up.

"I didn't mean that."

"Oh hell," he said, "tell me what's going on around here."

"Nothing," she said, "nothing ever does."

"Okay," he said, "I'll tell you the news . . . the bastards I nearly had a fight with—what's their name?"

"Livaudais."

"Well, they went out somewhere in Hector's boat, with a couple of pirogues. And then, maybe a couple hours later, Hector comes back alone, and picks up his crew. You know, the crippled man, and your boyfriend, with the tobacco name."

"Not my boyfriend," Annie said.

He lifted one eyebrow and winked.

She was uncertain, so that it was an actual pain. She could not look at him. "I got things to do," she almost whispered and turned away.

"You have a mean hangover?"

"No," she said.

"Man, I did."

She was moving quietly away when he said: "You want to have a drink with me tonight?"

They had a drink at the Rendezvous, which was almost empty on a Monday night—only Story LeBlanc playing a game of pool with Lacy Livaudais.

"You're extra pretty," Inky said, "when you don't have that scared look."

"They listening over there."

"Okay," Inky said, and stood up. "I know another place."

*

THEY were gone, the two Livaudais and the two Songy men, hunting for Henry, nearly three days. First the *Hula Girl* took them across the bay, then up a small deep bayou to a second smaller one, and finally to Catfish Bay—they had taken the priest there only the day before; and if they had looked they could have found some of the floating blocks of wood with bits of candle still stuck to them.

They changed to their pirogues. And the *Hula Girl* turned back. From here on, it would be too shallow for the lugger.

They paddled up through the low salt marsh, looking for some sign, all the way up to the heavy swamp. They spent the night there on the edge. And in the morning, soon as it was light, they went in far as they dared. They went in far as they knew, any of them, and then a little farther, marking their own way carefully. And every hour or so, they fired the shotguns in the air or down in the water. There was never an answer. That night, they lit the cypress torches they'd brought. And Mike Livaudais sent up the flares. They all watched the red and white colors stream out, way, way over the vine tangle tops of the big cypress trees. And they'd waited.

Mike sent up four different flares, all that he had. And there was only the faint hissing and the sharp searing smell.

Chep Songy scratched his chin. And in the swamp silence the finger over his beard made a rasping sound.

And finally Eddie Livaudais lowered his head from the empty night sky where the flares had been. "Let's us go back," he said.

They took the shortest way, and they paddled all night, taking turns now, for they were dead tired. But more than that, they wanted to get out of the swamp—out of the stifling, sulphur-smelling air, the slime-coated water.

By daylight they were back in the marshes behind Isle aux

259

Chiens. The cranes were still asleep in the little ponds in the grasses: eight or ten white shapes clustered together.

The still heavy water streaked back from the paddles in a long v. . . . When they got near the end of the marsh Chep Songy grunted to his boy to stop paddling and motioned toward the shotguns in the center of the pirogue. He fired both barrels from his; the boy added a third.

"Maybe," Chep said, as much to himself as to anyone else, "it is three shells wasted, but maybe somebody, they hear and come."

Perique Lombas heard them, and got his own boat, the *Tangerine,* and crossed the bay to meet them. He got there first, cut his motor and sat down to wait. While he waited, he changed the plugs, which had needed doing for some time.

Perique and Robert Cheramie had built the twenty-foot hull a couple of years ago. They'd worked at it all one summer, getting up before daylight so they'd have a couple of hours cool. And Perique had taken the engine out of his old Ford, which he'd kept for a while on the island, and spent nearly a month working on it, tuning it up, in the shade of the chinaberry tree in his back yard.

The rest of the car he had pushed back up against the little chicken house, way back in the hackberry bushes. And a storm that September had torn off a limb of the old oak there, and smashed it down on top the car and jarred the doors all open. During the winter storms the grasses blew in and made drifts on the floor that went halfway up to the windows. And that spring, his mother moved some of her hens in.

He saw the two pirogues finally, put on his motor and went over to pick them up. He didn't ask once about Henry. And they didn't mention it. They all knew that he didn't have to, that he had his answer already.

When they came into the dock, there was a kid, standing back a little, by the icehouse, watching them. Only before they had landed, he turned around and disappeared. And they weren't surprised about that either. It was Pete Livaudais.

The *Tangerine* swung into the dock. Perique left the wheel and grabbed the mooring-lines.

"I'm going back, me," Eddie Livaudais said. The other men were ashore now, but he hadn't moved.

"Ain't no use," Chep said.

The two other men were so tired they didn't bother talking. They picked up their shotguns and the empty sacks which had had food and water in them, and moved off, dragging their feet and stumbling on the uneven boards.

Eddie started to get up from the deck. He put his hands on his knees and pushed. But he slipped sideways. Perique put the last loop in his mooring-line and jumped back aboard.

"My legs, they cramped from being in the pirogue this long," Eddie said.

"Sure," Perique stuck out his foot for a brace and got one arm around the older man, and heaved him to his feet.

"Got to get some sleep," Eddie said. "Then I'm going back."

Perique got him to the dock. "Leave the stuff," he said, "I got to go right by you house anyways."

Eddie held out his hand, motioning for Perique to pick up the sack. "I be back by morning, me." He lifted the almost empty sack across his shoulder. "Vec tou mo drigail," he muttered.

"Lemme bring that," Perique said. "I'm going right by you house."

Eddie did not seem to hear. Perique followed him down the wharf a little, not quite sure what to do. Finally Perique stopped and stood watching him—moving rapidly, with short little steps like a woman's, and leaning forward at such an angle you thought he was going to fall any minute.

He went out again the next morning alone. Like he said he would.

HE had found nothing, when he came back two days later.

He dragged his pirogue only half out of the water and left it. (The Songy boys came down later and carried it the rest of the way up the shell ridge.) He didn't bother with the gear either, taking only the shotgun and the shells. It was all he could carry. His arms had turned weak as a woman's. And he had to go home.

When he got to the house, his wife was out on the back porch, cleaning shrimp. He could see the shells flipping over into the yard, where the chickens and the cats fought for them.

He knew it was his wife; not many people on the island could work that fast.

He felt his feet get heavy and just scuff the ground. He put the shotgun and the cartridge belt on the front porch. He stood for a while chewing on his lower lip and scratching his jaw: the two-day stubble was beginning to itch.

"Maybe Pete, he seen me come in and he already told her," he muttered to himself.

Then he went around the house.

Pete was there all right, sitting in a corner of the porch, back to the railing, smoking a cigarette.

"I told you," Eddie Livaudais said, "you too young for that."

"He ain't all that young," his wife said.

He was standing staring down at this woman he'd lived with for thirty years. This tall, thin woman with olive skin and straight black hair that was beginning to turn gray on top. Just on top, like a gray cap.

"Let me handle the boys, my way." He was angry at her. Angry at the way her face was so calm.

"You done handle the boys your way, all this time, and I ain't said nothing." She didn't stop with the shrimps, twisting off the heads, popping the meat out of the shells and flipping the rest over the railing to the yard.

Eddie took off his cap and hung it on the back of her chair.

"Only now," she said slowly, "you ain't got but one son."

He could feel that hurt, somewhere in his chest.

"Pete done told you."

"He don't got to tell me," she said, still slowly. "I got so I can feel it in my blood, me."

Eddie walked over and with a quick move of his hand yanked the cigarette out of the boy's mouth and flipped it over the railing with the shrimp heads.

The kid half rose, then stayed where he was, his knees bent. His father reached out, taking his shoulder, pushed him back down on his heels.

The head of a shrimp flashed by Eddie's nose, not two inches away. He jerked his head around, but his wife was working quietly. Only, she was flipping the shells to the other side.

"You taking to pushing kids around?" she asked without moving her eyes from her work.

"If he old enough to smoke, he old enough to get pushed around."

"Hey . . ." Pete said.

His father looked down at him, drawing back his hand. "If there is just one more single line out of you, I going to twist your head around, just the way the old woman there does with them shrimp. And that is for sure."

"Look at him," she said, "Eddie Livaudais, done lost one son, and getting ready to beat up the other."

"Maybe he ain't the only thing around here I got to lick back in place, me."

"Listen at him, Pete," she said, "him that comes back empty-handed. Listen at him."

"Quit that," Eddie said.

"He don't come home with Henry. He don't even come home with a dead body, him."

Eddie sat down on the top step and began to take off his shoes. "This here is the first time I had my shoes off in near three days now."

"We are right sorry for you."

The boy Pete stared at him from under his eyebrows. He looked so much like his brother there for a minute that Eddie had to shake his head.

"Why you come to quitting?" his wife asked softly.

"I ain't quit."

"You come back, didn't you?"

He shook his head.

"That's quitting, ain't it?"

He put an elbow on each knee and rested his weight on them. "You get tired, going for two days and nights."

She sniffed.

"With hardly no sleep."

"Henry, he ain't sleeping neither."

He looked down at the ground. There was a doodle bug working his way across the bare sun-cracked stretch. He stared at it hard, at the funny ridged shell and the little horns: he hadn't really looked at one since he was a kid.

"Me, if I'd stayed a couple of hours longer, I never would found my way out. I'd been too tired to figure."

She didn't answer, just whistled through her teeth.

He put his shoes one alongside the other on the edge of the porch. Then he began to pull off his socks slowly. His back was hurting him, in waves, like. It was the paddling.

"I ain't so young," he said, "not any more."

The words seemed to run off and echo on the hot afternoon air.

"I'm getting on to be old," he said, and he shivered. That meant somebody was walking over his grave spot. "Getting old."

One of the chickens spotted the doodle bug and gulped it.

"Haaaaa," Eddie hissed. The chicken fluttered away. He put a hand to his back and straightened up. "I should have took you," he told Pete.

"I ask you," Pete said.

"He did, for sure," Belle said.

"Shut up."

The boy looked at him without blinking.

Eddie looked from one to the other. "What you got against me?" he said. "I ain't told him to go out."

The brown stubby fingers cleaned the gray, almost transparent shrimp. "You ought to stopped him."

Eddie rubbed his back. Funny how he hadn't noticed it until now. Not until now. "He wasn't no little kid that you could lock up in a room till he forgot."

The cats were fighting for the shrimp heads. There was one down there he hadn't seen before, a small tom, black and white.

"Where that one come from?" He pointed.

Neither answered for a while, then the boy said: "Where they all come from, I reckon."

"I ain't never seen him before."

"We heard you," Belle said.

Eddie rested his head in his hands, and bent his body forward a little to try and relieve the ache in his back.

"Pete," he said, "go see if we ain't got some liniment." He began to rub the small of his back with both hands. He stopped, hearing no sound of movement behind him.

"Enfant garce!" he said softly. He plopped his hands on his knees but did not turn around. "Go get that there stuff."

He cocked his head, listening until he heard the soft pad of the boy's feet as he got up and crossed the boards, and then the creak of the spring on the screen door.

"Why I got to fight for everything?" he said aloud.

His wife did not answer. He heard her shuffle the cleaned shrimp in their big iron pot. He rested his head in his hands. The afternoon sun made a long black streak of shadow from the house. There wasn't a bit of breeze; long strings of spider webs hung straight down from the edge of the porch railing.

Pete came back with the bottle of liniment. He put it next to his father on the floor, then went back to the corner of the porch and sat down.

Eddie picked up the bottle and held it out at arms' length, reading the label carefully.

"That's it, ain't it?" the boy asked.

Eddie put the bottle down, stretched his back slightly, arching his neck, then bent forward again, elbows on knees. He closed his eyes, but all he could see was the swamp: the edges where the roots and grasses came and disappeared into the water. He'd looked at miles of it, carefully, keeping his eyes moving slowly along, the same speed as the boat, looking almost from blade to blade, jumping each time a fish broke water or a frog splashed, jumping when a turtle craned its head or a bird squeaked, and hunting all the time for something that would be a trace. . . .

He rubbed the back of his neck. He was getting old, for sure. Or he wouldn't be so tired.

Behind his closed lids, the grasses kept slipping past, one reed after the other. He shook his head and opened his eyes: he'd have to keep awake then.

"Get me a drink," he said.

In the pause one of the cats yeowled. Then his wife said: "You want a beer or whisky?"

He tapped his open palms on his knees. "I ain't said that. I ask for water, me. Plain water out the cistern."

He heard the boy get to his feet.

"Why you send him all the time?" he asked. "Why you ain't gone to get me something?"

She spat noisily into the side yard. "With my hands smelling from shrimp? You wouldn't do nothing but scream louder."

"Okay," he said. "Okay. So Pete go."

The spring on the screen door creaked.

"Don't brace it that way," Belle said. "The house fill up with flies."

When the boy had come back, a couple of minutes later, she said: "I hope you fixing to catch all the bugs you let in."

"Oh sure," he said, "sure. . . . Here, Pa."

He reached the glass over his shoulder. Eddie took it, started to drink, then stopped, looking at it.

"What is the matter now?"

"It ain't got no ice."

"It ain't supposed to have none," she said. "You too hot for it to be good for you."

"Since when you know what good for me?"

She tossed a whole shrimp down into the yard and bent over the rail to watch the cats fight for it.

"That little black and white, he a scrapper for sure."

"Where he come from?" Eddie said, "I ain't never seen him before."

She threw another whole shrimp, high this time. The cat leaped after it, arching his small body, and missed. She laughed shortly, a snort, more.

"You throwing away good shrimp there," Eddie said.

"I know it, me."

"You losing your head to be throwing out shrimp."

"It ain't all I'm losing."

Eddie opened his mouth to answer, but heard someone walking around the house. So he just rested his chin on his hands and stared straight ahead.

Story LeBlanc came and put one foot on the bottom step. He held a duck in each hand, cleaned and pink.

"I come on these this morning," he said.

Eddie closed one eye and looked at them. "They look fine, for sure."

"Man," Story said, "there ain't nobody on this here island like duck much as you."

"Well," Eddie said, "I don't know that's a fact, me."

"Sure . . . ain't nobody."

"They out of season," Pete said, from his crouching position in the corner of the porch.

Story grinned: the front teeth were missing. His tongue rubbed back and forth, very quickly, fluttering in the opening. "And who going to tell the government?"

"I didn't say nothing like that," Pete said. "I just said they was out of season."

"These here was two of the prettiest pintails I never did see." Story put them on the railing. They hung over the wood bar, dripping a little blood. The cats circled around, their eyes big and flat.

"They going to get them," Pete said and giggled, like a girl; his voice was still changing.

"Not while I'm sitting here," Eddie said.

"Man," Story said, "I never did see a man like duck much as you."

Eddie threw out his hands, "Maybe . . . it is good, for sure."

"So I give it to you. The both of them. Because you enjoy it most."

Belle flipped the last of the shells into the yard and got to her feet, carrying the half-full kettle. She snorted loudly. "Lose his son, and he get him a pair of duck."

She slammed the screen after her. They could hear her in the kitchen, banging the pots around.

Eddie did not move. He sat staring straight ahead. Story started to say something, then changed his mind, and stood with his mouth open, the tip of his tongue just sticking through the hole in his teeth. Pete got to his feet, swung over the railing and, almost without a sound, dropped to the ground. One of the cats jumped up to the porch and crouched, tail over nose, eying the ducks.

Eddie said: "They look real fat."

"They was the first pintails I seen this year."

"They real pretty, for sure."

Inside they could hear her begin to sing: "Mary Mother, pray for me. . . ."

"You know," Eddie said, and he rested his chin on his hands, "you know I done everything."

Story nodded. "Sure," he said.

"Kept going out there, until I couldn't stand it no more."

"Sure," Story said.

"Any farther, I'd got lost too, and not come out."

"I know that, me."

"And she know that. She know it like any of us."

"See you," Story said and walked around the corner of the house.

"She know that," Eddie said to the cats. They sat and looked at him, the tips of their tails twitching.

"She got to know that."

A mockingbird came down and sat on the edge of the roof, squaaking. Eddie lifted one eye and squinted sidewise at him. "What's the matter with you?" The bird hopped up and down, sliding along the gutter.

Eddie got to his feet, very slowly, and stood for a minute looking out across the back yard, hitching up his pants, tightening the belt. He'd knocked the bottle of liniment over, but he didn't stop or notice or look down. He turned and opened the screen door, then stepped back again and grabbed the ducks off the railing. "You ain't going to get them yet," he told the cats. He went inside, letting the door slam after him.

His wife was right there, on the other side of the small kitchen. He blinked for a few seconds until his eyes got used to being inside. She was chopping up some onions, holding the big heavy blade of the knife in both hands.

He walked over and put the ducks in the sink. She did not say anything.

"Couldn't do nothing more," he said.

She did not lift her head.

"You know it."

"Can't even find his boy's dead body."

"You know why."

"Comes walking in here, bringing some dead birds with him."

"I hunt until I couldn't stand up no more."

"Don't come crying to me."

He flopped the ducks in the sink.

"It ain't my job, to go find him."

"I done tried."

"I drop down dead, before I come back with no sign, me."

"Leave the shrimp alone," he said, and wiped his bloody hands on the seat of his pants, "and let's us have the duck tonight."

"You want a party too?"

He stared at her, his head bent very slightly, and wobbling just a little bit on his neck.

"I'm glad I'm bushed out," he said. "I'm right glad."

She kept chopping the onions, short even movements.

"Or I twist you head right off."

She put the knife down and with the flat of her hand swept the onions from the board into the pan. "Talking," she said, "seems like that all you can do."

"No," he said.

"Now you go round thinking about food, like nothing happen."

"I know something happened, me, only I don't see no reason to starve to death."

She hissed at him, between her teeth.

"We going to eat them duck tonight."

He walked out of the house, and she shouted at him from the window. The words were so blurred he did not understand.

He went down to the Rendezvous, dragged a chair over by the front window, under the fan where it was cooler, and had two beers.

"You look green, man," his cousin Lacy said after a few minutes. "Come here in the back."

Eddie got up, swaying a little on his feet.

"Man, you don't look good for sure," Lacy said and scratched his scarred, naked head. "Stretch out there on the bed."

Eddie's back was hurting him so, from all the steady paddling he'd done, that he could hardly talk. And he wasn't sure which hurt more: lying down straight or sitting up and hunching over.

Lacy called his wife, Andrée.

"Mary Mother!" she said, "go get a bottle of whisky."

There was a pint bottle on the dresser, next to the picture of the Infant Jesus of Prague. Lacy held it to Eddie's lips. He swallowed, choked, and began to hiccup.

"Pull off his shirt," Andrée said, "and grab some of this stuff." She poured some liniment in the palm of her hand.

While they were working, Perique Lombas came in and began to pound on the top of the bar with his fists, whistling.

Lacy Livaudais lifted up his head without stopping what his hands were doing and he yelled: "Get your own stuff and leave the money on the counter. I got all I can do back here."

His wife got some towels and wrung them out in boiling-hot water and put them still steaming on Eddie's back and chest.

When Lacy finally went back in the bar, his face was bright red and dripping with sweat. Perique was still there, with two empty bottles on the counter.

"Jesus Christ," Lacy said and tried to wipe his face on his shirt-sleeve.

"Now who you got back there?"

"Eddie."

Perique whistled softly. "I seen him when he come back."

"Lacy, hey." His wife stuck her head through the screen door. "Come here quick and talk to your cousin."

Eddie was sitting on the edge of the bed, swaying back and forth a little. They had taken his shoes off when they put him on the bed, and he was trying to find those shoes now: he swung his feet in big uncertain circles, the toes pointed down, hunting. "I got to get my shoes," he said, but the words didn't come out clearly.

Perique had followed Lacy. He stood just inside the screen door that led from the bar to the Livaudais's bedroom and kitchen.

Eddie saw them, and blinked his eyes rapidly. "Perique, boy," he said, and lifted up one hand to point at him, "I got to go out again and hunt . . . you going to come help me, no?"

"Sure," Perique said, "I come with you."

Eddie's head was so heavy he had trouble keeping it straight. It kept falling to one shoulder or the other. "I ain't going to ask Lacy here, account he too old. Don't want no old men."

"Sure," Perique said. "They get tired out too quick."

"Listen at him," Lacy said, "him talking about the *dos gris*."

"Shut up," Andrée put her lips to his ear and hissed.

"You got to be young and tough. If I wasn't so old I could found him."

Eddie stopped moving his feet around. He stared at Perique and his eyes were big and almost round. You could see the long red strain lines at the corners, deep almost as cuts.

"You coming, Perique man, no?"

"I said I was coming, me." Perique swung the screen door back and forth. "When you want to go?"

Eddie stopped moving and sat very still. "I don't know, me."

"Don't know when you want to go?"

"Ought to get some sleep first, maybe."

"Sure," Lacy said, "you can't tell what you doing without that you got some sleep."

"Look, man," Perique closed the screen behind him and came one step farther into the room. "You go get some sleep and I go get everything ready."

"We got to have somebody else," Eddie said. "Not just us."

"Okay," Perique said. "I go find them. Who you want?"

Eddie fell asleep sitting there, sitting straight up on the edge of the bed, with his head resting over on one shoulder. They tipped him over, very slowly, until his head was on the pillow; then they picked up his feet and stretched him out. His mouth fell open and he began to snore.

They tiptoed out, closing the wood door behind them.

"Man," Andrée said with a sigh, "man, man, man."

"You ain't serious about going out with him, no?" Lacy said to Perique.

"If he say so."

"In the morning, when he wake up, he going to see that ain't no good," Andrée said. "It be just for nothing."

"Maybe he still want to do it," Perique said.

"He ain't going to."

"I don't reckon he is," Perique said.

"I sure don't want to be in his place, when he comes to waking up."

He slept only a couple of hours, until about five o'clock. They weren't sure what woke him. Maybe somebody slammed the front screen door, or maybe a kid yelled under the window. Or maybe it was his own dreams. Andrée had looked in at him once, when he'd been asleep about an hour. (She got the idea, somehow, that he might have just stopped breathing, lying there on her bed.) He was sleeping heavily, muttering a little and his shoulder was twitching. She said when she'd tiptoed away: "He is still paddling, him."

After a couple of hours he sat up, with his eyes swollen and half closed so that it was hard for him to see. He got down on his hands and knees and found his shoes. The strings were knotted. His fingers were too stiff to loosen them, so he stuck his toes in, slipper fashion. The canvas heels flattened easily under his weight.

He did not go through the main part of the bar. He hesitated for just a minute in the center of the room, then went out the side door, quietly.

The screen had a heavy spring on it. It got away from his clumsy fingers and slammed. He blinked at the sudden sharp noise, but he did not turn or stop. He kept walking, down the little path, in the direction of home. The shoes dragged along the ground.

Behind him he heard Andrée's sharp voice: "He ain't here. He done gone out the side door, him."

And then she was right alongside him, panting a little with the sudden run—she wasn't young any more, for all that she had the thin figure of a teenager.

"Why you ain't sleeping?" She had hold of his arm. "Why you go running out?"

He just shook his head slowly and kept walking.

She kept pace with him. "You come back and I give you some supper. I got some real fine shrimp, me."

He looked at her slowly through his puffy lids. The skin on his cheeks and chin was beginning to turn bright red and crack from the sun. "Belle, she got some shrimp, too."

"We got good cold beer, man," she said. "And that go with shrimp for sure."

"I got to get home," he said.

"Wait and put you shoes on straight."

There was a mockingbird right over them, screaming and diving at their heads. She waved her hand at it.

"Rest a minute."

He did not answer.

She kept running alongside him, with her quick little nervous steps. "Come take a cup of coffee with us, no?"

He ducked his head and kept on moving. Her legs stopped making their quick pecking little movements and she stood still. "Ga-ga," she whispered to herself.

He kept walking, listening to the little white bits of shell grind away from under his feet. It was beginning to get cooler—just a little—and the wind had dropped. It must be about five o'clock. Shadows were criss-crossing the shell path; he walked over them.

It took him such a long time to get home. He was surprised how slow he'd been walking.

There was a cat sitting on the edge of the path, sitting, tail curled over feet, one paw combing bits of cobwebs out of its whiskers. A yellow cat, with yellow eyes and white whiskers. He wondered if they had got his duck: they slipped in the house sometimes. He kicked at the cat and sent it yeowling away. His shoe fell off. He started to bend to pick it up: he was too stiff. His back ached just bending a little way over. He slipped the shoe on, without looking. Some of the shell had got inside, but he hardly noticed.

He opened his front gate; it swung crookedly from one hinge. Henry had been promising to fix that since the winter. Only he'd never got to it.

Eddie swung the gate back and forth, listening to the scraping sound. He would have to fix it, or get Pete to do something. They'd be a lot of things Pete'd have to do now, that he hadn't before.

Eddie closed the gate carefully. The small white dog came and smelled around his flapping shoes. "Get away."

There was the gray shell of a shrimp right there by the front walk: one of the cats must have carried it. He crouched down slowly and painfully and picked it up. He turned it over and over, just a piece of shell, slightly curved. He tossed it over his shoulder.

His wife said from the porch: "Supper is fixed, if you want it."

He looked up slowly: he hadn't noticed her. She wasn't doing anything—there wasn't a sign of work near her. She was just sitting there, rocking slightly in the cane chair.

"I don't want nothing," he said.

He started up the steps, very slowly, putting both feet on each one. He crossed the porch and opened the screen, letting it slam behind him. The house was full of the odor of duck cooking. He sat down in the big armchair in the living-room, put his elbows on his knees and rested his head in his hands. It was so quiet all he could hear was the creak of the rocker on the front porch.

CECILE BOUDREAU had been crabbing. It had taken hours —the crabs weren't biting—and her head was swimming with the heat. Under the very first tree that was big enough to give shade —the small oleander bushes weren't much use in a sun like this —she stopped and squinted out over the bay to the marsh, to the shifting grasses and the little chênières.

And she'd seen Eddie come back, not half an hour ago, hunched over and leaning so hard on his paddle that it seemed he'd go overboard each stroke. And she could tell by the way he held himself that he hadn't found the slightest sign and that he wasn't going to look anymore—that he was beat.

The shells of the crabs rustled together and the basket shook. She'd have to be getting them home before they ate each other up. But she didn't feel like hurrying, not today. She sat down instead. The ground was hot through her cotton shorts. She reached out one hand and patted the brown burned grass. She picked up a shell and tossed it over her shoulder.

She heard it snap against the trunk of another tree and then fall. A couple of gulls passed overhead, squaaking and fighting. Then it was very quiet, even the dust still under the heat from the sun.

She rubbed her eyes slowly. The basket shook. She sat up took a deep breath, put two fingers in her mouth and whistled, four short sounds. Then she leaned back, fanning herself, and waited.

The close-clipped black head of her son peeped around one of the chinaberry trees. She saw him, winked. He made two enormous one-legged hops and landed behind her.

"Don, boy," she said, "take that basket home, che'."

Flat on his stomach on the grass he squirmed over to the basket and lifted the cover.

"Put that down," she said.

He hesitated, his hand raised, ready to reach in.

"They going to take a piece out your fingers." She stood up, looked briefly at the bluish shells and put the cover back on. "Now take this home, bougre, before I got to lay my hand to your rear end."

When he had gone she still hesitated, putting the hat back on her head, patting it slowly in place with her palms, and looking out across the back bay. The sun was so bright—and there was no wind, no wind at all—the water was flat and reflecting like a mirror, it was hard to see the grasses on the other side.

She gave the hat a final pat, tipping it forward over her eyes and started home, shaking her head just slightly.

Her father was standing on the front porch of the store. She waved and then went over to him.

Without getting up, Julius Arcenaux hooked a toe over another rocking-chair and pulled it toward her. "Sit down, Cecile che', and pass some talk with the old man."

She sat down and gave herself a little flipping rock.

"I been crabbing."

"So," he said and scratched the top of his bare head. "You been lucky?"

"Enough . . ." she paused, looking down at her own hands, that were picking at the splintered cane of the chair seat. "Only I couldn't help wondering. Sitting there, you begin to wonder."

Her father stopped rocking and let his face rest in the palms of his hands. "Henry, no?"

A big yellow tomcat crossed the edge of the porch. He had a bird in his teeth.

"I seen his papa come back."

"I heard tell about that."

"And he was nothing but a kid."

Julius picked up the cigar and lit it again. "He ain't much younger than you."

She looked away, down the shell path, toward her own house, out of sight there, behind the oaks and the oleanders and the summer hibiscus.

"I reckon," she said, "only with kids you feel older."

He puffed hard on his cigar, making the tobacco gurgle.

"Maybe I just plain feel old."

Perique and Therese came by, waved but did not stop.

Julius nodded after them. "Perique now, he seem to get over losing his girl quick."

Cecile looked after them. "Annie didn't ever like him much."

"Maybe," Julius said with a grin, "she like him better when she don't have him."

"You think he sleeping with Therese?"

Julius shrugged. "You think he sleeping with Annie?"

"How I know that?"

"I seen Inky out washing the covers one Sunday morning."

"You don't know nothing," Cecile said.

"Maybe," Julius said. "Only Annie got herself another man, and Perique got himself another girl. And everybody is happy."

Cecile stood up and stared along the path, back the way she had come. "And Henry," she said, "it don't change anything."

"Some," Julius said.

"Except maybe for his family, everything keep going like he never was here."

Julius scratched his cheek. "Can't go stopping," he said. "Just one crazy kid."

"Get all upset, and then we forget it. . . . And he ain't even buried here to remind nobody."

Julius got up. "I got to change my shirt," he said. "Wringing wet."

She heard him cross the store and then heard him talking briefly to her mother back in the living-quarters. She walked around the building, outside.

"Tell Mama I be back." She remembered all of a sudden that she had sent Don home with the basket of crabs. "I got to go look at something back home."

She trotted off: the weight of her swinging breasts was almost distasteful to her in the heat. She was up the steps in two hard jumps that shook the house and woke Hector who was dozing, a newspaper over his face, in the shady corner of the porch.

"Hey," he said.

She stopped with the screen door open in her hand. "Ain't seen you." She let the door slam shut and went over to perch on the rail by him.

"To look at you," he said, "you think the whole island was sinking down in the Gulf."

"You hear about Henry?"

"I hear Eddie come back."

"Didn't find anything."

"You expect he was going to?" Hector asked quietly.

Cecile sat down. She took off her straw hat and rubbed a hand across her neck. The back of her head was tingling: she'd had too much sun, she thought. It came through a hat, even. She'd have to be more careful, and maybe put a handkerchief inside.

"You not getting sunstroke?"

She shook her head, and her ears buzzed.

"Don come home with some crabs."

"I told him put the basket in the kitchen."

"You know," Hector said, "you can't take the sun like you used to. You look groggy."

"No," she said.

"I got to put the water on, if those crabs going to be done by suppertime."

"I get it, me," he said. "Big tubful of water's too heavy."

"I lift it before," she said, "and I reckon I can lift it again."

"Quit," he said, "I plain said I do it."

"Maybe I better go see if the kid left the cover on tight."

"If we got to chase crabs all over this here house," Hector said, "I'm gonna warm his tail for good."

He filled the big tub and put it on the stove. Then he sauntered down the steps, stopping to pat the big black dog whose name was Grandpa. "Reckon I get back to work," he said.

She nodded.

When the water finally began to boil she dumped in the crabs. And then began to wash the dishes she'd left from breakfast, working slowly in the water that was left in the dishpan from that morning. She did not think of heating it, though she had to rub the plates harder to clean them in the cold water. She wiped them and put them away.

She lifted the cover and looked at the crabs: they were still now and turning bright red. Good fat ones, she thought.

The afternoon sun made the house stifling, even with the shutters all closed on the west side.

She put some of the baby's diapers to soak in the big galvanized tub in the back yard and lit the little charcoal pot under them. Outside she felt better; there were thin streaks of shade from the oleander bushes and there was a little breeze moving. She pulled a sprig of parsley from the little plot by the side of the house and chewed on it. The clear, almost peppery green taste made her mouth feel cooler. She pulled the last of the oleander flowers and stuck them in her hair.

She started up the back stairs, but turned and came down again when she smelled the close hot odor of the house. She stood quiet for a minute, thinking, then turned and cut through the oleander bushes. She put her hand to her head, when she remembered that she'd left the hat inside.

"I can stay most in the shade, me," she told herself aloud. And she circled slightly to stay in the shade of the oaks. The kids weren't out playing, though there'd usually be half a dozen of them whooping and yelling back in here. The ground was smooth and sandy under the thick shade. You could see where they used to play: the deep hopscotch marks and over there, a little farther, the small baseball diamond, a circle of oyster shells to mark each base.

Maybe it was too hot for the kids too. Or maybe it was something else, she thought.

She kept going, passing the LeBlanc place. Somebody waved from the window; she waved back but did not stop. "I'm going to fetch the kid from Mama," she called to explain.

A yellow and white dog lifted his head to peer at her with yellow eyes. He started to bark, changed his mind, and stretched out again.

Cecile climbed over one of the big branches that a hurricane had ripped off an oak. The winds had dug it deep in the earth, and so it was rooting now, with tall feathery green shoots.

Cecile hurried; she was more tired than she had thought. She'd been silly to stay so long in the sun. Hector was right, though it would never do to tell him, she thought. She wondered if her mother would have a coke in the icebox. There'd be coffee for sure, there always was a pot on the back of the stove; but she didn't want anything hot. And her mother was too old-fashioned to stand for her putting ice in hers.

She ducked between some blueberry bushes, and stopped, her

mouth open in surprise. She had not expected to find anyone.

Annie Landry was stretched out full length on the ground, face up, her hands behind her head. Her hair was tied back in a bandanna, and there was cold cream on her face, and little packs of cotton over her eyes. Not more than a foot away, next to three little blue jars, a small portable radio was playing softly.

Annie sat up, suddenly, surprised and scowling.

"So this where you hide out all day long."

Annie smiled with one corner of her mouth. "Now I reckon I got to find another place." She reached up and shut off the radio.

"Where you get that?" Cecile pointed.

"Borrowed it."

"Who from?"

"Layovers to catch meddlers."

"Bet I know," Cecile said. "Bet his name is Inky."

Annie shrugged.

"And this here is where you been coming, and we don't see you around no more."

Annie began to brush the little bits of grass off her back.

"What you find to do?"

"Nothing."

"Come on," Cecile said, smiling. "I ain't goin' to bite you or tell anybody . . . what you do?"

"Listen to the radio."

"Besides listen to the radio."

"Think."

"About Inky, I bet."

"No."

Cecile bent and pulled up one of the long thin grasses and stuck it between her teeth, sucking. "Always did like the taste of these things, here."

"Yea," Annie said.

"Always taste sort of good—green and tart. You wouldn't think eating grass would be so fine."

"I wouldn't think nothing," Annie said.

"Oh lord, lord," Cecile said with a grin, "if you ain't in the lousiest humor this day here."

Annie did not answer. She concentrated on a little piece of dirt under her fingernail. She fished in her pocket and took out a pocket knife.

"You know," Cecile said, "when I was a kid, we used to come here too."

Annie did not answer or move.

"And you know, Mamere Terrebonne . . . that old woman, she told me once that when she was little they used to come here, too. Ain't that something?"

Annie looked up. "Here? You come here?"

"Oh sure," Cecile said, and waved out her hands. "Only I forgot about it, it been so long ago . . . or anyhow it seem that way."

"And what you do?"

"Oh nothing very much . . . we didn't have a radio, like you. We just sort of come and hid out."

"Right here?"

"Sure," Cecile said. "You had to pull aside the oleanders and then slip through quick, before they snapped back together. They grow in a circle around here, almost like somebody planted them . . . but they were thicker when I was coming here. There was a freeze once, I remember, that burned them out."

"I like it," Annie said, "because its the one and only place where you can't hear anything."

"The trees do that," Cecile said.

"Today's been real quiet anyhow."

"I reckon," Cecile said, "they don't feel like yelling and horsing around with the news about Henry."

Annie began to rub the cream off her face. "You think he'd have better sense than to go getting so far in he couldn't find his way out."

"I don't reckon he intended to go get lost." Cecile sucked the piece of grass in and out of her mouth, thinking.

"He was the ugliest guy," Annie said, "long, with big old saucers under his cheeks and pimples all over his chin that'd all bleed when he tried to shave."

"Look," Cecile said, and she threw down the little weed she'd been chewing, "nobody asked you."

Annie did not answer or move.

Cecile turned to push aside the bushes. "You said what you

think. . . . But just quit screaming." She stepped through the branches and let them pop back together.

Her mother had the baby out on the front porch, in the little cradle they had all used when they were that size too, and she was rocking it slowly with her foot—one nudge to the cradle for every two rocks of her own rocking-chair. Cecile swung astride the porch rail and sat there, grinning.

"You just ought to have some more kids, Ma, you like them all that much."

Her mother laughed, the soundless wheezing, and her three chins bobbed up and down, one against the other. "Been a long time since I could have a kid, me."

"I don't know," Cecile said.

"Don't go laughing at me. I am an old woman, for sure."

"Take one of my kids."

"Sure . . . if you are willing to let them go, I will take him, this one right here."

Her mother was so fat, the least little movement in the heat made the sweat pour down her face. Just standing up and bending down to the baby's crib and clucking her lips in the sleeping face —and she had to wipe her face off with the handkerchief she carried in her bosom.

Cecile said: "You heard about Eddie coming back, no?"

"Sure," her mother said, and slipped the handkerchief inside the top of her dress and wiped around.

"You got a coke, Mama?"

"There is coffee on the stove."

Cecile grinned.

"Now what is so funny?"

"Mama . . . you'd have coffee on the stove if the whole place was blowing over with a hurricane."

Her small mouth grinned in its heavy fat cheeks. "Maybe that be the time you want some most, no?"

Cecile threw up her hands. "I give up," she said. "You want me to get you some coffee, when I get mine?"

"If you are going back there . . ."

"Okay," Cecile said, "I bring you some."

Cecile walked back through the house that had not changed

since she was a child. Even the bunch of yellow straw flowers in front of the picture of the Sacred Heart was the same. She poured the two cups of coffee, put three teaspoons of sugar in each of them. She stopped a minute to admire the new washing-machine. Maybe, she thought, her father chased the girls, but he was good to his wife too. There weren't many people on the island could afford a machine like that.

She brought the cups to the porch. "That is sure a pretty machine, Mama. You still like the way it works?"

Her mother's eyes slanted a little, the way they did each time she thought about her husband. "At my age it is a great pleasure."

Cecile patted her mother's shoulder. "Stop talking like you an old decrepit woman."

"I am old," her mother said. "You the baby and you got children. Five sets of grandchildren I got—they growing up and pushing me into the cemetery."

"Mama, you don't feel good, or you ain't started off talking this way."

The woman sighed, a hissing wheezing sigh. "You get heavy sometimes and tired of living."

Cecile threw back her head and laughed, loud, so that the birds in the chinaberry tree started up, leaving a flurry of feathers drifting to the ground. "If you ain't the darndest one. . . . Now I plain know you don't mean that."

The woman looked hurt. She began to fan herself more rapidly. "You think they ever going to find Henry?"

"No."

"Well . . ." Cecile was silent, staring down at the coffee cup and the brown stain around the rim.

Her mother tapped the fan gently on the tip of her nose. "I seen it before." She finished the last bit of coffee and rested the cup on her thick high breasts.

"Maybe," Cecile said.

"I seen it before, more than I remember, me."

It was funny, Cecile thought, talking to her mother she could hardly wait to get away. But when she got home, she could think back and remember her with affection, tenderness even.

Her mother repeated: "More times I seen this."

Cecile nodded. "I reckon you are right." She picked up the baby, who gave a single sleepy cry. "I left supper sitting on the stove, me."

"You don't want no more coffee?"

Cecile shook her head. "I ain't got the time now." She picked up the cradle in her free hand.

"Just leave that be," her mother said. "I will take it in when I go."

"I can set it inside."

"I am not that old," her mother said.

"Okay," Cecile said. "I bring you some of the crabs tomorrow."

Her mother patted her forehead with the fan. "I got no need for crabs."

"They look like good fat ones."

"Your papa, he always bring plenty food to the house."

"I didn't mean anything like that," Cecile said, "and you know it."

"If you got any left," her mother said, still tapping the forehead with the corded edge of the fan, "you make gumbo, hear?"

"Sure," Cecile said, "I can always use them."

"So don't be giving them away."

"I'll be darned," Cecile pointed to one of the little banana trees, "you got some bananas."

Her mother wrinkled her nose. "I done tried one of them yesterday."

"What's wrong with them?"

"They don't taste like nothing. They ripe but they don't have no taste."

The baby burped on Cecile's shoulder. She flicked it off with the tips of her fingers and grinned at the little pinched face. "I ain't got a single shirt that don't smell sour from you."

She looked up at her mother and was astonished to see what a perfect pyramid her figure was: the enormous legs, the heavy hips that hung over the rocker like folds of cloth, the enormous breasts like a solid shelf (she had rested the coffee cup there, while her hands were folded on her stomach) and the small head with its tight, high knot of hair.

"Seems like he know when I got a clean shirt on," Cecile said. "He go and spit all over it. Keeps me washing."

Her mother said: "Bring the stuff over here and use the ma-

chine. It don't get used enough as it is." The cup perched on her
bosom vibrated with each word.

Cecile hefted the baby to her other hip. "Maybe I will," she said,
"but I ain't got too much to do now."

She did not go home. Her legs felt cramped and tingling. She
began to walk, using a long, slow loping stride that made the little
shells of the path rattle off behind her feet. She kept going until
she got to the little shell ridge at the north edge of the island. She
scrambled up through the long tough grasses and then sat down,
cross-legged, at the top. A couple of mosquitoes sang around her
legs but did not bite. She waved her hands limply at them.

The baby burped again, this time down his chin and on his own
shirt. "Miss me this time," she told him. "This time you got you
own self dirty."

She settled him on her lap and looked around. Behind her was
the island. From this angle you couldn't see any of the houses:
just trees and bushes, green-brown in color, all burned by the salt
spray, and all twisted and stunted by the wind. Ahead of her the
ground fell off into a short little marsh, not more than a couple of
hundred feet of grasses; beyond them was the bay. She squinted
as she looked out across it. There was a boat over there, coming in.
It was too far away to see clearly.

A big red ant crawled over her toe and she flicked it away.
She leaned back on her hands so that the grass prickled her palms.
And she tipped back her head until she was staring straight up into
the sky, the hard blue sky, whitened a little by the sun. She stared
at it, thinking how hard and solid it looked, like a blue cup put
over the ground. By tilting her head way back she could see the
thunderheads that sat on the rim of the Gulf, black heaps with
little lightning flickers. They seemed to stay there—never coming
closer—day and night.

She sat up straight again, rubbing her eyes: the bright light had
hurt them.

When she was little, very little, she had seen a face peep out
now and then from behind clouds: the same face, which she knew
was God's. Sometimes she'd lain flat on her back staring up into
a clear sky, staring at one patch, staring and staring, trying to make
her eyes reach through the solid blue and see what was behind it.

And sometimes when she had reached through a great distance she would catch just a glimpse of that face, before it vanished a thousand miles ahead.

She stared off across the bay at the fringe of salt marsh, and just barely in sight beyond that, the swamp. And she thought of Henry Livaudais, and how he had nothing to look at but alligator grass and salt cane and oyster grass and cattails waving in the wind. And how there were mosquitoes that came in clouds and moccasins that swam through the water without a sound. And the sour-sweet odor was so strong it made you dizzy.

And she thought how Henry had seen all these things and how he was seeing them now—in the hot bright sun. If he was seeing anything. . . .

She scrambled to her feet. Her sudden movement woke the baby, who began to cry, short peevish wails. Cecile did not notice. She stood, trembling slightly, turning her head from side to side, looking first across the bay and then over the island. And then she lifted her head and stared straight up in the sky: it was clear and empty and flat.

Hearing the baby for the first time, she stopped and picked him up. His cries trailed off to hiccups.

"I ain't going to let you go out alone," she said, "no matter how much you want to. Not as long as I can stop you."

A big brown pelican flew clumsily across the sky and landed with a splash on the bay. A couple of mockingbirds squaaked and fought in the twisted limbs of the chinaberry.

"He ain't coming back," Cecile said slowly. "He's dead right now. And nobody can find him—except the gars."

The baby hiccupped. She lifted him to her shoulder and patted him gently. She went on whispering to herself.

"It don't matter why. It end with the gars working on him."

Her lip began to tremble. She rubbed the back of her hand against it hard as she could.

"It don't matter that we get caught and die, us."

The baby gurgled and burped and began to cry again. The lugger was closer now: she could make it out: the *Belle Helene*. She watched the little white bow wave.

"It don't even matter that we been alive."

The baby was wailing steadily now. She swung on her heel in a circle, squinting as far as she could in all directions. Her jaw was trembling and she was beginning to cry. The tears were running down the side of her nose and putting their salt taste in her mouth.

"Damn," she said, "damn, damn, damn."

With the tears she couldn't see clearly. Her whole body was shaking. The baby began to scream. She bent down and searched until she found the largest rock around: a half-brick. She rubbed her eyes against her shoulder. "Damn, damn." She threw the brick hard as she could, at the sky, then turned and ran home, not waiting to see it fall.

THE OTHER ISLAND

AFTER that week-end everybody went back to work.

When he was unloading at Petit Prairie, Hector met three men from New Orleans. They chartered his boat right then and there. He charged them nearly twice what he could have made fishing. That was what the rest of the island called Boudreau luck. But they weren't starving either, just then. It was almost as if Henry's death had brought good luck to the island—but people didn't let themselves think of that.

And there were things happening; there always were.

Robby Livaudais fell out of a tree behind the LeBlanc house and twisted his ankle and broke three fingers of his left hand. And Stanley Bechet was cleaning out his big cistern (it was the time: everybody was doing that; at the end of the summer half the cisterns were stone-dry) when he thought he'd have a look at his second cistern, to see just how much water there was left and how clean it was. He took the cover off, to let the sun in a little. And he fell in. He wasn't quite sure what happened himself. Only he nearly drowned before anybody found him, for the water was so low he couldn't reach the top to pull himself out, but it was deep enough to be over his head. And this small cistern had no ladder nailed to the inside. So he yelled and treaded and stared at the small wigglers that scooted like lightning through the water. It

288

was an hour before anybody found him, and he was getting pretty tired by then.

They got the cisterns scrubbed out just in time too. A couple of afternoons later the thunderheads moved over and dumped a couple of inches of water into them. And during the lightning one of the tall palms got split right clean to the bottom so that there was a smell of burning all over the island. By the next morning the sun came up bright and hot again and the wet ground and leaves steamed away until they were bone-dry.

The day after this storm Inky was running up his main—to let it dry—when his fingers slipped off the winch handle. He'd forgot to put on the brake too—he was just careless that day, all around. The winch spun free, the sail dropped—the halyard ran in evenly and did not jam—the handle, whirling around, slipped off its pin. It missed Inky's jaw by a fraction of an inch and whirled in a long arc down the dock, smacking finally into Perique's leg and knocking him down flat on the *Hula Girl*'s deck.

That was a day's excitement. They thought at first his leg was broken. But after a couple of hours of hot towels the pain was mostly gone. By the next morning there was a tremendous bruise. But even that went away when they put a couple of leeches to it.

But that one night, Inky drank coffee and stayed awake, his revolver close at hand. Annie laughed at him. "Nobody going to think it's deliberate," she said. And they didn't. But Inky was not sure. And he didn't want to take any chances.

The next morning Inky went down and called Arthur in New Orleans, while the grocery listened. And explained what had happened to him.

Two days later there was a check for fifty dollars. Inky brought it over to the Lombas house himself. "Hell," Perique said, "for this I go do it every day."

His mother looked at the amount and then shook her head. "For a bruise."

"He's loaded," Inky said. "Anyhow you could sued him."

That was the end of that. Except that Perique stayed home for four solid days, sitting on his front porch with his leg propped up. And Therese Landry stayed with him.

And that, Ferd Lombas said, was real tough living.

Another thing the island took calmly—the way Annie slipped

down to the *Pixie* every night. They hardly noticed any more. And they didn't even talk.

Annie ate supper at home, early and by herself. Sometimes Inky came and stood at the front gate waiting (he never came in, though Adele had once or twice asked him: Annie had made him promise not to). Sometimes they met down at the Rendezvous. And sometimes she went down directly to the boat.

Annie was almost never in the house any more, except to sleep. And whenever she went out she carried a large pad of white paper and a couple of pencils stuck over her ear. Al asked about that once.

"I'm learning to draw," she said. "Inky, he's teaching me." And when he insisted, she showed her sketches—some were of the island, the twisted oaks and the palm trees; and some were things she had carried in her head from the novels she'd read at the convent: castles perched high up on hills above a river that was broad and smooth as a ribbon, and little houses almost buried under their climbing roses.

Al looked at them, and clucked his tongue in admiration, and called for Adele. When Annie tried to gather up the pages quickly he stopped her. "Look at this, che'," he said to Adele. "Look what our girl, she is doing."

Annie had to stand quietly by while they went through the pictures again.

"And there's another one," Adele pointed to a sketch held to the walls with straight pins: a girl's head.

"Didn't notice that," Al said.

"That's me," Annie said.

"Says who?"

"Inky did that."

Al squinted at it. "Only it don't look like you."

"Sort of," Adele said quickly. "Look around the mouth there."

While they were arguing, Annie picked up the pad, walked around them and out the door.

That evening Inky said: "Twenty-five pictures at five bucks is over a hundred."

She nodded.

"All while I been sitting on this boat."

She nodded again.

"Funny the money you can make out of a pencil and a couple pieces of paper."

"I won't be able to sell mine," she giggled.

"No," he said, "bet you don't."

"My old man didn't like the picture you did of me."

"You know what he can go and do."

She just giggled. "Keep your head still." She was sketching him. She had covered a sheet with small heads, and now she was trying a large one.

"I'd do some more," he said, "only it's no fun without a model."

"No," she said.

"You can keep right on sketching, while I'm making some money."

"I told you no."

He got up and turned on the radio, grinning over his shoulder. "You think your papa will find out."

"No."

"Bet that's it."

"I don't care what he thinks."

"Then you're ashamed to have me look at you."

"I don't care."

"Okay," he said, "don't do it, just because I ask you." He found the station he wanted and turned it on loud. "Don't do anything I ask you. I don't need it."

Over the noise of the radio he didn't hear her answer. But he did see her walk over and pull closed the curtains on the land side.

The sketches were good, among his best. And he had even got a face that looked like her. When she had gone he sat smoking and looking at them.

Boy, he told himself, you wouldn't make a bad artist.

He lined them up on one bunk and sat down on the one across from it. He closed first one eye, then the other, studying. Ought to get more than five bucks for those, he thought. But it wasn't likely. It wasn't that kind of a business.

He snapped off the radio and stretched out on the bunk. The figures watched him.

"Too hot down here," he said aloud and taking a pillow tossed it up to the cockpit. He had started to follow it, had one foot on the ladder, when he turned back to the pictures.

For the first time he noticed, really noticed, what a good body it was. Legs you'd see on a calendar. And a pointed behind. But the face now, it was a child's yet. Well, not a child's, but a young girl's.

Alone, Inky laughed. Imagine Annie, now, little Annie, looking as seductive as Eve herself.

He went up to the cockpit, under the mosquito net, put down his pillow and stretched out. But for the first time, for the very first time, he couldn't get her out of his mind. Once he even got up to lean down the hatch and shine a flashlight on the pictures to see if he'd remembered correctly. Annie, undressed, undressing, raced through behind his closed eyes until he finally fell asleep.

In the morning he gathered up the pictures. Maybe, he thought, he wouldn't sell these. Maybe just these, he would keep for himself. He could do others.

All day long he was quite irritated, though he couldn't figure out why.

And then one Friday night, when he and Annie were down at the Rendezvous (it was still early and there weren't many people yet), Perique and Therese came in. They just waved and went to stand at the bar.

Inky found himself staring at their backs, at the tall thin figure of Perique in its faded jeans, at Therese in jeans too, tight jeans that creased over her large rear. A good figure all right, heavy hips, heavy breasts and a small waist in between—she didn't look as bad in pants as you'd thought. The sort of figure a guy'd gone nuts about fifty years ago, but it didn't do so well right now, Inky thought.

Then, as he watched, he saw Perique's arm slip around that waist, and his hand come to rest lightly on the broad hip.

Alongside him Inky felt Annie stiffen. And he sat back in his own chair, surprised: she was jealous. He was almost sure of that.

"You want him back?" he said in a whisper.

Annie jumped—like she'd been slapped, almost—and yanked her eyes back.

"You can go see about getting him back," Inky said, "when I'm gone."

Before he knew quite what had happened, he was furiously angry. He sulked all evening, until Annie went home very early, almost ready to cry.

She'll be back, he said silently to the empty cabin as he gathered up the empty paper cups and the cigarette butts to toss them into the bay. She'll be back.

And if she isn't, he thought, and then pushed that answer away. . . . She'd be back.

WEST of Isle aux Chiens, over a mile of shallow water, speckled here and there with tufts of weeds and filled with whitecaps at the slightest breeze, is Terre Haute. A small island, not quite two miles long, a ridge of shells sticking up like a turtle's back, and covered thick with little oak trees and hackberries and oleanders. Thirty or forty people live there, in tight little unpainted houses under the trees, people with names like Svboda and Tortorich and Pivach. They are oystermen, all of them; they keep the boats at a little dock behind the island. On a Saturday night, when they are drinking, you can hear them over on the nearest point of Isle aux Chiens. On Caminada Point, which is nearest, you can hear the accordians and the singing, so clearly that you could make out the words, if you knew the language. Kids sometimes memorize the sounds and yell them back across the pass. And once the people from the other island got so mad that they sent out a skiff—with an outboard—and a couple of men with shotguns. But they hadn't dared come close enough, they'd just gone cruising up and down in the pass, cursing. And finally they'd pointed the shotguns to the island and pulled the triggers. The shot spattered down in the water. The kids, who hadn't moved—they knew the range of a shotgun—hissed and laughed and yelled: "Sal bougre-là!"

And sometimes there would be fights at Petit Prairie when both groups went in for a big week-end. It was after one of these, not three years past, that the icehouse at Isle aux Chiens burned down. And there were those who said they saw a pirogue moving rapidly out the harbor and across the pass. And sometimes kids from Isle aux Chiens would go out and, just for the hell of it, churn up the oyster beds or steal some oysters. They'd come home drenched with sweat and tired as puppies, but they'd be grinning. And those same kids sometimes would think it fun to dare somebody to sneak over to Terre Haute and peep in the windows of the houses and maybe kill a dog or a chicken. And the kids from Terre Haute, they would come over too, when it was a dark night, or a stormy one. They stayed to the western end of the island, pretty much, not daring to come down to the end where there were houses and shotguns. They'd build big fires on the west beaches with gasoline they'd brought over and then slip away before the men could get there. Once Yvonne Meynier, who knew better, saw the pirogues coming over, and instead of getting the hell out of there, she'd slipped behind a clump of hackberry bushes to watch. Only, they'd brought a dog with them, and the wind was right, it caught her scent in no time at all. They sent her running back without a stitch of clothes on. They took her clothes to Terre Haute and hung them on the outhouses. That was maybe ten years past, and Yvonne Meynier was an old maid. Though she swore they hadn't touched her, nobody believed it. And there wasn't a man on the island wanted to come after a Yugoslav kid.

It went on that way. And during the war, people at Petit Prairie used to grin and say that they hadn't heard of a fight with the Germans. The only war they knew about was the one going on across the pass. One thing just led to another, that was all.

Hector Boudreau, who was loafing near the chute of the ice-house, pretended not to notice that morning, along toward noon, when Anthony Tortorich, from Terre Haute, edged his outboard up to the wharf at Isle aux Chiens. Tortorich tossed a line around one of the posts, made a quick knot, and stepped to the dock. He stretched and hitched up his pants. He was a short man, with a very heavy body and very thin arms and legs. His pants didn't close in front; he left the top three buttons open and hung them under the curve of his belly by a pair of checked suspenders. But across his chest and his slightly hunched back was the thick band of muscle the old oystermen had—from a time when oysters were raked up by hand.

He looked around, saw Hector and went slowly over, walking like a potato on toothpicks. "Hey," he said. Hector turned around. "You tell me where old Livaudais house is?"

"Why?" Hector said. The old fellow was alone, he could see that.

"I got talk to him."

"What for?"

"I got talk to him."

"What business you got over here?"

Anthony Tortorich walked away. At the end of the dock, he hesitated a minute and then turned to the left. Hector followed right along beside him.

Some kids who were playing catch stopped and stared. "Sal cochon!" Tina Roualt yelled.

The old man looked sidewise out of his eyes and spat a yellow stream of tobacco juice down at his feet.

Hector said: "You don't know where the house is at, but you sure going in the right direction."

The old man stopped and turned. "I go all right?"

"You know for god damn sure you are."

"I ain't come to have fight."

"No, huh?"

Anthony Tortorich shifted his tobacco slightly and sucked on it with a plopping sound. "I am old man."

"What you come for?"

"I want talk with the old Livaudais."

"You keep telling me that."

"I want talk to him." He began walking again, slowly putting his heels down hard, the way old men do.

The kids were following behind them, at a little distance, giggling and scuffling.

Tortorich said softly, almost to himself: "I talk to him about his boy."

Hector stared at the broad hunched back under the faded plaid shirt. He looked at the little puffs of dust the old man's heels raised. "What you know about the boy?"

Anthony Tortorich turned very slowly; but this time he kept walking, speaking over his shoulder. "I want talk with him."

"Okay," Hector said. "And I hope you ain't starting nothing."

"I am old," Tortorich said. "I have my belly full with fighting."

Hector pointed out a house to the left. "The white painted one, there."

They walked together to the gate. Hector called, "Eddie, hey man, come here."

And Tortorich planted his elbows on the gate post and called, "Old man Livaudais, I got something say to you."

Belle came and stood in the screen door. Then Eddie pushed her aside and stepped out on the porch.

"Look who just come here," Hector called.

Eddie came down the steps, scratching his chest slowly through the thin undershirt he wore. His wife followed him.

"What you want?" Eddie said.

"I got something say to you."

"Huh?" Eddie reached inside the undershirt, to scratch better.

"He just come in," Hector said, "and I fetch him here."

"Your boy," Tortorich wiped the dribble of tobacco from the corner of his mouth, "he is gone."

Belle was standing without moving a single muscle, her hands folded across her stomach.

Tortorich leaned harder on the fence post. The wood creaked lightly.

"He know right where you live," Hector said.

Still leaning on the fence post, old Tortorich pushed up the brim of the baseball cap he wore. It was an old cap, stained by sweat and faded by sun, the sort cafés all along the bayou sold. They kept long lines of them hung over the bar on clotheslines and pinned with clothespins.

"Who?" Eddie said.

Tortorich did not answer, he stared off into space, his brown eyes squinting just a little in the glare. He pursed his lips until they stuck straight out. "I got a son."

"So?"

"And he got a girl, name of Niccolene."

"That is a stupid name for a girl," Belle said. "For sure."

"You cannot shut up for nothing, huh?" Eddie said without turning his head.

"And Niccolene does not come home either."

It was so quiet then that they could hear the old man's heavy wheezing breathing, slow and even. Eddie's fingers had found a tear in his undershirt; they were twisting and pulling at it. The sparrows fluttered and squaaked in the mulberry tree.

"Belle, hey," Eddie said, "go get us some chairs."

She got two cane chairs from the porch and carried them out to the front yard. She plunked them down behind Eddie. "There," she said.

Eddie opened the gate, pushed it open wide. Then he took the chairs by the backs and put them down, facing each other, about four feet apart on the shell walk that led to his front door. He sat down in one. Tortorich pushed the baseball cap even farther back on his head, came in the yard and sat down.

"You get back in the house," Eddie said to Belle. She did not even move. She stood behind the chair, hands folded on her stomach, her eyes jumping from one to the other. Hector squatted down on his haunches.

"You got ears, you can hear," Tortorich said, "but you got minds to think?"

The kids came close up to the fence, giggling and kicking at each other. They had long daisy chains around their necks and they were chewing on the heavier reddish flowers.

"Fi' d'ici!" Belle yelled at them. She bent and scooped up a handful of gravel and threw it. They scattered in all directions and disappeared.

"Niccolene she does not come back," Tortorich said. "We find this out."

Loretta had said nothing about her daughter that evening. She went quietly about her business, tending the baby and washing the clothes and cooking. Nick, her husband, was working very hard then in the oyster beds over in Marsh Bayou. He came home so tired that he could hardly lift up his arms or see. And when he had eaten, he wanted nothing more than to lie down on the front porch where the night was a little cooler. She sat alongside him, fanning him with a palmetto leaf. Once she started to tell him about Niccolene, but he fell asleep in the middle of her first sentence.

So she left him there on the porch and went to bed herself.

And that night her second to the youngest who was called Josef woke up with a malaria chill. When she saw him there, shaking so hard that his teeth clacked together like an old man who is dying, she wrapped him in a blanket and held him tight in her

arms. And she forgot everything else. She began to yell for Niccolene to get out the other blanket and heat some water.

Nick went into the little back room to wake the girl. He came
out with a hard look on his face, saying: "She ain't here." And
then Loretta remembered and clapped her hand to her mouth.

He lit the stove and got the blanket himself. He didn't ask
Loretta anything until nearly an hour later, when the spasm had
passed and the boy was asleep again.

"I ask you," he said, "and I still continue to ask you. Niccolene,
is she living in this house no more?"

Loretta wiped her hands on the apron she had tied over her
nightdress, very slowly. "I have meant to tell you."

Nick waited.

"She go this afternoon."

Nick said: "Where she go?"

"She tell me not to say nothing at all."

"Where she go?"

Loretta shook her head. "My heart been aching with her gone
and never coming back."

Nick lit his pipe silently. No one had ever seen him angry.
"She ain't coming back?"

"She gone with the boy." And Loretta bent her head over into
her apron and wailed.

"What boy?"

Loretta tapped her heels on the floorboards and sobbed. "She
gone for good."

"What boy?"

"She meet him at Petit Prairie. And she never say his name."
She ain't never told you?"

"It ain't a boy from this place," Loretta said.

Nick's pipe went out.

"One from over there."

He kept turning the black stained pipe in his thick calloused
fingers. Finally he put it away.

"You see why she ain't told me," Loretta said.

He stood up.

"But they ain't there now," Loretta said.

He leaned against the door frame and waited.

"I know you want to get her back."

His face did not move. "Where they go?"

She shook her head. "Isle aux Chiens, no. She know you come for her there."

"What did she do?"

"Not to the other island . . . but you know the little bayou that is back of there, the one they call the rabbit?"

He nodded.

"She meet him there."

"And how she got there?"

Loretta ducked her head. "I ain't ask her."

Nick squatted down and began to tie the laces of his shoes.

"What I could do," Loretta said, "is nothing."

He finished the knot methodically, stood up and lit a cigarette. "I come back to deal with you."

He went down the steps very slowly and walked away, the cigarette in his hand now. She sat and watched the yellow glow swing back and forth until it passed the bushes and disappeared.

Henry was at Rabbit Bayou early. There was a little half-circle in the marsh there, where the bayou drained into the bay. He slipped his pirogue out of sight, backing it in through a passage so narrow the reeds brushed hard on each side of the shell. And he settled down to wait.

Niccolene did not come until nearly twelve o'clock. By then the wind was up, and there were small flat pieces of cloud scudding low across the sky. Henry was just beginning to wonder when he heard the distinct crisp sound of a paddle in water. He kept perfectly still until the girl came into the mouth of the bayou. The first thing he recognized was her eyes—they were very large and close-set, and the shiny irises looked always as if they were full of tears.

She had stopped in the center of the little open space and was turning her pirogue in a slow circle, looking. She was panting; he could hear that even from where he was. Hard going in the wind out there in the bay, he thought. He pushed his way out of the grass.

She swung her pirogue over to meet him. "I didn't see nothing."

"You have trouble out there?"

She nodded. "I been thinking the wind was coming up."

"Yea," he said.

There was a small sloping bank, a tiny beach not more than four feet wide. They pulled the pirogues up there and put the bundle and the two brown paper bags from hers into Henry's. Then, together they lifted her pirogue and ran it even higher up the shells.

"That ain't going nowhere," Henry said.

"My old man be fit to tie, and something happen to it."

It don't matter any more what he do, Henry started to say. But didn't."

His pirogue, now that Niccolene was in it, rode low in the water. He paddled it about a bit, testing. Finally he shook his head. "We ain't going out in this." The mouth of Bayou Verde was a mile north on the circle of the open bay.

"So we go the other way," she said quietly.

Up Rabbit Bayou to Timbalier and then along its snaking route until it reached Bayou Verde.

"Longer."

"We ain't that hurried."

"We better not be."

"My old man going to think I gone out fishing when he don't see me there in the morning."

He nodded and headed the pirogue up Rabbit Bayou.

Later that night, when it began to storm they had to stop, and cut back some grass and push the pirogue into the empty spot to steady it a little because the wind was very high. They pulled a tarpaulin over their heads and waited a couple of hours, holding to the heaviest of the reeds to steady the canoe against the stiff wind.

"It getting cold," Niccolene said once.

"Bottle whisky there."

She got it and offered it to him first. He took it, surprised as he always was. Girls on Isle aux Chiens, he thought, would have taken a swallow first. But on the other island they didn't. The women didn't even eat with the men. Niccolene had told him that.

He took one gulp and handed it back. "Take it easy."

"So cold my insides shivering."

"Scared?"

She screwed the top back on the bottle and put it carefully away. "Nothing to be scared of," she said.

The lightning rolled in around them. Even under the heavy tarpaulin they saw each other's faces clearly in the bluish light.

"Don't worry about it hitting you none," Henry said. "I'm feeling real lucky, me."

"I seen lightning before," she said.

They were both silent, only shifting their weight slightly to balance the pirogue.

Finally she said: "Tell me what it like in New Orleans."

"I told you," he said, "all I got to know."

It was daylight when they reached the end of Timbalier and turned up Bayou Verde. The sun was just barely up, but it was burning hot already and there were little steaming dazzles of heat mirages on the water ahead.

They were both paddling now and the heavy pirogue moved rapidly. The water ran smoothly past a half-inch below its gunwales.

They heard the lugger nearly half an hour before it appeared, heard the thump and bang of its gas engine echo out over the marsh grass.

To the right, maybe thirty feet back in the grass away from the bayou, was a little chênière, a shell ridge, covered with salt-burned slanting oaks, and vines, and palmettos. Without looking behind, without once saying anything, they swung the pirogue's bow over and threaded through the little passes in the grass until they were behind the chênière. Then still without saying anything, Henry left the pirogue and, with his cane knife, cut his way to the top of the chênière.

Henry looked back over his shoulder once to be sure the pirogue was hidden in the grass and saw that Niccolene had come up silently too and was standing at his elbow. He motioned her back. She shook her head. They both peered out at the bayou from under the fringed leaf of a latanier.

The lugger went past so close they could read the name on the pack of cigarettes that a man squatting on the deck was holding. The lugger was going full ahead and the grasses on each side shook and quivered with its wake.

"So," Henry said finally when it had disappeared around a turn of the bayou and all you could see was the very top of its wheel-house above the reeds. "You know who that was?"

"I seen that boat before."

"And whose it is?"

"My uncle."

They were silent for a while. And she said: "Maybe they just gone up to sell something."

"They was six," Henry said. "And all of them ain't happening to go in selling something."

She went back to the pirogue and sat down. Henry followed. "Let's us eat breakfast," he said. "No use starving."

They had some sausage and bread and a jar filled with coffee.

"She told," Niccolene said finally, thinking of Loretta.

Henry just shrugged.

"They going wait in town."

"Yea," Henry said.

If they'd made the early bus, he thought, the way they planned. If that wind hadn't made Niccolene so long coming. If the storm hadn't held them up in Bayou Timbalier. If the wind hadn't been so high they had to come the long way. . . .

"They's always winds coming up from nowhere this near to September," he said aloud.

"We can sneak in town," she said.

"Sure," he said, "and then where we are?"

She finished with the sausage and wiped her hands on her shirt. "Then we get the bus like we planned."

"Hell," he said, "they just going to be sitting where that bus stops."

She hesitated a minute and then nodded, sadly. They would.

Another lugger went by in the bayou. Henry did not bother getting up this time to look. "More," he said.

Niccolene went up to the top of the chênière and watched. When she climbed down, she didn't say a word.

"We ain't never going to get in there," he said.

She had picked up a bit of oyster shell and scratched with it on the rough gunwale of the pirogue.

"You want to go back?"

"Where?"

He jerked his finger south.

She looked down at the old oyster shell her fingers held. And she shook her head. "No."

"You can all right."

"No," she said, "no, I can't."

It was so quiet they could hear the stir of the grasses and the little animals out in the marsh and the steady rubbing of the hyacinth bulbs.

"We could go to Port Ronquille," Henry said. "We could wait till dark and go down the bayou again and be across the bay by daylight. And they wouldn't never think to look for us over on that side. And we just go on up Bayou Maringouin to Port Ronquille pretty as we please."

Niccolene tossed the shell from hand to hand. "Except for the wind, maybe."

He squinted up into the clear sky. The wind was still high. "Blow for three or four days, times."

She nodded.

The heavily laden pirogue would never make it. Even the lightest one would be too risky now. The onshore wind would have kicked up little breakers. And they would have to cross the bay and skirt along the edge of the open Gulf, broadside to the wind, for a good many miles before they came to the place where Bayou Maringouin emptied into the Gulf.

"We don't got to go out in the open," he said finally, "we go up through the marsh just behind the bay."

She still played with the shell. "They's oyster beds back in there," she reminded him, "and nothing but grass around. Somebody's sure to be working around and we going to get seen."

"Jesus God," he said and got the bottle of whisky. This time he did not offer her any.

"I ain't going back," she said.

"Maybe at night . . ." He took another swallow and then shook his head. "Me, I couldn't find my way through back in there in the dark too," he said. "You could?"

"I could, for sure. But only one way I know in the dark."

"So?"

"It go all the way around, past six or seven beds, almost far up as we are right now, before it come out at the bayou."

"Yea," he said. "I get it."

"Going that way, only one I know, we ain't going to be through by light either, account of we can't leave here before dark."

"And they see us that way, like nothing so easy."

A couple of gulls circled overhead, curiously.

"And they don't go away," she said nervously, looking up at the gulls, "and they going to look suspicious to somebody coming along."

"They go away all right, soon they see we ain't something for them to eat."

After maybe ten minutes, the gulls tired of their watching and spiraled away on an updraft.

"Maybe," he said, "we just walk right into town. Got a couple shotguns." But he knew he didn't stand a chance. One man against so many.

"You got family there," she said. And waited.

He did. Sure he did. And they had cars too, some of them. All you would have to do would be sneak into town at night and get one of them to drive you up as far as Millaudon or maybe even a little farther to Colyell City.

If they would.

He shook his head. "They wouldn't do nothing like that."

"Account of me."

"Hell," he said, "we don't got to have them."

She tossed the shell away into the alligator grass.

"Now look," he said, "we can go straight on through, right straight on to Port Ronquille."

She had folded her hands on her lap and was staring down at them.

"We go straight across." Through the marsh. "And then we go right straight on through the swamp."

She jerked her head up.

"If you ain't scared."

"I never been in there," she said.

"I been hunting there. Lots, me. I been way up in it. One whole day long."

She was watching him with her large eyes that always seemed full of tears.

"One whole day I spent going in," he said. "Another day and

maybe a little more and we come out back of Port Ronquille."

"We got the food," she said slowly.

"There bayous big as anything back in there, wide as nothing you seen, two, three times wide as the road at Petit Prairie."

"You find the way?"

"Sure," he said.

After a minute she stood up and retied the cotton scarf that covered her hair. "You find the way?"

"Hell," he said, "I been telling you."

"Nothing else to do," she said.

Old Tortorich sat with a hand on each knee and stared straight ahead. Hector began to make little lines in the dusty ground with the tip of his finger. Belle walked away.

"So," Eddie said. "Like that."

Tortorich said, "Nick gets some of his brothers and they go to Petit Prairie. And they ask around and they find out Niccolene ain't been there. And they sit down waiting."

Eddie nodded. Belle had begun to sweep the side yard clear of twigs and grass, the way she did every day. She had a special broom of rushes tied to a long handle. The ground was dusty and cracked and hard as a floor.

"And we see you take the priest. And we see the candles you burn in Catfish Bay." Tortorich smiled. In his brown face his teeth were long and pointed and yellow. Rounded teeth, like an animal's.

"We did that," Hector said.

"Only us, we find something."

"What?" Eddie asked.

"Where they camp that first night—over by Muscat Lake." Tortorich stopped, waited for them to understand.

"Ain't in direction to Petit Prairie at all," Eddie said.

Tortorich nodded.

"So they was heading for Port Ronquille," Eddie said very slowly.

"Son of a bitch," Hector said.

"They try," Tortorich said, "straight through the swamp. Three, four days. With luck."

"While you looking for them in Petit Prairie." Out of the corner of his eye Hector had seen Pete Livaudais come to the

front door, and stand there, half hidden by the black screen.
He thought he saw something else too, but he wasn't sure. He
didn't move his head, or give any sign, but he kept watching.

"Don't believe that, me," Eddie said.

Tortorich sighed and scratched the side of his brown crinkled
cheek. "We find." And he took out of his back pocket a folded
paper box, and held it out on his palm.

Eddie took it. The paper box from a tube of Squibb sunburn
cream, on it a little red-and-white sticker that said Arcenaux
Grocery.

Eddie held the crushed pieces of cardboard between his fingers,
staring at them.

"He buy that, all right," Hector said. "Julius tell me how he
couldn't figure out why."

"You believe now?" Tortorich said.

The screen door slammed shut and Pete came running down
into the yard, shotgun in his hand. Eddie did not move, but
Hector stepped out to meet the boy.

It was over in a few seconds, so fast that the gun did not even
go off. The boy's body, tense and muscular as it was, went down
under Hector's weight.

Tortorich looked over and grinned. Eddie did not turn his head.

Hector held the boy down with his knees, and punched him a
couple of times, not too hard, but enough to make him grunt. Then
Hector got up, nudged the boy with his toe. "Get away from
here."

Pete disappeared at once. Belle was standing at the corner of the
house, her broom still in her hand. Hector avoided looking at her.

"They ain't there now," Eddie said in a half question.

"We ask and we look," Tortorich said, "and they ain't there
now."

"They coulda left. They coulda take a bus or hitchhike."

"They ain't left," Tortorich said.

He stretched his baseball cap on his knee, carefully working around the band. "The road," he said, "five mile out the
town, the rain that come wash out the little bridge. So they got to
ferry the cars across." He put the cap back on his head. "And the
man there, he marry my wife's cousin's girl. So he tell us. And he
say there ain't nobody come along."

Eddie said nothing.

"They don't even get there," Tortorich said. "We know."

They went back to the dock, the three of them. The old man first. He had taken off his cap again and was fanning his half-bald head with it. Four or five feet behind was Eddie. He had rolled his undershirt up under his arms now and he was scratching at the prickly heat that peppered his body. Half-a-dozen yards away, Hector followed, still holding the shotgun.

Tortorich freed his line and dropped it into the bow of his skiff. The water was still, and the hull sat on it almost without moving, while he fiddled with the outboard. Eddie came and sat on the edge of the dock, looking down. Hector stood with his head tilted back, looking at the gulls and the single brown pelican that circled in the white sky.

"They was intending to go right straight through the swamp," Tortorich said. "Maybe you could make the way through?"

Eddie shook his head slowly.

Tortorich slapped the motor with the flat of his hand, and then began to wrap the cord tightly around the starter. The skiff moved slightly under the dock; he gave it a shove out into the open. "Crazy," he said. "Nobody find the way through."

"I don't get this," Hector said. "Why you come all the way over here to tell us when you know all about it?"

"You go back to looking one day," Tortorich said. "Maybe you find."

"I don't reckon we be looking," Hector said.

Tortorich went on. "You find something of her, you give it to us." He yanked at the starter rope. The motor sputtered and died. "If we find, we give him back."

Eddie just nodded.

After a few more tries, he got the motor started. He adjusted the throttle and then swung out. The pelicans splashed up, beating the air with their clumsy wings.

They stood watching until he disappeared around the point. The pelicans came back and settled on the water, swimming their tight circles.

"Waiting for their fish guts," Hector said softly.

Eddie was looking out across the bay, across the still sun-polished water to the line of saw grass. "Two out there." His head was hurting; he rubbed it slowly. "I plain crazy to come out in this sun with no cap."

Out in the bay four or five mullet broke water in a series of frantic leaps and disappeared.

"They really chased, them," Eddie said. He felt himself begin to shiver, even in the hot sun, and he rubbed his hands up and down his arms.

Hector put the shotgun down on the wharf and lit a cigarette.

"A crazy kid," Eddie said, "from the time he could walk."

"Some born like that."

"He didn't say how old she was."

"No," Hector said.

"Maybe she was pretty." Sometimes those girls were, with their black hair and their big black eyes. But it wouldn't matter any more with the fishes and the insects working at her.

Hector was cracking his knuckles gently.

Eddie sat down on the top of a piling which was covered by a hammered sheet of galvanized tin. He felt peculiar, sick at his stomach sort of. He stared down at the water. It was thick and heavy, almost oily. It was that way in the bayous sometimes.

"He didn't have to go running off like a tramp," he said.

Hector nodded.

"He could brought her back," Eddie said, "and gone up with one of the boats, the regular way."

"We coulda got him on that bus for New Orleans all right," Hector said. "Ain't no family going to stop us."

"A crazy kid. Born crazy."

"Yea," Hector said.

Eddie sighed and rubbed the palms of his hands down the length of his thighs. "No," he said, "I don't believe he could come back, him. We wouldn't done that."

"Maybe."

"Musta thought he could figure the way through."

"Seems like."

Eddie looked up and over at the distant marshes again, and he squinted and rubbed his face in his hands.

"She must been pretty," he said.

Hector nodded.

"He always had eye for pretty girls."

"Yea," Hector said.

"He didn't got to go sneaking out across the swamp. . . . August Claverie going up the next morning. He'd took them."

Hector didn't answer.

"He'd took them," Eddie said. "And we'd gone along to make sure nothing happen."

Still closer the pelicans were riding on the water, brown ones and gray.

"They still waiting," Hector said, pointing to them.

"I don't reckon they could come back," Eddie said, "after all."

Hector kept his eyes on the pelicans.

"We wouldn't done it."

Hector just nodded.

"There wasn't no way to go but through the swamp."

"He ought to been sure he knew which way he was going," Hector said.

"I never seen her," Eddie said.

"Yea," Hector said.

"Cottonmouths out there . . . they the only thing don't bother running when a man comes along."

"I know, me."

"You figure it was a cottonmouth?"

"I don't know. How'd I know?"

"You can see the trees from here, just barely."

"I never noticed that before," Hector said.

"Those'd be the ones just east of Rabbit Bayou, no?"

Hector nodded. "Around where we got the crawfish last March. The black ones, that was all heads and no tails."

"That wasn't fit for nothing more than bait," Eddie said.

Hector said: "I wonder, was she pretty, her?"

"She ain't now," Eddie said, "not after she been feeding the gars and the crawfish." And because he couldn't help himself, he shivered, shivered hard, his whole body shook.

Hector didn't look, trying not to see.

When the spasm had passed, Eddie said: "You figure they bring him back here, if they do find him?"

"Yea."

"You believe the old guy?"

"Yea," Hector said.

Eddie looked down at his hands. The skin on their backs was still prickled. "Shivering in the sun," he said, "maybe I got the malaria again."

"Maybe," Hector said.

"You got things to do," Eddie said. "Why you don't go do them?"

"Me?" Hector said. "No. And I'd just as leave stay here."

Eddie reached in his pocket and found a pack of cigarettes. They were bent and crumpled. He put the pack on the top of the piling and took a single cigarette. He smoothed and straightened it between his fingers, then took a light from Hector's butt just before he threw it away.

They spent all afternoon there, smoking. Every time they dropped a cigarette down into the water, there was a flash of small transparent fish up to the surface to nibble on it.

IT hit young Pete Livaudais hard. He wasn't home for a couple of days. He stayed down in the west end of the island. Annie saw him once, but it was only at a distance and only for a second before he ducked behind some palmettos.

"Leave him," Eddie said. "He don't want to see nobody."

The people who lived in the most western of the houses—the Cheramies—they thought they could hear sobbing and crying. But it was so far away they couldn't be sure.

Cecile said: "If he don't come out soon, somebody got to go get him."

And Hector shook his head. "He got a right to it."

Cecile looked at him, squinting. "You know something? You been strange ever since it all come to light."

"How strange?"

"If I could tell," she said, "maybe I wouldn't be worrying."

"Nothing wrong with me."

"I guess so, maybe."

"Tell you what," he said suddenly and began to grin, wide and bright, "let's us go in to Petit Prairie."

"Now? In the middle of the weektime?"

"Sure," he said. "I'm gonna borrow the *Tangerine* from Perique. And him and your old man, they can work if they want to without me. Or they can get somebody else."

"Right now?"

"Sure," he said, "we ain't that hard up for money."

"What we do?"

"What we do?" he mimicked. "See what going on. Go to a movie."

He was on his feet. He flipped a cap on the back of his head. "You never done this before."

312

"So we do it now. . . . I'm gonna talk to Perique."

She called after him: "You got to shave."

Adele felt dreadful. She had a headache, and four aspirins had done nothing for it. Al was out working; he had left at three o'clock that morning. There was no telling when he'd be back—it always depended on how his luck was running.

She walked down to the grocery and bought a small pack of tea bags. Julius Arcenaux put them in a little paper bag and rang up the cash register. "Somebody sick?" he asked.

"No," she said. "Why?"

Julius grinned. "Nobody buys tea, unless somebody's sick."

He had a good smile, she thought, very gay. And his reputation as a lady's man, she thought, well, maybe . . .

"I was thinking it might be nice."

"It is, for sure," he said.

He wasn't making any play for her . . . but Al said he liked the young girls. . . .

Claudie tugged on her skirt. "What?" she asked.

He kept tugging, giggling.

Julius leaned over the counter. "Hey there, brother-in-law!"

Claudie looked up and began to grin. One thing about Julius: kids liked him, liked him at once.

He reached over and swung Claudie up to the counter. "You getting heavy, brother-in-law," he grunted.

"He's growing up," Adele said.

"God damn," Perique said.

Adele jumped. He was over in the corner, behind the counter, and he was looking through a series of small paper boxes. "Jesus God," he said, "you old bastard, it ain't here."

Julius did not even bother to turn around. "I bought some, not five months ago. And they got to be there." He said to Adele: "He looking for a special kind of screw."

"Oh," Adele said.

"I hope Al is having good luck."

"Thank you."

"They went down to the west," Julius said. He had a pair of field glasses and he would often watch the boats—to see if they put over their nets or to see what direction they were going in. "And you going to go fishing, dogaree?" he tugged at Claudie's hand.

"Mostly he follow Annie around all day," Adele said with a small smile. "The other kids don't play with him."

Julius scratched his belly. "Kids go slow," he said, "they will one day coming."

Adele tapped Claudie's bare leg. "Let's us go, beau."

He whimpered and would not jump down from the counter.

"I get him," Julius said. "And how you going to be a fisherman, and afraid of such a little thing?"

"He's not going to go fishing," Adele said quickly.

"So . . ." Julius said and put him on the floor, "after Henry, nobody want their kids to go out much."

"Yes," Adele said. "Maybe he will get a job in New Orleans." And she went home.

While she waited for the water to boil, she walked around the living-room. Too much furniture, she thought.

"Claudie," she said, "now your papa's away, you help me, huh?"

He grinned and nodded.

"And we going to move furniture, if you do what I tell you." The water began to boil. She raced out and poured it, then brought the cup back.

"How we have live with this so long, I don't know . . . a month since I been here and it never occur to me!"

They tugged the two chairs out into the middle of the room, she pulling and Claudie pushing. "Now," she said, "we get down the pictures. . . ."

She stopped to drink the tea. Claudie dropped down on the floor and panted, pretending to be a dog, lolling his head from side to side.

She grinned at him at first and then the smile faded off. He paid no attention to her but went crawling around on his hands and knees, growling and panting.

"You going to want to get married," she said, not so much to him as to herself, "one of these days, if I am alive to see it, and no matter who you got, it going to be all right with me. And if they don't like it where we living, I give you the money to go somewhere else. . . . You hear?"

He looked over at her. And began to bark.

"You not going to go sneaking around, you hear?"

He threw back his head, and howled, the long hunting howl.

"Quit!" She put the teacup on the window sill. "Now let's us go back to work."

Perique slammed out of the store. "You find the fucking bolt," he said. "God damn if I can."

Julius shouted after him, "You said screw, man. You ain't said bolt. . . ."

"You find it!" And Perique turned and threw the piece of metal.

Julius caught it and held it up between his two fingers looking at it. "That what it is, for sure," he said. Perique was gone. He sighed and went back in the store. He put the bolt down on a shelf carefully: Perique would be back for it. Maybe, Julius thought, if he had time, he'd look too. That might be a good thing to do. . . . Everybody was so nervous. They'd all be having strokes if they didn't calm down.

He sat down and turned on the radio.

He'd have to remember to pull closed the heavy shutters on the front of the store. With everybody in a mood like that, there were liable to be fights. And the store windows might get broke—just for fun. It had happened before: smashed both windows, just to get a couple of packs of cigarettes. Left the money on the counter. It was a penny short too.

He'd close those shutters.

Annie came home in the late afternoon. Adele found her in the middle of the living-room.

"I didn't hear you," Adele said. "I got a start."

"I forgot," Annie said, "you were so delicate."

If Al would just come home, Adele thought. It wouldn't be so bad. But if she had the girl all evening alone . . .

And she was immediately furious with herself for thinking that. She put on her brightest smile. "You like the room?"

"I was just looking at it," Annie said.

Claudie had heard her too and came scooting into the room. He grabbed her legs. "Go way, stupid," she said.

"He likes you," Adele said and was surprised how silly that sounded.

"You got paint in your hair," Annie said.

"Painting the back steps." She reached up, trying to find the place.

"Probably have to cut it out."

"I got lots of hair," Adele said, "it don't matter."

"When we going to eat supper?"

"I was waiting to see when your father come back."

"We all going to starve waiting for him." Annie scratched at her forearm. "I'm going get something out the icebox."

"There's some cold brisket."

"I'll find something, don't worry."

Adele bent forward looking at her arm. "That's poison ivy."

"No," Annie said.

"That big patch there. Put some soda on it."

"I don't get it," Annie repeated. "I keep telling you."

Adele leaned back again. "You see any sign of your father's boat?"

"I don't keep track of him," Annie said; "he's a big boy now."

"Oh," Adele said, "I was just wondering."

She sat down in one of the armchairs and began to unravel the sleeve of a maroon-colored sweater.

Annie finished letting her eyes run around the room. She brought them back to Adele. "What you ripping up the sweater for?"

"The elbow wore through." Adele held it up. "I'm going to knit it up again. Cuff'll be a little narrow, that's all."

"Lopsided."

"You won't notice it."

Claudie had got his ship model. He stood in the door, holding it to his stomach, looking from one woman to the other.

"Kid's beginning to get a pot," Annie said without looking at him.

"Kids do," Adele said.

"His's worse." Annie crinkled up her nose. "And he does smell," she said, "phew."

Claudie giggled. "Don't."

"Get out here," his mother said. "Go take the boat on the front porch."

Claudie hesitated.

"Go on, stinky," Annie told him.

He grinned over his shoulder. And went.

"You oughtn't to talk to him like that."

"It's true," Annie said.

Adele went back to her ripping. Her fingers went too fast. The yarn knotted. She held it up close to her eyes, trying to untangle it.

"You need glasses, huh?"

Adele shook her head.

"Sure you do."

"It's just—hard—to—see—this color." And she shook out the tangle. "Now."

Annie turned on her heel, studying the room, again.

"You like it?" Adele asked without looking up.

"Nope."

"Oh," Adele said. "Why you don't like it?"

"Looks like a whorehouse, that's why."

It was so quiet you could hear the butterfly bushes on the side of the house brush against the boards.

"Oh . . ." Adele said softly.

"You ask me," Annie said.

"I never been in one," Adele said, still softly, "so I don't know. . . . But I guess maybe you have."

You could hear Claudie singing to himself on the porch. It was a minute before Annie understood. When she did, she flashed out of the room, kicking over the closest table as she went.

When Al came home, Adele had not quite had time to get the puffiness and the red away from her eyes. And the powder which she put on quick when she heard him coming, did no good at all.

"Now look," Al said, "you going to stay still and listen to me, if I got to hold you."

"Okay," Annie said. "Okay. Quit yelling."

He found her coming along one of the paths not far from the house.

"You ain't too big for whipping now," he said. "And I got to, I do it right out here."

"Oh hell," Annie said. She managed to swagger her shoulders.

"You give me just one good reason you got for walking in the house and calling Adele a whore."

"Oh Jesus," Annie said, "I didn't call her that."

"Don't go lying."

"I *didn't*."

"You say it look like a whorehouse in the parlor."

She tilted her head and squinted at the top of the young palm trees.

"Answer me."

"She asked me if I like it."

"What you tell her?"

"Told her the truth."

"What?"

"Looked like a whorehouse."

Al lit a match against his nail and touched it to a cigarette. "Now I got something to tell you."

"What?" She screwed up her mouth and tried to look uninterested.

"You going back to the house and make you' apologies. And you are going to start being polite."

She shrugged and looked away.

"And you are going right now."

"Can't make me."

He looked at her.

"I'm going to make the biggest yell you ever did hear."

"And who going to interfere . . . Inky?"

She jumped a little. She had been thinking that, though she had not realized it.

"That what you thinking?"

"Not thinking nothing," she said.

"He ain't going to do nothing."

"I don't need him," Annie said. "I can take care myself."

"You going back if I got to carry you."

"Okay," she said, "okay. But don't be surprised if one of these days I'm gone."

"Where?"

"None of your business."

"With him, no?" He jerked his thumb over his shoulder toward the north side of the island and the wharf.

"None of your business."

"Well, maybe," he said. "Maybe you get to starve in New Orleans. But if I was betting, I give odds you ain't going to get there."

"Shows how much you know." She tried to pull free and did not succeed. "If my mother was around, you wouldn't go acting this way. . . . Leggo!"

He didn't pay the slightest attention. He was dragging her steadily along the path to home.

"Leggo!" she yelled.

And Claudie came scuttling out of the bushes to stand wide-eyed.

"You going to be surprised," Annie said. "I wouldn't stay around here for nothing."

It was easier to walk. And her feet began moving. "Wild horses wouldn't keep me here."

"Maybe," her father said quietly. "Maybe not."

"I'm telling you!"

Therese Landry stood leaning on the door of the kitchen talking to her mother.

"Jeez," she said. "They sure fighting. . . ."

Her mother looked up from the peas she was shelling, the last of the season's peas. "What?"

"I was coming home and what do I see?"

"What?" her mother asked patiently.

"Old Al just dragging Annie along like she was a sack of feed."

"That been coming for a long time," her mother said.

Therese scratched her ear. "It sure here now."

Her mother popped a couple more peas into the dish. "You hear what they was fighting about?"

"Adele."

A few more pods emptied their scant loads.

"Poor peas, for sure. But I can make a soup outa these."

"I was going to go closer to the house. So I could really tell what was up." She hesitated. "You don't have to look at me like that—you'd done the same thing."

Her mother shrugged. "So?"

"Claudie was sitting on the front steps, big as life. And there wasn't no way to get closer without him seeing me."

Her mother shook her head, a large head with a heavy mat of gray-streaked hair. "Second wife. . . ." she said. "It don't ever work smooth."

Therese took a handful of the pods and began to shell them. "Do you reckon," she said after a while, "she is going to go off with him?"

"Who?"

"You know who I'm talking about."

"Annie?"

"And Inky what's-his-name."

Her mother lifted her shoulders, high up, so that they almost reached her ears, and let them drop again. "You are asking me . . . and what should I know."

"Just wondered. That's all."

"It come out," her mother said. "In time. It all work out. The way it is going to work. Sooner or later."

"Still wish I'd heard," Therese said.

*

FIFTEEN minutes later Annie came hurrying out the front door. She gave the screen a hard swing behind her so that it almost jumped off its hinges. Her father yelled. She started to take the steps in one leap. Just at the top her ankle turned, and she fell down them, ducking her head under, bouncing once on her shoulder, landing on her hip and arm.

She was up in a minute, half running, half hobbling, but moving. Claudie, who had had himself pulled up into a tiny corner of the steps when she came by, got down and trotted after her.

She went to the tiny field of clover grass that was completely surrounded by thick oleander bushes. She pushed her way through, carelessly, hearing her blouse rip.

When she got inside, she sat down, on her good hip. And she looked at her arm. There was a long brushburn from her elbow down to her hand: it was bleeding, slightly. She sat staring at it, until Claudie wiggled through the tangle and sat down beside her.

"God," she said, "get out of here."

He didn't move.

"Beat it," she said and lifted her good arm.

He moved out of reach, sliding along the grass on his rear. And waited.

"Now I know what happen," she said, spitting the words out as if each one tasted bitter. "You sitting up there at the top of the steps so innocent and quiet . . . and you trip me. Yessir, I'm getting to see it now."

"No," Claudie said.

"Jesus!" she lifted her eyebrows. "You can talk. . . . Maybe you human after all."

He watched her, a little uncertain, and staying well out of reach.

"Trip me," Annie muttered. She felt her hip carefully and then began rubbing it softly. It hurt—so much that her eyes began to water.

"Don't cry," Claudie said.

"God damn it . . . go away!"

He pushed himself back a couple of feet.

She stretched out on her back and doubled up her legs. And the little wires of pain ran all through her body.

Maybe I'm going to die, right here, and the crows'll come and eat me. . . . "You wouldn't have the sense to go call anybody."

They'd never find me. It would be like Henry. Only right on the island.

Even she did not quite believe that, so she gave up the thought.

She rubbed her shoulder, in small circles. That made it feel better. She closed her eyes and felt the warmth of the sun on her face and the warmth of the ground at her back.

Adele's face passed in front of her closed eyes: the plain face, with its smooth olive skin and its smooth brushed hair.

Annie put up a hand and rumpled her own hair fiercely. Bitch, she thought, bitch.

If my real mother was alive. . . . She tried to remember her mother, but she couldn't seem to remember very much. She couldn't seem to find the details she wanted, the details that made the image real. . . . It was the sun. For sure.

Somebody was whistling. They would be passing, and not too far away. She recognized the tune: "Tennis Shoes." The sound faded and stopped. She wondered idly who it was.

Her leg was burning, and she thought she could feel a little dripping. She had scraped that too—she was furious. Always did have weak ankles, she told herself, and you couldn't expect anything else from them.

She opened her eyes once: a brown rabbit was chewing nervously at the grass, not twenty feet away. She let her eyes slide closed again. Claudie giggled.

"What?"

"Gone."

She opened her left eye. The rabbit was gone. "Nothing I can do about it."

Her fingers patted the grass that the rabbit had been nervously chewing. It would be nice to live out here . . . in a tent or something like that, so you could be near to the ground. You could find some bricks and make a little fire and cook over them. Except when it began raining, in February.

"I won't go back there." She could hear Claudie stir himself to listen.

She peeped at him. He was bent forward so that his chin was almost on the grass, he was listening so hard.

"Lots other places."

Claudie nodded, eagerly.

She opened both eyes. "You don't look much like her," she said. "Maybe you're not her son. Not really."

Claudie shuffled a little closer.

"You going to have the greenest behind, moving around like that."

A crow circled way up in the white-blue sky. His gigantic shadow flicked over them.

"Maybe she just found you someplace."

If you had a floor to your tent it wouldn't be bad out here, even in February. But somebody owned it. Had to. Somebody owned all the land, even if it was only marsh and no solid spot on it, and even if it was only the state government. . . . If you just had your floor a little off the ground so the water would run under it. . . .

"I'd live all alone. I wouldn't have a soul with me."

You wouldn't have to work, you wouldn't have to have money to buy things. You could live on the things you could find.

She rolled over on her side and squinted up at the sky through the blades of grass and weed. She stopped pretending. She wasn't hurt. She didn't feel anything. Even the little ache of her arm was gone and the anger that had been like a fist doubled inside her.

I'll go back, she thought. Maybe. No place else to go. Yet.

She thought about Inky and she didn't feel anything either. When she tried to imagine him, it was Perique's face that formed instead.

There were so many things going on inside her. She could feel them—tumbling around like clothes in a washing-machine, she thought.

*

ANNIE had her usual early supper that evening, only this time she hurried even more. She finished just as Adele and Al came back, and she ducked into her room without their seeing her. Then she climbed out the window. Claudie didn't follow her. Adele had found him and was making him brush his teeth—which he never did and which were getting coated with a yellow-white film. As Annie swung herself over the side fence she could hear the yelling begin inside.

And she went hunting for Inky. Without asking anyone. First she went down to the docks and walked along them. There was not a single person there. She went and looked in the packing-plant, but it was just an empty room, with long tables and a black wet floor. A couple of cats wandered around, looking for bits of shrimp. As she walked away, she noticed a half-shrimp still in the drain chute. It was covered black with flies. She picked it up—it was warm from the sun—and walked back to the door and threw it to the cats.

He was not on the *Pixie*. But then he wouldn't be—he wouldn't expect her this early.

Next she walked along the back path to see if he wasn't fishing from one of the little piers. She saw young Allen Cheramie, dozing there, with a pole in his hand, and two other poles wedged down and weighted with bricks. He had been asleep so long that a pair of sea gulls were roosting on a piling not ten feet away from him.

She looked up at the sky, squinting. There was something in its color, something that told you it was September, though it was just as hot as midsummer. She'd often tried to figure that out: it wasn't a change of color exactly, though that was close to it.

She walked quickly back over to the grocery, the sweat running

down her face. Ted Mitchaux was on the porch there, reading an
old copy of *Life*. He looked at her over his cracked glasses.
"Looking for somebody?"

"No," she said, and wiped the sweat off her face.

"You sure want him quick, running on a day like this."

"No," she said, "I just got energy, me."

"Running like Jean Sot with the wind. . . . You ever hear
that story?"

He took off his glasses and held them carefully between the
fingers of his right hand. His little shriveled face stared at her.
He looked like a prune, she thought, wrinkled up to nothing, and
just about the same color. His papa must have been a Negro, for
sure.

"You told me all your stories."

"Now I know I ain't done nothing like that."

But she had gone.

Annie saw Mamere Terrebonne working in her garden, bent
over, like a half-opened knife.

Annie went over. Now she could see that it was not gardening
at all. The old woman was carefully replanting the yellow light-
bulbs that lined the garden beds.

"How you?" Annie said.

The old woman did not straighten up; dipping her head lower,
she looked at Annie from under her arm. Like a chicken, like an
old chicken whose feathers are torn and mostly gone, her petticoat, dress and sweater, apron and shawl flapped and hung around
her.

"How you doing?" Annie said.

"You looking for the man, eh?"

Annie shrugged. "No."

Mamere laughed and coughed at the same time. She began to
straighten up. Annie went over and helped her pull the old stiff
back into place.

"I know you want him, me." She shuffled her feet in their
heavy men's army boots, and she stepped on the drooping hem of
her flannel petticoat that had once had a design but was now
faded into a kind of yellow-gray color.

"How you know?" Annie asked.

Mamere patted the wide-brimmed gray hat that she had pinned on by her old long hatpin with its tarnished little silver knob. "One man gone, you go looking for the other."

"Lord," Annie said, "how you talk."

"Shu . . . I talk true, maybe? No?"

"Lord, Lord . . ." Annie said, "I got no man."

Mamere planted her thin hands with their heavy cords of veins on her hips. It was hard to tell if she were a man or a woman. The body had no shape, though it did wear skirts. The shriveled, wrinkled face with its little straggling gray mustache would give no clue.

I'll never get that old, Annie thought; hope to God I never get that old.

Mamere said: "You got a man che'. Me, I know it. And everybody know it."

Annie swung her foot back and forth, knocking off the tops of the long raggedy grasses.

"Me, I don't know or not he was your first. . . ."

They know everything so fast, Annie thought. And how do they find out. . . . There's nothing they don't know.

She pushed the hair back from her forehead, noticing too that it had a little sour odor.

Been so long since I washed it, she thought. And . . . I bet they know everything: how many times I been down to the boat. I bet they can count the just right number. And how many times we did it.

Nothing to do but watch and figure out things, she thought. I bet they counted.

Mamere giggled. "So small, che' . . . but I know."

Annie walked away then. Mamere turned slowly, the iron heels of her boots digging in the soft mud, and watched her go.

Annie slipped into the long thick line of bushes that grew in the shell ridge just to the back. She was still wearing shorts and the blackberry vines scratched her thighs. Damn, she thought, I oughta go back. But she just pushed her way through more carefully and a little more slowly. After a couple of dozen feet there was an oak. She climbed to one of the broken branches and looked around.

She didn't see Inky. She didn't see much of anything. Just a couple of kids playing dollhouse under a tent of palm leaves. She watched a few minutes before she picked her way out.

She went on looking, up and down the tangle of the connecting shell paths, slower now and not hurrying, never hurrying, but moving just the same.

The island seemed quiet and empty. Most of the boats were out working (the *Mickey Mouse* was the only one back early), and most of the men with them. And the women, they weren't walking around. They'd be gathered in little groups of three or four in kitchens somewhere.

Annie could have found them fast enough. If she'd wanted to. She kept strolling on, hands in the back pockets of her shorts. The only one, except for the kids and the animals, moving.

She had covered most of the paths on the eastern end. Finally she headed out along the single straight path that went out to Point Caminada to the west. Minute she came out of the trees she saw him, sitting on top of the tumble of concrete blocks where the light had been once.

"Hey!" she called. She was afraid to come on him by surprise. Afraid of what his face might look like, if he turned it on her suddenly. Stupid . . .

He looked over his shoulder. And lifted his left hand slightly. There was a little breeze out here, even in the sun. The big old straw hat tugged at its strings under her chin as she scrambled up the blocks and squatted down by him. "Crabbing?"

"Hell, no."

"You shouldn't be out without a hat."

"Yea, I know," he said.

She felt the top of his head. "You get sunstroke."

"What are you doing down here?"

"Looking about the crabs," she lied. "I didn't want to lug all the nets and bait down here for nothing."

"I been seeing some," he said.

"I see one right now."

"Where?"

She pointed. Down almost directly below them, in the rocks and seaweed, a single big blue claw.

"Man I knew in New Orleans could catch 'em with his bare hands."

"I wouldn't try it, me."

"He could all right."

She half-closed her eyes against the glare from the water. "What were you doing?"

"Going crazy."

"Huh?"

"Look," he said, "I got a sailboat that don't belong to me. And I been on it how long? And it's hot as hell there and there ain't room enough. . . ."

"It's a beautiful boat."

"Sure," he said, "only a sailboat's no good unless it's moving and there a breeze going through it.

"A real unusual hot summer—they call 'em weather breeders."

"Yea?"

"Say it's a sign of hurricanes coming."

"Hell," he said, "a hurricane would be cool."

"Don't go joking."

"I mean it," he said. "Where's your shadow?"

"Who?"

"Claudie."

"I got away from him."

A young gull—soft brown color—settled on the water and waited, watching them.

"The boy they been looking for," Inky said, "he a friend of yours?"

"Who?"

"The kid who didn't come back—"

"Henry?"

"Yea."

"Sure I knew him," she said. "You know everybody on this island or you're blind, deaf *and* dumb."

"I guess so."

"Why?"

"Just wondering."

"Wondering what?"

"Nothing special."

A clump of seaweed with bright orange berries washed up and hung on a cement projection, gleaming under the sun.

"You know," Inky said, "place where I was last summer, had six- and eight-foot tides?"

"No tide here," Annie said.

"Few inches," Inky said.

"That's what I meant."

"You didn't say that."

My head hurts, Annie thought. And my back too. Maybe I'm going to have a period.

"The gal was from over there, huh?" Inky pointed ahead toward Terre Haute.

I got no reason to feel bad, Annie thought, except maybe the heat. I ought to feel fine.

"Over there?" Inky repeated.

"Huh?"

He pointed to the low rise of trees across the pass.

"Oh," she said, "yea."

Inky wiped the sweat off his forehead with the back of his hand. And then he closed his eyes against the glare.

She yawned, and hunching over settled her forehead in her hands. She tipped back the hat so that the sun did not burn her neck.

"Look," he said without opening his eyes, "haven't you got anything else to do?"

"No," she said.

"Don't you have to wash the dishes or mop or something?"

"Where?"

"At your house."

"Hell," she said, "Adele does all that. . . . Anyway, it's her house."

"Oh."

"You want me to go away?"

"Hell, no," he said. "I was wondering if you wasn't bored."

"Nuh-uh."

A kingfisher shot right over their heads, screaming.

Annie said: "When are you going into New Orleans?"

"With the *Pixie?*"

"Uh-huh."

"Jesus," he said, "I don't know."

"You don't like it here?"

"Not the most exciting place I've ever been."

"I know," Annie said.

"I bet you don't get bored."

"But I do . . . awful sometimes."

She opened her eyes; he was shaking his head.

"I do," she said. "Can I come in to New Orleans with you?"

"What?"

"I can get a job," she said. "I saw the want ads just last week."

He scratched his head: the sweat tickled.

"At the telephone office," she said.

"Bet you could at that."

"I just don't want to go in all by myself," she admitted slowly.
"And looks like we going about the same time."

"Hell," he said, "I didn't know you wanted to leave here."

"Only I don't want to go in by myself . . . kind of scary,"
she said and felt ashamed. "You don't think I can get a job?"

"Hell," he said, "there's lots of jobs in New Orleans."

"You going to take me in?"

"Sure," he said.

She felt herself relax. She stretched, slowly, carefully, all over,
like a cat.

*

AND that next day Pete Livaudais came back from the western end of the island where he had been hiding. Story LeBlanc saw him first, walking along the main shell road, which was just a little wider than the other paths. He looked sort of hungry, and there was a growth of spotty kid-beard on his face—but he didn't look bad, except for his clothes being muddy.

When he saw him, Story wondered what he should say or if he should take himself back into the brush and disappear. But when they passed, Pete Livaudais just lifted his hand in the half-gesture he had had since he was a child, and said: "Hi."

And Story LeBlanc spent the rest of the afternoon telling people what he had seen and how it looked like the kid was over the worst of it.

"Without losing his wits," Mamere Terrebonne said when she heard, "yes?"

"Look all right to me," Story said.

"Sometime . . ." and Mamere touched one yellow wrinkled finger to her forehead.

When Eddie Livaudais came down to the Rendezvous for a drink later on, he didn't have to be asked questions. He knew what everybody was wondering and so he told them. "Had to get over the worst," he said, "and the kid had to do it by himself. Had to go out there where there wasn't nothing but dogs and animals to watch him."

Coming over to hear the news, Annie met Perique just outside the Rendezvous. She hadn't talked to him for a couple of weeks. "Where you been keeping yourself?" She was glad to see him now.

"Working," he said.

"You going to ask me in for a beer?"

"If you boyfriend don't object."

There was a little twinge, a little hurt. But she laughed. "I got no boyfriend."

331

"No?"

"How's Therese?"

"Okay."

"Haven't seen her much either, lately."

"She been around."

His face had gotten more serious in the last couple of weeks, she thought. But maybe it was just the dark. "You look different," she said.

"Me? No."

They went inside. Over in one corner of the bar, Eddie Livaudais was talking to a little group. Perique went down to the other.

"You don't want to hear?"

He shook his head.

"Why not?"

"Don't like listening to other people's miseries, me."

"I never thought of it that way . . . but I guess it is so."

Perique went around behind the counter and got the two beers himself. "Too busy down there to give us any attention."

"They're interested, all right."

"Forgot the glasses." And he went around the counter again and fished the glasses out from the ice locker. He shook them out, then put them up on the counter.

"It's interesting," she said, "for sure."

"You go listen."

She shook her head.

"That what you come over here for."

"In a way, but I can hear it later."

She poured the beer carefully so that there was no foam. "I'm glad Pete come back, anyway."

He nodded.

"You don't look happy about it," she said.

"There's all sorts of ways of coming back."

"I don't get it."

He leaned sideways against the bar. "You seen Pete yet?"

She shook her head.

"Well, I see him."

She brushed the hair back out of her eyes. "So?"

"He don't look good to me."

"What's wrong with him?"

"You ask me," Perique said, "and I tell you what I think. Only I can't tell you why I think it."

"What's he look like?"

Perique shrugged.

"Everybody say he look tired to death."

"He was plain crazy about that brother of his," Perique said. "Maybe nobody ever figured out how much until just now."

"He took it hard."

"Still taking it hard," Perique said.

"Everybody say he's coming out of it."

"Maybe," Perique said.

Annie turned and squinted into the cracked mirror behind the bar, a mirror trimmed with red and green feathers and some that were just plain gray-brown (that had come straight from ducks). Annie looked at herself and at Perique.

"You never come by the house," she said.

"I thought you was busy."

"Not all the time."

Down at the other end of the bar, Eddie Livaudais straightened up and pushed his way through the people around him. "I got to get home," he said over his shoulder. He crossed the room in that loping bowlegged gait of his. "Hi, love birds," he said to Annie and Perique. And then again over his shoulder to the group that had re-formed in a straight line along the bar, he said: "I got to see how he make out . . . tired as a puppy dog he come in."

"It's a funny thing for sure," Perique said quietly, "how getting one back after two days makes him forget how he lost the other one for good."

Annie went back to staring at the feathers that fringed the mirror. You could see the lacy work of cobwebs linking them all together.

"I wish I knew what I thought," she said.

"You having trouble?"

There was a little mocking twist in his voice and she was very sorry the words had slipped out.

"I haven't been feeling too good, lately."

"Sick?"

"My head hurts all the time."

"It's all the thoughts," he said, "swirling around inside."

"Quit making fun of me."

Like colors, all mixed. And how would you straighten them out? And how would you make sense out of them? Or did you just wait?

Perique did not come by the house to see her. For a couple of days she thought he would. Then she didn't expect him anymore.

*

THE pictures had done it. Inky kept thinking about her now. First he spread them all out carefully on the port bunk, except one which he pinned to the wall with scotch tape. Then the next day he gathered them all up, and got them set in his hands for tearing up—only he stopped just at the last minute. And put them under the cushions. By the next day they were back out again.

Still, when he spotted her coming, he ducked below and gathered them up and put them in the big locker. When she got there he was back on deck, polishing the brass lamps. They were lined up on the dock with the little heap of rags and the bottle of polish.

"Hi," she said.

The dock was empty. Mid-afternoon—most people would be home taking a nap after dinner if they weren't actually out on the boats. Even the September sun was too strong around noon. She could feel it now, burning through the straw hat she had perched on the back of her head.

"Can I come aboard?" she said.

He waved his arm. She came. The varnished wood burned the soles of her feet. And when she sat down beside him—he had not put out the cushions—the wood stung the backs of her thighs with its heat. She lifted up her legs, hugging them with her hands.

"It's too hot to sit."

"Want me to get you a cushion from below?"

"No," she brought her legs down, sitting half on her hands. "It get cool in a minute."

"You think you ought to be coming out here in broad daylight?"

"Why not?"

"People'll figure out something's been going on."

335

She watched his face with the prickles of light brown beard. He hadn't shaved that morning. And he was frowning as he looked at her. "I reckon," she said, "most everybody know I been sleeping with you."

His pipe was out. He stopped and relit it.

"They ain't going to mind that," Annie said.

"Look," he said, "if your old man's coming after me with a shotgun, I want to know it."

She smiled, very slowly. "He ain't going to care about it."

"Yea," he said doubtfully.

A big brown pelican skimmed over the top of the mast and settled on the water.

"Want me to help you?" She jumped up suddenly and scrambled out of the cockpit to the dock. Let's us clean up the lamps."

"I'll be damned," he said softly as he picked up the polishing rag.

She crouched back on her haunches, holding the lamp against her thigh. By the time they had finished there was a big black smear reaching almost all around her leg.

She giggled. "Look what I done."

"Got some on the front of your shirt too. And on your face."

She rubbed her face with the back of her hand. "Off?"

"Hell, no." A single fat tom cat swaggered past them and sniffed the polished lamps. "Come on down below and I'll get a washrag."

They tried to carry all six lamps at once. The sponge fell overboard. They stood and watched it float on the surface of the water and giggled.

"It ain't no good," Annie said. "Let the gars have it. . . . This deck is burning my feet off." She ran down the ladder hastily. "Owwwww."

"Take the damn lanterns." He handed them down to her, two at a time. Then he swung down himself, not touching the ladder, but lowering himself by the arms. His leg brushed by her shoulder. She stepped aside.

They hung the lamps in their gimbals. "Now," Annie said, "that looks nice and neat, no?"

"Shipshape, all right."

"I wonder, me, sometimes, what you can do on a boat like this all day."

"Me?" He scratched his head. Little trickles of sweat were running along his scalp. The cabin was hot and close. "Let me see. I fixed up that air scoop, over the forward hatch, so I could breathe down here better. Then I cleaned up the lamps."

"Those old lamps was just sitting on the dock when I come along. I cleaned them as much as you."

"You win." He started to pass her; in the narrow way between the bunks, he brushed hard against her, his shoulder against her breast.

For one minute she wondered if he felt that as much as she.

He was stooping down opening the little refrigerator door. "Can I get you a beer?"

"I don't want anything, me."

His face was so close that she could see the little flecks of black in his blue eyes. "Have some brandy . . . I'm not paying for it."

She pulled away and sat down on the bunk, tucking her feet under her, keeping her thighs pressed tight together.

"Ever taste brandy?"

She shook her head.

"Here." He poured an inch or so in the bottom of a tumbler and handed it to her. "Taste it."

She took a mouthful, swallowed and sputtered. Two tears came to the corners of her eyes. She brushed them away and rubbed at her throat.

He was laughing. "I didn't tell you to go take a big mouthful."

With one hand still rubbing her aching throat, she threw the rest at him. He caught the glass neatly. But the brown liquid formed a trail across the polished floor, up the blue-and-white-striped cover of the bunks. Some even splattered the portholes and ran down the white-painted wood.

"Jesus Christ," he said. "The varnish!"

"Clean that up, Mister Funny Rabbit. I got other things to do."

She had one foot on the ladder when he grabbed her around the waist. "Honey, if I wasn't crazy about you, you'd end overboard, for sure." He backed up, holding her, and sat down, still holding her so that she sat in his lap.

She laughed, a short quick little giggle. "You never got that drink."

"Nope." He was nibbling at the back of her neck, pulling the hair between his teeth.

"Lemme get it for you."

"Hell, no," he said, "I got enough to clean up now."

"Crazy old man, I ain't going to spill nothing." She pulled free, and getting the brandy poured it out in the same glass. "Like this?"

"Plenty."

"And I got to fix one for myself," she said. She mixed a little Bourbon with a glass of water and bounced down on the opposite bunk.

"That all?" he frowned. "That wouldn't make a baby high."

She giggled again, the same way. All her laughs sounded exactly alike.

"Come here." He patted the bunk alongside him.

She shook her head.

"Okay," he said.

"I was planning to do just exactly that."

He swallowed the brandy. "Be a good girl and reach me that bottle."

She brought it. He yanked her down beside him. "You're the damndest girl. A guy's got to play tricks to get ahold of you."

She settled back against the pillows, smiling. "I didn't want you getting any ideas."

"I got them already." Outside a gull gave its wailing openthroated call. "I just got to look at you wiggling that behind when you walk, and I get ideas."

She giggled again and leaned farther back. Since he kept his arm around her waist, she leaned in a semicircle over it.

"That all you got to say, just giggle?"

"Sure I got something else to say—lemme go."

He closed one eye. "Honey, you don't mean that—right now you're leaning back like that so I can see your tits through your shirt."

She sat up abruptly.

"I like you anyway," he said. With one hand he held her head steady, as he kissed her. "Tastes like sugar to me."

She tried to pull and squirm away. Her body only rubbed more closely against his.

"Honey," he said, "the tips of your nipples are real sharp."

"Lemme go." She slapped him.

He only grinned. "Nothing I like more than a woman fighting mad."

She slapped him again.

"Now quit," he said. "You're beginning to hurt."

She drew back her hand again. He caught it.

"When you start scratching like a cat, that's no fun."

"Enfant garce," she said and blew in his face. "Lemme go."

"I don't know what that means. But I can figure it's no compliment."

She got one hand free and jabbed for his eyes.

"Jesus Christ," he grabbed her, "I'm likely to end up tying you down."

She was quiet. A little shudder she couldn't stop ran along her back. Her body quivered and twitched.

He laughed, so hard that he had to lean back, and release his hold. She scrambled up.

"You little bitch . . . that's what you like."

"No," she said, panting. She stood across the cabin, one hand holding to the railing on the other bunk.

"Come here."

She shook her head.

"You're dying to come."

"No."

"Okay." He stretched out on the bunk and, reaching one hand back into the little bookshelf, got a copy of *The Saturday Evening Post*. "See you." He flipped a couple of pages, found a story and settled down to read.

A couple of gulls were fighting. And the water sucked very quietly at the hull.

"You mad?" she asked finally. She hadn't moved.

He did not look up from the magazine. "Hell, no."

"You are."

"I learned never to bother about a woman."

She came and sat beside him. "I don't want you to be mad with me."

"I'm reading."

"Stop and listen to me." He did not move. "Stop, huh?" She pushed down the magazine.

He looked up, squinting one eye. The radio station was not quite clear and he lifted one hand over his head, adjusting it. "First you throw alcohol all over the varnish, then you try to jab my eyes out—why don't you just try letting me alone?"

"I don't want you to be mad."

"Look," he said, "go home."

"No."

He pulled the book back up over his face.

"I can't go nowhere, with you feeling like this."

"How'd you expect me to feel?"

"I don't know," she said miserably.

He dropped the magazine, grinned up at her. "Baby, you sure don't know how to take a joke."

She was still hesitating, when he pulled her down and kissed her.

"I thought you was serious."

"No." He nibbled gently on her lower lip, found her tongue and bit it softly. His hand began to move up and down her leg, brushing back and forth.

She pulled herself upright. "I can't do nothing like that."

He smiled wearily. "Why not?"

"I couldn't do anything with anybody watching. Not even a kid."

"What the hell are you talking about?"

"With Claudie sitting up there, and making faces at me, I just couldn't." She pointed up to the hatch. He twisted his head around and looked, just in time to see a faded pair of pants disappearing.

"Jesus Christ!"

He jumped to his feet and was up the ladder in a minute. But even as he was climbing, he heard the quick sound of the little feet as they flashed across the carriage roof, under the boom, and then the rattle of the boards on the dock.

By the time he had got topside, the boy had disappeared. Only, the shells around a half-dozen or so kegs were still rattling and rolling. He stared at the barrels for a while. Then he went slowly down the ladder again.

He sat down and put a hand on each knee. "Why the hell did you bring him?"

Annie sniffed. Her eyes were heavy with tears. "I didn't. He just come along. And there ain't nothing I could do about it."

He sucked back his lips and whistled. They waited. There was the faintest little whispering sound, hardly a sound.

"There he is again." And the little face peered in the window.

Inky got to his feet and went up into the cockpit. Not bothering to hurry this time. He stared at the kegs, at the tool shed, at the heap of old lumber.

"Which one do you suppose he's hiding behind?"

Annie had followed him up. "I don't know."

"Oh Christ." He threw himself down on the cockpit seat, propped up his legs and reached in his shirt pocket for his pipe.

"I guess I go home."

"Might as well," he said.

"I couldn't help Claudie following me."

"Sure," he said.

"I'm going."

"See you around sometime."

When she was halfway down the dock, walking slowly, curling her bare toes at each step, the little boy slipped from behind the farthest of the kegs and followed her, his skinny legs moving rapidly.

She heard him, spun around, stamping her foot, and lifting up her right arm, with its fist clenched. He veered off, still at a trot, and ducked around the tool shed.

She kept on, walking the full length of the dock. At the end she hesitated a minute, and glanced back over her shoulder at the boat. Inky had not moved: she could see only the back of his head. And there was a brown pelican sitting right on the top of the mast.

She started home. She went along the path, feeling how hot the shells were to her feet. Then she crossed the little fields where the grass was prickly, but cool. She did not look behind her, but she could hear: the little boy had appeared again. And he was trotting along, not ten feet behind.

*

PETE LIVAUDAIS stayed quietly around the house for a few days, seeming to rest, though he didn't sleep much: any time of the day or night that you passed the place you could see him on the porch, in a chair, his feet up on the rail. It looked like he was waiting for something.

But when anybody passed, he would look over and wave and give them a big smile. And unless you went over to the front steps to have a word or two, you didn't notice how deep and heavy the circles were under his eyes.

That Thursday evening three of the luggers were out: the *St. Christopher,* the *Hula Girl* and the *Captain Z.* The *Mickey Mouse,* coming in, said their luck had turned bad. So they'd be staying out until late that night.

It was a thick heavy yellow twilight. Any of the women who had clothes to bleach spread them out on the grass so the very first of the morning sun could get them: best thing in the world for a stain.

The mosquitoes were coming over in waves from the marshes across the bay. The cows snorted and churned their tails around, while the kids drove them back to stalls that were covered with mosquito netting.

Cecile Boudreau had finished feeding the baby and was sitting down to supper with her oldest boy. The table was under the window and when she glanced out she saw Pete Livaudais. He was walking in the slow heavy way he had got, like an old man, bending forward a little from the waist as if his back was hurting. Cecile was surprised. It was the first time she had seen him come off the porch. And the sight of the bending back put a sharp little pain in her stomach—she could almost see the other boy, Henry, going there.

342

So she yelled out through the window; "Hey, Pete!" And he stopped short, hesitated a minute trying to figure out where the sound had come from, then turned.

She could remember the flash of his teeth in the steadily darkening light. His face was not clear.

"I got a cup of coffee here with your name on it," she said.

"Thanks," he said. "Got to get some things down at the dock."

"No coffee?"

"Promised Ma I'd get straight back."

"You got to hurry for sure," she said, "or the mosquitoes drain you dry."

She waved and sat back down at the table. And yanked her boy's head up out of his plate. He had fallen asleep, one cheek on the rice.

Al Landry was leaving the *Mickey Mouse*. He was tired, and his luck had been bad, not enough to pay for the gas this time. When he heard the clatter of hollow cans he looked up.

It was Pete Livaudais, dragging a cart, a boy's wagon with bits of the flaked red paint still on it. There were two five-gallon cans jouncing on the bed.

"Hi boy," Al said. "What you doing?"

Pete waved a hand. "Got all this."

"You doing that the hard way, boy."

"Maybe."

"Why you don't bring the engine around to the pump?"

"Never did do things the easy way," Pete said.

And the rusty mildew-spotted wagon jounced along the uneven boards and right along past.

The kid looked tired, Al thought, real out-and-out tired. Bone-tired.

"Better take it easy," he said to the blue-shirted back.

And Pete said, soft and whispered, without turning: "Hell. . . ."

Fornest St. Clair was reading an old copy of *Good Housekeeping* under the single unshaded globe by the gas pump. "What you say, kid?"

"You want me to fill 'em?"

Fornest got up and stretched his short stocky frame, carefully. Then he unhooked the hose. He pointed with the nozzle to the magazine he had left, face up on the chair. "Look at that."

Pete looked but did not answer.

"That what I come to read."

"Yea?"

"Recipes, and babies . . . man, I'm an expert, me." He scratched his chin, long slow strokes, enjoying every one.

Pete waited, stooping a little, his arms hanging straight down at his sides.

"My old lady, she say if I don't get me a shave, she going to walk straight out the house."

"Yea?"

"She do it, boy. She go right straight over to her brothers'. . . . They never did think she shoulda married with me. . . . Bastards. Like Dagos, man."

"I want the gas," Pete said.

"Sure . . . sure." He plunked the nozzle down. "Lemme get you some lube."

"No," Pete said.

"Huh?"

"Just the gas."

"How you going to use that in an outboard?"

Pete took the nozzle and began filling the first can. Fornest grabbed it away from him.

"You spill any," Pete said, "you ain't charging it to me."

"Never did spill a drop in my life."

"Don't go starting now."

With his ear down on the can to listen to it fill, Fornest said: "How you going to use this without no lube beats me."

"Got lube back at the house."

"Huh?"

"Got lube."

"Where from?"

"How'd I know?" Pete said. "It's just there."

Fornest began the second can. "Reckon you can always come back for it," he said. "Tell you what, man—bet you a dollar bill, there ain't no lube back at your place. Ain't like your old man to keep more stuff around than he's going to use."

"Okay."

"Plain gas ain't no use." Fornest screwed the top on the last can and stood up.

He stopped arguing, all of a sudden, when he saw Pete's face. The boy looked like he was about to cry.

WHEN the *Hula Girl* came back, around one o'clock when there was an old moon just beginning to rise, the men did not notice anything. Maybe it all happened after that. And maybe they weren't looking. They were beat and just wanting to get to bed. Old man Boudreau and Hector and Perique did only the things they had to on the boat and then went their three separate ways.

Old Boudreau limped slowly up his steps: his crippled hip hurt more than ever when he was tired. Wore out like a bull, he thought, at the spring servicing. Just inside the kitchen door, he stepped on the cat, which yeowled and scratched at him. He kicked at it, but without any real energy or direction. His wife did not even wake up.

There was a light in the little back room where Hector's son slept. Even as he came up the steps he could hear Cecile explaining: "There ain't no painter here, che' . . . open up you eyes and look now."

So he'd been having another dream, Hector thought. And why did kids always have the worst ones? That boy now, he'd seen his whole body shake . . . just like a branch somebody was beating.

Hector dropped his pants and shirt alongside the bed. The sheet was still warm where Cecile had been lying. He stretched out waiting for her: she was still talking to the boy. "Open you eyes. Come on now."

His hands were full of grease and dirt, Hector thought. But he'd probably marked up the sheet already. And it was such a long trip to wash them.

The light went out—he could see that through the cracks of the boards. And he could hear Cecile close the door softly. She was talking to herself. "God damn," she was whispering, "god damn to hell!"

And wouldn't she be surprised, Hector thought, when she found him.

Perique wiped the sweat off the back of his neck. The nights weren't even cool. But that was September. It was always like that.

He had taken off his shoes and tied them by the laces to his belt so that they flopped against his thigh. He stopped now and loosened them.

In the room where he slept, Jesus, it would be hot. The screens kept out more air than mosquitoes.

The houses had their doors and windows all wide open, and those who had them had the electric fan going all night long. If you stood still and listened you could hear the buzzing all around. And just walking past the houses, you could smell the heat and the closeness that was coming out of them. Odors hung in the air like ribbons. And you could tell what they had had for supper.

The Robichaux place, he was passing that now, they'd had meat, fried meat. Tina Robichaux always used lots of onions and garlic. And if you stopped you could hear the old man snoring away like somebody was choking him.

And the Landry place, that was shrimps for sure. . . .

He found himself staring at the window he knew was Annie's. He found himself trying to remember—he'd been in only once since he was a man grown: that evening he'd been drinking with Hector. . . . Wasn't much over a month ago, but it seemed longer. He kept staring at the dark window, wondering.

He put down his shoes, carefully, one next to the other in the very center of the path, slipped open the gate. There was a bucket by the front steps—the shrimps would have come in that—and he picked it up, carrying it in both hands so it wouldn't rattle. He walked around the house carefully until he came to the window, which was slightly over his head. Then he up-ended the bucket and stood on it. It sank a bit in the soft ground, but held. He put both hands on the sill and peeped in. He couldn't see much through the mosquito netting, not with the moon behind him.

He reached out one finger and moved it slowly, wondering if it would catch on anything inside, lifting one fold after the other. He had it up finally, and he held it back with his left hand. Now the moon fell straight into the room.

He leaned on the sill, sniffing the warm heavy female odor which hung on the still air. He blinked his eyes quickly, getting used to the soft half-dark. The bed was under the window, but pulled out a little, to get the best of the air. Annie was there, feet toward him, sleeping on her side.

She wasn't at the boat. He felt relieved.

He let the netting fall back across the window and, quickly as he could, he put the bucket back by the steps and slipped out the gate. His heart was pounding, the way a kid's would, who's just had a beating.

Son of a bitching fool, he told himself silently.

On his own back porch, on the railing there, was an extra piece of netting. His mother had left it there a week or so ago, intending to use it for something. . . . Whatever it was, Perique thought, it would die waiting for her.

But the net would do for him now. He took it and headed for the oak grove not too far behind. The smell of houses made him sick, there in the back of his throat.

He hung the net—carefully so it didn't tear—on the lowest dead twig of a little oak. Then he held out the edges with pieces of brick he found. He took off his shoes and crawled under. There were a few mosquitoes left. He set about killing them, and then he fell asleep.

He was too tired to notice the sky to the west.

Story LeBlanc saw it first, coming in on the *St. Christopher*. But by then you couldn't miss it, if you had any eyes in your head.

"Jeez," he said, "they got a hell of a fire over there."

And Placide Arcenaux looked over and grunted.

Beyond the west tip of Isle aux Chiens you could see the low hump of the other island, the low bumpy outline of its scrub trees. You could see it outlined dark against the red glow.

"On the north side, huh?" Placide asked.

"Somebody got careless."

"Yea," Placide said.

But by the time they had gone in and were fastening their lines, there was another sound, a sharp flat thudding sound. Shotguns.

Placide Arcenaux looked at Story LeBlanc and scratched his ear. "Look like they having a real fight over there."

And Dick Milliet shook his head. "I'm too old to go bothering about what they doing." He went stumping off: he had rheumatism all down one side. He carried a big bottle of aspirin; when the pain got too bad, he would gulp three or four.

Placide and Story took the skiff with the outboard and went down to the west to have a look. They lay just off Caminada Point, and they could see plainly from there: the fire was on the north side, along the wharf. They could see two boats standing off, and there might have been more in the dark behind them. And they could hear the yelling.

"Jeez," Story said, "they got themselves a beaut."

There were a couple more outboards coming up from Isle aux Chiens: they weren't the only people who'd been curious. The skiffs bobbed there, softly in the gentle swell. And the surface of the water reflected in broken planes the glow of fire.

Back at the island most everybody had gone to the north side. They stood watching very quietly on the long shell mound that was the island's backbone.

The older kids were running up and down, yelling at the glow in the sky.

"Burn the crap out them!" Tim Milliet yelled and his mother gave him the side of her hand on the back of his neck.

"Jeez," he yelled, "you going to kill me."

His mother just lifted her chin and didn't answer.

In the houses under the trees, the babies were screaming. Nobody seemed to pay much attention to them.

The *Captain Z* put in, the last of the luggers. As he swung his bow in, Eddie Livaudais called: "They roasting over there for sure." And he was chuckling so hard that he fumbled his stern mooring-line and dropped it in the water. So that the kids on the dock had to throw it to him again. He caught it this time, but it left a smear and a spatter of wet and seaweed on his pants.

.   .   .

Perique was over on the north side, looking, like everybody else. The noise had got him up. But he hadn't seen anything interesting much. And he was turning to leave when Cecile spotted him.

He grinned briefly at her round eager face. Hector had himself a girl there for sure, he thought.

"Where you going?" She was breathless and panting and grinning.

Like a baseball game, Perique thought, and she was having a grand time. "Nowhere," he said, "in particular."

"You want to do something for me?"

He squinted up into the sky. It wasn't a very clear night after all. The stars were misty. Or maybe it was smoke.

"Like what?" he said.

"Take me over there to see what going on."

Perique sighed. "And me so beat."

"You want to see, no?"

"I been working," he said. "And I don't give a god damn if the whole place over there burn up."

Adele was passing them. In the dim light she hesitated before her timid hello.

"You want to come with us?" Cecile asked.

Adele looked from one to the other.

"Tell her where we going," Perique said.

"Perique is taking us over to see what going on."

Adele was looking at him. He could feel her steady calm brown eyes. "Maybe," she said softly, "Perique don't know that."

He snorted. "She call you bluff, che'."

"But then," Adele said, "maybe you will take us?"

He thought: pretty eyes, pretty teeth, in a face that wasn't much and a body that was too thin.

She reminded him of his mother. Not because she looked like his mother—she didn't, not at all. But because she looked just the way his mother should look.

"Okay. . . ." He gave up. "We going to use the *Tangerine?*"

"Nope," Cecile said, "my old man's outboard."

"Go get it," he said. "Me, I'm going home and get some coffee or I fall asleep."

He walked home, not hurrying. Let 'em wait, the bitches. He

was swearing softly under his breath all the way. A man didn't work twenty hours and then go chasing around. "Sal au pri," he told himself aloud.

In the houses he passed the lights were all on; some of the kids had got tired of watching already and had come back home. The littlest ones sat on the front steps, nodding with sleep, but not going to bed. And some of the older ones played Devil on the Banquette on the shell walks.

The night was hot and still. The roosters had got mixed up: they were strutting and crowing just as if it were dawn.

"Mammyjammer," Perique muttered to himself, "getting talked into something when I'm beat up enough."

His mother had made some fresh coffee. It was standing on the back of the stove. He took the pot and a cup over to the oilcloth-covered table and sat down: he'd have this much in peace, for sure. He drank two cups and was pouring a third when he remembered something.

All the houses had lights on, except one. Except one . . .

He was sure of that. He had noticed it, but it hadn't meant anything to him at the time. One house where nobody was up: the Livaudais house.

He turned it over in his mind. Eddie Livaudais, now, he'd be still down at the boat, or talking with the people along the wharf. They hadn't come back more than ten minutes ago. But there was Belle, and there was Pete. And they were, neither of them, ones to miss an excitement.

Perique finished his fourth cup of coffee. Maybe he should go see . . . but it wasn't any of his business.

He headed back to the wharf.

Even as he climbed down in the skiff and yanked at the cord of the outboard, Perique kept wondering about that dark house where the people were such hard sleepers. . . .

There were five outboards bobbing in the little pass off Caminada Point. Perique headed over for them and cut the motor. They sat watching silently for a while. There was a little current here and the skiffs were drifting slowly back into the bay, but it was so slight a movement you hardly noticed it. And behind them, on

Caminada Point, some kids were yelling. "They run all the way down here just to see," Cecile said.

After half an hour they turned and went in, all the skiffs together.

By this time most of the people had gone back to bed. Only some of the older kids, the ones in their teens, were still wandering around. And they wouldn't be likely to go to bed at all.

Perique noticed that the lights in the Livaudais house were on now, every single one was blazing out.

And the surrounding houses were beginning to go dark.

They just didn't seem to catch up, Perique thought.

He would have to go over tomorrow and see if anything was wrong. But right now he was too tired. And so he forgot.

*

THE kids who were still up did not pay any attention to the outboard. They heard it, they remembered later, but they hadn't been interested. It was a hot summer night and they had a bottle of whisky—and they were more interested in each other. They felt excitement burn between their legs. And so most of them crossed over to the south shore to build a big bonfire on the sand.

Inky heard it too. He was almost asleep under his netting-tent in the cockpit. But he listened carefully: that outboard wasn't too far off. By its sound it would be running in fairly small circles: the rudder must be jammed over.

"Jesus God," he muttered, "what's the damn fool trying to do?" He lifted himself on one elbow and stared out. But he couldn't see much through the white netting. And he didn't lift it to have a better view: the mosquitoes were bad out that night. And enough of them got through the netting without any help.

He stretched out again. In a few minutes the motor sputtered and stopped.

Eddie Livaudais heard nothing—he was on the other side of the island, over in the Arcenaux Grocery. The fire had him excited so that even before he went home he stopped and had a drink with Mike and Julius. They were playing Black Jack when Guidry Olivier stuck his head in.

"Too late for you, kid," Julius yelled at him.

"Lay off," Guidry said, scratching the mosquito bites along his arm. "But all the lights is on in Eddie's place."

"So?" Julius lifted one eyebrow in the way he had.

"So nothing," Guidry said. "I'm just telling you what I seen."

"The old lady," Eddie said, "is waiting up for me, and wondering where the hell I got to."

"Prenez un coup!"

And Eddie poured himself another shot.

In half an hour or so, they went home, Eddie and Mike together, feeling their liquor a little, because they were so tired.

"Jesus," Mike said, "the place is lit up for sure."

Eddie squinted. The windows were yellow.

"I turn them out, me," Eddie said, and turned in the gate. Mike plodded along, putting his feet down heavily, lifting clouds of white shell dust after each step.

Belle was lying in bed. Only instead of her nightgown, she was fully dressed.

Eddie stood in the doorway. "So," he said, "you go to bed with the clothes on now. And the lights on in the house, burning up money."

She glanced down at him without moving her head and then back up at the ceiling again.

"You know maybe it is not an hour until daylight?"

"Tant pire," she said quietly.

Outside a rooster began to crow. "See," he said, "what I tell you?"

"Near morning."

"You gone ga-ga? Burning lights all night." He walked over to the foot of the bed and stared at her. "Who going to have need of all that light?"

"Pete."

"Hell," Eddie said, "where's he at?"

"Over there," she said. "The other island."

THEY got up again, Mike Livaudais and Chep Songy and Jerry, got up slowly and heavily from beds that weren't even damp from their sweating bodies. They gulped left-over coffee while the kids woke up and screamed and their wives slapped them into silence. Then they followed Eddie down to the dock.

Christine Bartels and Charlie D'Abadie were still on the wharf, arms wrapped around each other. They looked up when Eddie came along, slowly got to their feet, and disappeared into the trees. Charlie looked back over his shoulder once, mad at having been disturbed.

Eddie had not even seen them.

The red glow over at Terre Haute was gone now, and the sky was a steady, even black. The four men found some kegs and settled down to wait. It was the only thing they could do—no use trying to find anything in the dark.

Chep Songy noticed the skiff first. It was just barely beginning to be dawn and he had to blink his eyes and shake his head to be sure. And then he yelled and pointed.

The skiff was a couple of hundred yards out in the bay, motionless on the dead still water in the flat gray mist of the first light.

He yelled to the others, and he swung himself down into the skiff and picked up the oars. He had just fitted them into the locks when Eddie dropped down into the bow.

Julius, who'd been out for a walk, heard the shouts (he'd had a restless night and he was up far earlier than usual) and he went hurrying over, almost running, so that his paunch jogged up and down and he had to hold it in his hands, the way a woman holds her breasts. By the time he got there Chep had already got the skiff a hundred yards out.

355

It was getting steadily lighter now. In just a little while you'd see the sun swing up, white hot, over the rim to the east, and it would be full day.

Chep was rowing fast, pulling so hard on the oars that the bow went lunging up at each stroke and then smacked down again, sending the water flying off in flat sheets.

"And he went slower," Mike said softly, "he go better."

Inky had heard the yelling and he stuck his head up out of the cockpit, rubbing the sleep out of his eyes. "Hey," he called, "what's happening?"

Nobody answered. Julius went rushing right past to join the other group.

"Wasn't hard to find," Jerry said. "Leastways."

"Lucky he didn't run straight into the pilings," Mike said, "and drown."

Inky left the *Pixie* and stood at the edge of the circle of men. No one talked to him, or gave any sign of noticing. It was something in their faces and their bearing that kept him from coming closer or repeating his questions. It was the same sort of feeling that sometimes told him to keep away from neighborhood gangs, back in the hibiscus-lined streets of New Orleans. That there was something going on in which he could have no part.

Inky stood and waited. The two skiffs were closing now. Chep had softened his stroke, and the boat moved more smoothly. Eddie got to his feet and bent forward, straining to see better.

The two skiffs came abreast. Chep glanced over his shoulder, briefly, then pulled hard on one oar. His bow swung around and touched the other. Almost before the wood had touched, Eddie Livaudais was across.

"Hope they ain't killed him," Jerry said.

"Yea," Al Landry said.

"Damn fool . . . crazy jackass of a damn fool."

Eddie Livaudais gave a wordless shout of relief.

Mike said: "Hear him?"

Eddie tipped up the outboard and got the oars in the locks, and headed back.

"He ain't dead," Mike repeated. And the three men on the dock looked at each other and grinned.

"Ain't so bad, man," Julius said.

The smile disappeared. Mike said: "Leave us wait and see how bad he is hurt."

The skiffs slid under the wharf. Eddie Livaudais stood up, holding to the piling for balance. "Gimme a line."

"What happened to him?" Mike said. "Leave Julius here have look."

The men squatted down, peering over the dock. A little to the back and to one side, Inky squatted down too, without quite knowing why he did.

Eddie Livaudais took off the baseball cap—the one he always wore, that had been white once but turned almost brown from sweat and rain and dust—and he fanned himself with it, two or three times.

Julius stared down, trying to see. In the half-light he could hardly find the boy. The bottom of the skiff was shadowy and his skin seemed to have turned dark, like a Negro's.

"Get him up here," Julius said.

Eddie got up on the wharf and stood back. Chep let himself down into the boat gently; Jerry followed him. Together, easily as they could, they lifted the boy up to the dock. His head swung down, loose, almost as if his neck were broken. Mike slipped one hand under it, steadying it as they lowered him down to the boards, and the boy groaned.

Chep and Jerry scrambled up and stood around while Julius got down, slowly, and wheezing as his knees dug into his stomach.

He saw now why the boy's skin looked so dark. He had covered himself with black axle grease, and he wore a pair of black bathing-trunks.

Julius bent down until his nose was only a couple of inches above the boy's body. And he caught the sharp clear odor of blood.

There was a cut across the forehead and down past the ear. Looked like a piece of that was gone. The loose flap of skin had fallen back into place, making a puffy fold. Blood was clotted into crusts all around it.

Blow like that, Julius thought, a man was lucky to live through.

He couldn't see too much with all the grease. There was a deep cut along the ribs, the kind of crease a bullet or a shotgun pellet would make. And lower, on the side, that was some kind of shot wound, for sure.

Julius put out one finger and then drew back. He was afraid. "No job for me," he said. "You got to get him to a regular doctor."

Eddie stood by swinging his head from side to side, not seeming to hear. Mike said to Jerry: "You go get the shotguns and some bread and sausage and a bottle of whisky. And you go by and get the purse and money from Belle."

"Hell," Jerry said softly, "all I get to do is run around." But he went.

"I get the blowers going on the *Captain Z*," Mike said.

Pete was talking to himself now and moaning. They had to lift him up again and put him on board, on the little bunk in the wheelhouse. They did it gently as they could, all of them together. Just as they got him down on the bunk, his moaning stopped. They stood without moving for a minute, scared, all of them. Julius bent his head and listened, and whistled with relief. "Ain't done nothing more than pass out."

Eddie had stood on the dock watching, and not moving. Julius left the boat and walked over to him. "Ain't bleeding too much," Julius said, "leastways not that I can see."

Eddie just nodded.

Julius said: "You want me to get the doctor on the phone, while you going?"

Eddie looked surprised. "I had forgot that, me. I had forgot clean about it."

"You coming?" Chep called.

Eddie did not seem to hear.

Julius took his arm and started him walking to the lugger. "Come on, man. You got to get going."

Eddie stumbled when his toe brushed the cap rail.

"Watch it, man, watch it."

"Ain't had no sleep this night and I'm falling on my own feet."

"You go be with Pete," Chep said, "soon as Jerry come we shove off."

Julius went and released the bow and the springline, then held the sternline, waiting.

Eddie had gone into the wheelhouse and perched on the edge of the bunk. He was staring straight ahead.

Mike and Chep stood on the forward deck. Mike said: "No use both of us going."

Chep nodded.

"If Jerry, he come with me, we can manage."

Chep nodded again and stepped to the dock. "And I come in, when?"

"Day after tomorrow."

"I be there."

Jerry came back at a run, carrying a couple of paper bags. "You going," his father said. The kid nodded and grinned and jumped aboard.

Mike yelled. Julius released the sternline. The *Captain Z* swung out and headed across the bay.

Chep and Julius coiled the mooring-lines and hung them on the pilings.

"His papa and two men," Chep said slowly, "the boy be safe enough."

They understood. If the boy lived, the people from Terre Haute would try again, almost for sure—if he had done any real damage with the burning. And that wouldn't be so easy if there was a man with him all the time, sleeping on a cot or on the floor right next to his bed in the little hospital.

The sheriff at Petit Prairie wouldn't interfere. He always stayed clear of feuds: a man could get killed meddling.

* * * * * *

THE WAY BACK

~~~~~~~~~~~~~~

THAT night there were two men down at the boats: Stan Schesnaydre and John Olivier. And one had a shotgun and one a deer
rifle. They played cards and drank coffee. Every so often one of
them would walk down to the end of the brightly lit section (people
had strung up some big spotlights on temporary poles) and squint
out into the dark. Mostly they sat and cursed the Livaudais boys:
Henry for being such a fool over a woman; Pete for getting even.

When Rose Schesnaydre brought her brother (he wasn't married yet) more coffee and some cold boiled shrimp around ten
o'clock, she found they'd set up a kind of target of an old board
propped against a sawhorse. They were tossing knives into it.

She played a couple of hands of cards with them. But after a
while she had to go home too. And there was nothing more for
them to do all the night long except walk around a little and
listen and be sure the lights were on.

Annie had come down to the wharf after supper, the way she
always did. And she had taken her favorite seat: a pillow up on
the cabin top. Inky was stretched out along the cockpit seat.

"Took me a hell of a long time to find out what was going on,"
Inky said. "Wouldn't anybody talk to me."

"They get like that," Annie said.

"I was asking them point-blank, and they didn't give an answer."

360

"Sometimes," Annie said, "you can't shake a word out of them."

"And they just going to stay there?"

"Don't ask me."

"Looks like the army around here."

She slapped a mosquito on her ankle. "I'm sick of talking about the whole thing."

"You just can't keep a guard out."

"You know," Annie said, "Somebody was after the boats in my grandfather's time, and this was before I was born or anything near to it, and they had two men out here, and two shifts, just like this, all night long—and there wasn't near so many people on the island then."

"How long?"

"I forget . . . couple of years."

"Don't believe it," Inky said.

"Okay, mister smart jackass, you go ask my papa."

"Oh hell."

"Ask him and see what he says."

"Okay I will," Inky said.

"You forget, I bet."

Inky got to his feet. "Right now."

"What?"

"Let's go ask him."

"Where?"

"He's home. Let's go ask."

"At the house?"

"Where else?"

"No," Annie said. The word was flat and hollow on the still night.

Inky hesitated for a minute, remembering Adele with her smooth brown hair and her gentle ways. "She isn't bad," he said. "Don't take her so hard."

"No," Annie said. The tone got flatter and more hollow.

"Looks to me like . . ."

"I can go be alone," Annie said, "I don't have to stay."

"Jesus," Inky said and stretched back out again, "okay."

"Tell me if you want me to go away."

"Christ sake," Inky said, "stay here, will you."

. . .

Al was taking a bath in the tin tub in the back yard. He was scrunched up in it, comfortably, and he was smoking his pipe and staring into the quiet dark. Now and then it would go out and he would yell and Claudie would come running to light a match for him.

Between trips, Claudie sat on the porch with his mother, on the screen porch where the mosquitoes wouldn't bother them.

"Now you listen to me," Adele told him, "you listen to me good. In the daytime, when you go playing around, you know?"

He nodded, trying very hard to understand what she was saying. The tone already told him it was important.

"You go playing around and with one thing and another you don't notice where you going and where you are. . . ."

He nodded again.

"You don't do that any more." Her voice was deep and sudden and sharp.

"No?" he offered uncertainly.

"When you play you watch where you are and you don't go far off. Or the old men of the woods'll get you. And they feed you to the loup-garous, just one little piece at a time."

Claudie shivered. From the back yard Al yelled, "Hey, towel . . ."

"Go on," Adele told him. "Towel's on the chair in the kitchen."

"God-damn fool kid," Hector said, "son of a bitching fool."

Cecile said: "His mama, she call the clinic and they say he going to make it, most likely."

"No," Hector said, "she tell you that?"

Cecile shook her head and grinned.

"Who told you?"

"I was over talking to Papa, when she comes in and wants change because she's going to use the phone." Cecile spread her hands. "So I know."

"Used to tell me your ears would drop right off from listening."

"They didn't," Cecile said.

"I'm right glad to hear that."

"Wonder if he did much," Cecile said.

"How the hell would I know?"

Cecile gave a quick grin. "Thought maybe you been over and ask."

"Oh sure," Hector said with heavy irony. "Can't hardly wait."

She was putting buttons on a shirt of Don's. "And what you think they fixing to do?"

"Nothing," Hector said, "with somebody watching the boats all the time. Can't do nothing much."

Perique had brought Mamere Terrebonne a present: a small bottle of anisette, bright-red-colored. And he stood on her porch a minute talking to her.

"There is some doings, no?" Her yellow-toothed smile flashed at him. And her little eyes disappeared in the crinkly folds of skin.

If I get old, Perique thought, I be glad to see somebody too. "We had some excitement for sure," he said.

She tilted back and forth in her rocker. "I have seen excitement before."

"The same thing?"

"Or another . . . just alike."

"Tell me."

She grinned again. And shook her head. "You got to find out for yourself."

"Okay, cherie."

"I seen before . . ."

"What you predicting?"

"Nothing."

"You predicting hurricanes this year?"

The corners of her old mouth turned down and she sulked.

"Tell me now what you predicting?"

"Layovers to catch meddlers," she muttered.

Perique had a date. He had put on a fresh shirt and a clean pair of pants. Therese was waiting for him too, in the swing on her front porch. She was wearing a bright pink dress and she'd done her hair different too. It was pulled up on top and drawn through a ring of pink flowers.

She's expecting to marry me, Perique thought suddenly. And stopped perfectly still. When Therese turned around and called to him, it was all he could do to get his feet moving in the direction of that porch. When he finally got there, he sat in the rocking-chair where her mother usually sat.

She was looking at him with a very hurt expression, but he didn't care.

Finally she said: "You thinking about Annie, no?"

He jumped. "No," he said, truthfully. He hadn't been at all.

She didn't believe it. She looked even more hurt. Finally they went back into the kitchen and found a bottle of her father's orange wine. After a couple of glasses of that, he felt better. And went back and sat in the swing with her.

Her parents went to bed. They turned off the porch light. The dark hit him like a sharp jab. He rubbed at his eyes.

"I brought the wine out here," Therese whispered, "so Papa wouldn't find it."

There were no glasses so he drank out of the bottle.

He put one arm around Therese. The other one slipped in the neck of her dress.

For a minute he thought of Annie and her high hard breasts. Then he forgot. Therese was the softest woman he'd ever felt.

*

THE next few days were still and hot. But there were certain signs
that made people shake their heads and wonder.

The Gulf had the restless uncertain feeling of a storm on it
somewhere. And the surf on the south side of the island was much
higher.

"Nervous, for sure," Cecile said with her bright fierce grin.

The sky was still blue-white overhead, but the thunderheads
had moved closer. They looked higher and thicker now too, and
their underbellies were darker. Long ragged streaks of lightning
reached from one to the other and sometimes flashed down into
the gray water.

None of the boats went out. The men had been making good
money lately; now they were tired and they had enough. They
wanted to lay around the house for a while, sleeping in the afternoon. Some of the younger unmarried kids took Dan Rivé's boat
and went into Petit Prairie. They went to see Pete Livaudais in
the hospital. They all tiptoed down the ward and crowded around
his bed and made jokes in whispers. And Pete answered them best
he could from under the bandage. He was very pale under his
sunburn, a kind of muddy color. But he grinned with the good
side of his face.

After a while the nurse made them leave. So they went to have
a couple of drinks and see if they could pick up some money
shooting pool. And that night they got into a fight. Nobody
knew if they started it, but around nine o'clock everybody was
fighting and yelling over at Rose's Café, and it was a miracle pure
and simple that the big front window didn't get broken. The
fighting spilled out on the street. And the deputy sheriffs came
and looked at it and wondered what they should do. And finally
did nothing.

Free-for-alls always ran down. There was a time when people stopped swinging and blinked and straightened up and looked around. And felt kind of sheepish and sneaked away off into the darker streets.

They even went back to the island a whole day earlier than they'd intended to. The fight had been depressing.

Back at the island the family men nailed up shutter hooks and patched screens and cleaned drainpipes. It was as if the feel of a storm in the air had reminded them that the houses could stand a little fixing.

Hector sat cross-legged on the flat tin roof of his house. The last brief rain had shown a leak up there, and he had to find it. He had got it now, and after two hours up there he was almost finished. His leg went to sleep. He stood up, stretching it, and knocked the hammer to the ground.

He looked down at it and yelled: "Cecile, hey, Cecile, hey!"

She came out of the house and stood looking up at him, hands on her hips.

"Reach me the hammer."

She did. "You going to get it fixed?"

"We got a bottle beer?"

"Sure."

"Reach me that too."

"Up there?" she said; "in the sun?"

"Hell," he said, "sure."

While she went to get it, he began to hammer again, but this time the noise made his ears ache and he stopped.

He drank the beer slowly, while Cecile stood below and watched him.

"Got nothing to do?" he asked her politely.

She just grinned.

"You making me nervous."

She went away. He balanced the hammer across his thigh and rubbed at his eyes with the backs of both hands. The sun was getting to him—always the same place, the back of his neck, on the old scar there.

But he'd have to get the roof finished. He tossed the empty can down into the yard, and began again. After a few minutes he stopped again and stared into the greenish brown tops of the trees. He yawned.

Cecile came out again. "You finish?"

The silence has worried her. "When I finish," he said, "I come tell you."

The other island—he'd been thinking about it a lot lately. And wondering what the people over there were going to do.

That Livaudais kid, he thought wearily. Somebody should locked him up.

He took off his cap, fanned himself with it a couple of times and flipped it back on his head again.

He found himself thinking about Cecile, about the soft, heavily fleshed curves of her body, the faint musky smell of her skin. A smell that could drive a man clean out of his mind.

There was another aching in his body now, apart from his tiredness. He got up and scrambled down the ladder.

If she'd just let him alone . . . if she just hadn't gone running in and out every half-minute . . . he'd have finished.

He picked up the beer can and heaved it along the side of the house into the grove of hackberries at back.

He'd go find her. And he wouldn't be able to finish the roof today. Tired as he was he wouldn't be able to get out of bed again.

He shrugged. Some things a man had to be glad of. And this was one of them. The roof could wait.

He let the screen slam after him. "Cecile," he called. "I got something to show you. Come quick."

*

THE following evening nothing seemed different either. Story Le-Blanc had started painting the inside of the wheelhouse on the *St. Christopher* and he worked for a while on it after supper. Dan Rivé and Ozzie Pailet were being guards that night, and they sat on the edge of the pier and told each other jokes for a little while. Then Dan got out a handline and dropped it over, not looking to catch anything particularly, just wanting something to do.

Hector came down and got a screwdriver off his boat. Don came with him. They stopped and talked for a while, until Don got so sleepy he began to cry.

About eight o'clock Annie came down to the *Pixie*. Inky was waiting. They took a short silent walk—it was too hot a night to go far—and came back to the boat. It was a bad evening. Inky was restless. Annie was angry, furiously angry, only she wasn't quite sure at what.

"Jesus," he said, "I'll be crazy and talking to myself if I stay here much longer."

That was when the cold heavy feeling had started in her chest. "What been happening to you?"

"Get so I talk to myself," Inky switched on the little radio so hard that the knob came off in his fingers. "Jesus God!"

"If you went slower," Annie said, "that wouldn't happen."

"Jesus. . . . You keep out of it."

She waited a minute. She was not sure whether she felt hurt or not. "You call Arthur again?"

"God damn it," Inky said, "how the hell do you think I talk to him?"

"You didn't say you talk to him."

"The hell I didn't."

"What he say?" Annie asked quietly.

Inky screwed up his mouth, mimicking. "Can't get anybody . . .
can't get away himself. . . . But he's trying like hell . . . and
he's going out to the yacht club this afternoon because he thinks
he's got a line on a guy. . . . Horse shit!"

"Well," Annie said and rubbed her hands up and down her
thighs, "maybe he will."

"Another week," Inky said, "and I'm leaving the boat right
here and going in myself."

"You wouldn't."

"Hell," Inky said, "I've had it."

"You can't take it back alone?"

"Jesus!" Inky said and threw himself back, full length on the
bunk.

"Maybe we could get somebody from here to take you up the
bayou."

"They too busy," he said. "I been asking around."

"Maybe," she said, "I can ask."

"I got enough trouble," he said, "you stay out of it."

There was that funny little twisting pain. "I was just helping."

He sat up then, surprised by her tone, and patted her shoulder.
"Don't pay any attention to me, honey." He got up and rummaged
around the medicine cabinet. "You like perfume?"

"Sure," she said.

"Here." He found two bottles, the ones that had belonged to
Helen, the ones he had put away weeks ago. "Don't know anything about it, but I bet this is good stuff."

Annie held it up, sniffing at the tops.

"Go ahead," he said, "put some on, put some of each on,
smear it around."

"I never heard of this kind . . . *Balenciaga.*"

"There's some more around," Inky said, "I'll find 'em and you
can have them too."

"This is plenty."

"Hell," he said, "I'm sure not going to use it."

"Me, neither," she said. She put a little of one bottle on
carefully, behind her ears. "You know what?"

"What?"

"I know the channel, and I could help you take the boat back."

He laughed shortly. "Don't make funnies like that."

"I could."

"For God's sake," he said, "quit, will you. I don't want to fight."

"I'm not trying to fight," she said and her voice was very small.

"Here," Inky said and took the bottle away from her, "lemme do that. You're not putting enough of the stuff on."

"Don't waste it."

"Hell," he said, "you got to put it all over. Or it's no good."

Annie went home very late that night. She didn't notice anything. But then she was too tired. And she felt sick. All over. In spite of the hot night she shivered every few minutes. Her ears were singing.

Maybe I'm getting malaria, she thought. Her legs ached. They felt heavy and swollen and she kept stumbling. When she did get home she fell down on the bed, not bothering to undress.

She lay in the dark and wondered, breathing in the heavy musky odor of the perfume.

She heard the yelling, vaguely and far off. But she didn't get up. It was coming to her from miles away. It didn't matter to her. It didn't matter at all.

*

PEOPLE on Isle aux Chiens slept heavily that night. Maybe having a guard out on the boats made them feel safer. Maybe they just couldn't quite believe anything would happen. It was such a quiet still night, dark with just a flickering of heat lightning off to the south. Occasionally a bird would squaak or a kid would call out or a hot tomcat would yeowl. But you could almost feel the sleep all around, thick, like a fog.

They were expecting them at the boats on the north side of the island, if they came at all.

And they did come.

The men from the other island slipped quietly over to the west tip, Caminada Point, in the heavy dead hour just before it began to get light. Not even the dogs there put up a cry, just a couple of sharp sleepy yelps. Ozzie Pailet heard and woke Dan Rivé up. They both listened: but the barking seemed to come from scattered animals. There was none of the steady howling that meant they had found something. So the two men stretched themselves and looked out at the bay and saw nothing. They settled down to have some more coffee.

After all, the dogs were always shifting around. There was always some sort of racket coming from them.

An hour later the yard dogs began to cry. First there was just one dog (the old spotted hound at the Roualt place) barking, slow and not too sure. Then another took it up, then four or five until the whole sleepy night was full of their calls.

Archange Boudreau stuck his head out the window and saw something moving and his three dogs dancing around the yard like they had a deer cornered. And he saw something else too, a little flash of yellow flame, and then a bigger one. So he gave a yell, and began to scramble into his pants.

. . .

371

Al Landry had been dreaming. He had waked up twice already with the roaring of a dream in his ears, roaring that was like the Gulf in a storm.

The first time he woke up, Adele had sat up and leaned over and looked at him. Even in the dark he could see the little crinkle of worry on her forehead. So he reached out one finger and rubbed out that line. "Don't pay mind to me, che'," he said.

And so she slipped back, turning away from him, turning gently with the funny little murmur of a child. And he could tell that she was asleep before her head was down.

For a minute or so he sat bolt upright, feeling the animal pleasure of being the man and the only one awake in the house. Then he dozed off.

The second time he woke up, Adele did not stir. He eased himself back down in the bed, very gently, like a boy sneaking home. But the dream which he had forgotten followed him and he lay staring up at the ceiling, not being quite able to close his eyes.

And it was against the faintly cracked and streaked ceiling that he saw the flickering light. And for a couple of seconds he watched it, wondering what sort of a dream this one would be. A yellow-orange light. And the dogs began.

And then he understood and went up out of the bed in a big arc. Like a wrestler, he thought briefly, bouncing up from the mat. Like a television wrestler, me. Even at the time he thought that was funny. But just for a minute. Then all he could think of was what his eyes saw.

The grass in the side yard was burning—or that was what it looked like. The palings of the fence were short straight lines of flame. Heat hit him under his chin and he yanked his head in. He was shouting now too, all of a sudden he was conscious of that.

He turned in time to see Adele vanish through the door. He raced after her, past her to the kitchen where the two small round glass fire-extinguisher bulbs hung on the wall by the stove. He snatched them down and looked around again for her. By this time she had got Claudie out of bed. She was heading for the kitchen door with the boy, only half awake and crying, under her arm. In her other hand was the silver coffee pot.

That was fast going, he thought. Her face was calm; she was hurrying just the way she'd hurry to catch a ferry that was leaving shortly. Not many women would behave like that, he thought. He'd have to tell her so later.

The brick foundations of the house on that west side seemed to be burning—and he understood then, finally. It was no ordinary fire. There'd be kerosene or gasoline. And somebody had thrown it—from outside the yard, beyond the dogs' reach.

Out of the corner of his eye he saw Adele come running down the kitchen steps again. This time she was carrying his shotgun. She had figured it the same way.

He took the gun away from her. "I got to go see about the boat." Maybe they had been down there. In spite of the guards.

He handed Adele the shovel. He didn't like leaving her, but there might be trouble down at the wharf.

She was already at work with the shovel, digging a little path through the burning grass to get to the side of the house. Annie turned up, alongside him, with a spade. And he realized that he'd forgot about her. He was so ashamed that he hesitated a second.

"Keep it off the house," Annie said quietly to her stepmother. She looked heavy-eyed and sleepy.

Al ducked back then, and raced along the path. He glanced over his shoulder, just once. The two stooped figures were outlined dark against the fire. What a target, he thought for an instant, if anybody was figuring that way.

But they had to save the house. And he had to be sure the boat was safe. So he ran harder.

"Shovel it under around the foundations," Annie said.

Behind them were a couple of hollow popping sounds from a shotgun.

"I got to see about that," Adele muttered, "when I get through here." Al had put the little glass balls of extinguisher liquid on the back steps. Now she ran to get them and tossed them into the worst spot.

"Gasoline," Annie said. "Burning on the bare ground."

They shoveled as hard as they could in the hard-packed mud of the yard, shoveled a path through the burning area alongside the house, smothering out some of the flames.

Annie felt her eyebrows begin to scorch and she stopped for a minute and rubbed at them.

"Hurt yourself?"

Annie shook her head.

"Be careful," Adele said. Her spade had not stopped.

She was stronger than she looked, Annie thought. She was working like a man. And you had to give her that: she wasn't the least bit upset or nervous-looking.

Adele dropped her shovel to drag over a wheelbarrow load of sand: Al had brought it yesterday to make a sandbox for Claudie. She shoveled it now, carefully, on the flames that burned on the ground under the house itself.

Annie pointed. "Look there!"

Gasoline had splashed up the side of the house, almost up to the little loft window and it was burning.

"I get to that in a minute," Adele said; "got to get it from under first."

Al came back, still at a run. His face was brilliant red and his mustache hung down over his mouth like a piece of wet paper. He put the shotgun carefully aside and took a shovel.

In the end it was Annie who had the idea, had it all at once. And she turned and grabbed up two big buckets, the biggest she could find. She had remembered the pigpen and the little spring that turned the mud into liquid, a thick syrupy liquid that could be thrown by handful or bucketful.

She kicked down the bars. If the pigs got out, it was just too bad. She heard them down at the far end, snorting. They wouldn't go too far, and with the ear notches she could find them again.

Full, the buckets were heavier than she'd expected. She staggered uncertainly, then, bending her body forward, she got herself moving at a half-run.

"Al," she yelled, "hey, Al!" That was the first time she'd called him by his first name. She was a little surprised how natural it had come to her.

Won't call him Papa again, she thought. And then: that's a stupid thing to think of.

"You throw it," she said, "I can't."

In a second he had scooped up one bucket, moved as close as he could, and splashed the syrupy mud down the side of the fire.

"That got it," Adele said and grabbed the empty bucket and ran off with it.

Annie was throwing the mud by handfuls and listening to the

splat and sizzle. Al yanked the bucket away and slung its contents in a heavy stream like molasses against the wall.

"Get another one," he said to Adele.

As Annie left, Adele was coming back with two full buckets.

In five minutes the path of the fire was covered with the sticky, slop-filled mud. Where little flames still flickered—at the edges— they threw double handfuls. Adele was giggling like a kid. "Going to be weeks before we get the smell out the house."

Annie just looked at her.

"Well," Al said, "we got a house left, che'."

Annie wiped her hands on her sleeves. "We don't have a fence."

Al shrugged. "Let it burn . . . ain't worth the trouble saving now."

"Oh," Annie said and scratched at her head, "one of the dogs got bashed in the head or something. Down by the pen, I noticed."

"God," Al said, "I got no time for that." He crossed the yard to the place where he had leaned the shotgun. He checked the shells. "I got to go see," he said, and waved his hand toward the other houses—you could see the faint red glow through the trees.

"It's out all right," Adele said. "Here, leastways."

"You watch it, che' . . . so the fence don't catch nothing else. Me, I'm going to take a quick look to see there ain't nobody hanging around here. And then I leave the gun with you, no?"

Adele nodded.

When he had gone Annie said: "If there was anybody around wanted to shoot us, they'd done it when we was standing in front of the fire, fighting it."

She couldn't stop herself. She shivered, hard and all over.

Adele noticed. "It's done with." She put out her hand to touch Annie's shoulder, then changed her mind.

And Perique was there, all of a sudden, standing just the other side of the burning fence. "You all right?" he asked Adele.

She laughed, such an easy relaxed laugh. Annie hated her for it.

"I'd come before," Perique said to Adele, "only my old man went out chasing something or other he think he see. And he leave me to put out the fire in the henhouse."

"Al is looking around just this very minute," Adele said. "Back by the pen, there."

"Okay," Perique said. "I'm staying here, me. So he don't go shooting at me."

Annie shivered again, even harder this time. And just when he was looking at her. She stomped her feet and then bent to examine her bare toes. "I got something in my foot," she said.

"I reckon it's over," Perique said.

And his tone—she was furious—he thought she was afraid.

"Who was it?" Adele was asking.

And Perique was just shrugging. "Didn't see nobody but I got a good idea."

"I wasn't scared," Annie said.

"Huh?"

"She was wonderful," Adele said. "You shoulda seen her."

"Bet she was," Perique said flatly.

Al came back. "Ain't nobody around. . . ." He stared at Perique. "How's it at your place?"

"Burned up a couple chickens."

"Nothing more?"

"Didn't come near the house. . . . Maybe the dogs stopped 'em."

"They killed one of the dogs," Annie said. And she was still panting though she shouldn't have been. "I saw it. Only I didn't see which one."

Perique looked at her and she had to hold her under lip with her teeth to keep it from trembling.

"Which one?" Adele asked softly. "You see?"

"Tantine," Al said. "Smash her head in."

"I'll kill 'em," Annie said.

"Jesus God!" Al said, "where's Claudie at?"

And Adele chuckled a little and pointed up to the big old chinaberry tree in back of the house. "Told him to climb up there and stay out of the way. . . . Claudie!"

And his reedy little voice came back: "Claudie. . . . Claudie!"

"See?"

"Don't she beat hell," Al asked proudly, "don't she now?"

"Look," Perique said, "you stay by the house before you get hurt."

"Quit telling me what to do," Annie said.

"You stay close to the house, bébé, no?" Al asked her.

She just shrugged.

"Hold onto this." Perique handed Annie his shotgun. "I'm gonna have a look."

The cistern was on this side of the house, behind the kitchen at a little angle. It was the biggest cistern on the island: they always had water, and plenty, even during the long dry Octobers and Novembers. There was a kind of ladder up the side, just cross-pieces nailed there: they used them for cleaning or repairing.

"What you see?" Al called.

Perique climbed up and looked. "Over by LeBlanc," he said, "something burning for sure."

"We gone already."

"I keep an eye on the fence," Adele said.

"Grab a bucket, man," Al said.

"Don't have to tell me, none," Perique dropped down. "I brought one over here when I come."

There were a couple more faint popping sounds. Al and Perique disappeared beyond the light of the burning fence. Adele walked once around the house, slowly, looking. When she had made the circle, she said to Annie who had not moved, who had stood staring straight into the flaming posts: "It looks all right."

"They'll burn out in a while."

From his tree, Claudie said something.

"You stay there!"

Her tone frightened him so he did not even answer.

They could hear people yelling. "That's your father," Adele said.

Annie scratched the side of her face. She was beginning to be terribly sleepy again. Her legs were aching.

"What could we do," Adele was asking, "if they come back this way?"

"Huh?" Annie got her eyes away from the fire. She almost had to reach out with both hands and pull herself free.

"If they come back . . . listen there." Some more of the hollow shotgun sounds.

"Those are way off," Annie said, "down by the west end. I bet they just shooting out at water, empty water."

"I guess everybody's up by now."

Annie giggled. "With all this racket, they either up or dead."

The nightgown made Adele look thinner than ever, a seer-

sucker nightgown printed all over with little sprays of flowers.
"Don't let that thing catch," Annie said.

"I want to see could we do something with the fence."

"Hell," Annie said, "let it burn; it's mostly gone now."

Adele went over to the front steps. "I'm going get a dress on,
and I'll be right back out."

"Hurry up," Annie said.

She waited. It wasn't more than two minutes before Adele was
back.

"Okay," Annie said, "you watch it now."

As she was walking away, Adele said, very quietly: "And your
boyfriend does not come to see how you are. . . ."

Annie felt herself stop breathing. She had been thinking that
and wondering. "He knows I can take care myself. . . ."

Annie crossed the island, scarcely noticing where she walked.
And when people yelled at her, she answered them without really
knowing what she said.

The shore lights at the wharf were off—she was a little
surprised. The telephone wouldn't be working either, she thought.
One of the luggers, it looked like the *Bozo* from where she stood,
had its big searchlight on, shining it right down the line of the
boats. And at the other end, the *Pixie's* high spreader lights were
on.

She squinted in the glare: the boats had not been touched,
none of them.

"Inky," she called, "Inky!"

"By the icehouse."

She went over, her eyes drooping against the glare. "Quit playing games," she said.

"Come around the back."

She didn't see him until she was close enough to touch him.
He was sitting on a box, leaning against the wall. She blinked
rapidly to get her eyes used to the dark again.

"Figured you'd be coming down," he said.

Adele's question was still echoing around in her mind: he
does not come to see how you are?

"How's the boat?" she asked.

"They didn't even come close to this side." He answered her
slowly, not understanding her angry tone.

"What are you hanging on to that for?" She pointed to the automatic in his lap.

"In case they get over this way."

"They gone," she said. "And everybody's putting out the fires."

A boat cost a lot of money, she thought. And it didn't belong to him. So he had to be careful. More careful than he'd be for himself.

"Won it off a guy, couple years ago. Out at Milneburg one night." He rubbed the short blued barrel.

You always had to be more careful of things that weren't yours. And if it hadn't been for the boat, he'd have come. . . .

"We had a fire," she said.

He whistled. "I wondered about that!"

"Side of the house got scorched."

"I figured that you weren't exactly all alone, with your old man right there, and your stepmother."

"We put it out in no time at all."

"They didn't come near the boats, none of 'em."

"Burnt down our fence."

"Jesus," Inky said, "it's beginning to look like a war."

She shook her head. "They had to, I reckon."

"Huh?"

"With Pete Livaudais and all."

"Hell," he said, "it's getting too rough for me."

"They had to."

"The electricity's off."

"Line down, I bet."

They could hear people yelling, and toward the western end of the island more shots.

"What's that all about?" Inky asked.

She shook her head.

"Look how red it makes the clouds right up there."

"Rain clouds," Annie said.

"Time for it."

"You going to take me with you?" Annie asked.

"When?"

"When you leave."

"You still want to go?"

"Seems like."

"Okay," Inky said.

She squatted down on the shells. "Give me time to pack, huh?"

He bent forward and peered at her. "You feel all right?"

"I'm tired," she said; "I been working."

"Sorry," he said, "but I couldn't help it."

Her little finger was aching, just the way it always did when she was terribly excited. She rubbed at it, hard.

"You going to stay here?"

He nodded. "Me, and the one guy down in that lugger there: Ozzie something-or-other."

"Pailet."

Inky nodded. "Just in case."

"Where's Dan?"

"Went home to see what was going on."

"I better go back," Annie said.

"Sorry I can't go with you."

"Nothing much to do back there now."

"Okay," he said, "so kiss me good-by."

Annie went back to the house. The fence was still burning. Claudie, armed with a long green leafy branch was watching it.

"What are you playing at, stupid . . . King of the May?" she asked him.

She stumbled through the house until she came into the kitchen where there were two kerosene lamps lit on the table. Adele was bent over at the stove, trying to see if the coffee was dripped.

"I wish they'd make a glass pot," she said, "so you'd know."

"I been down by the boats."

"I was thinking you would."

"They didn't even go near any of them."

"I have heard that," Adele said.

"How?"

"People passing by."

"I'm sleepy," Annie said, "I'm going back to bed."

"You watch the fire and Claudie for me," Adele said. "I heard the LeBlanc roof is burning."

"Jesus," Annie said, "what could you do?"

"You just sit on the front porch and watch the fence, no?"

"God!" Annie said and scratched over her ear. "I'm going to bed."

"You just sit and watch."

"All the same to me if the whole island burn up."

She found her way to her room in the dark and stretched out on the bed. She was yawning and arching her back when the door opened. The fire flickering outside gave just enough light for her to recognize Adele.

"Jee-*sus!*" And she waited.

"Are you fixing to leave here?" Adele asked.

"Huh?"

"Way you acting nobody's going to want you around here."

On the tin roof overhead began the first little knocking thuds of the rain.

"There it comes," Annie said, "and that is going to solve your problem."

Adele was quiet for so long that Annie lifted up her head to see if she was still there.

She was. "When people find out what you do," she said slowly, "when . . ."

"Jesus," Annie said.

Annie did not hear her leave; but she knew by the silence that she must be gone.

The first thick fat drops of rain were plopping into the dirt and smashing into the flat sides of leaves. A sharp clean odor began to come from the ground.

With a flashlight Adele hurried along, noticing only: there's no lightning, none at all. And it's coming down a little faster.

A couple of dogs were growling and snapping in the underbrush. All of them, Adele thought, and not a one began the barking in time.

She passed the Arcenaux house and waved to Philomene Arcenaux who was sitting on her front porch, rocking, as if nothing had happened. There was a kerosene lantern burning on the floor by her.

"Nothing happen here?" Adele called to her.

She shook her head, slowly, so that even in the half-dark Adele could see the fat chins tremble. "Didn't come this far in."

"Didn't do no real harm with us."

"Over by LeBlanc's now," Philomene said, "they have some doing and some trouble."

"I was going by there," Adele said.

"I don't go," Philomene said. "And I be no use, leastways."

"I got to see," Adele said.

It wasn't more than a couple of hundred yards away. She could see the glow over the trees. But when she finally saw it, there wasn't a house any more, just the outlines: the studs dark against the yellow flame.

She stood staring, fascinated by the light, shaking her head slowly.

"You left the kid?" Al said.

She jerked her head around.

"You leave Claudie?"

"Annie's there."

His shirt was torn and a long black line of soot smeared across his forehead and down his left cheek.

"This here was the only one," Al said. "The only one."

There was a ring of people standing back from the fire, quietly watching.

"They went after this one," Al said. "And they done a job with it. Never had a chance saving it."

"Oh," Adele said, "they got a lot of their stuff out." She pointed to a pile of things, "Even the icebox."

"Everybody here was carrying. Even the kids."

"I meant to come down," Adele said. "Only I was afraid to leave till Annie got back."

"Feel rain, no?"

"Maybe that stops the fire?"

Al shook his head. "And even if it does now, it ain't no use. They still got to start over and build a new house."

"It's coming harder."

Al said: "They starting to move that stuff to a dry spot. What the fire didn't get the water ain't going to ruin."

There was a crowd yanking at the stuff. Al grabbed the end of a sofa. "Vieux couillon . . ." he yelled, "gimme a hand." Adele tried, but he pushed her away. "Go get something light."

She got herself a market basket of china. And she found herself following two girls who lugged a baby's crib between them. At night the paths still confused her, and she didn't quite know whose shed they turned into.

The girls put the crib down in the far corner. She stood at the door hesitating, until she recognized them: the Schesnaydre twins.

"Put that in the crib, and it be safer," the one whose name was Polly said.

Adele tried: the basket was too heavy.

"Here we come," Polly said. And the two other pairs of hands got under the basket and lifted. "Maybe we didn't break just all of it," Polly said. And her twin giggled.

They ran back, the three together. It was really raining now, hard, big drops that splashed cold on your hot skin. But the rain hadn't made any difference yet to the fire: it had only set up a little sizzling sound.

The pile of chairs and tables and pots and clothes was gone.

"That was quick, so quick," Adele said, to herself, but aloud.

"For sure," Julius Arcenaux said, patting himself on the belly. "Lots of hands carrying it in all directions, so it go poof!"

Adele could feel the rain on the back of her neck now. She stepped back under the shelter of a broad-leafed mulberry tree.

"Good," Julius said, "the harder the better."

Cecile was standing there too. The rain had slicked her short black hair down until it shone like patent leather in the firelight. "They didn't do no more than pitch some gas at the rest—over by us they burn up one old skiff." She nodded to the burning house. "They fix this, dirty mudders!" She spat down between her own bare feet.

Adele's hair was hanging in wet, tickling strings over her ears. When she pushed it back her hands were trembling. She tried not to have it show.

Julius noticed; he had a quick eye. "Why you don't go home?" he asked. "Nothing much more to do here, and plenty people still around to do it."

"Maybe." All of a sudden she was very tired, as if she'd been up for days: her legs were aching.

"Why they pick this one?" she asked.

"Wrong house," Julius said and pointed fifty yards to the west. "That the house they really want."

"The Livaudais place," Adele said.

"Bastards got the wrong house," Julius said. "Simple like that."

She nodded and moved off. Once out from under the tree, she felt the rain slap into her face, she felt the shoulders of her dress go soggy in half a minute.

Just where the path turned, she stopped again and looked back. The rain was beginning to have an effect: the fire was dimmer, much dimmer, with a kind of orange color. There were columns of blue steam rising straight up. And over the rattle of the rain a steady hissing.

She could only see one figure standing out in the teaming rain (the others would have got back under the trees for shelter): Story LeBlanc. Straddle-legged, arms folded, watching his house burn.

A L took a bottle of whisky and two packs of cigarettes and went out on the front porch. It was raining harder than ever; you couldn't see ten feet ahead, you couldn't see the burned-out sticks of the fence line.

Looking out to where he knew that fence was, Al shivered, unscrewed the bottle and took a drink. They'd been in too much a hurry when they threw the gasoline, or maybe they'd stood too far back. Most of it had gone in the yard or on the fence. But for that the whole place would have gone up like the LeBlanc's. Just that one side was burned. He'd have to rip out those clapboards—but that wasn't too bad.

They hadn't got to the boats. Hadn't even tried. Down there it was like nothing had happened. And that was the best news of all. A house was easy enough to build—maybe they could even use those same foundations—but a boat now, that was a different matter. When you didn't carry insurance. And who could afford insurance? He'd seen people live close to the line when they'd lost a boat.

He started a cigarette. They had got wet, somehow. And they weren't drawing. He used another match and shrugged to himself: But they will dry.

Beside the rain, there wasn't a sound. Though there wasn't a person on the island asleep, except maybe the kids . . . and Adele, he added. Passed out, almost, on the sofa. She wasn't all that strong, he thought. He'd tell Annie that she'd have to do the heavy housework.

And Annie now. . . . She wasn't in the house. She'd gone out again.

He yawned, and stretched his back in the chair. He ached all over, inside and out, like a tremendous hangover.

Would she be marrying him, he wondered. And what sort of a

guy was he? Would he take her off to New Orleans, and after a while walk away, leaving her stranded and having to go on the Welfare to get back home?

That was the trouble marrying away.

He stretched again and sighed.

It would be light before too long now. And a man could see what was really happening around him. Flashlights and lanterns and even spotlights—they didn't do much good. Wherever you put them, you saw only one little place and the others were just that much deeper. You'd almost be better without any.

He rocked slowly back and forth and waited. . . . That Livaudais kid, he thought, done it all. And what for? . . . Somebody shoulda figured on that. And somebody shoulda watched him.

Al finished one cigarette and started another. It was funny, he thought, moving the words carefully and slowly through his mind, when he'd been younger he'd never been one to think of missing a fight. He'd looked for them, for sure. Maybe it was part of getting old. . . . He didn't want them now. But he had them, they all had them this time, unless he could talk down the LeBlancs . . . and they wouldn't be likely to forget about that burned house. . . .

"I'm getting too old for all the fighting," he said aloud.

And he could add, silently: But there plenty kids to do it.

The rain was falling so hard that there were little rivers of it running through the dry grass of the front yard: he could see that much by the little yellow square of light from the kerosene lamp in the parlor window.

The whole island smelled burned out. He wondered if Terre Haute had smelled that way too, after Pete Livaudais had been there.

It wouldn't be long before daylight.

*

SOON after Adele had gone, Annie slipped out the back door. The
rain was just starting then: a couple of fat drops sprinkled her
hair. She started to go down to the dock, but then changed her
mind and began walking west on the little shell ridge.

It was very still, the way it always was before a rain. The
slowly dripping clouds were right close overhead. She wanted to
stretch and see if she couldn't touch them. Instead she reached
down and flicked away the piece of shell that had got caught between her toes.

Good thing my feet are tough, she thought, or I'd have to wear
shoes all the time.

In spite of that thought, she snapped on the little flashlight she
was carrying and, squatting down, inspected her big toe. It was cut
all right, there on the side. She sat down, put the flash still burning on the ground beside her and, taking her heel into her left
hand, lifted her foot to her mouth. She sucked at the little cut,
tasting the salty blood and the rather sweetish dust.

She sucked and spat. Wonder, she thought, would I have stuff
enough to do this with a Congo bite? If Inky got bit?

Holding the foot up to her mouth, she stopped and imagined:
Inky in a pirogue. And the long dark snake that they sometimes
called a Moccasin. She saw it, on the low hanging branch, and
with one quick jab of her paddle danced her pirogue aside. Inky
was looking at her; he didn't see. She opened her mouth to call
to him, to yell to him: get out, get out the way, don't you see,
can't you see? But the top of his head brushed the branch. And
the long dark shape fell. . . . She heard him cry and she saw
the pirogue shake and ship a little water. And the shape went over
the side and into the dark oily hyacinth-spotted water. . . . And
she could see herself: crossing over in a couple of strokes. She

387

could hear the rough wood sides of the pirogues rubbing together. And Inky was holding his thigh, just below his bathing-trunks, holding it with both hands, pressing with all his strength. And he took his hands away and she could see the little round holes. She watched him take his knife and make slashes over the holes, x-shaped slashes and the blood came out red as ink. But he couldn't reach to suck it. He couldn't reach. She ran her tongue around her mouth, to see if there were any cuts or sore places for the poison to enter. And he was looking at her, asking her. . . . The pirogues bumped together, very gently, and she couldn't figure what was making the dead-quiet water move in little swells. She looked and could see nothing but the swamp. He was watching her, asking her. She started to, she bent forward to begin to suck the poison into her own mouth . . . but she couldn't. She couldn't. She stayed bent over, staring at the ink-red wound, but couldn't touch it. . . . The pirogues began to slide apart and she was staring down at the water, the thick slimy water.

Annie sat on the crushed shells, still holding her cut toe in her hand. The rain splattered around her ears.

A man shouted: "Over by LeBlanc's!" She jumped and the dream was gone, leaving only the heaviness in her stomach. She put out her hands, one on each side of her, and patted the sharp shells.

They were clams once, she told herself, and oysters. Clams swim but oysters don't, somebody'd told her that. And her father now, he'd told her: the Indians left those little heaps of shell and stuff; garbage heaps, a man from the state university had told him.

Annie flicked a crumbled piece of shell away between her fingers. All the stuff the Indians had thrown away. A long long time ago: a thousand or a million years.

She flicked another shell away. And tried to imagine the Indians. They'd eaten the shellfish or maybe they'd used them for bait. It was so far back she couldn't even imagine.

She stood up and shook back her hair. The rain felt almost cold. And it would put out the fires too, if it came much harder and nobody would have to bother. . . .

Inky now, he would think she was completely crazy walking around in the rain. Not even a hat. . . . She could just hear him now: "You lost your god-damn mind?" And those close-set blue eyes of his would be staring at her and there'd be just a touch of impatience in his tone.

She got to her feet and began walking along. There wasn't a soul out, though she'd expected to meet lots of people. The rain had sent them hurrying inside. Annie snapped on the flashlight and pointed it straight up at the sky, into the rain that was more streams than drops.

"Oh, hell," she said and snapped off the light. "Nobody can stop me. If I want to be out. Nobody can."

She put her hands to her waist. Even my stomach's wet, she thought, even that.

She moved down toward the west, going slowly, feeling her clothes get wetter by the minute.

Wasn't nobody could stop her. Not if she wanted to be out. She took a big swallow of the wet air. Wasn't nobody . . .

She heard the dogs off in the bushes to the right. There weren't more than one or two. But they had something and they were worrying at it. Not fighting, no. But she could hear their rumbled growlings.

She listened for a minute, balancing the flashlight on the tip of one finger. Just the sound of the dogs. And the heavy rustle of the rain on trees and grass and ground, a sound that was almost like breathing.

That was what they told little kids sometimes when they took them to the window: listen to the world breathing.

She went on. This was the highest point of the island: a little mound. If you climbed up any of the trees here, you could see all over the island and way out to sea. The pirates had kept a man here, all day and all night, people said, those days when their ships were moored safely back in the curve of the harbor. And down there at the foot of the hill, not more than two feet under the ground, Leon Caillet's father had found six gold coins. That was all; just the coins. The bag or the purse they'd been in had decayed clean away.

"You know," Annie whispered to herself, "if you could just take off the top layer of this island here, you'd have yourself a lot of money. A real lot."

She was standing on top the mound now, the thick grove of wind-shaped oaks to the south. On the other side the mound fell off sharply, giving way to the marsh that fringed all this side of the island, a little strip of marsh, and beyond that the wide now-smooth expanse of the back bay.

"Bet there's a lot of money on this island," Annie said to the rain. "You just can't ever get at it." There were little flickers of lightning, way off there to the north, maybe way over by Petit Prairie, but it wasn't very much.

"A lot of money." If you could just take the top layer off, the way they could do with a muskrat. Just one slice down the middle, and one on each leg, and pull it off. And the things you would find. . . . "And the Indians too," Annie said, "skeletons maybe." She shivered in spite of herself. "And the pirate money, all the things they hid and won't ever find."

She thought of climbing a tree. She went over and touched the trunk. Then changed her mind and went back the way she had come. She went very quietly. The same dogs off in the under-brush were still at it, still growling. She was passing them when she heard something else: muffled curses, which she didn't catch, and then a dog's yelp. A growl and another muffled word.

She stood absolutely still and bent her head forward, straining to hear. Just rain moving the leaves. And then the dogs started again: a low steady growl.

"Micmac. . . ." she whispered to herself. "Du micmac. . . ." She moved a few yards up the path so that she could turn back and come at an angle to the spot where the dogs were. She stepped off the path, moving slowly and carefully. There were a whole mess of old blackberry vines back in here, and they could tear you to ribbons, just those little thorns could. And back in here, too, were all the trenches Oliver Robillard had dug years ago when he had his idea for growing terrapins in his own back yard. That hadn't worked. But the trenches and pits did fill up with fresh water—not salt, the way some people predicted. And he finally put crawfish there. He spent a good day paddling around in the rice fields south of Petit Prairie just to get the crawfish that grew there, the light gray-green ones with the thick tails. He brought them back and dumped them in his trenches. And it worked. It worked fine. Only, one dry July the water had shrunk all back into the main pool. And when the rains finally did come, the ground had cracked and changed so the water never did run back into the proper trenches. They were still there, but covered over by Jerusalem oak: rabbits lived in them now mostly. They were a couple of feet deep and you could go sprawling in them before you had time to think—flat on your face in the bushes. And maybe even poison ivy at that.

She moved very carefully, feeling with her foot ahead of her. There—the first trench. She could follow it down now easily: the connecting trenches were all on the other side.

The dogs were snuffling not too far ahead. "What you got?" she called. "What you got there?"

One of them began to bark, short snapping yaps.

"Okay," she said. Jesus, she thought, nothing but poison ivy and me with bare feet. Jesus Christ.

A tangle of little mulberry trees and chinaberry trees and creepers grown all over everything—bread-and-butter vine with its thin mean thorns. She saw the rear quarters of a dog, a brown and white dog. "What you got, hey?"

The dog backed out and stood, barking. She stepped around him. The clump was thick and matted with old grape vines. One of the dead twigs scratched her cheek. "Damn." She got down on her hands and knees to peer through the little hole the dog had found. It was too dark to see. "Jesus," she said and, standing up, began to tug away the vines and clear a spot.

The second dog had come out now, a white animal, fair-sized. It sat very quietly, waiting, and working at its muzzle with paw and tongue.

"Hurt yourself, huh?"

The dog went on licking; he had begun to whimper softly. The brown and white one went over and stood alongside him, head cocked, ears pointed up.

Annie cleared the vines and pushed aside the little trees and snapped on the flashlight.

It was a small light, a narrow beam. But it picked up the black T-shirt and threw a faint glow on the face above it.

Annie was not surprised. It was as if she'd known what she would find. She was only curious.

She didn't lift the beam into the face. She could see it clearly enough: not young, not old, a wide square face with slanting cheek bones, and wide-set eyes.

They all look alike, Annie found herself thinking. Those people from the other island.

Not too far off a woman called: "You seen Tina?"

"That's a kid," Annie said to the T-shirt. "Wandered off, I guess. Or hiding somewhere, scared right stiff."

Behind her the dogs snorted and licked. There was the soft lapping sound of their tongues. Softest sound she'd ever heard, Annie thought.

"A Congo bite you?" she asked.

And then she remembered herself. No dream, this.

The man had not moved.

"What happen to you?"

She held the light steady, staring at the smears of brown and black on the shirt.

"Nothin'," he said finally.

One dog whimpered again. "You hit him? No?" Annie pushed back her straggling hair. In the shelter of the bushes, the rain was not falling so heavy, but you could hear it roar. "But maybe they bit you," she went on. "Sometimes they bite anything that's out flat on the ground."

The same woman's voice called: "They want you down by LeBlanc's."

Annie stared into the narrow stick of light that was speckled and criss-crossed by the falling rain. "Goes on raining like this, you going to be swimming back here."

She stopped and waited. The man said nothing.

"How come you got left behind? What you waiting to burn down?"

He snorted, shortly, and with his left hand wiped the rain off his face.

"Yea," Annie said, "I reckon I know, me. I reckon I can put it all together. You want to hear?"

The man still did not move.

"Running in the dark," Annie said. The glass of the flash was streaming; the light was wavery and crooked. "You thought it was the same way you come in." She could see it now, plain as if she were there. . . .

She wondered whether a leg breaking made any sound.

"People died from broken legs before this."

He grunted.

"Hurts I bet."

She shivered.

"Broke my finger once . . . hurt all the way into my back."

He still did not answer. And Annie, uncertain, snapped off the light, felt her way back to the path and started home. She did not quite know what else to do.

The rain was coming down so hard now you couldn't hear anything else. Her jeans were soaked through and they stuck to her legs and made it hard to walk. The force of the rain on her head was like a weight.

I got to go home, she told herself. Her thoughts paraded very slowly across the front of her mind so that she had time to size up each one before it disappeared.

I'm so tired I can't hardly tell where I'm walking. And there's a burning in my head. Like I had a fever, only not quite. Like I had a fever behind my eyes. It felt sort of like this back when I had the malaria, and how long ago that was that, back when I was a kid, and a little kid too, small enough to be lifted up out of bed. Somebody lifted me up, only I don't remember who. And it felt like this, the burning. . . . You'd think the rain now would cool it off, only it doesn't touch it. Maybe it's getting near my period, and getting wet now'll stop it for sure. And cuts you get during your period are always three times slower to heal, I can tell that, me. . . . Or maybe something went wrong, and I'm having a child. Maybe this is the way you tell first. . . . Haven't been to sleep at all, just a little doze. I kept dreaming then that somebody was looking in the window. If it wasn't raining I could sleep out here. I'd rather sleep out here. The whole house . . . she's got such a musky smell. You can tell it even on the front porch; you could tell it anywhere. If it wasn't raining I could stay out. . . .

The rain's been slow coming. For September. There's no lightning. Just a little, maybe. Not much for storm season. September storms.

And back there, just a little way back there, is a guy from Terre Haute. And when they find him, when it gets light in the morning, I don't want to see what they do. Won't look. . . .

She stumbled: a plank across the path. She looked up, squinting into the rain and recognized: a fishing-platform. Sure. Arcenaux's. He like to fish, him, and crab. And he built this one specially strong for himself: he must have weighed 250 if he weighed a pound.

And she saw something else: under the walk a faint whitish shape. The dinghy, the one from the *Pixie,* the small one, the one without an outboard. She walked out on the platform, keeping her balance carefully. No oars. She bent down and squinted closer: but the oarlocks were there, dangling by their chains.

Then she was running. She could feel her feet moving and she could see trees and bushes race past her. But she didn't seem to be within herself any more. She was going along for the ride. Like a hair ribbon that's perched on top a head, looks out and flutters.

The Manint house was closest. They had the lamps on in the kitchen. And they'd be sitting there, coffee or breakfast. The yard dogs were gone, scattered. The gate stood wide open: it had even got pulled off one of its hinges.

She wondered how that had happened.

The oars were under the house, on little racks, right where everybody kept them. There were several pair: she took the closest to hand. A little scraping sound when she pulled them out, but nobody seemed to notice.

She had them over her shoulder and back to the landing, at a steady jog this time: they were heavy and she was beginning to be winded.

She put the oars quietly in the dinghy, loosened the line, and stepped down into it. It was unsteady. And she had stepped in wrong. The shell ducked and shivered and shipped a little water. She grabbed at the sides, and nearly fell over; a little of the brackish bay water splashed into her mouth.

She spat it out, wondering if what her grandmother used to say was true: if you drank five glasses of bay water it would kill you.

She settled herself and fitted the locks into their rings. She pushed off with an oar and began rowing down the island, going slowly and very quietly.

If there was any wind, she thought, I'd swamp in two minutes. Inky said this dinghy wasn't good. But there isn't any wind.

I'm glad it isn't his boat, she thought. If it was his, I couldn't take it. Even with an insurance company to pay him back. I couldn't do it.

She found the place, though it was hard to tell in the rain and the dark. And she rowed in. The dinghy struck bottom a good fifteen feet off shore.

And me with no shoes, she thought. She took one oar and churned up the inch or so of water and reeds. "Congos get away from here," she whispered. "Get away from here."

She threw over an oar, and clinging to the round handle with her bare toes, walked its length. The rest of the way she picked along over the sharp reeds and shells.

She found the man, not in the spot she had left him, but a good ten feet away.

"You walk?" she asked.

He held perfectly still.

"Look, stupid idiot, there's a dinghy just over there."

He was rubbing his jaw now and squinting to see her.

"Get yourself over there and I'll give you a shove off. There's nothing wrong with your arms, you can row."

"You don't turn off the light, I can see nothing."

She snapped it off.

"Why?" he asked. "Why you doing this?"

There was a sharp ache across the back of her neck, just the way it had felt, years ago, when one of the boys had rabbit-punched her.

"Get yourself up," she said, "I ain't coming close enough for you to get a finger on me."

A dog howled, short and close by.

"It's this way," Annie said. "I'll wait up by the path for a little while."

She stood in the middle of the path and waited. She held her left arm out in front of her and watched the heavy drops bounce off. The oar was floating in the very shallow water, not even seeming to move.

I'll wait a little while, she thought, and then I'll go call people. If he doesn't come. . . .

But he came, sliding himself backwards along the ground, in wormlike movements.

If his leg is broken, Annie thought, it must be nearly killing him.

He got himself to the path and stopped, one hand clutching his leg. He wasn't making a sound but you could tell from the arch of his back that he was screaming.

"Gimme you shoes," Annie said.

He didn't answer. He just waggled his head back and forth a little.

"Oh hell," she said and waded out after the oar.

She brought it back to him. "You can use this to stand up with."

He took the oar. And she stepped back.

He jammed the handle in the ground and shifted himself for balance. The oar slipped away and almost fell on his leg. He hesitated again, panting.

"Quit stalling," she said. "I ain't coming near you."

He planted the oar more firmly this time, got his balance and stood up. For a minute he swayed so she thought he would fall. And she snapped on the light. He stared into it and made a hissing sound, like a sick animal. She turned it off, quickly. But she had seen his face: it was red, bright red, and sweat, not rain, was pouring down it.

He got himself set firmly, and wiped off his chin with the back of his hand.

"I can't get it any closer in," she said, and pointed.

Using the oar for a crutch, he moved out into the shallow tangle of reeds and water. Each step the oar sank deeper and he had to yank it out.

Already back in the tangle of chinaberry trees the birds were beginning to squaak sleepily: it was that near daylight.

He got himself in the dinghy, and down on the seat. He gave one short muffled cry and the oar dropped from his hand and went overboard.

Annie waded out, wincing against the shells. She got both oars and put them in the locks.

"Hold onto them. Just hold on and I'll give you a push off."

His weight had sunk the boat slightly. She pushed and nothing moved. She had to get down, kneeling in the oozing mud, put her shoulder to it and push with all her strength. The boat floated free, and she landed, chin first, in the muck. She scrambled up—thinking: If there're Congos here, they get me sure—and ran back to the solid ground, this time not noticing the shells and afraid to look down, afraid of seeing the long black shape.

On solid ground she took a deep breath and wiped the mud off her chin. They miss me, she thought, they miss me. She wanted to laugh. Instead she called, still softly: "You clear now. Go and start rowing."

A shape turned gray by the rain, he pulled once on the oars: the boat moved. Then he leaned forward, holding the oars high up in the air like wings. "Bitch," he said clearly, "bitch." And spat toward the land.

*

IT got light very slowly with the clouds. There was just a kind of faint gray glow over the rain.

Annie was going home, hobbling slowly because her feet were cut and hurting. Even as she walked, her eyes kept slipping closed.

As she was turning off the back path to the one that would lead to the house, she met Julius Arcenaux. He had just got up and just come out: she noticed he was wearing a pair of dark blue tennis shoes that were only beginning to get spotted and splashed with the rain.

"Bébé," he said, "how come I find you out here?" He was wearing a black raincoat and a wide-brimmed straw hat. Annie could smell the strong odor of fresh coffee on his breath.

"I was all nerves, me," Annie said.

"Rain is good for nerves, huh?"

She shrugged.

"You been out long?"

"I didn't bring a watch."

"Wet straight through." She could feel his eyes fasten on her breasts, so hard it was like a touch.

"I was chasing Gigi, me. She got loose last night."

"Ain't a dog on this island in his yard," Julius said.

"And her about ready to drop too."

"Come on by the store and get warm."

She shook her head, "No thanks."

"You need a drink."

"Not before breakfast I don't need nothing."

"I got coffee down there," he said and winked. "And a bottle of rum too. Good rum."

"Lemme pass."

"Taste mighty good. Taste real good for sure."

398

"Look," she said, "I got to go home. . . . Move!"

He stepped aside. As she passed, he patted her behind.

"And that going to be the closest you get too," she said.

He scratched one side of his nose. "You ain't been looking for no dog."

"Go to hell," she said and walked away.

At the house the lamps were all out and the kitchen was empty. That shaking feeling in her stomach now, it might be hunger. But the table was clear except for a blue box of Morton's salt and the stove lid was down. She went over and touched the oilcloth, with the tips of her fingers. Then, holding her head a little sideways, she went to her room. The singing in her ears was so loud now that she couldn't hear anything else.

The room was just as she had left it: the unmade bed had its sheet creased into little puckers. The window was open too, as she had left it, and the rain had come in, leaving a dark smear on the wallpaper under the sill and a puddle on the linoleum.

It was still coming in. She went over and closed the window, hard, so that the glass shivered and almost broke. She stood, head against the frame, looking out. The day was the silvery-gray luminous color of the underside of a pompano. The trees were black wet stems splotched with green. And the yard was gumbo mud: a single brownish-yellow puddle, churned by the drops and completely empty except for a couple of floating sticks and little specks of floating white chicken feathers.

She took off her wet clothes. They clung to her and she yanked at them, bruising her own flesh. She found some dry ones: a long-sleeved cotton-flannel shirt and another pair of jeans. And she let herself drop face downward on the bed.

She was almost asleep. One thing was nagging at her, keeping her awake. She sat up, scrubbing at her eyes. The bed . . . that was it. The bed was wet. Even this far from the window . . . there must have been more wind than she thought. The sheets were soggy, and the moss inside the ticking was giving off its faint sweet-sour smell.

Oh God. . . . She climbed out of bed. She got the two towels that were hanging behind the door and threw them on the floor in the corner farthest from the window. She took a couple of shirts from the drawer and threw them down too. Then she emptied the drawers completely, pushing the clothes into a heap with her bare toe.

She stopped and stared. There was a long cut across the instep. Blood and mud were smeared up to her ankle. She'd have to do something about that. Later.

She stretched out on the mattress of clothes, face down. She smelled the cold paint odor of the linoleum. And then nothing else.

The opening door hit her thigh and stopped. She rolled over from it and peered up. Inky slipped through the small opening.

"Jesus," he said, "what are you doing there?"

She moved her tongue slowly. It felt heavy but all right. So she said: "The bed got rained on."

"Oh." He squatted down on his haunches beside her. "Poor kid," he said, "you really had a night."

It was hard work to talk, very hard work. So she just nodded. And her eyes slipped closed.

"Look," he said, "will you wake up and listen?"

She got her eyes open. And not quite knowing why she said: "I hear somebody in the kitchen."

"No," he said, "you don't. Nobody in the house at all."

She wanted to ask: Where did they go? But her throat was tight and stiff.

Inky said: "Are you listening to me?"

She nodded.

"Sit up then."

She pulled herself up and propped her back against the wall. "Okay," she said thickly.

"Couple of things," he said, "now listen. They took my dinghy. The one I was keeping at Arcenaux's pier."

She remembered. . . . She wouldn't be likely to forget ever. But it was so faraway.

"Didn't touch another thing on the island far as I can see. Just my dink."

She swallowed a couple of times and said: "Yea."

"We're taking the *Pixie* in."

She thought, if I could feel anything, that would surprise me. She said: "Who'd you get to take you in through the channel?"

"Jesus," he said. "I knew you weren't listening."

She didn't argue. Just went on staring straight ahead at the wall. There was a mosquito squashed there, a dry black smear.

Inky took her chin and turned it in his direction. "You real punchy."

She shook her head but he held on. "So I'm telling you again."

She nodded, blinking her eyes rapidly because they were so dry they stung.

"Sure enough Arthur gets one of the guys from the club in New Orleans and pays him to come down to Petit Prairie—and I bet he's paying him good for that too—and this guy picks up somebody in Petit Prairie who knows the channel and who wants to make some easy money. And early this morning they start out and not ten minutes ago they get here. . . . See? Got it?"

She nodded.

"That's luck, huh? . . . Once we get to Petit Prairie it's no trick to get on the Intercoastal right to New Orleans."

Her eyes were slipping closed.

"Hey, look now," he said, "I thought you wanted to go."

Yes, she thought. Sure.

"God damn, keep your eyes open."

She hadn't noticed. So she put a finger to the corner of the left one, holding it up by the lashes.

"You look sorta sick. . . . Nobody's been that tired just from staying up all night."

She said: "I'm just tired, nothing else."

"I thought you wanted to go."

The wallpaper was beginning to peel off too, behind the door. Maybe the roaches were eating the paste behind it again. "Maybe," she said.

"I don't get it," he said, "first you want to and then you don't."

She swallowed and got ahold of her voice. "I been up and I been working and I hadn't been asleep more than five minutes."

"Sure," he said and rubbed her shoulder, very gently.

"I won't fall apart." And she was surprised how her voice whined and complained.

He pulled his hand away.

"You can't expect people that haven't had more than a minute's sleep to make perfectly good sense."

"Sure, honey."

The rain had driven the ants inside. There was a train of black ones around the door frame. When she was little, she'd liked to take a lighted match and hold it right in the path.

"When you leaving?" When she was this tired, she had the accent of the island. *Cap-cap,* she thought with a sneer at herself. *Parle cap-cap.*

"Along about one."

She nodded and took her fingers from her eye. It slid closed. She lifted it open again.

"You sure you're not sick, huh?"

"Tell you what . . . I don't make it down there by one, you go ahead."

"It won't make a difference if we got to wait a little while."

"I'm not down there then, you go ahead. Account of I won't be coming."

"I don't get it," he said, "you wanted to. Why'd you change your mind?"

"Don't wait for me, that's what I said." She turned herself around and stretched out on the tumbled clothes. "Only I think I go crazy if I got to stay awake much longer."

"Listen," he said. "What's the matter? What changed?"

She stretched on her side, feeling the cold hard floor through the little heaps of clothes. She patted it with one hand, vaguely. Nice floor, she thought. Nice old floor.

"Nothing," she said, "nothing matters. Not now. Not one bit."

"You get hurt?"

She crooked her arm under her head. "Nothing. And nobody." She could tell she wasn't making sense. So she said: "I got to get some sleep." And she stopped fighting and let her eyelids slip closed again.

When he had gone—in spite of what she had said—when she'd heard the outside screen slam shut, she did not go to sleep. She lay without moving because it was easier that way while her mind turned over and over slowly. Like a turtle dragging along through the marsh grass.

I could go now, she thought. If I'm going at all, I'm going now.

That was it. It came on you all of a sudden. And it wasn't the way you thought it was going to be. There wasn't anything wild about it or strange. It was just there, like lots of other things. And you took it. Or not. And only looking forward or back you saw how important it was, really.

Now, she thought, either I put my stuff in a suitcase or I don't. It's that simple. Now. Only when I look back on it tomorrow, I'll see that it wasn't.

The room was making small tight circles. She was thinking, I'm going to throw up, when she fell asleep.

She could hear the rain still and smell the damp coming up from under the house through the floorboards. And Inky was back.

"You just stay here, waiting for me to doze off?"

"It's near half past eleven," Inky said.

She sat up and began to rub her jaw. There was a pimple there and she scrubbed at it.

"You awake?"

"Sure," she said, "sure I am."

"Just want to tell you," Inky said and stared at the things jumbled on top of her bureau. He picked up her powder puff and dusted it against his fingers nervously. "If you want to get married, it's all right with me."

Again there was that faint far-off tingle that would have been a shock if she hadn't been so tired.

She stared at his dripping raincoat, and at the little puddles beginning to form on the floor. And when she spoke, it wasn't her speaking at all.

"I got one bed full of rain water," she said. "Don't wet up my other one."

"I forgot," he said. "I'll take it off."

He put it in the hall and was back in a few seconds. "You hear what I said?"

"I'm beat but not deaf."

"Jesus," he said. "I think you musta got hurt last night."

"No."

"You didn't get hit by anything? Or fall down?"

"I smell coffee now, for sure."

"She's out in the kitchen, your stepmother."

"Oh," Annie said.

"I said it's all right with me."

"I heard you."

She got up and stuffed the shirt inside the jeans. "I had a belt somewhere. . . ."

Inky found it and handed it to her. Then she began brushing out her hair in front of the little bureau mirror.

"I had a . . ." She forgot to finish the sentence. She turned slowly on her heel, looking around the room. She found it on the little table by the bed, a bottle of cologne. She sprinkled some on the brush and went back to brushing.

"Maybe this'll get the smoke smell out."

Inky had forgotten to take off his cap. He wore it backwards like a catcher's, and water was still running down the long bill and dripping to the floor. "That all you got to say?"

She took her lower lip in her teeth and held it.

"I thought maybe that's why you weren't coming."

"I wasn't thinking about it," Annie said.

"I'd like for you to come."

She began to clean the brush of loose hairs.

"And I thought you wanted to live in New Orleans. Or did you change your mind?"

"No," she said.

"This is what I was figuring." He scratched his ear. "Soon's we get there, we borrow this car from my brother and head for the Coast and get married right there. And I got my back pay from Arthur and we drive anywhere we want to."

She held very still listening.

"Sound good?"

"I'da wanted to do that once."

"Not now?"

She put an elbow on the bureau and leaned her head against her hand. "Things change and I feel all thick and heavy."

"You don't want to come?"

"My throat's so dry," she rubbed at it, "I'm going get some coffee. You know your dinghy?"

"The lost one, sure."

"Nothing." She shifted her head so that her forehead touched the wood.

"If you don't want to, that's all there is to it."

She didn't lift her head. "I don't know what I said."

"Look," Inky said, "we got to leave by two, the latest. And I'll come ask you just before we leave."

Annie nodded, feeling that her head was moving through a mess of cotton. "I'll get some coffee."

"Never thought to see me proposing to a girl," Inky laughed nervously. He came up behind her back and hugged her, hard, his hips pressing into her behind. "Never thought of an answer like this, either."

She felt a responsive quiver begin in her. The wire-thin twitch.

"Quit," she said.

"Hope you come along. I'd miss you for sure."

"Quit," she said.

He stepped back. "Settled, huh? I come back and ask you before we go."

She lifted her head just enough to nod.

When he had gone she moved out into the center of the room and looked around. There wouldn't be much to take, she thought. If I went. If.

And why didn't he come looking for me last night with the fires?

And she could feel her face turn heavy and sullen, like a bad make-up.

I don't know, she thought. I don't know. . . .

There was that time Claudie had followed her. And Inky had yelled at her to go home.

Not the marrying kind, she thought. And where'd he be next week? And why'd he ask? And why'd he ask?

And she remembered Julius, remembered seeing his black slicker, that pulled tight across his belly, come popping out the mist. And he hadn't believed about the dog. And he'd gone and poked around, for sure. And he was a sharp one; maybe he put some things together.

Though there hadn't been any signs, she thought. But maybe he could guess.

And if they guessed. . . .

I need some coffee, me, she told herself.

She moved steadily, putting one bare foot in front of the other.

She moved straight through the kitchen to the stove. The pot was there, and a cup too. She poured, noticing without particular interest that there was a puddle of sugar left at the bottom of the cup.

"Wait," Adele said, "and I'll get you a clean cup."

Annie had not noticed she was there. "Look, I'm all right."

"I been using that."

"You got anything contagious?"

Adele put a clean cup out.

"Okay," Annie said, "you drink this one."

She poured another cup, feeling for the first time against the warm handle how very cold her own hands were. She filled the cup and then held her hands to the blue enamel sides of the pot.

"Hands cold?" Adele asked.

"I just like to feel the warm."

"You getting sick?"

"I'm just beat."

"Sit down."

"No." Annie stayed leaning against the stove, warming her hands.

"Your papa didn't get to bed at all."

"Tough luck."

"He had something to eat and went right back. . . . They looking to see if anybody's hiding still."

"There's nobody around."

"They're looking."

"Wouldn't be so stupid to stay around." Annie lifted her head with difficulty and stared out the window. The chinaberry trunk was black with rain, its mold splotches bright yellow-green. "Still raining."

"Didn't you notice when Inky come in he was dripping wet?"

Inky. . . . "Come to think of it, guess I did."

Cats were yeowling under the house. Annie stomped on the floor and they were silent.

"He was telling me," Adele said, "how they finally got fixed up to leave."

Annie was still looking at the splotches of mold. "Who?"

"Inky."

"Oh, sure . . . he wants me to come."

She said it so flatly she surprised herself. She hadn't intended to say anything. "But that's nobody's business."

Adele reached up both hands to smooth back the hair that was already pulled tight over her ears. "I figured it was something like that."

"Nobody's business."

Adele kept patting back hair that hadn't moved.

"How'd you get it to stay in place so?" Annie asked.

"What?"

"Your hair."

"I wasn't thinking about that," Adele said.

"I was just wondering."

Claudie came out on the back porch. You could hear him riding a rocking-chair back and forth, talking to himself.

Adele asked: "You going?"

"I don't know. Maybe. Maybe not."

"I was wondering."

"I'll be back," Annie said.

She went back into her room, closed the door carefully after her. She opened the window, held her head outside, and vomited into the swimming mud.

*

SHE WAS BACK

HALF an hour later, Annie slipped out the back door. She had not taken a raincoat or a hat, but the rain was beginning to slack off a bit. She hurried. Remembering that she hadn't combed her hair, she stopped under the shelter of a palmetto leaf and took a comb from her pocket. She fixed her hair best she could, and ran her finger over her lips to smooth her lipstick. And she went on to the Lombas house.

Walking this way, she'd approach it from the side, around by the chickenhouse, she remembered suddenly when she saw the tangle of blackened slats. Carrie and Ferdinand Lombas were working back there, picking around among the ashes. They looked up when they heard Annie.

She thought: I should have come the other way—they'll all be talking.

But it was too late. So she reminded herself that it didn't matter. And went over to lean on the fence. "The side of our house got burned."

Carrie Lombas nodded. "I been by there."

"Chickens in there?"

"Some."

"Oh," Annie said. "Perique around?"

"By the front."

She walked around, outside the fence. Perique was sawing some boards in the shelter of the front porch. He stopped when she came over.

"Hi," he said.

"I been looking for you," she said, and smiled her best smile.

He looked very tired. There was a long scratch across his fore-head. "I been here."

"Where you get that?" She pointed.

"One place or another."

"Last night?"

He nodded. His hands were dusty with sawdust as he wiped them across his sweating chin.

"I been meaning to thank you for coming to see how we made out."

"Wasn't anything."

"Just last night," she said and ran a hand over her damp hair that was glued to her head, sleek as a seal's. "Seems longer somehow."

"A lot been happening, maybe."

"Yea," Annie said.

"You want something from me?"

Annie jammed her hands down in the pockets of her jeans. "Nothing more than talking to you."

Perique tested the blade of the saw against his finger. And waited.

Annie walked across the porch, wiggling her hips slightly under her tight jeans.

He did not seem to be watching her.

She climbed up on the rail, and glanced toward him. He was squinting down the blade.

It was so quiet, just the rain, and the little shuffling sound, muffled from the back yard, of things being dragged and dropped.

Annie stared down at the faded knees of her jeans, and waited for Perique to say something. Finally she gave up. "I got to decide something," she said.

He put the saw down and came and sat astride the rail, a few feet from her.

"Something real important." She turned facing him. She'd left the two top buttons of her blouse open and she wasn't wearing a bra. She hunched her shoulders just slightly so that the breasts would swing forward and push against the cloth.

She couldn't tell whether he noticed or not—he used to. Once. But today his eyes were absolutely steady, looking into hers. His eyes were milk-chocolate colored.

Still he might be looking. . . .

She had to go on. "Real important," she said finally.

"Like what?"

That she'd got him to answer at all made her feel better. "If I'm going to New Orleans."

She didn't know exactly what she had expected. But it wasn't this.

He didn't so much as blink. There was lots of yellow in his eyes, she noticed, pointing out from the pupils like sunrays. It was funny she'd never noticed that before.

"Thought you want to go to New Orleans, me," he said.

"Maybe," she said automatically, "maybe not."

"I was plain sure you want to."

The brown eyes turned away from hers and reached out into the gray day.

"I was plain sure."

She swung her body forward catching her weight on her hands. "I'm not sure." She sounded miserable; she knew it. And she knew she hadn't intended to.

A mockingbird settled himself on the top branch of the sweet olive and shook the water from his feathers noisily.

"Look at him," Perique said.

Annie didn't turn her head. "I'm not sure," she repeated.

Perique whistled softly to the bird.

"Nothing to keep me here," she said.

Under the porch the chickens shifted and squaaked. The bird flew up suddenly and disappeared.

"Scared him off," Perique said.

"Nothing to keep me here."

He put one foot up on the railing and brushed the bits of grass off his tennis shoes. "No," he said, "I reckon not."

"Maybe I'm gonna get married."

He went on brushing the top of the shoe. "That right?"

"No reason not to."

"Yea."

"Only it's a lot of trouble to pack."

"Yea."

"For two cents I wouldn't do it."

Perique shrugged. "What's keeping you?"

She didn't believe it. She just didn't believe it. Even when she knew she should stop, she tried again: "You want me to go?"

"Maybe you got a taste for New Orleans now."

"You don't want me to stay?"

Perique was smoothing his left eyebrow with his right finger. "None of my business."

"Why not?"

"Free country."

Annie got down from the rail. She stood at the top of the steps. "I reckon you won't miss me," she said. "I don't reckon nobody will."

"You tell me."

"Okay," Annie said and because she had a choice of crying or getting mad, she almost yelled the words across the porch. "I'm telling you: I'm leaving."

"I be surprised, me, if you didn't go—if he be willing to take you."

"There a lot of things you don't figure out." She put one finger to her lips, sucking slowly. "You figure nothing right in your whole life."

"Maybe."

"Okay, Mr. Smart Jackass. . . ." She stopped for a minute and caught her breath. Then, quietly, almost without realizing that she spoke: "You going to miss me, for sure . . . and you going to want me to be back. . . ."

She walked down the steps and out the front gate. She could feel Perique watching her. But he did not follow her, or call.

*

SHE went back to the house, slowly, scuffing her feet in the mud, kicking up the puddles. She wasn't feeling or thinking clearly any more. She passed her cousin Therese, and stared at her for a minute, not recognizing her.

By the time she had focused her eyes, Therese was a few steps past. Annie turned, but Therese went hurrying off.

("She look like she going crazy," Therese said to her own mother. "And I don't know, me, should I say something or what I'm going do. So I just walk faster."

"It's a man, for sure," her mother told her. "You got to be real extra careful or you get more aching than fun from a man."

Therese shivered a little, and it was exciting.)

"Neigre," Annie hissed at her back. But she wasn't really angry. She wasn't even surprised. It was like she expected it.

She was a little surprised when she saw the house in front of her—the gray house where she'd been born and where, except for one year, she'd always lived. She walked all around, staring as if she'd never seen it before. She waded in the half-flooded yard but she hardly noticed until she felt the mud ooze over the top and squish inside the shoe. She took them off and carried them, one in each hand.

"Annie?" Adele called.

She went up the back steps to the kitchen, because suddenly she noticed she was hungry. She dropped the shoes by the door.

"You just miss your papa," Adele said.

Annie looked at the dishes still on the table. "Anything left?"

"Jambalaya," Adele said. "Only it's been standing a while."

"You always nervous about your cooking," Annie said and went to get a plate. "All the time."

"Standing don't help rice," Adele said, "nobody can tell me it does."

412

There was a clean plate on the drainboard. Annie uncovered the frying-pan, took what was left. When she finished, she left the plate unwashed on the table and went to her own room. In a few minutes Adele followed her.

Annie was dragging the suitcases off the shelf directly over the door. They barely missed Adele and clattered to the floor with a puff of dust.

Adele sneezed.

Annie grinned, only it seemed more like she was drawing her lips back across her teeth. "Haven't been down since I came back from the convent."

"You going?" Adele said.

"Hell," Annie said, "I been wanting to get off this stinking island. Ever since I saw what New Orleans was like."

She yanked the suitcases open and then went over to the clothes rack which was hidden by a curtain of yellow cotton. She pulled it aside and a couple of the thumbtacks which were holding it up came loose. "God damn," Annie said and gave a couple of harder tugs, dragging the whole curtain down, leaving a little ruffle of ripped cloth.

Her three good dresses were there, one cotton, one soft gray voile (she had brought that back from New Orleans and had never worn it on the island) and one green print silk.

"Haven't got enough for New Orleans," she said. "Inky'll have to get me some more there."

She took the three dresses and put them in one suitcase. "What you staring at?"

Adele was still in the doorway. "You really going with him?"

"What it look like I'm doing? Going fishing?" She scooped the clothes off the floor, the clothes she had used as a mattress and jammed them into the second suitcase, and then went over to the little dressing-table and took her make-up and powder and the two bottles of perfume and packed them on top. She got her hat— a round-brimmed one with blue cornflowers around the crown— out of the paper bag and looked at it, turning it carefully around on her finger. "It'll do," she said, "for a while. For the wedding."

"I better go see I can find your father."

"Sure," Annie said.

She went over and pulled a box of scented soap from under the corner of the bed. When she looked again, Adele was gone. She could hear her out in the kitchen, talking to Claudie.

Briefly, Annie thought, she's going to like having me gone.

And for just a minute she hesitated. . . .

She'd wanted to get away. She'd wanted to. And here it was, all here, all at once.

And she'd be getting married too. She'd wondered about that, off and on for years: could she find anybody for a husband? Was there going to be anybody around who'd want her? And she had that too, and not just an island man, nor even one from Petit Prairie or Port Ronquille. But one from the city. One who'd seen a lot, a whole lot. And still wanted to marry her.

That was something you couldn't forget.

But it was strange now, because it wasn't at all exciting. It wasn't sad either. It was just something you had to do because you'd planned it that way a long time ago. If it wasn't exciting now, you knew it was just because it was too close to you. You'd had a good look at it from before. And decided you wanted it. That was what you had to remember now. And go ahead.

But still . . . She sat down on the soggy bed and ran her fingers through her mud-splattered hair. . . . It was lonely now.

Annie got dressed. She put on a bra and tucked the tail of her shirt into her jeans. She took out a pair of leather shoes, then, remembering the water outside, put them in the suitcase, and got her sneakers. They were still wet but she slipped into them and tied the strings carefully.

And she remembered something else too. She went to the big armoire in the parlor, opened one of the doors, and reached up into the top shelf. It was there, of course; nobody would ever think of moving it: the big heavy cut-glass decanter that was one of her mother's wedding presents—from a cousin of hers who'd struck it rich in the bootlegging business. Annie held it up to the gray light from the window; it was thick with dust and the stopper wouldn't come loose. (She remembered her mother intending for years to get it loose; but she hadn't ever got around to it.)

Annie put it on the window sill and stepped back. In spite of all the dust the crystal glowed faintly. So she took it back to her room, opened the suitcases again, and wrapped it up, as careful as

she could, in slips and shirts and blouses and skirts. Then she put
it in the very center of the suitcase and packed the other clothes
around it.

If it breaks, she thought, I'll feel awful. But it won't, she
answered herself.

Then she heard her father and Adele coming in the front door
and she wondered if they were going to notice that the bottle was
missing. But they didn't. And she felt better about it.

Al was very calm. Adele was not. (On the way back to the
house, she'd wanted to run. But he'd insisted on walking, holding
her arm tightly to keep her with him. "Slow down there," Al said.
"We don't want to go falling on her neck.")

They walked through the center hall, and Al stopped in the
door of his daughter's room. "I hear you are leaving, no?"

Annie was a little startled to hear it put into words. "Yea," she
said.

"So," he said, "come on out to the kitchen and we have a drink
on it."

"Oh," she said, "okay."

The three of them went to the kitchen and Al got down a bottle
of red-colored anisette and another of Four Roses. "Which is
yours?" he asked Adele.

"Nothing, I don't think," she said.

He poured a glass of anisette. "Good for you," he said, "And
what you want, che'?"

"Whisky," Annie said.

"So. . . ." He poured. "Now we drink to you."

Annie tossed hers off.

"Is that good for you," Adele asked, "when you were sick this
morning?"

"Settles the stomach," her father said.

"It does," Annie said.

"Have another," Al said. "Do you marry him or just go to the
city?"

"We're getting married," Annie said stiffly.

"I was just asking," Al said. "You get packed?"

"If I need anything else you can send it."

Al was curling both ends of his heavy mustache. "I was thinking,
me, here we have a wedding and the groom is not here."

"I can go tell him," Adele offered.

"No," Annie said too quickly. Then she added, "They got an awful lot to do." It sounded lame, even to her.

Al tugged his mustache harder. "I'm not one for forcing anybody."

"He'll be coming up, anyhow," Annie said and stared down at her hands.

"What?"

"He'll be coming to get the suitcases."

"And then we have the drink."

"No," Annie said, "I keep telling you. We haven't got time. We just want to leave."

Al pursed up his lips thoughtfully. "And maybe you like it better if we don't be here at all when he come."

Annie waved her hand at a circling fly. "Maybe," she said softly.

"What?"

"I said maybe."

"So we do it that way." Al finished his whisky. The one umbrella in the house was hanging behind the kitchen door. He handed it to Adele. "Where is Claudie?"

"The back porch," Adele said, hardly more than whispering.

"We go out that way." And he was holding the screen open for her. Claudie was there. Al reached down and picked him up.

When Annie looked out the window, they were just turning out of sight on the path. And she yelled out after them: "I just want you to quit pushing me, that's all."

She was sorry they'd gone. She couldn't think of a way to get them back.

She got her bags, lugged them into the kitchen, and sat down to wait. There was only the unsteady drizzle on the tin roof, and the soft calling of the cats around the foundations. She poured herself a drink, and sipped at it. She wasn't thinking anything. She was just waiting.

Finally she heard Inky at the front door. "I'm in the kitchen," she called.

He came through the hall, carefully so he wouldn't track mud.

"I been waiting for you," she said.

*

THEY went down to the Rendezvous, with Adele holding the umbrella carefully all the way, trying to keep it over their heads. The rain was hardly more than a mist now.

Al was walking rapidly, with the boy in his left arm. Claudie started to squirm once and he had told him, sharply: "Quit a minute." And the boy was very still, staring out of his wide blue eyes.

At the Rendezvous Al went in first with Claudie, leaving Adele on the porch to close the umbrella. She had trouble: the catch was rusted stuck. She had to put the handle down on the edge of the boards and step on the catch.

"I was wondering if we had lost you," Al said when she finally went inside.

He had taken one of the tables near the front door. With the windows all closed (the way they were now) the back of the room would be hard breathing. She put the folded umbrella down on their table, then changed her mind and moved it to a near-by chair.

"We all ready and waiting for you."

"It wouldn't work," Adele said and then stopped, staring at the table. There were three glasses on it, a pint bottle of PM whisky and in front of Claudie a bottle of beer.

"He going to try some beer," Al said. "We going to see how good his stomach is."

"You think . . ."

"Got to learn sometime," Al said. He poured a half-glass and, as the boy reached for it, pushed the hand away. "Wait for you mama."

"In the morning?" Adele asked uncertainly.

"Never a morning like this," Al said, "after last night."

"Hell," Lacy Livaudais said from behind the bar where he was whittling an English soldier for his youngest grandchild, "you ain't seen nothing, if they start doing the things they say they going to do."

417

"Who?" Al asked.

"LeBlanc, for one."

Al fingered his mustache. "I expect he believe that."

"He got reason to be mad, him."

"Hell," Al said, "I didn't say he ain't."

"Leastways, lots people around here talking tough."

"Hell." Al poured the whisky.

"Maybe," Lacy said. "But if they just went and did half of what they was saying in here not so much as an hour ago. . . ."

"Talk," Al said.

"What they say?" Adele asked.

Lacy shrugged. "I can't remember for them, me."

"Don't pay any attention to them," Al said. He added Seven-Up to the whisky. "Here."

"More people been in here drinking," Lacy said.

"A good idea, no?"

"But now most everyone home eating their dinner."

"Except us."

"That is right."

"They don't do nothing for a while."

"Why?" Adele said.

"They going to have some good storm to keep them busy."

"When?" Adele asked, "when?"

"Oh hell," Lacy said, "always get storms in September. Nothing peculiar in that."

"Who said it was?" Al took his wife's hand and put it around her glass. "Only it'll keep people too busy to think of fighting for a while."

Claudie gulped his beer, sputtered and rubbed his face hard with both hands. Then, because they were laughing at him, he went back and tried again. This time it was a little better.

They finished the bottle. Al pulled his watch out of his pocket and looked at it. "Take the boy and go home," he said.

"Where you going?"

"Me?" Al said. "I think maybe I go take a walk down to the boat and have a look at it."

Adele opened her mouth to object.

"Go on."

"I feel the likker," she said.

"Go home and lay down."

She nodded, short little jerky nods, grabbed Claudie by the hand and went.

Al checked the mooring-lines of his boat. They were secure. But then he had checked—and reworked them—just a few hours before.

When he had finished, he put his hands to his back and for the first time let his eyes run down the line of moored luggers. The mast, the one tall thin mast that shot over the stocky clumsy rigging of the workboats—that one was gone. Then, no longer trying to be casual, he went up on the high pointed bow, stood on the thick wood rail, and looked out at the bay. The boats were not very far out, the sailboat and the little launch that was guiding her in. The *Pixie* was going on power, its mast a naked stick against the low clouds. Without sails it was unbalanced. The hull wobbled and pitched in the little swells.

He could see Annie's yellow shirt, see it quite clearly even in the mist. She was standing in the cockpit, standing upright, on the port seat, and leaning at a little angle, one arm wrapped around the boom. She must have been looking back. She must have seen him. She went below. And there was just a gray-blue smear, Inky's shirt, left by the tiller.

When Al got home, Claudie was in the front door, swinging back and forth on the screen door. He could put just one foot on the bottom of the frame, and he could push off with the other. The door would sag slowly out and swing slowly back, creaking.

"You want to break it off?" Al asked. And then he heard the sobbing.

Adele was sitting in the living-room, sitting in the middle of the sofa, head in her hands, crying. "I made her leave," she said.

When Al sat alongside her and tried to comfort her, she put her head in her lap and cried harder.

"It's the likker," Al tried to tell her. "It does some people that." It had made him feel levelheaded and had given him a little glow. So that in spite of Annie's leaving, he felt pretty good.

Claudie swung back and forth on the screen with a strange

frightened look on his face. And Al went right on patting Adele's head and wondering what the hell had made him give her that much whisky.

When she was too tired to cry any more, she sat up and poked at her eyes with her fingers.

"Now look," Al said, "no use to take it like that. I been expecting this, halfway. And it wasn't but time till she find a way to go back."

A few minutes later Perique came down to the dock. The *Pixie* was blurred now and indistinct. Even as he watched, she disappeared. And only the sound of her engine remained, clear and loud, echoed by the fog.

*

ANNIE came up to the cockpit again. The island was out of sight in the heavy mist, and the other side hadn't come into view. "You want the compass?" she asked.

"They got a compass." And he tipped his chin to the little launch a couple of hundred yards ahead.

"Don't look like we're anywhere."

Inky looked back over his shoulder. "Can't see anything."

Annie settled down in the corner, facing the stern, back to the cabin. The heavy mist gathered and ran down the wood in little streams. The boom dripped water steadily. She could feel her cheeks turn wet and she wiped at them impatiently.

"You ought to have a cap on," Inky said.

"I don't want to go after it."

"Take this," he said. "I'll go get it."

She slid down the seat, getting wetter and not caring. She took the end of the tiller, lightly.

"Got it?"

She nodded and he crossed over, balancing himself against the roll of the boat, and dropped down the hatch.

She squinted after the launch ahead. And around into the soft gray-white fuzziness. She moved the tiller, hesitantly. The boat responded, clumsily, heavily, the way it would always do under power.

"Hold her steady," Inky called. "Where's the god-damn cap?"

"On top the locker." Her voice sounded sleepy and muffled. She could feel her hair begin to cling to her head, wet and close. A gull squaaked somewhere, very far off, and she lifted her head to look. There was just light gray overhead, not even a round spot for the sun.

The clouds were right on top now. Around her shoulders like a coat. But over them, if you went high enough, it was always clear —sun or moon—clear and warm or clear and cold.

421

That part didn't reach you, wasn't the one you had to worry about. The lower part of the sky now, the part that touched your head, touched the ground—there was trouble in it: storms and rain and wind. Things like that.

She had swung off course. The launch was over to the right. And one of the men (she had met him at the dock, not even an hour before: what was his name?) was waving at her. She pushed the tiller over.

"What's going on?" Inky called, feeling the bow swing around.

"I was dreaming," she said, "I'm back on." You won't lose me, she told the man in the other boat, silently. You can't lose me. Not when I'm going to New Orleans. Not when I'm going to get married.

"Be damned if I can find the cap."

"Maybe," she said, "I left it up by the anchor."

She could hear him swearing softly as he went climbing over the baggage. The cabin was littered, her stuff mostly. But there wasn't room to put it away.

Not my fault, she told herself. Not at all.

"Got it," he yelled. He did not come right up. She could hear him rattling things around up there.

She sat holding the tiller, feeling the nervous vibration of the engine and the heavy dull pull of water on the rudder. If I put it over hard, she thought, and step up the motor, we'd be out of sight in no time, and there'd be just us, and the fog all around, nobody but us.

Until we got stuck, she thought with a little laugh. Maybe she didn't know her way around good as some, but she knew that much.

"It's a stupid boat to have," she told Inky when his dark sleek head came out of the hatch.

"For around here?" Inky said. "You're telling me?"

She caught the rubbery faintly sour odor of the pale blue coats he held on one arm. "They stink."

"So they stink. Put 'em on." He handed one to her. "Just the tops."

She held out the blue jacket and shook it violently.

"Put it on," he said. "We want a wedding instead of a burying."

She pulled it over her head. And pulled up the hood.

"Jesus," he said, "we're way off course."

"Well, come take it. I was putting on this stuff."

He took the tiller, and swung the bow around again. "You were really off."

"There's enough water way out here."

"But if we lose them, what happens then?"

"We could find them again."

"Sure we could," Inky said. "Only I don't want to have to do that."

She slid along the seat until her back touched the cabin. Then she swung up her feet and wrapped her arms around her knees. Mist condensed on the boom dripped steadily on her hood, with a kind of flat plopping sound, like batter hitting the sides of a bowl.

"They're wavin'," Inky said once, and lifted his arm to wave back. "Everything's okay!" he yelled.

They were both quiet. Her legs went to sleep and she had to stretch them out and rub them, hard. The gearshift began to rattle in its slot; Inky got out his pocketknife and tightened the bolts on each side.

The swell died. There was no wind and what you could see of the water was flat and glossy, except for the two wakes.

After a while Inky said: "Look at me. Getting married and liking it, too. Man, man, how strong is that. . . ." He sounded nervous.

"I was thinking," Annie admitted, "about that."

"It sure is funny."

"I guess so."

Inky scratched behind his ear. "I'm sure glad to get off."

"Me too."

"It's nice and all that," he said, "but it's not the most exciting place in the world, you know what I mean."

"I been living there, remember?"

"Can I show you some living in New Orleans! Man . . . is it good."

"I want to," Annie said.

"Maybe I won't go back to the boats for a while. There's this guy I know has a place on Iberville, always can use a man at the bar."

"I can get a job too," Annie said.

"It's going to be fine," Inky said, "it's going to be real fine."

That gull was still calling, somewhere overhead. She tried to see through the drizzle.

"You won't see him," Inky said, "less he comes down and sits himself on the mast."

Annie stood up and stretched. "Not being able to see where you're going always makes me kind of nervous."

"They using a compass, so we know.".

"Annie walked up to the bow.

"Stay on board," Inky told her.

"Don't worry about me."

The decks were slippery and her sneaker bottoms were glassy, so she kept one hand on the lifelines until she could swing around the forestay and settle herself on the railing of the pulpit. The water was directly beneath her now and she stared into it for a while, watching the lines of the bow wave go curling up on the hull. She felt peculiar and she held on to the stay very tightly to keep from falling.

It was not being able to see backward or forward. That was it.

After a while she got up and went back to the cockpit.

"I'm always glad when you make it back here," Inky said.

"Look," she said after a little, "you don't have to."

"To what?"

She clicked her tongue. "Get married."

He lifted the tiller and scratched his chin on it. "Suppose I want to?"

"You didn't want to last week."

"That was last week."

"I meant . . . it's all right with me if you just drop me off in New Orleans."

He was resting his chin on the polished wood tiller. "I don't get it."

"I just don't want you feeling you got to do anything."

"Oh for Christ's sake."

"I'm being serious."

"Look," Inky said, "if you don't want to you can get off at Petit Prairie."

"That's not what I'm saying."

"So I don't get it."

The shift began to rattle again. "Damn," Inky said, and pulled out the handle. "Get up a minute," he said. And lifted the seat to check the dial for the r.p.m.'s. "Okay."

"I guess I don't get anything," he said. "Maybe. I thought they'd make a lot more fuss over your leaving and all."

"Huh?" she had only half heard him.

He lifted the cover again and pointed. She peered in: his automatic was there, on a carefully spread piece of canvas.

"What for?"

"I thought somebody'd object, with a shotgun maybe. A lot of shooting around the last couple of days."

She reached in and touched the cold steel of the handle and then the barrel. She straightened up and he closed the compartment. She stood looking at him.

He shrugged and settled down cross-legged. "Look," he said, "how was I to know? I thought maybe your father or what's-his-name? Perique? They would go making trouble."

Annie just shook her head.

"Well, it figures. . . . He was an old boyfriend of yours."

"Who?"

"Perique."

"In a way," she nodded.

"He wanted to marry you."

"For a little while." She rested her forehead against the cool wood of the boom and closed her eyes, remembering. Remembering, or trying to remember. There was something there, a feel maybe. She tried . . . a color, maybe, or a smell . . . the times when Perique had hung around the porch, shoving himself back and forth slowly in the swing. And when the swing had broke, when the hook had pulled clean out of the beam overhead, he had got a new hook down at the store, and then dragged up a ladder and put it back in, and when he saw that one of the slats had been broken falling, he fixed that too. That time then . . . there was more between it and now than just a couple of month. . . .

There had been a feel to those days, for sure. . . . It wasn't so much that she longed for it, as that she wanted to remember. . . . She was irritated, and she shifted restlessly from one foot to the other.

"Maybe you are sorry," Inky said softly.

She looked down at him, surprised. "I never thought of that."

It was true. She hadn't. It hadn't once occurred to her that there was a way back. She thought about it now and shook her head: there wasn't. And the reasons why were just as vague as her memories. . . . The happenings of last night, just last night, were as far away as those days before Inky had come.

"I wanted to tell you . . ." But what? She wasn't sure. Just last night. And it was the dinghy. "I had to."

"What?" Inky asked. "Get off the island?"

That too. That too.

She would tell him someday. When she had gotten some sleep, and she knew more exactly what had happened. She would tell him that she had lost him part of his precious boat. Or maybe (she thought with a sudden burst of shrewd woman-thought) she just wouldn't.

And her mind went back to those days before Inky had come, trying to find them, trying to find some detail that she could hang a thread of memory on.

There wasn't any. She felt cheated. She didn't want to go back. But she didn't want to forget. She wanted to have Perique tucked away carefully in a corner of her memory. . . . And again woman-fashion, she recognized that this memory would be a comfort: when things did not go well with Inky: she could conjure up another image and hide behind it. And if things were ever really rough, she could tell the children about the man who nearly was their father.

She'd remember more about him, she thought, when she wasn't so tired, and when things stopped happening so fast.

And there was Inky. She loved him and there wasn't anybody else.

Maybe, she found herself saying silently, she loved him because there wasn't anybody else. Yet.

She was surprising herself, this last half-hour. Thinking things that had never come to her before. She was surprised but she wasn't shocked. Things were the way they were. And she was what she was.

She stepped up on the seats, and stood leaning on the boom, her chin buried in the green canvas of its cover, and thinking. Thinking the way she had never done in her life before. The drizzle dripped down her forehead and ran in a little arch around her eyebrows.

Things happened, she thought, and you did whatever it was you had to do to meet them. And they went on past you.

And what you were came out in the way you handled them. And what you were changed from one month to the next and maybe even from one hour to the next. And no use quarreling with the way things were. Or the way you were.

She wasn't sorry she'd left the island. Not now. Maybe she would be some day. Maybe she'd even go back. You couldn't tell. But right now was what mattered. She couldn't remember the past very well. And she couldn't imagine the future.

So what did that leave her? she thought, and she almost smiled to herself. There wasn't anything back there. Only there didn't happen to be much here either. . . . The suitcases in the middle of the cabin, one of them with the fancy decanter that had been a present to her mother. And Inky.

He was stretched out almost flat, listening to the motor. His hair was so wet now that it looked like he'd gone swimming. He straightened up and put the boat back on course and glanced up at her, a little puzzled, a little worried.

She stepped over and tickled the top of his head with her fingers, the hair was greasy and wet to the touch. And even out here she could smell his hair oil.

She wasn't happy. But she certainly wasn't sad either.

She was waiting, waiting for things to happen to her. Things that could be handled and changed. And things that could just be handled. She felt herself grow great and passive in her waiting.

Yes, she thought. It's Inky now. We'll go to New Orleans, and we'll get married. I can get him to do that. He wants to now, but even if he doesn't. . . . And we'll live there, we can have an apartment or maybe even a house.

It's Inky now. And maybe it will go on being Inky. But maybe it won't. And if I believed in cards or palms I'd say I could tell.

Maybe it will stay. And maybe, she thought calmly, it won't.

"What you so busy thinking about?"

"Way things go and change."

"Don't you worry about it."

"I wasn't," Annie said.

* * * * * * *

THE LOWER PART OF THE SKY

~~~~~~~~~~~~

IT rained for four days.

People wondered if a storm was coming. They listened to the weather broadcasts carefully and they squinted up into the sky and tried to tell. If it were going to be a big storm, the men would have to take the boats away. The harbor would not be protection enough.

During the worst storms, there are very few men on the island: they have gone with the boats, the most valuable things. They take them as far inland, up Bayou Verde, as there is time. The old, old men remain but they are not much use, for they have to be looked after, and their brittle old bones are likely to snap. And the children. And the women. They stay and pull in the wood shutters tight. (Under the clouds the air turns cold and rain comes in swirling eddies, so that the littlest kids cry from cold as much as fright.) And they save what they can and lose what they must.

They have been doing it that way for nearly two hundred years, ever since there were sailing-ships in the harbor, part of Jean Lafitte's pirate fleet.

But the rain stopped. And the lower clouds blew off and there were just the high black ones, smeared across the sky, like the wind had flattened them over. Every now and then the sun came out, a little weak maybe, and a sort of sick yellow. But whenever it appeared, the women grabbed up the loads of wet clothes they had

428

hanging on their back porches and over the stoves in the kitchens. They hurried to spread the clothes out on the gallery railings in the sun, or they went rushing down to hang them on the lines, even if they had to wade in mud up to their ankles to get there. Everybody knew that clothes dried inside never did smell clean.

Mamere Terrebonne came to the edge of her porch and squinted at the sun, held out her wrinkled old hand and looked at its shadow, and then turned it over and over, feeling the little warmth. Then she went back inside and got her rubber boots: she was going to the grocery and wet feet gave her rheumatism. She brought the boots back out to the porch and sat down in her rocking-chair. She had not had them on since the past spring. She shook each one carefully: a lot of dust and some dead roaches and beetles fell out. She bent down and looked at the shriveled shapes, grinning. "Nothing to eat in there," she said aloud, "for a ravet, no?"

They were not mates either, these boots, but they were both black and they were both about the same size. She had found them years ago on the beach: she was always finding things. She had a quick eye for an object half buried in the sand. She found the left one first, and people laughed when she came home one day carrying only one boot. But she'd just put it on a shelf in her back hall, along with a couple of old eel traps and a bottle of stuff that was supposed to keep the gars off the dragues, the trot lines. And she forgot about the boot. Until one day, nearly five years later, when she found another. It was a right one, this time. She brought it home, and took the left one down, and stood the pair behind her front door. She had used them ever since.

She put them on this time, and, taking her cane, made her way carefully down the steps. She stood for a minute right in the middle of a puddle, the mud oozing over the tips of the boots, and she grinned a toothless smug grin to herself. Then she made her way to the grocery, the boots making plopping, sucking sounds each step.

She stopped on the grocery porch and cleaned her feet carefully. Inside she could hear Julius laughing with some girl. She grinned to herself. That Julius now, he was some hand with the ladies, for sure. Coeur comme un artichode . . . leaf for everybody.

She went inside. When he saw her Julius threw up his hand, and ran out from behind his counter to kiss her on both cheeks. Mo tante, he called her jokingly . . . they were related someway, vaguely, the way nearly everybody on the island was related.

"You look so fine," he said, and pinched her cheek.

She took the muddy tip of her cane and poked at his chest. "You keep that for the young girls." She looked around the room to see who else was there—Cecile Boudreau and over there, going through the piles of sweatshirts on the table, trying to find one for his kid, was Hector.

"Look who's here," Cecile said to him.

Hector turned and waved. "Hi, Mamere, what you say?"

She grinned at both of them. "I got a check, no?"

"Sure," Julius said, "you been having a check ever since the fifteenth when they always come for you."

"I didn't need nothing," Mamere said. "Why I should come get it?"

Julius had got the welfare check out of the wire cage that was the post office. He put the envelope down on the counter. "There."

Mamere bent over until her nose was almost touching it. Then she straightened up. "Ah."

"For you, huh?" Cecile said.

Mamere nodded.

"People brought you so much you didn't need it, huh?" Hector said.

"Popular gal," Julius said, "for sure."

Mamere sniffed at them, wriggling her nose like a rabbit. Then she began to make her rounds of the grocery. It was always the same. She would begin at one end of the shelf, and stand right in front of it, her nose almost touching the cans. Then can by can she would study the shelves. As she got lower and lower her knees kept bending until, for the last ones, she was crouched almost on the floor—then she would yell for help getting up. Julius would get behind her and put his hands under her armpits and lift her up: she was so light it was easy. Then Mamere would shake herself out and begin on the next section of shelf. When she found a can she wanted she'd take it off and hold it out behind her, not looking around, but clearing her throad loudly. And Julius would take the can and put it with the others on the counter.

"You always was a great one for the women," Mamere said suddenly.

"Which one?" Cecile said.

"Him. Julius," Mamere half turned around. "You going to tell me, no?"

"You say so," Julius grinned, "and it's so."

Mamere went back to her careful search of the shelves.

"I can tell you what you was thinking," Hector said. "Bet me?"

"No," Cecile said and tossed her head. "And let's talk about something else."

"For sure," Hector said. "Like what?"

"We just had the biggest kind of excitement, and you don't remember."

"I'm tired as hell talking about the fires and what we going to do to them," Hector said, "and I'm sick and tired trying to figure what they going to do to us."

"I didn't mean that," Cecile said impatiently. "I meant Annie going off with her guy."

Mamere had been holding out her hand with a can of Spam in it, but nobody had noticed this time. So she had turned around and brought it over to the counter. "Ah," she said, "Annie, she leave. And before her some more of them leave. And maybe they come back. And maybe not. But me, I am always here."

Hector and Cecile waited while Mamere finished her shopping. Then she carefully and slowly signed the check, and Julius cashed it for her. What was left, she put into the bag that dangled by long green strings from her belt. Then she looked up, and her wrinkled old raisin face grinned happily. "So now we go home."

Hector took the two largest bags, and Cecile the smaller. And they went.

"Jeez," Hector said. "This is real heavy—you stocking up for the whole year?"

Mamere did not answer. She was walking fast as she could, the shoes slushing in the mud. Her head was bent down, and she didn't appear to have heard.

Hector shifted the bag. "Don't spill anything," Cecile said.

"Watch out yourself," he told her.

They put the stuff on Mamere's kitchen table.

"Got a crick in my arm," Hector said.

"Got a hitch in my back," Cecile giggled.

Mamere peered into the bags.

"Look at her," Hector said, "stick her head clean down in them."

"Yea?" Cecile said, "look at us—going to get wet."

It had begun again—flashes of gray rain. They went over to the door and Mamere followed them. It was coming down steadily.

"And me, I got a line full of clothes out," Cecile said.

Mamere chuckled. "Ca mouillasse."

"Too late to go worrying about them," Hector said.

"They was most dry when I put them out."

"Say, Mamere," Hector said, "what you make of this funny weather?"

"Seen this before," Mamere said calmly.

"Bet you have."

"And I know what coming."

"What?" Cecile asked sharply.

"Ha!" Mamere said. "So you are so serious now."

"Sure, I'm serious."

"I can feel it."

"I'm asking you what."

"I can feel it begin to blow and rain."

"You can?"

"Storm too."

Cecile had turned her back to the outside and was staring at the old woman. "You mean hurricane?"

"Me, I can see a flag already flying at the station at Port Ronquille."

"No fooling?"

"See it so clear."

"Come on, honey," Hector said.

"I don't want to get wet."

"Make a dash," Hector said and got hold of her left arm.

They began running, trying to pick their way through the puddles of the path. Cecile landed squarely in one, and started laughing. She stopped for breath under the broad leaves of a latanier. Hector, who had gone a few feet ahead, came back for her.

"What the matter with you?"

"That one splashed clean up me."

"Yea?"

"That why I don't like skirts, none."

"Let's go."

"Got to catch my breath," Cecile said, "it felt so funny."

"Okay," Hector said. He stepped under the tree, and held a leaf carefully over his head.

"Do you reckon," Cecile said, "there's anything to that?"

"To what?"

She pointed with her chin in the direction of Mamere's house. "That."

"Hell," Hector said, "means she heard the radio, that's all."

"Huh?"

"Means she been listening to the weather report out of Port Ronquille, same one I heard."

He took her hand again and they ran the rest of the way home. The very minute they were up on their gallery Cecile asked again: "They say there's a storm coming?"

"They say maybe."

"God damn," Cecile said.

BELLE LIVAUDAIS wiped the last dish and put it away. She spread the cloth to dry over the back of a kitchen chair and took off her apron. Then she left the house, walking in her determined, stiff-shouldered way.

Marie Livaudais was carrying the plants from her porch to shelter inside. "What you say?"

"I got to talk to you," Belle said.

"Come have some coffee."

Belle shook her head. "Where is Robby at?"

"Huh?" Marie shook her head, shocked. It was the first time Belle had ever spoken of the child. The very first time.

"Eddie's boy."

"Huh?" Marie stalled. And to herself she thought: She went and blew her top, for sure.

"We got need of him."

"Where's Eddie at?" Marie said. "I ain't seen him around."

"At Petit Prairie," Belle said, "with Pete."

"I thought maybe he come back."

Belle shook her head. "He got to be there."

"Ain't really thought he be back yet."

Belle sat down on the railing. "We got room at our place," she said, slowly. "And I come to get Robby."

"I don't know, me," Marie said hesitantly.

"We got place," Belle repeated, "for him now."

"Okay," Marie said. "I pack up this stuff."

That was the way Robby Livaudais came to his father's house.

It was one of the things the island would have talked about for weeks, if they had had time. But too many other things were happening.

. . .

434

They took his things up to the attic room that had been Henry's. He put his clothes away and he hung up the board stuck full of the butterflies he had caught.

Then he slipped out and stayed away until dark. Later, as he had always done, he went for supper to Marie Livaudais's.

She shook her head and sent him right back to his father's house. His father's wife was waiting for him. They had supper and then he went up into the new room, up the narrow stair, that was really just a ladder, tripping over his own clumsy feet.

The whole attic was empty. He listened. There wasn't a single sound of breathing. He had never been in a room alone before.

For a while he walked around, jumping on the other bed, fingering the fishing-tackle that stood in the corner, opening drawers and looking in.

"Thought I told you to go to bed," his father's wife called up to him.

And so he had to go into the little front compartment. He stretched out on the bed, still dressed, and kept very quiet. But he kept his eyes opened and he kept the light burning, the one that stuck out of a socket on the wall.

Until his father's wife called up again: "I can plain see that light burning through the cracks."

There was no help for it: he had to reach out and switch off the light. He stared straight at it, trying to keep a little bit of light stored up in his eyes—but it turned into a red worm and disappeared.

"You ain't a kid no more," she called.

He kept his eyes open in the dark. And listened to the strange sounds as the house swayed slightly in the wind. The sharp cracks as the furniture popped and settled. And the smells that were unfamiliar. . . .

He shivered and made himself stay very still.

The morning would come, the way it always did, and he could go out. And he could go see what Gus Claverie and Joey Billion were doing. And wouldn't they be surprised when he told them he had changed his house. Wasn't one of them had done that. Most people, they just stayed in the house where they were born. And none of them changed. The way he had.

He would tell them that in the morning. And he would tell

them too about the room that was his now. A whole room all for him.

The shutter rattled. And he wondered if a loup-garou were banging away out there.

With his eyes and his ears closed it was just like any other place. He could imagine. . . . He tried. It worked.

He kept at it. And after a bit he convinced himself he wasn't there at all.

*

IT wasn't the storm that was bothering Mamere Terrebonne on the following day. She'd seen too many of them, been in too many of them to bother any more. It was the winter. She could tell that it was coming. Already the wet, black nights felt different. It wasn't just that they were cooler—the rain would make them that way—but they weren't the same. The air wasn't the steady even air of summer, not any more. It was quivering and nervous.

And the man—his name was Jean Cheramie, she'd been married the same day as his grandmother or his great-grandmother, she couldn't remember which, in the old church, the one with the real gold cross over the altar, bright and gleaming that morning—had stopped coming. She didn't hear him any more, didn't hear the soft rubbing of the wheels of his little cart on the sandy road, nor his voice calling out the names of the vegetables he had brought over from Petit Prairie and wanted to sell. She missed his shouting; a voice like his you could hear all over the island, nearly.

Mamere Terrebonne lifted her head and stared up into the branches of the pecan tree. She didn't do that often; her back had grown so stooped it hurt to straighten it out now. She could remember, just barely, when her whole body had been slim and bending as the new branches on the oleanders. She could just barely remember. . . . Now she put both hands to her back and straightened it slowly, staring up into the highest branches of the tree. As she watched, the wind pulled a handful of leaves away.

It was blowing for sure. . . .

But the wind didn't bother her. The house had stood steady before, even when water came right up to the level of the floorboards and her father had got down on his hands and knees and with an awl bored holes in the floor to let the water in—to keep the house from washing clean off its foundations.

The house would stand.

437

And if there was a storm—that was nothing. Maybe even a hurricane—that was not much more. It wasn't the storms. It was what the storms indicated: the beginning of winter. It had nearly sneaked up on her. But she had found out in time, and everything was all right.

Every winter Mamere Terrebonne had had a struggle with death, every winter for the past ten years. Though she locked the windows and put the heavy bar across the door, he still managed to find his way inside. She had seen him so plainly once—by the light of her kerosene stove. Each year he came earlier. The first time had been in January, when she heard him rattling the shutters and pounding at the door in the heavy salt winds before he managed to slip through a crack somewhere with the winter cold.

Each year earlier—and she wasn't going to take any chances. She had got the food from the grocery. And now she would have to get the shutters up.

Up in the sky now, the gray heavy clouds broke up for a minute and the sun came out. She held out her hand and felt the warmth. And shook her head. Sun was hot, hot as summer. But it was a winter-colored sky. No mistake. In summer it was a soft gentle blurry blue that stretched from tree to tree. It pulled farther away in winter, until it was very high and very blue and very hard and winds came out of it.

She sighed and let her body relax into its bent arc, the position that was natural for her now. No mistaking a sky like that. . . .

There were other signs too, now that she came to look for them, signs that she had been seeing for weeks and had not wanted to interpret. The yellow leaves lying curled like pods under the gardenia bush. The red flowers falling off the Rose of Montana. The wild honeysuckles that had finished blooming and pulled back close against the shelter of the house foundations. The yard was empty, except for the dead things: the burned-out yellow light bulbs her great-grandchildren brought her from the grocery store and which she stuck in the ground to edge the walk. Their smooth yellow glass was gleaming under the bright sky. Mamere stood right over them and saw her ownself reflected, the sun over her shoulder small and flat like a dime.

Somebody passed by. "Hi," they said, "what you say?"

She didn't bother looking closer. She lifted one hand in a half-wave. And, since that hand was up, she lifted the other, and they both pulled down firmly on the brim of her hat.

It had been a light gray hat once, but time and rain and sweat had stained it almost black. She remembered when her husband had bought it, she could see him standing out in the garden, wearing it. She could see him clear as anything, the felt of the hat soft to the touch and glowing. He'd been a man; the only man for her. Even after they'd had that one big fight and he'd gone off, she hadn't even been able to look at another man, even though she'd wanted to—when the pain had turned into anger and she'd wanted more than anything else, more than breathing even, to hurt him, even if he didn't know it. But she hadn't. Though she had been pretty then and young still and there'd been men who were willing. People would have understood too—even his own family—and they wouldn't have blamed her: when a man leaves his wife he can't complain about what goes on in the house. But she couldn't, anyhow. Though she hated herself and lay on the bed for hours crying. Nothing her mother had said could quiet her. Finally they'd got the priest to talk to her. That had done no more good. She lay very quietly, her face buried in the pillow while he was there; the very minute the door closed behind him, she had started crying again. She had stopped only when she could cry no more. Then she got up, her face still swollen and ugly, and she'd gone out to the garden.

She began working with a man's shovel—it was early spring then—and she planted a garden. It was a garden like the island had never seen before—things sprouted overnight from under her hands. He walked over them when he came back, carelessly, not seeming to know that they were there—the beans and the corn and the peas that she'd been so careful of. "I been to Houma, me," he said and came inside. He hooked his thumbs in his belt in the way he had, and looked around the house; his eyes stopped at the colored picture of the Virgin that was hung over the dish cupboard. "I got that in church on the Feast of the Assumption," she said. His eyes moved from it and finished looking over the rest of the house. Nothing else had changed. "Houma's a good place," he said. And he took off his hat and dropped it on the oilcloth-covered table. It was all he had to show for his six months' work. But it was a beautiful hat. And it was new then. . . .

Mamere Terrebonne went down into the yard. The front walk was dry; but then it had been made that way specially. It was really a shell bank, raised a couple of inches above the level of the rest of the yard. She walked on it now, and the bottoms of her boots were dry while the rest of the yard swam in mud.

A levee, she thought, I'm walking the levee.

Just outside the front gate there was a little boy, three or so. He was squatting down, digging at the sandy ground with a sharp piece of slate. He wore only a plaid shirt, and under it was his naked bottom, mud-caked and streaked.

She was a little surprised to find him here. Most of the kids ran when she appeared. He was so busy he hadn't even noticed. She watched him for a minute, one of her crippled rheumatic hands rubbing her face. Then she prodded him in the middle of the back with her cane. "Go tell your mama she got to put some clothes on you." He scuttled off sideways, looking at her all the time, one hand raised up, grabbing for his back.

Like a touloulou, she thought suddenly, just like a touloulou crab.

He looked familiar. He would be one of her grand-children's children. She could not remember just which one now, there were so many of them living in the houses built around hers, built any which way so that the paths to her house were all twisted as they passed around the yards and fences and cisterns and privies.

She raised her cane and shook it at the boy. He began to run on his quick unsteady legs. He had pulled the shirt high up and bundled it against his chest as he ducked around a tree.

Mamere Terrebonne stood staring at the twisted bark of the pecan tree, and the last bloomless sprouts of the lilies around it, the white spider lilies that in summer had a heavy sweet smell, even on this island where the sea winds carried off most odors.

There was the steady sound of the surf, Mamere could hear that —not summer's sound, the quickened nervous insistence of September. She sighed and shook her head. She had come so close to forgetting the job she had to do.

She made her way slowly around the house, putting her feet one after the other carefully along the brick walk. The bricks were sinking in the sandy soil; parts of the walk had almost disappeared.

Around in the back of the house, behind the cistern that her grandson last year had painted bright red, was the mirliton arbor, the vines bare now, the wood of the arbor showing still new—it wasn't more than a couple of years old, the one that they had built for her after a storm had taken down the other.

She put out one hand on the arbor as she walked along its length. There had been fine mirlitons—big and a good light green, their meat soft and tender as a flounder. They didn't grow so big on the second arbor; they didn't like new wood; she could have said that, but it had been nice of the boys to make it for her. And it didn't really seem to matter so much to her whether the mirlitons grew fine any more.

She had reached the end of the arbor and stood holding on to it with her left hand, not because she was weak but because she liked to feel things under her hand.

Things had changed in the garden since she had planted it first. So many things, not just the leaves and the vines that you expected to change each season or each year, but the things that you wanted to be permanent, arbors and trellises. The iron-pipe trellis—low and fan-shaped—that her husband had built so carefully, built to stand, it had come down, in the same September hurricane that had lifted the church and dropped it piece by piece into the back bay, the pretty church with the real gold cross on top the altar dome.

It seemed that when you built things up again they were less good. The church was smaller and nobody put up a gold cross for the winds to throw into the bayou. And her husband hadn't even bothered to go find his trellis; they had let the climbing roses spray upward and then down again to run along the ground.

She reached the hollow chinaberry trunk. In it were the heavy wood shutters from her house. She peeped in, her eyes blinking from the dustiness. They were there, the shutters with their wood so worn that the grain stood up in it like veins. She took one and tried to drag it out; it was too heavy; there were warnings twanging up and down her back. She turned away with a sigh. She would have to wait until somebody came to fix it.

Not ten minutes later her grandson Ferdinand came. And inside an hour, he had all the shutters up and the big storm doors too.

She sat on her porch and watched. When he had done, he came over—the brown-black mud spattered to his waist—and talked a bit to her.

"Some fighting, no?" he asked.

She shrugged. She wasn't sure she was going to talk to him.

"What you think of all the fighting?"

"Me?"

"Yea," Ferdinand said, "I was just asking."

"I think maybe it is a good thing for men to fight. They got to fight."

"It could be," Ferdinand said.

"They like to fight."

"I got everything up," Ferdinand said, "and I braced up the chimney."

"Always fighting," she said.

"I got to get going," Ferdinand said.

She closed her eyes and listened to her words echo round and round in her head.

"Even me," she called out after him, "even an old one like me."

When he was gone, she walked once around the house to be sure that everything was snug. It was getting cloudier now and the wind was cooler. She pulled the sweater up around her neck. Then she went into her house, closing the shutters and locking them from inside.

*

BY Saturday morning Al Landry had almost finished fixing the
worst of the burned side of the house. He had been working fast
and he was tired. So that when he saw his wife come back from
the grocery, he stopped and followed her inside, looking for a cold
beer. She was just putting the basket down on the table and she
said to him over her shoulder: "You finish?"

"No," he said and got a can out of the icebox, "but it won't rain
through."

"You think it blowing harder?"

"No," Al said.

"Seems like it is."

Al shook his head. He punched a hole in the can and began to
drink directly from it. "That is real fine," he said.

"Mamere Terrebonne's is all shut up, like nobody lived there."

Al looked at her in surprise. He forgot sometimes that she
hadn't come from the island, that she'd only been there a little over
a month. He couldn't remember when he wasn't married to
her. . . .

"What so funny?"

"Nothing," Al said, "I forget you didn't know."

"About Mamere?"

"She stay inside from the minute it get a little cool."

"With the shutters closed and all that?"

Al nodded and smoothed out the curve of his mustache. "She
stay like that. And at night the kid that going to stay there slips in.
And her family bring her food and oil for her stove. And sometimes they go visit her."

"All the time?"

"Nobody making her," Al said. "This here is her idea, plain and
simple."

"Oh," Adele said. She began to pat her hair into place, her sleek
smooth brown hair that never moved.

443

"A funny island, che'," Al said.

She began digging among the groceries in the basket. "While I was by Arcenaux's, there was this mail." She found it finally and gave it to him.

It was a postcard, from New Orleans. On one side a picture of a single big oak tree. On the other, four lines of writing: "A real great town. Nothing like it. Annie."

"So," Al said, "you have read it?"

Adele nodded. "It don't say if they are married."

"Same thing as."

Al went into the living-room and propped the card up on the mantel. He felt a little lost.

By the time he went back to the kitchen, Adele had the groceries put away.

She asked him: "If there is a big storm coming, you will take the boat away?"

"Got to," he said.

"Oh."

He wondered for a minute what she meant by that. Then he thought he understood. "You come with me, no?"

"And who will stay with the house?"

"House don't matter."

"What do people do?" she asked. "Didn't hear any talk of leaving."

"They stay," Al said. "But nobody think bad of you for going. When you never been in a storm out here before."

"They stay, all of them?"

Al nodded.

"And if you got to go," Adele said, "I will stay here. And watch out for things. With everybody else."

Philomene Arcenaux sent word to two of her sons, Placide and Florian, that she had need of them.

The three of them went over to the Livaudais place, walking very slowly—because of Philomene. Even so, though it wasn't more than a hundred yards or so, she was puffing like a porpoise by the time she heaved herself up on the porch.

Belle was working in the back yard. She was alone: Eddie was still in Port Ronquille with Pete. She came around the corner of the house to see who was there—and she was so covered with mud it almost seemed that she had slipped down in it. Even her hair was caked.

"I been getting the shutters out," Belle said. She sat down too, put a hand on each knee and swung her body's weight over against them, sighing a little. Robby peeped around the corner of the house. Mud was dripping off his arms and legs like water.

"We come for that," Philomene said.

Belle shook her head.

"Your men," Philomene said, "they are not here."

"The boy," Belle said, "he is here. And we got no need of help."

Story LeBlanc and his three sons were clearing the burned house. They had been working all morning and they had a pile of studs cleared out. It was hard going. The timbers were burned and ruined, but they were still solidly set. They had to use crowbars and axes. They didn't talk at all. But each time they put their muscles into an ax swing or bent their backs over a crowbar, they'd get a peculiar light in their eyes. It was the other island they were thinking about.

The clouds were much lower today and grayer. But none of the LeBlancs looked overhead.

*

DOWN at the dock Hector Boudreau stretched himself full length on the *Hula Girl*'s deck. Even in the shade from the cabin it was hot: with one shirtsleeve he wiped the sweat off his chin.

For a minute he stared straight up into the bright gray cloud-filled sky. Far up, under the smeared gray clouds were four birds, big birds with angled tails and black wings, moving fast. They were man-of-war birds and they always headed in before a storm.

He'd come down to the boat very early, and tinkered with the engine and cleaned out the tiny cabin. He'd dragged the little mattress from the single bunk out on the deck for airing: it smelled faintly of mildew. He'd taken the stripped cover off the pillow, the cover that was stained with greasy fingers and smelled strongly of hair oil. He'd tell Cecile to wash that some day or other: not that it was going to do much good, with the couette so dirty. But, maybe. . . .

He dozed for a moment, but so lightly that he knew he was dozing. Then he was wide-awake again, the hot day burning in the back of his throat. He was worried.

It was the feel of the water under the hull, the nervous movement of even the sheltered waters of the back bay.

"It does not need my knowing of it," he muttered aloud.

Stan Schesnaydre, loafing on the *Star of the Sea*, not twenty feet way, called: "What you say?"

Hector did not answer. He looked up at the sky, at the steady high band of clouds and the low bits of racing ones.

"You studying something, no?" Stan persisted.

"Maybe."

"You ain't working."

"I ain't loafing, me."

Stan shrugged. A thin stream of saliva shot over the side from the gap between his front teeth. The cigarette in the corner of his mouth did not move.

446

Hector rested his chin on his palms. There was only the soft plop of a fish jumping and the faint creak of the mooring-lines and the sound of water on wood, on the hull, on the pier. And still he couldn't rest.

They said, some people, you could tell how far a storm was and how bad it was just by looking at the waves. I can't, me, Hector thought, though I seen plenty.

Almost the first thing he remembered—the morning after a hurricane when his mother gave him a boost up to the roof to see what had been torn away. He'd seen how the wind had peeled back strips of tin-like pieces of cardboard or tin foil. He'd stood and stared and very slowly he'd put out one bare toe and touched the crinkled strips. And the inside of his stomach was just as crinkled.

A hurricane once every seven years, people said.

It was past due, Hector thought.

He stared down at his oil-streaked sneakers.

The clouds had a funny color, he thought. A funny color. . . .

His ears singled out two new echoes on the wood pier: the light barefooted scampering of his son and the irregular but quick step of his father.

Hector grinned as the old man came aboard. "You ready for work, no?" It was funny how a crippled man could walk that fast, be that light on his feet.

The little boy giggled and Hector glared at him. "You go see what you mama doing, you."

The boy did not move. He stood shifting from one bare foot to the other, his small close-set black eyes glinting.

Hector lifted his arm. "Fi' toi!" And the kid was gone with long leaps down the pier, all the time looking back to see if he was followed.

The old man leaned against the cabin, to take the weight off the bad leg; he had gotten that habit: almost like a big cat rubbing up against things.

"You rip up the nets this last time I am not with you." He'd gotten a belly since the accident. The top button of his pants was always open.

Hector put out the mending equipment, the heavy shuttle and the ball of tarred twine.

"This going to be some storm, for sure."

His father did not answer. His fingers fumbled for the twine; the ball dropped and rolled across the deck, unwinding a little as it went.

"Better a man dead than a cripple," his father said. He'd been saying that for the last two years, and he did not mean it. His hold on life was as tight as an old crab's on bait.

"Maybe," Hector got the ball and put it in place; "and maybe not." He picked up the net. "Here, see?"

His father did not look interested; he stared off down along the bay where there was nothing but a fringe of marsh grass and a couple of brown pelicans fishing and way high up, a man-of-war gliding with wings straight out.

"There plenty of wind in those clouds."

"I said that, me."

"You got to have somebody hold the other side, if I going to fix it." His father nudged the heap of nets with his toe.

"I going to hold, like this here."

"You can stand with you arms out like that for a long time?"

"For long enough I can."

His father threaded the heavy bobbin and his fingers began the quick intricate knotting that would repair the net. Hector had never had the patience to do that himself. He held up the nets and let his eyes wander around the boat: overhead the draping black nets, their lines wrapped around the winch, lead weights swinging in the wind; and underfoot the paint-chipped deck.

He wished he had an arm free to wipe his face. He could feel the little trickles of sweat working down his cheeks, through the stubble of his day-old beard.

"There always storms in September."

His father's fingers did not stop moving as he clicked his tongue between his teeth.

"This time it will be a hurricane," Hector said flatly.

"You have said that before," his father reminded him. He let his eyes wander around the boat, but his fingers still did not stop the knotting.

Hector said: "I will take Cecile and the kids with me." He dropped the net from his fingers.

"Jesus Maria," his father threw down the shuttle. "I say you can't hold anything steady enough."

Hector picked up the net again without a word.

"She will not go," his father said.

"She will go if I drag her."

"No woman ever goes."

"They will be safer with me."

His father grinned slyly. "Do you remember Philippe Robillard?" Heading for the bayou during a small storm, the *Bonne Femme* had disappeared. There were not even bodies.

"Just because you are not on the island, you are not safe as in a rocking-chair."

"I will take care of them."

"Cecile can take care of herself here, if nobody can."

"No," Hector said.

His father stopped working and looked up into his face. The corner of his mouth was twisted and his eyes were puzzled. "But you going to need her here."

"No."

"You have seen what happens to houses in storms with nobody to watch them."

"Yea," Hector said. "I have seen that."

"She got to stay here."

Hector said: "If we take the boat, they will come with me."

His father sniffed as if he had got a cold.

"They coming."

"It is all equal with me," his father said.

They finished the work without talking. Hector, with his eyes half shut against the glare, remembered, kept remembering, back to when he was a kid, older than his son now, but not much. Seven or eight at the most, he decided, that September.

There weren't any radios in those days—just the sky and the wind and the Gulf to tell them what was coming. He'd hidden behind hackberries and scrub-oak bushes, crouched under the planks of the docks where the big cats rubbed and mewed against him, and watched the men, the little groups of men, as they talked and studied and finally one night took the boats away. He was asleep when they left; that next morning he'd waked early and gone sneaking out of the house (he wasn't supposed to do that; his mother always told him never to go out in the morning damp with an empty stomach). The docks were empty; not even the cats were there, just the big mooring-lines, hanging over the boards, trailing in the water.

At mid-afternoon, when the wind came up sharply and it began to rain, his mother called him and his two sisters inside into the main room of their house that was parlor and kitchen and bedroom for him. They sat, and hardly moved, listening to the sounds outside: the swishing of the oleander bushes and the creaks of the hollow chinaberry trees, and from the windward side of the island, the steady sound of the surf.

At six or so, his mother stood up and beckoned to him. "Come help me." They went outside in the steady falling rain and pushed closed the heavy wood shutters. The wind was already so strong they had to fight them closed, the two of them, until his sharp wiry shoulder was bruised and cut under the thin shirt. And, with the rain stinging his eyes and the muscles shuddering in all his body, he'd wished that he had a big brother. Thinking that, he felt ashamed of himself and put his weight against the wood and pushed harder.

Five shutters had taken them nearly half an hour. His throat was aching from the strain.

Inside his two little sisters were crying. "Shut up," he told them sharply. They had crawled up in a corner of the bed, the two of them and they were sobbing open-mouthed.

Inside there it was dark, only the faint hairline of light around the edges of the windows and the one strip down the middle where the shutters met. "Fix the door, che'," his mother said; her voice was deeper than usual, breathless and panting.

There were iron hooks on the door for a crossbrace. And over in the corner was the bar, an old piece of iron that his grandfather had found years ago on the beach at Isle Timbalier, a thin flat bar of iron, rusted but solid, that might have been almost anything. Hector would spend hours sometimes staring at the bar, trying to imagine what it was from, and how it had got on the beach at Timbalier, where there was only white driftwood and sand crabs scuttling like white shadows across the sand.

He got the bar and dropped it into place and then carefully, because his eyes had not yet got used to the dimness, felt his way over to a chair. It was a rocker. He began to tip it softly back and forth, dipping his head up and down, resting it on his chest, then throwing it back as far as he could.

They sat there, the four of them, with just the sound of his rocking and the rattle of the wood beads of his mother's rosary. They did not make a light; the dark seemed safer.

Outside was the sound of thousands and thousands of bushes rubbing together, being pulled and twisted together; and the plopping of heavy drops of rain into the sand; and farther, the sucking of the water at the beach. His mother lit the vigil light in front of the statue of St. Christopher.

By eleven or so the tone of the wind began to change; it got higher and clearer too, like a bell almost, or a set of bells. There were small sharp crashes when flying things—branches or bits of wood or pieces of other houses—smashed into the walls.

"It is here now," his mother said.

The wind seemed to be scratching against the outside of the house. They could hear it run up and down like fingernails on a washboard.

The chimney went; the bricks rattled down along the roof. The house was swaying. On the south side a shutter gave way. It didn't blow in or hang rattling. One of the wind's fingers found it and pried at it. Like a cork out of a bottle, almost, it popped open and was sucked away.

All the loose things in the room rose up toward the ceiling in the flood of wind. The house was quivering, the roof straining at its beams.

"Hector, open the windows," his mother shouted. "Vite!"

He clambered across the bed and smashed his fists at a shutter until it flew open. He realized he was kneeling on his sister, which one he couldn't tell. She was wailing. He slapped at her, clambered down and threw himself at the last closed window.

"We got to," he heard his mother telling him, "or the roof or maybe the whole house goes."

They caught at the flying things, odd bits of cloth and paper. Nothing looked familiar to him or felt familiar. The vigil light had

gone out; there was only the peculiar color of the sky. Only the
rain pouring in through the open windows and his clothes sticking
to his body. He thought for a minute that the whole island had
slipped into the Gulf and he began to whimper.

He thought his mother said something to him, but he couldn't
make out the words. The vent pipe from the cook stove fell
clattering to the floor; they began to cough from the soot that
sprayed upwards. And very distinctly, far off somewhere, he heard a
cock crow.

His sisters were scrambling around the room, hunting for a
place to hide. Even in all the noise he could hear their fierce little
scurrying as they tried to wedge themselves behind the big old
oak armoire.

He was standing in the middle of the floor, crying, with rain so
hard in his face he could not catch his breath, when the armoire
toppled over.

For that half-second he heard it falling, heard something falling,
and would have run but wasn't sure of the direction. And caught
his breath to scream but didn't have time: one of the wide-flying
doors clipped him across the back of the head.

He still had that scar, a thick gray line. It was sensitive to the
sun and tender; he had let his hair grow long and heavy over it.

His father looked up briefly. "Except you hold the net, I will not
finish this for two or three weeks."

"Okay," Hector said; "okay."

A yellow and black cat that has been fishing under the pier
paddled lazily out to an isolated post—all the island cats swim—
clambered to its broad top, a couple of inches above the water,
stretched, shook, and settled down, eyes half closed but watching
the water.

"You remember old Isabelle Guillot?" Hector asked.

"Perhaps. Maybe. She been dead a long time."

"Sure," Hector said, "back in that storm." They'd found her
under the smashed cistern in her yard.

And the Guidry boy, there wasn't even a trace of him. He was
just gone. Nobody ever did know what had happened.

Hector shifted on his feet, but held the net steady. "I have
made up my mind fast. They coming with me."

"Oui?" his father did not look up from the work. "Wait any-how until the radio tell us what is there."

When all the nets were finished, they went over to the grocery and sat on the porch there, drinking beer. There were some other people: Al Landry, Perique Lombas, a couple of the Arcenaux boys. And after a while Story LeBlanc came by. Therese Landry was there too, sitting very still and not making a sound, only now and then she would peep, out of the corners of her eyes, at Perique.

The radio was on full blast, hillbilly music and every hour a weather-news broadcast.

In an hour or so Ozzie Pailet came up on the porch. "I seen the boats from the other island going in."

"That don't mean nothing," Archange Boudreau said.

"I'm just telling you," he said. "What the radio say?"

Archange shook his head.

"You going hear soon enough," Perique said.

At four o'clock the crisp voice read off the formal hurricane-warning and gave the last course of the storm. Without saying anything, they went inside the grocery, over to the north wall, where there was a government navigation chart. Julius snapped on the little light he had pinned over it. A little lamp with a wood ship's wheel for a base and little sailing-boats around the shade—Hector jerked his eyes back to the chart.

Julius was saying: "Halfway between Point Sarrat and Lost Bay," he put his finger down, "here." Right under his finger was the island.

The radio voice was still repeating, emphasizing the words in a flat unconcerned way, "We repeat, hurricane precautions should be taken in this area. The course of the storm is estimated . . ."

Hector did not bother to listen any more. He went outside. There were things to be done now.

The church bell had begun to ring. The minute word had come Perrin's daughter had scurried off—she was part crippled at birth. She jerked the rope unevenly so that there was a kind of choking clang.

The light top sand of the road was blowing like smoke along the ground.

Without turning Hector asked: "You going with me?"

His father was trying to light a cigarette in the wind, leaning with one arm wrapped around the porch post. "Why you think I ain't going with you?"

"Don't know, me."

Perique shouted: "Hector, hey, what you say?"

"What?"

"You going right away?"

He nodded.

He and his father began to walk along the path to their houses. The wind was not any stronger, yet. There was never a slow rise. But all of a sudden when the storm was very close, the winds would come swirling down out of the clouds. And that would be it.

His father turned aside and pushed open the gate to his house. Hector went on to his own place, close by. One finger rubbing the thick whitish scar, he climbed his steps. The house was empty. "Hey," he called, "hey." In the crib in the bedroom the baby answered with a squawk. Hector studied the angry little face.

"You look like an old man," he told the child, "just like an old man, you." He walked through the living-room again and then into the tiny half-room that was the kitchen. "Cecile, hey!"

A scuffing sound right under his feet—he stuck his head out the window, looking down, studying it as if he'd never seen it before.

His house was built off the ground, not as high as most old places but four feet or so on brick foundations. Under it were the things they wanted to keep but were not using just then—nets that were too old to be patched (bits of them could be used for kids' crab nets). Two pirogues that he used when he went hunting (he hadn't been in over a year, the fishing had been so good). Some empty barrels he forgot just why he was keeping. A tiller from a dinghy that had gone to pieces long ago. Some washtubs and washboards and a charcoal pot. All of them with the white streaks of spider webs.

His wife was emerging, rear end first, from under the house. Without looking up at him, she began to pull out a heavy storm door, cross-braced. His son scrambled out, pushing on the other end.

"This kid here is screaming his head off," Hector told her.

She looked up, her eyes bright green-blue and startling in her brown face. "I got plenty enough to do out here."

He stared at her, not moving.

"You heard the hurricane bell same like me." Her face was streaked with dirt; there were gray shreds of spider webs in her black hair. "You got nothing to do but stand there? Ain't you got a boat to take out . . . ain't you got the bars to put up or you house goes blowing away?"

"The kid is shouting like he is going to die."

"You nurse him." She bent to her work again, dusting the cobwebs off her feet and ankles. "If I going to do your work."

But she came in anyway, walking like an angry cat, stiff-legged. The baby was tiring from his yelling already. She tucked a sugar-tit into his sagging mouth.

Hector followed her, admiring the set of her broad hips.

"I got no time to be thinking like that," he said aloud.

"What you muttering about?"

"We got to get the storm door up."

"I been telling you that." She stomped down the steps and around the side of the house.

"We got to get it up because we are leaving."

"What you saying now?"

"You coming with me."

"And leave the kids here?"

He sighed patiently. "You coming. All of you coming."

He lifted the door into position.

"No."

"Huh?" He turned and looked at her. "Let's us fix the back door now."

She did not move. "I ain't going."

"Gimme a hand."

They put up the back door in silence. In a space between the trees they could see the black-squared hurricane-warning flag go up on the flagpole in the middle of the island.

Inside again, he took down a large zipper canvas bag. "You can just put the kids' stuff in here."

"No," she said. "Somebody got to stay and take care the place." She turned around, looking at the room, with the new red upholstered living-room set they had bought only one winter past.

She had half finished tucking canvas over the chairs. "Somebody got to stay or water ruin everything."

"You going," he said, "if I got to take you by the seat of the pants and throw you in."

She sat down, so hard that the springs made a little squeaking sound. "Everybody else, they going to stay."

"Everybody else is crazy."

Al Landry went home, almost running, stopping only once to talk to Therese. His own house, shuttered tight, looked strange and different. He tried to get in the front door, but that was barred. He had to go around to the kitchen.

The first thing he noticed was his little bag in the middle of the table. It looked like it was stuffed full. Adele was sitting in a chair right next to it, waiting.

"We got to take the boats," he said.

"I hear the bell."

"So. . . ." He wasn't sure what to say or what to do. "Therese, she will come over to stay with you."

"You ask her?"

He nodded.

"I can manage alone, me."

"Sure," he said, "but you ain't used to it yet."

"I been in storms before at Port Ronquille."

"Well," he said, "I feel better with somebody extra here."

"I fix you some sandwiches," she said quietly, "and some coffee."

He squeezed the canvas bag.

"And some sweaters, that I find."

There was some extra coffee on the stove. He poured some and tossed it off, like likker, neat. Not because he wanted it so much, but because he was nervous.

"You going right now, no?" Adele asked.

He kissed her on the top of the head, and left. She did not get up until Claudie, who had been playing in the parlor, upset the tabouret. Then she got the broom to sweep up the pieces of the ash tray.

.   .   .

Hector Boudreau went out on the porch and sat down. The chairs had all been taken in, so he squatted on his haunches, his back against the wall.

"I'm through talking, me," he said. "You coming." She did not answer, but he knew that she had heard, even though he did not turn his head. "I'm waiting here, me, for five minutes. Then we going to lock up all the doors and go."

He heard a few soft movements, then nothing.

Over beyond the trees, men were shouting, but so far away he couldn't make out the words. Funny, he thought, the way trees muffled sounds. He hoped the storm did not blow down too many of them.

That other hurricane—when he was a boy—had swept some places clean, like a thousand people had gone through with knives and brooms. And at some other places there were heaps: against a tree that had been too strong or too lucky to go; or against a house that was still standing. He remembered following the sound of dogs—he'd run to keep up with the others, his legs had been dropping off, but he'd kept going, not knowing what they were after, but going all the same. The dogs had gone yapping around one of the piles of brush and wood, where a big chinaberry tree had been torn up from the ground. And his mother got him by the shoulder and pointed him home and gave him a swat on the rear end to help him along. It had taken him two days to figure that out. Nobody spoke of it before him. He'd heard the kids whispering about it, whispering about the people under there. And when he understood, he began to shiver all over, so much that his mother thought he had malaria and gave him a big dose of whisky and quinine and put him to bed.

Hector rocked back and forth on his heels and toes. "You near ready?" he called.

Over to the left, somebody was hammering, boarding up windows: that would be Julius at the store.

Two kids ran past, one of them with an air rifle. "You going to shoot a hurricane?" he called to them and they giggled.

His father came ambling down the path, the printed cloth bag in his left hand swinging even more sharply with his uneven walk.

"You need some help?" Hector slapped his hand to his fore-

head. "Mary Mother, but I just forgot to ask if you and the old
woman needed some help over at the house."

His father dropped the bag and leaned against the porch railing.
"Non," he said, "the shutters is all closed and the plants in off the
porch and the old woman, she is lighting a candle next to the holy
palm. Let's us go."

"Cecile," Hector called, "let's us go."

She turned up in the doorway so suddenly they both knew
she'd been standing just behind it, waiting. "I ain't going."

"God almighty, woman," Hector said, "ain't I got enough to do
without dragging you to the boat?"

He went inside, checking all the windows; she stood without
moving in the middle of the door. "There stuff in that there bag
on the table for you, if you want it."

He looked inside the bag briefly and then picked it up. "Least
you ain't so lost you senses, you forgetting food."

She came into the living-room and sat down on the edge of a
chair, her hands still on her hips.

"Okay," he said. She did not move. "Get the kid before I lose
my temper and bat you over."

"He ain't here." Her face was perfectly blank. "Ain't neither of
them here."

He glanced in the crib: it was empty; and he shouted out the
window, "Don!" There was no answer, just that hammering far off.

"What you done with them?"

She shrugged.

"Where you put them, you?"

"Where you ain't ever going to think to look for them."

"You want the boat gets smashed to pieces, with us all wasting
time hunting for the kids?"

"You leave me here to look out for things."

"You crazy. You crazy."

He spun on his heel and dashed down the steps to take a few
steps in the trees, shouting: "Don!" There were so many places
she could have hidden the baby, any place inside half a mile.

Perique passed. "Hey, boy," he called. "We got to be going."

"Jesus Christ!" Hector jammed his hands in his pockets, "ain't
you got nothing to do but pester me?"

Archange said: "Don't pay a mind to him." He took Perique by the arm and whispered in his ear: "Don't get hot with him. He don't mean what he saying, him. He got wife trouble."

Perique grinned shyly. "I be down at the boat, me."

The old man followed Hector who was walking back and forth peering in each clump of hedge and oleander. "You got no reason to talk to Perique like that. What we do, us, if he got mad and wouldn't come out with us? What we go and do then?"

"We ain't going out."

His father did not answer.

Hector turned around. His face was flushed with anger. He kicked at a small white periwinkle plant. "I told you we ain't going out."

"I ain't saying nothing."

"I ain't going to let nothing happen to those kids, me."

"Oui."

"And her, she can go drown in the bay, for all I care, her."

"Oui." His father was still following him. For all that he was a cripple, he could move fast on the uneven ground.

"I don't care none if the boat get smashed."

"You ain't going to eat then."

"I going to take them with me."

They had stopped walking abruptly. "You hear something?"

They were in the middle of an oleander patch. In the wind the leaves and branches bent and lashed down in their faces.

"No," his father said, "you ain't ever going to find them in time."

Hector leaned against one of the largest oleander trunks. "That kid got to get hungry and then he going to start to yell, and then we know."

His father thought about this for a moment. He caught one of the branches that pounded his face and pulled it off. "Jesus God," he swung the twig like a switch in the air around him, "that kid ain't going to get hungry for three hours or four maybe. And the longer you wait, the rougher it get."

Hector was staring at the ground, rocking back and forth on his heels, just a little.

"So." His father rubbed the side of his nose with the little twig.

"You wait any three or four hours, or any time like that, and I ain't going with you. And Perique ain't neither, him. Then it just too late. Ain't neither of us that crazy."

Hector squinted up into the sky, one eye closed. His father whistled softly and tunelessly between his teeth.

Hector swung his eyes slowly back to his house. "Jesus!" Following the path of his eyes he walked back, slowly, until he took the steps in a single jump.

Cecile was just where they had left her, sitting on the arm of the living-room chair that was covered with canvas. She half closed her eyes when he came in; her heavy underlip was curled and pouting.

"You so crazy you don't go hide from me." He slapped her across the cheek. She was up in a second, kicking at his stomach, reaching for his eyes. Very carefully, using his left arm to shield himself, he beat her. He used only the flat of his hand.

He finished with a push that sent her slamming back into the chair and the chair smashing into the wall. She sat quietly, glaring at him.

"Eyes of a bitch." He was panting. "Ain't going to let you ruin my boat, me."

Archange stood waiting outside, swinging the little bag from his left hand.

"She ain't even had sense enough to run and hide from me. . . ."

His father tucked his upper lip inside his teeth and whistled.

"It is the same to me." Hector yelled as he picked up his bag and slung it over his shoulder. "But I will come back, me, as soon as I can, and if the kids, they are not all right, I will take you to little pieces and feed the crabs with you."

She hissed through the door after them.

Therese let herself drop full length across her bed. She had just been down to the dock: the *Hula Girl* was gone. And Perique had not come to tell her good-by. . . . She cried until her head hurt. Then she got up, washed her face, put fresh make-up on, and, with a piece of tarpaulin over her head, started for Adele's. The cool wet air made her feel better.

.   .   .

Claudie was nervous. He held on to his mother's leg and whimpered.

"Quit," she said, "this ain't the storm."

He only held her tighter.

"Look," she said, as much to herself as to the boy, "we ain't going to be alone. And even that ain't so bad . . . nothing to it. Just a little wind and some little rain."

The boy was listening to her carefully. She loosened his fingers and walked around the rooms, which were almost pitch-black with the shutters closed.

Claudie began to wail, frightened at being left in the kitchen alone. She ran back there, and because the sound made her skin creep, she slapped him, harder than she would have used to do.

For the very first time, she saw fear, and then hate come into his eyes.

"I never tell you it was easy," she yelled at him. "I never did, me."

When Therese came, she felt calmer. She even gave Claudie the couple of Tootsie Rolls that she'd been hiding in the china jar on the top shelf of the pantry.

Julius put down his hammer and took the remaining nails out of the corner of his mouth. He'd finished boarding up the new big front window, the one he should have had sense enough not to buy. He began to take things off the floor and pile them on the higher shelves. He put the sugar and the rice and the flour on the very top. You could never tell when you'd have water inside.

From the rooms at the back he heard Philomene puffing as she pushed things around. It struck him all of a sudden that he was winded—he had put up the storm door but he hadn't barred it yet —so he went out on the front porch for some air.

It was blowing about the same. The clouds seemed a little darker, but that might be imagination. It would be four, five, six hours before anything much happened.

It was beginning to rain, you could smell it. Julius sniffed at the air. It gave him a funny feeling, this standing on his porch and knowing that he was just about the only able-bodied man on the island. He liked that very much.

His daughter came along the path; she waved briefly at him

and went around to the back. She had left her two kids there, not much more than half an hour ago. . . .

And now so soon. . . . He ducked back through the store to talk to her.

She had the baby in one arm, and Don was already down the steps.

"Hey," Julius called after her.

She turned and he saw the cut at the corner of her lip, which was beginning to swell, and the bruise on her cheekbone.

"What happen to you?"

She grinned with the good side of her mouth. "Shutter fell down on me." She left with a wave.

Julius said to Philomene: "You don't reckon Hector done that?"

"And would she look so happy, if they had a fight?"

Julius had to scratch his head and admit that was true.

The *Hula Girl* was the last boat out. The harbor, when they had left, was like the harbor that Hector remembered from his childhood—empty posts and lines dangling down into the water, and splintered, weathered boards that looked worn almost through.

Even the sheltered waters of the bay were rough. The hull shuddered and rolled. They headed straight across, the wind astern.

Perique sat down on the little bunk next to Archange Boudreau and let his body shift back and forth with the boat's motion. There was nothing more to be done for a while. Now that he had time to catch his breath he remembered Therese. . . . Jesus, he thought, Jesus Christ. . . .

He'd have to bring her something, a present from Petit Prairie. That would make it all right again.

And all of a sudden he found himself wondering what a hurricane was like in New Orleans, where Annie was. . . .

He shook his head and got rid of the thought.

Archange Boudreau eased himself into a comfortable position on the bunk, stretched himself carefully, tucked a fresh piece of tobacco in his cheek and began to chew it gently.

A flock of gulls passed overhead, coming from the south, their feathers a dull white gleaming. They were riding the wind, hardly moving their wings.

"Là-bas," Archange said, pointing.

Through a break in the mist, a boat, almost out of sight in the beginning dark.

"Was wondering where they all got to, me."

"Can't tell who it is, this far."

"They must about turning up the bayou right now, this minute."

"We ought to be up there with them." The mist blew back and the boat disappeared.

"We going to get there," Hector said. "We got the wind running with us."

"All the same," Archange shifted the tobacco, "we can't go no faster and I wish we was there right now."

Perique laughed and crinkled his little eyes. "We going to make it. Or maybe we drown."

The old man pulled a knife from his shirt pocket and began to clean his fingernails.

Hector motioned Perique to take the wheel. He went on deck. They were taking a little spray; there was a trickle running out the long slit scuppers.

With one hand for balance on the lifeline they'd rigged around the cabin, Hector stared back the way they had come.

"Hey, boy," Perique called, "ain't nothing you see out there you can't see from in here."

"You go over," his father said, "and there ain't going to be any use even trying to find you."

"Why she stay, in place of hiding with the kids? Why she didn't save herself no beating?"

Behind them the island was just a clump of trees with a clump of storm-colored clouds resting right on top of them. The heavy rain was almost there, too; you could tell by the color of the haze. The trees would be lashing around like crazy, he thought, and for a minute he saw it all clear: the people running for cover, slamming doors after them, putting in the bolts. She'd be doing that too. He could see her; she'd have stayed on the porch until the last minute, after she'd sent the kid inside. Maybe she'd even stay out in the rain for a while, because it would be cool.

But she wasn't one to do that, he thought. She'd be inside, making sure the covers were tight under the furniture, and that the kids were in bed. And then she'd sit down, rocking and waiting.

He cocked his head at the gray clouds streaming overhead and listened to the wind that was carrying them.

He was grinning when he turned and closed the cabin door behind him.

THE KIDS were the last ones inside. They had been running around, excited all of them, in groups, like packs of dogs.

They had been yelling and singing all through the little drizzle. When their mothers came out on the porches and called for them, they paid no attention. None at all.

The first drops of rain sent them scurrying home for cover. By this time most of the doors were closed and bolted. And their mothers weren't in any hurry to open them up. . . . Let them stay out a while, they thought, get soaked to the skin, be a good lesson. And so the kids kicked at the doors and screamed with fear before they got inside.

From the Gulf rain moved in on the island, gray and thick.

The wind whipped it around corners and across open places like streams from a fire hose. Stripped leaves flew by in bunches, like handfuls.

There was a little rattle of slamming shutters all over the island—all of a sudden. Those were the people who liked fresh air, who hadn't closed up until the very last minute. Until the rain began coming from every way all at once—so that even the undersides of the porch roofs got drenched.

It slacked off finally after an hour or so, and then the whole sky filled with a network of lightning threads, like a spider web. The gray air was fresh with the clear odor of ozone. On Isle Cochon the one dead tree was split open and two parts fell away so that there was only a splinter left standing, like a toothpick. The dogs down at the western end were howling without a pause—you could hear them over everything else.

People stayed inside, behind the closed shutters and the barred doors. Some lit candles and fingered their beads. Others began to drink, carefully, knowing that their supply might have to last a long time, and careful too that they didn't get drunk, but only felt warm and comfortable. Some people played cards and learned new tricks or practiced fancy dealing.

The lightning passed over too. In the silence the kids squinched their eyes up to the cracks around the doors to see what was going on outside. For a couple of hours there was nothing very much, not even rain. Nobody went out. They were waiting to see what would happen. . . .

The clouds shifted and swirled and darkened to a kind of dull greenish color. Under them the winds were very much higher.

A NOTE ABOUT THE AUTHOR

SHIRLEY ANN GRAU describes herself as "a New Orleanian by birth (twenty-eight years ago), an Alabamian by upbringing, and a New Englander by summer adoption."

"I like," she adds, "anything outdoors, whether it's as organized as tennis or as disorganized as a duck hunt down in the marshes around New Orleans. . . . I like to sail, love to swim, love to go fishing. . . . I hate the cold and love the steamy heat of the tropics and semi-tropics."

Miss Grau is married and is at present moving from a New Orleans apartment to a house in the suburbs to make room for the thousands of books that she and her husband have accumulated. She says that she is not too selective in her reading, enjoys tremendously the westerns of Will Henry, the stories of Henry James, many travel books, the Maigret novels of Simenon, and has recently been immersed in Trollope.

Since the publication of *The Black Prince* Shirley Ann Grau's work has appeared in *The New Yorker, New World Writing, Mademoiselle,* and *Holiday,* and she is already at work on a second novel.

A NOTE ON THE TYPE

The text of this book was set on the Linotype in Garamond (No. 3), a modern rendering of the type first cut in the sixteenth century by *Claude Garamond* (1510–1561). He was a pupil of Geoffroy Tory and is believed to have based his letters on the Venetian models, although he introduced a number of important differences, and it is to him we owe the letter which we know as Old Style. He gave to his letters a certain elegance and a feeling of movement which won for their creator an immediate reputation and the patronage of the French King, Francis I.

Composed, printed, and bound by Kingsport Press, Inc., Kingsport, Tennessee. Paper manufactured by S. D. Warren Company, Boston. Designed by George Salter.